# THE
# WOMAN
## IN THE
# PHOTO

By Mary Hogan

*The Woman in the Photo*
*Two Sisters*

Young Adult novels:

*The Serious Kiss*
*Perfect Girl*
*Pretty Face*
*Susanna Sees Stars*
*Susanna Hits Hollywood*
*Susanna Covers the Catwalk*
*Susanna Loves London*

# THE WOMAN IN THE PHOTO

## A Novel

# MARY HOGAN

WM

WILLIAM MORROW
*An Imprint of HarperCollinsPublishers*

Photos courtesy of the Johnstown Flood Museum Archives, Johnstown Area Heritage Association and courtesy of the National Railroad Museum.

HarperCollins books may be purchased for educational, business, or sales promotional use. For information please e-mail the Special Markets Department at SPsales@harpercollins.com.

FIRST EDITION

*Designed by Diahann Sturge*

Library of Congress Cataloging-in-Publication Data has been applied for.

ISBN 978-0-06-238693-9

16 17 18 19 20   OV/RRD   10 9 8 7 6 5 4 3 2 1

*To the resilient people of Johnstown, Pennsylvania.*
*Past and present.*

*"You and your people are in no danger
from our enterprise."*

—Benjamin F. Ruff, President of
the South Fork Fishing and Hunting Club

# THE
# WOMAN
## IN THE
# PHOTO

# HORRORS OF HORRORS.

## The City of Johnstown Completely Swept Away in an Awful Rush of Waters.

## THOUSANDS OF LIVES ARE LOST.

## The Dam of South Fork Broken by a Swollen Stream, and an Immense Volume of Water

## SWALLOWS EVERYTHING IN ITS REACH.

### For Hours Hundreds of People Are Seen Floating Along, Shrieking For Help.

Some of the Scenes Indescribable—The Work of Rescue at All Points—No Trains Able to Reach the Scene of Desolation and All Other Direct Communication Cut Off—The People Warned, but Ineffectually—Familiarity With Their Danger Had Made Them Careless—Touching Incidents of the Work of Rescue at Bolivar, Lockport and Blairsville.

THE PITTSBURG DISPATCH

*1889*

## ⋅⋅◦〗 CHAPTER 1 〖◦⋅⋅

*The previous day . . .*
*Memorial Day*
*May 30, 1889*

Elizabeth, *please.*" Mother looks away from the train window long enough to eye me sharply. "Why do you test me?"

I frown as she grips the gloves in her lap and returns her gaze to the branches flickering past. It's Memorial Day. Yet the weather matches my mood: stormy. It rained all morning. More is on its way. Even now, in a dry patch, the gathering clouds are the shade of dried lobelia. It's destined to be the dreariest week of my life. I can barely breathe. The air in the Pullman is as dense as Connaught pudding.

"All I'm saying is that the newest styles from France don't choke the very life out of yo—"

"No daughter of mine will dress like a Parisian trollop."

The crease between Mother's eyebrows mars the creamy skin that was once a smooth canvas over her legendary aqua-colored eyes. I've come to begrudge that scolding expression as much as the two words that often accompany it: "Elizabeth" and "please." As if I were a naughty child.

"It's eighteen eighty-nine," I mutter. "Not eighteen-fifty." Then I cross my arms over my chest, knowing Mother dislikes such a common gesture.

Tears threaten. Not only was I awakened this morning too early to be agreeable, I am now stuck on the Pennsy with my mother and six-year-old brother on our way to Lake Cone-maugh. No one will be at the lake this early in the season. The clubhouse will be deserted. The sculls will be locked in the boathouse. Not a single stable hand will be there to saddle a horse. Plus, the timing couldn't be worse.

"You can plan your debut at the cottage as well as here," Father had said, leaving me speechless. My quadrille lessons in Pittsburgh require *daily* practice to reach perfection. Would Father have me embarrass the family by stepping on a gentleman's toes? Did he think it was easy finding a gown that would be the envy of everyone? One that Mother would allow? With matching shoes that didn't pucker? There isn't a moment to waste. Especially after the unfortunate events of last summer—and my current predicament—so much is at stake. Certainly Mother has reminded Father—as she has *me* endlessly—that my entire future depends upon a flawless performance.

I sigh. It's more than any eighteen-year-old girl should have to bear.

"How much longer, 'Lizbeth?" Henry asks.

"*E*lizabeth," Mother corrects him.

"Two more stops," I say, curtly.

On the seat next to me, my little brother makes figure eights with the toy train he brought along for the ride. "Whoo, whoo!" Ruddy-cheeked, he gazes at me with adventure dancing in his eyes. "Mother says you might take me exploring around the lake."

I glance at Mother and she glances at me.

"It's too muddy today," I say.

"Tomorrow, then?"

"We'll see." I think, *What else is there to do?*

"Last summer, Albert Vanderhoff told me he saw a baby deer behind the clubhouse. But no one else saw it, so I think he made it up."

"Albert lied to you?"

"It's not lying if it's your imagination. That's what Albert Vanderhoff says."

In spite of my frustration, I laugh. To have such innocence. Such certainty! Twelve years separate my brother and me. Most of the time, it feels as if we were born into two different families. I am Elizabeth Haberlin, daughter of Dr. and Mrs. Stafford Haberlin, of the Pittsburgh Haberlins, of Upper St. Clair, Pennsylvania.

"You are a reflection of me," Father often tells me. Too often. When I look into a pier glass, I prefer to see my *own* face.

Henry is merely Little Henry. He is a boy who will grow into a man who will never feel the obligations that suffocate women like a spoon busk corset. Even as Father's patients are maligned in the newspaper—Mr. Frick's tug-of-war with his workers at the steel mill, Mr. Carnegie's battles with Mr. Frick, Mr. Mellon's public arguments over the value of his properties, and Mr. Vanderhoff's vulgar disputes with his working-class tenants—his daughter must be above reproach.

"Discretion and propriety are as important to your father's practice as a proper diagnosis," Mother reminds me constantly. As if I could forget that Father's position as personal physician to Pittsburgh's elite puts our family so close to the center of society.

"When we get to South Fork, will it rain cats and dogs?" Henry asks. His new favorite expression.

"If it does," Mother says, "we'll run outside and turn our umbrellas upside down to catch them."

"So they don't get hurt when they hit the ground?"

"Exactly."

"What if they fall into the lake? Will they drown?"

She shakes her head. "They'll swim ashore and we'll warm them up with Maggie's lima-bean soup."

Henry grins blissfully. Feeling a surge of affection, I reach my hand across the seat to stroke my brother's silky cheek.

"Don't slouch, Elizabeth, dear heart."

My smile disappears. My hand returns to my lap. I sit upright. Mimicking my exasperation, the train's whistle blares.

On the other side of the compartment, Mother reaches one slim hand up to tuck an errant strand of dark hair beneath the rim of her hat. Before we left Pittsburgh this morning, she chose an olive-green frock with a matching bonnet. She had her maid, Ella, style her hair in a low coiffure. Ostentation would never do when a woman was traveling alone with her children. Even the first-class compartments got dirty once the train wheels agitated all that soil on the tracks. Grit had a way of creeping between the seams of the railcar, the edge of the closed window. Best to dress for camouflage.

Personally, I don't care for camouflage. I had my maid dress me in my favorite apricot silk with the creamy satin embellishments from elbow to cuff. The ruffled edge dusting the floor is a shock of peacock blue, matching the trim on my hat. Nettie spent half an hour taming the humidity in my black curls and frazzling my bangs just so. Impractical in such soggy weather. But, if my parents are going to make me endure days of seclusion, I might as well look stylish on the way.

In a burst of energy, I leap up. Jostled by the train, I nonetheless manage to open the window latch. A glorious breeze rushes in, cooling my face and releasing the dank odor in the airless compartment. In spite of the dirt and dampness, I lean into the fresh air and *breathe*.

Predictably, Mother moans. I know what she is thinking: *Henry was unwell last week. He mustn't get a chill.* Pretending not to register her distress, I fill my lungs to their bursting point. I stretch to my full height. Mother will worry about Henry no matter what I do. Ever since his sixth birthday—the same age my uncle was when he was so tragically taken—her anxieties have flowered like butterfly weed along the rail tracks.

"Fresh air is good for the body and soul." I quote Father. His progressive views include the healing power of nature and tranquility. Why, the very reason we are banished to the lake cottage before the season has begun is so that Father can secretly treat Lily Vanderhoff's "moral insanity" with peace and quiet.

In his medical office behind our home in Upper St. Clair, I
overheard his conversation with Mrs. Vanderhoff's husband.

"It's as if two women reside inside her," he said. "At times,
she is blank in the face and unable to rouse herself from bed.
Other days, she takes over the maid's cleaning duties, scrubbing floors so furiously her fingers bleed."

Bernard Vanderhoff—a wealthy Pittsburgh landlord—
would no more consider the public humiliation of commit-
ting his wife to an asylum than he would arrive at dinner in
the striped trousers of a dandy. Instead, he asked Father to
treat her secretly. Naturally, Father did not have the option to
refuse. If one patient left his practice, others would follow. It
was their way.

"The only treatment poor Lily Vanderhoff needs," he told
Mother later, "is a peaceful week away from those indulged
children and her overbearing husband."

"Then why can't *she* go to the lake?" Mother had asked.

"At the moment, I'm afraid, a train trip is beyond her."

So that was that. To preserve Bernard Vanderhoff's reputation, Father arranged for us to depart for our family's lake
cottage without him. Several days before anyone else would
dream of arriving.

"Your hair will be a mess of curls, Elizabeth."

Thunder rumbles in the distance. The train slows as it climbs
the mountain to Horseshoe Curve. I cannot bear to leave the
breeze. With my head tilted back, I let my eyelids flutter shut. I
breathe in the mountain air.

"One more minute," I tell Mother. For the first time in
weeks, I feel free. The fear that I may soon be disgraced by the

so-called gentleman from Great Britain slips to a far corner of my mind.

"The loop!" Henry jumps up and joins me at the open window. His little fingers curl around the edge of the open sill.

"Henry, dear. Please sit down."

"One more minute," he says.

I needn't turn around to feel Mother's annoyance. "He's fine," I tell her. Then I press my palm against my brother's back as the train leans around the curve.

Standing on tiptoe, Little Henry pokes his face out the window to see the locomotive spew a blast of white steam. The railroad arc that loops around the tip of Altoona's new reservoir is his favorite part of the journey. One can feel the compartment list into the sharp circle cut into the mountain as the train curves in on itself. This high in the Allegheny Mountains, the view is spectacular, even on a day darkened by black clouds. The Pennsy snakes through swollen forests of white pine and black cherry, along foothills blanketed in yellow oxeye and lavender musk mallow. A deliciously woodsy aroma twirls around the floral scents in the air.

I feel my bleak mood lifting. Father is right. Fresh air is a tonic.

A porter taps on our compartment door.

"Twenty minutes to South Fork."

Once more, I fill my lungs with sweet air.

"Watch fingers," Mother says behind me. Henry obediently removes his chubby hands from the sill. Reluctantly, I shut the window and return to my seat as Henry hops over to join Mother on her side of the compartment. Nestling beneath her arm, he gazes adoringly into her eyes. His feathery blond hair dances about his forehead.

"Two stops, right, Mama?"

"Yes, darling." She kisses the top of her son's head.

"Will we see squirrels on the way up the mountain?"

Mother nods and grins. Then she glances across at me with a contented curve to her lips. In the tilt of her chin, she conveys the notion I know she's had many times before: *Oh, to have* two *children who wouldn't trouble her with minds of their own.*

## ···❧[ CHAPTER 2 ]❧···

SOUTHERN CALIFORNIA

*Memorial Day*
*Present*

The sun boiled Lee awake. Only a few hours into Memorial Day and North Beverly Park was already mired in the heat of deep summer. Like a cranky toddler after a drawn-out nap, Lee pressed her fists against her flushed cheeks and felt disagreeable. The towel she'd duct-taped to the wall of French windows had fallen in the night. Curtains were not allowed. A fan blowing on her face made more noise than breeze. Moldy smells rose up from the couch upholstery. Wet bathing suits and chlorine-soaked hair. The top sheet was kicked into an accordion at her feet. She flipped her clammy pillow to the cool side only to discover there was no cool side. Might as well sleep on a stack of pancakes.

"Good morning, adult daughter." Beaming, Valerie Parker emerged from the back room and kissed the top of Lee's head.

The humidity of sleep frizzed a halo of fine hairs down the length of Lee's long black curls.

"Pop-Tart?" Valerie asked. Dressed in beige Bermuda shorts and a striped tee, she seemed younger than her forty years, perpetually on the verge of bursting into a song from *Annie*.

"Mmph." It was the only sound Lee could muster. Trapped as she was in a nether land between wake and sleep, words were as yet unavailable. Her best friend, Shelby, once made her a choker out of letter beads that read NOT A MORNING PERSON. Frustration gusted from Shelby's lips like seawater from a whale's blowhole whenever she waited, yet again, at their corner. Once Lee arrived, she always attempted apologies, but it was *morning*. Sentences were still a jumble in her head.

Fluffing her coupon haircut, Valerie bounded into the kitchenette.

"Iced Raspberry Zinger?"

Lee bobbed her head and sucked in a deep breath to extract the last square inch of oxygen from the stuffy room. The air was as thick as Jell-O. Could a person die from carbon-dioxide toxicity so close to a wall of windows?

One glance outside revealed a palette of saturated blue. The turquoise water of the infinity pool met the sapphire sky. From this elevation in the hills above Mulholland Drive, the view was spectacular. If you stood at the edge of the ridge, the Valley looked picturesque. It was impossible to see the brown lawns.

"The bathroom is all yours," Val chirped. "I have time to lollygag."

Lee's shift didn't start until nine. Time for five more minutes. She rolled over and surrendered to the weight of her eyelids, inhaling the fusty air. Above her were the sounds of her particular morning: the creak of a cabinet door hinge, the rip of a Pop-Tart's freshness pouch, the bang of a microwave door open and shut, the *beep, beep* of its timer as her mother set it for twenty seconds.

"The day awaits, my sweet." Valerie leaned over her daughter and gently shook her shoulder. As she had since Lee was a baby, Valerie marveled at Lee's minky lashes, so long they curled in on themselves like the barrel of a surfer's perfect wave. Valerie joggled Lee's shoulder again.

Slowly, Lee opened her eyes. The microwave pinged.

In the white sunlight of another camera-ready day, Valerie stroked her daughter's soft cheek with the backs of her squat fingers. She smoothed Lee's tumble of black hair. Though the dread she'd been feeling as this day approached sat in her stomach like yesterday's oatmeal, she shook off all cloudy thoughts and returned to the kitchenette to open the minifridge and excavate the lone ice-cube tray from the frosted metal sleeve that was their freezer. Lee heard a crack and *plop, plop* into a plastic tumbler. The woodsy aroma of cinnamon braided midair with a sugary berry scent.

"Happy birthday, dear Lee-ee." Valerie's soprano pitch made Lee's heart clutch. Her mom's relentless cheer was her way of coping with the ocean of sadness within her. Val's natural buoyancy would never allow her to be sucked beneath the surf. They were as different as mother and daughter could be. Valerie greeted each day with determined bounce. Especially bleak mornings when she awoke to a refreshed memory of how badly her life had derailed. Lee was wired for catastrophe.

Things didn't always go wrong, but they *could*. Best to be per-petually prepared.

Over the years, Lee had tried to appropriate her mother's ruthless optimism, but it was no use. A black panther could never be a tabby cat. DNA was destiny.

With a grunt, Lee pulled herself up from the couch and into the day. She sleepwalked into the bathroom and shut the door. Eyes half closed, she avoided examining her face. She knew how she looked—irises like espresso beans, a jaw sharply angled in a determined sort of way, dark hair so dense it som-ersaulted down her back. She didn't even slightly resemble her champagne-haired parents or her brother with the Nordic eyelashes. They needed sunglasses when someone turned on a light. Even a stranger could tell she was adopted. Not that it was ever a secret.

Leaving the toilet unflushed to save water, Lee washed her hands and splashed cool water on her face. Twice. Shelby had nailed it. Lee Parker was not a morning person. Not even *this* morning when the world as she knew it was about to change. Again.

*New nonidentifying background information has surfaced regarding the medical history of the above-referenced adoptee.*

That sentence had tumbled through Lee's mind ever since the letter arrived from Social Services.

*Limited genetic information . . . after eighteenth birthday.*

Over and over, like a balled-up sheet in the dryer, phrases from the letter spun through her consciousness.

*Background information . . . above-referenced adoptee.*

Though the official envelope had been addressed to her parents and mailed to the house where they used to live, the letter was meant for her—the adoptee. Handwritten in the space below their zip code was Lee's previous name. No last name. No identifying background information. Just the original name her birth mother had given her: *Elizabeth.*

Valerie knocked softly on the bathroom door.

"Mrs. Adell needs me for a luncheon up at the house tomorrow," she said, her forehead pressed up to the jamb. "But I should be free by, say, two thirty or three. Is that too late to join you?"

Lee's shoulders drooped. A sarcastic retort popped into her head: *What's the rush to drive downtown in endless L.A. traffic to a government office that closes at four thirty?* Reaching for the knob, she curled her long fingers around it. Rotating her slim wrist, she opened the door.

"You don't have to come with me, Mom. I'm okay on my own."

A cloud passed over Valerie's eyes. "You don't want me there?"

"It's not that."

"I mean, if you'd rather not have your mother by your side . . ."

Lee frowned. Why did she test her?

"You know you'll always be my mom no matter what, right?"

"Right."

"And I love you. No matter what."

"Right."

In her mother's expression, Lee read her mind: *I can't bear another loss.* She understood the feeling. If you didn't cling to people, she now knew, they could slither away in the night. You could end up living in a moldy pool house with your sunny mother.

Lee reached out to encircle her mother's upper body. She felt the doughy softness of Valerie's upper arm, the padded ridge of her scapula. Curling into her, she rested her cheek on her mother's cushioned shoulder. The maternal pillow on which she'd leaned and cried and slept from the first day Valerie claimed her as her own. She inhaled the clean, uncomplicated scent of the only mother she'd ever known. Valerie Parker was the woman who applied Neosporin with a Q-tip so gently Lee barely felt it on her bloody scrapes; she jostled her tenderly when the alarm clock was beeping and young Lee was still floating atop a vast, warm ocean, buoyant, tucked into a blanket of stars. Not the slightest bit afraid of the gilled beings swimming beneath her. When she was sick, Valerie would press her forehead against her daughter's sweaty forehead to gauge her fever. She froze grapes to feed her when her throat was her sore. Every night she carefully folded back the top edge of her blanket and smoothed it over Lee's chest, whispering, "What fantastical journey will you take tonight?" She was *there* day in and day out, not just once on the day Lee was born.

"Tomorrow. Two thirty. I'll wait for you in the car," Lee said.

Tears rose in Valerie's light green eyes. She said, "We'll have an adventure."

Lee kissed her mother's cheek. She stretched to her full height. On her way back to the living room—such as it was—

she noticed that her mother's bed was already neatly made even though Mrs. Adell rarely checked before noon. Valerie's "bedroom" was really a dressing room in the back of the pool house; her bed was so skinny it was more like a padded cot. Their bathroom consisted of a toilet and completely impracti- cal pedestal sink. There was nowhere to put anything. They stored their toothbrushes in a mug on top of the toilet tank, which, Lee was pretty sure, was completely unsanitary. Don't toothbrushes need to be kept at least six feet away from free-floating germs? Didn't she read that in a dental pamphlet?

The shower was *outside*, surrounded by a brown picket fence. If they were anywhere but North Beverly Park, it would be woe- fully backwoods. While they didn't have to cart empty moon- shine jugs down to the creek, last week a baby skunk waddled out of the mountain brush while Lee was outside showering. When she screamed, it sprayed a lawn chair by the pool. How many skunk *families* lived in that hill?

It's fun to shower outside when you don't have to do it every day, even in the rain. Or worse, beneath the blaring Southern Californian sun. No lie, that shower sunburned Lee's shoul- ders. Plus, she felt more naked outdoors, forever worried that the mailman would pop his head over the shower's fencing with a certified letter flapping in his hand.

Seriously, Lee still couldn't believe they lived this way. Who could even imagine such a setup? Lately, it felt as if life itself was a sandbag on her shoulders. The events of the past year— and her current situation—were more than any eighteen-year- old should have be to bear.

As the clock ticked past eight fifteen, Lee walked over to the glass wall overlooking the pool, opened the door, and stepped outside.

"Aren't you too late for a shower?" Val asked, behind her.

Feeling the prickle of sweat beneath her cotton cami, Lee briefly pretended not to hear her. Then she nodded and replied, "I need two minutes of fresh air."

Tilting her head back, she let her eyelids fall shut. She faced the deliciously forbidden fire of the sun. Unscreened rays, she knew, could burn in less than fifteen minutes. Still, she expanded her chest and filled her lungs. For a fleeting moment, she felt free. Her heartbreaks slipped to a far corner of her mind. In twenty-four hours, Lee Parker would be reborn. When government offices reopened after the holiday, she would finally be allowed to meet the girl who had been living inside her for eighteen years: her biological self.

# ·∘❙ CHAPTER 3 ❙∘·

SOUTH FORK, PENNSYLVANIA

*Memorial Day*
*May 30, 1889*

The whistle shrills as the train begins its approach to South Fork Station: a weathered wood structure barely suitable for a lady. Unlike the summer arrival I am accustomed to, an odd quiet settles on the air despite the bustle of passengers onto the train at Altoona destined for the misty Memorial Day parade in Johnstown.

"We're here." Little Henry leaps up.

"Sit still, my precious." Mother settles her son down. I watch as her beautiful fingers flit about the front buttons of his velveteen Fauntleroy jacket. She fluffs his lacy collar and calms the flyaway strands of his hair. She plucks lint. Mother's spidery fingers are ideal for playing the piano. As are mine. We both excel at it. Last year, we entertained our holiday guests with a rousing duet of the most difficult "Mephisto Waltz." Mr. Liszt himself would have been delighted.

Obediently, Henry doesn't move. As I secure my hat with its pearl-tipped pin, I feel for my little brother. Surely his outfit suffocates as much as mine, yet he endures without complaint. As does Mother. Once she finishes her fussing, she slides her hands into her gloves, raises her chin, and sits as formidably as the Osterling bell tower. In silence, she waits for the train to stop completely. She lets her rigid spine speak for her. *Observe how a lady displays discomfort.* Not once have I seen Mother betray the expectations her fortunate union to Father thrust upon her.

"'Tis *I* who married well," he often says, embarrassing her. Implicit in the loving sentiment is the very real fact that Vera Sinclair married above her class. Her father—my grandfather, Silas—was a custom tailor near Pittsburgh's East End. Silas Sinclair was known well in the social circles of North Point Breeze and Upper St. Clair. Rare was the dining table that wasn't populated by men feeling the comfortable containment of a Silas Sinclair waistcoat. Though it was Grandfather's stunning daughter that kept Father returning for fittings long after his wardrobe was full.

"The moment I set eyes upon your mother, I could see no other," Father frequently sang in his baritone pitch.

Impeccably dressed Vera Sinclair had her pick of several suitors. Yet Dr. Haberlin was the most desirable choice. Grandfather said so often. While Father wasn't the wealthiest of Mother's admirers, he occupied an unimpeachable spot on the outskirts of society: a trusted physician whose loyalty was unquestioned. A man who could be counted on to keep secrets.

Amid the screech of the braking shoes against the locomotive's wheels, I gaze at my mother and see the woman I will become. Still a beauty, she has nonetheless aged beyond awe. Unlike my own kaleidoscope of inky hues, Mother's obsidian hair reflects fewer highlights. Faint creases fan out from the outer edges of her blue-green eyes and her hands are lined with delicate tributaries. Strict use of parasols and hats has preserved the paleness of her skin. The only cosmetic she ever uses is beet juice on her cheeks and lips and only sparingly on special occasions.

"Father told me not to play on the dock," Henry says, bobbing up and down on the seat, "but how else can I see the jumping fish?"

"They don't jump until summer," I say.

Mother and I exchange smiles. In summer—when all of Pittsburgh society relaxes in our exclusive mountain paradise— the caretaker stocks the lake with so many bass they can't help but leap over one another. They are so plentiful they often clog the spillway. The placid surface of our lake roils like bathwater forgotten on the stove.

Ah, summer. Glorious summer at the South Fork Fishing

and Hunting Club. My heart flutters at the thought of it. Weeks of fun and leisure. Croquet is my specialty, but water sports are my favorite. The way a line of sailboats slices the surface of Lake Conemaugh is as beautiful a sight as any I've ever seen. And when Mother allows me to race in a regatta, well, the thrill of heeling right up to the tipping point is unlike any excitement I've experienced in Pittsburgh.

Plus, last summer, in a clearing between the clubhouse and the South Fork Dam, James Tottinger from Great Britain first made himself known to me. And I to him.

"Do fish get cold, 'Lizb . . . Elizabeth?"

"No." I tug at the wrists of my gloves.

"Why not?" Henry's baby-blue eyes blink at me.

"Henry, *please,*" I say.

"Fish don't get cold because it is not in their nature," Mother calmly explains. "Biology is destiny, my darling. We all must be whom we are meant to be."

A quizzical look flashes into my eyes. Then a tiny grin curls the corners of my lips. Henry jumps up the moment the train stops moving. Mother and I wait for the porter's escort. I position my shoulders as befitting a girl of my breeding. Like Mother, I, too, am a beauty. And following in the Haberlin tradition, I shall marry above my station, as well. Only I plan to follow my mother's advice: I will be who I *am,* not who everyone expects me to be.

# ·∘꽃 CHAPTER 4 꽃∘·

## SOUTHERN CALIFORNIA

*Memorial Day*
*Present*

Lee was low on gas. Lately, the old Toyota seemed to be gulping fuel into its innards only to spew it out the tailpipe in gusts of white. Thankfully, the Encino branch of Bed Bath & Beyond was downhill almost all the way. She shifted into neutral and rode the brake.

"Do you feel different now that you're officially eighteen?" Valerie had asked before Lee left the pool house that morning. Lee was crouched behind the couch, folding her pajama pants and unfolding the tan khakis and blue uniform shirt she kept in a neat stack there. Next to the stashed sheets and pillow. Out of sight, as Mrs. Adell required. Valerie's face was so openly hopeful, Lee didn't have the heart to tell her the truth. Of course she felt different. How could she not? The speed of life's unraveling had left her dizzy. She had envisioned rising on her eighteenth birthday in her own bed, in her own home.

"Good morning, Mom and Dad," she would say as soon as full consciousness took hold. It would be a rare day when everything went right.

"Scott!" Her older brother would surprise her by coming home for the weekend. The family would be together in a TV sort of way. Valerie would hum a Sunday-morning tune while she scrambled eggs at the stove. Gil, Lee's father, would snatch a rippled piece of bacon from the greasy paper towel on the plate by the retro toaster. Valerie would playfully bump him with her hip. Scott would ruffle Lee's hair and call her "sis." Their twelve-year age difference would seem quirky instead of cryptic. Freshly ground coffee would suffuse the sunny kitchen with the irresistible smell of possibility.

After a loud and laughing breakfast, Lee would clear the dishes and wipe down the table and promise to be home in time for the Memorial Day picnic. Then she'd meet Shelby in Balboa Park, where they'd spread two towels on the grass by the lake and get started on their summer tans. Together, Lee and Shelby would fantasize about the fall semester when they would both rise from a *dorm* bed. Lee at Columbia. Shelby at Stanford.

"My roommate will be perpetually hungover," Shelby would muse.

"She'll stir yogurt and granola into a rinsed-out coffee mug," Lee would add. "And eat only half of it."

"Her hair will be sexily jostled."

"Unlike my morning fright wig!"

"I will kick *ass* in linguistics." Shelby planned to be a speech therapist.

"I will . . . do *something* amazing!" Lee was undecided. The only thing she knew for sure was that her future would shine as brightly as the lighthouse at Cabrillo Beach.

Even her most dire imaginings never pictured the current scenario: working at Bed Bath & Beyond and living in a cramped pool house with her mother, now a live-in maid. Her father gone, moved into a rusty trailer in Topanga Canyon, and her brother burrowed into a yurt somewhere in the Idaho woods. And Shelby—the best friend, who knew everything there was to know about Lee—in Malawi, spending her last summer before college building houses for the poor. Before, Lee never appreciated how heavy separations could feel.

"I feel extremely mature," she told her mom. Not entirely a lie.

In the sweltering car on the way into the Valley, Lee slowly rolled downhill with the windows open and the air conditioner off to save gas. She reached her hand up to the dashboard to practice the keys to the right of middle C. Just because she no longer had a piano didn't mean music wasn't in her head. This morning it was Giovanni Marradi. The high notes of his compositions soothed her like raindrops on a windowpane. Shelby used to call Marradi the Walmart Franz Liszt, but Lee didn't care. His music moved her. After school, she used to sit at their clinky old Baldwin and play Marradi's "Just for You" over and over until her fingers knew it by heart. Now she no longer had a piano or a dad or a proper living room. But her hands still knew the notes.

*Elizabeth.*

Inserting itself into the melody in her head was her birth name. As it did from time to time. She'd always known it. Her parents never hid the fact that she arrived with a label. And one with so many variants! Liz, Liza, Lizzy, Eliza, Beth, Betty.

"My child will be called *Lee*," Valerie had decreed. "A baby shouldn't have to cart around a name larger than she is. Lee is perfect. One foot in her original name, the other in her new life."

That was that. Lee had always been Lee Parker, daughter of Gil and Val, sister of Scott. The most wanted baby in the world. After a few years, she rarely thought about her beginnings at all. Well, hardly ever.

Then the letter arrived. Pushed through the mail slot in the door of the house in the Valley where she used to live. When her family was still intact and her future was unbroken. The letter sat on the floor with the water bill and bank statement and a tool catalog that her dad would tuck under his arm on the way to the bathroom. When Lee spotted the envelope, her breath caught in her windpipe. Its return address—California Department of Social Services—could only mean it had something to do with her. Why would they make contact after all these years?

"New nonidentifying information . . ." That's what she read that day, and *re*read a million times for months afterward. A national database had tracked her down. Limited genetic information, she was told, was recently discovered and would be made available after her eighteenth birthday. Since hers was a closed adoption, her history had been left blank. The only information Lee and her parents were ever given was that Lee's birth mother had drowned when Lee was a baby. Period. End of story. As if Lee's wondering would stop there, too.

It didn't. Of course not. As any adoptee knew.

Now, in one more day, her history would open up. A tiny crack. Still. It was something. A squiggle on her blank slate. Limited though it might be, knowledge was there for the taking. "If the adoptee so desires," the letter had stated. "Some do and some do not."

Lee did. Of course she did.

Birth kids never got it. That *simmering*. Like white noise, tiny bubbles were forever agitating her brain, fizzing about, not making too much of a fuss until one day, out of the clear blue, they enlarge and multiply and swim madly for the surface. All at once curiosity roils.

*Who am I?*

Innate belonging—the aura that genetic children feel so naturally they don't feel it at all—had remained a fingernail sliver away. Casual comments at the dinner table: *Scott, you are as impulsive as your father* pinched at Lee's chest. Not hard. No bruising. Just *there*.

*Am I as impulsive as my father? As sensitive as my mother? The spitting image of my aunt? Had anyone ever wondered what became of* me?

Lee hungered to know not just about her birth mother, but about her biological mother's mother, and *her* mother, too. Her entire lineage. More than one generation is lost when you lack genetic parentage. A whole ancestry disappears like hot breath on a cold window. Dad? Granddad? Great-grandfather? Had any male ever been more than sperm? Who gave Lee brown eyes that were so dark they looked black? Which ancestor wired her to be restless? A worrier? Had she, oh please, inherited resilience?

As Ventura Boulevard came into view, Lee shifted into drive and returned her piano hand to the steering wheel. "Green, green, green," she chirped, channeling Valerie by sending positive traffic vibes to the multilaned intersection. Just before she got there, the light turned red.

"Drat." Lights didn't always turn red on her, but they usually did.

*Did my birth mother have more red lights than green? Is traffic karma inherited?* Valerie rarely hit a red light. She didn't know what it felt like to be constantly kept out of the flow.

"Twenty-one, twenty-two, twenty-three . . ." Lee counted the seconds at the red light. Numbers calmed her. They were orderly and predictable. Most Los Angeles intersections, she knew, had up to two full seconds when all traffic was completely stopped. Yellow lights stayed lit for about four seconds, sometimes six, before the light turned red. It was based on some sort of algorithm designed to keep everyone moving. Unless you were late for work. In that case, red lights were endless.

"Thirty-six, thirty-seven, thirty-eight . . ."

The instant the green arrow lit up, Lee surged into the intersection and turned left onto the wide boulevard. As fast as possible, she raced to the parking lot in front of Bed Bath & Beyond. It was ten past nine. Already, the lot was crowded. Her favorite space—the far corner under the tree—was taken. Associates weren't allowed to park near the door. Lee groaned. By the end of her shift, the car would be an oven.

Swinging open the door, she leaped out, locked the car, and ran. As the rubber soles of her tennis shoes bounced across the soft asphalt, the irony of it all sprang into her consciousness: today was her birthday as well as Memorial Day. Yet *tomorrow* was the "birth" day she would never forget.

# ·◦⟩[ CHAPTER 5 ]⟨◦·

*Courtesy of the Johnstown Flood Museum Archives, Johnstown Area Heritage Association*

ABOVE JOHNSTOWN, PENNSYLVANIA

*Memorial Day*
*May 30, 1889*

In a flurry of movement, the train doors open and passengers flood the platform. Our porter exits first, and then extends his hand to assist us down the steep steps. *One, two, three.* Silently, I count my footfalls. A habit from childhood. For some reason, numbers are a comfort. A lullaby of sorts.

On the platform, the porter holds an open umbrella over our heads though the rain has yet to restart. Mother, Henry, and I are the only first-class passengers to disembark. Who else would come to South Fork off-season? The train station, however, is bustling with travelers. Muscular steelworkers, mostly, and their sturdy wives. The women carry picnic baskets; the men are dressed in their Sunday-best butternut trousers. All are on their way, no doubt, to the festivities one stop down the line.

"Hurry now," Mother says, with a linen handkerchief pressed to her nose. Quite unnecessary, I realize instantly. The distant smokestacks of Johnstown's nonstop steel mill emit only the faintest puffs of white, unlike a normal summer day in which the entire train station would be enshrouded in a murky blend of smoke and fog, smelling decidedly sulfuric. Today, the bosses at Cambria Iron must have cut the workday short so the men and their families could enjoy the Memorial Day parade.

I step out from under the umbrella and stand erect in my finery to breathe in the sodden air. Allowing, admittedly, a few moments for the townspeople to admire my dress.

"Elizabeth," Mother says over her shoulder. A carriage is waiting on the uphill road to the club.

"Miss Haberlin?"

Behind me is a vaguely familiar voice. I turn to see a face I haven't seen since last summer.

"Why, Mr. Eggar!"

He has the same puckish expression, though perhaps a bit paler in complexion since the summer's sun has yet to tint his skin. His shirtsleeves are unrolled and tight at the cuffs; his broadcloth vest lies flat against his torso. Atop the charcoal curls I remember well sits a shiny black bowler hat. It appears to be freshly brushed for the holiday.

"What brings you to South Fork on this gray day?" I ask, feeling a slight flush to my cheeks. How fortuitous I wore such a fetching frock.

Eugene Eggar grins. As I had last summer, I note the surprising evenness of his teeth. They are not unlike the ivory keys of my parlor grand piano in Upper St. Clair. He says, "Isn't it more surprising to see *you*?"

"It is, indeed." I return his smile. "Though I can't say I'm happy about it. See, Fath—"

"Elizabeth?"

Behind me, Mother stands with an alarmed expression. Little Henry's moon face peers out from the folds of her skirt.

"Mother, permit me to introduce Mr. Eggar from Johnstown."

"Mrs. Haberlin." Eugene removes his hat and bows slightly. Mother, I am distraught to notice, does not offer her hand. Thank goodness she drops the handkerchief from her nose.

"How do you do," she says, stiffly.

"And, Mr. Eggar, may I present my brother, Henry."

Little Henry steps forward to ask, "Did you ride the train, too?"

Eugene laughs. "Why, yes. Just a few moments ago I arrived to check on the state of the river." He looks at me, and I at him.

Mother says, "Our carriage is waiting, Elizabeth." To Mr. Eggar, she ends the conversation by wishing him a pleasant day and politely excusing herself to turn her back on him and make her way across the platform. Deep embarrassment descends upon me like morning fog over the peak of a mountaintop. It is clear that Mother is too perplexed by my association with a town boy to treat him with the respect I know he deserves. In the normal order of things, our paths would never cross. Especially not up here. Though mere miles separate the club from downtown Johnstown, its working-class inhabitants are as apart from us as heaven is from earth.

True to his character, Mr. Eggar nods at me in understanding. He is not unwise to the ways of the world.

At that moment, the train's whistle trills and the conductor shouts, "All aboard!" Departing passengers scuttle to the open doors. Umbrellas pop open over the heads of those who remain. It has begun to rain again. In the commotion, Henry extricates himself from Mother's skirt and scampers directly into the steam cloud still puffing from the locomotive at the front of the train. Its mammoth grille chuffs like an overheated Friesian stallion.

"Henry!" Mother shouts, but he doesn't hear her.

Supervising the final boarding of his passengers, the conductor stands near the engine. Clad in a double-breasted suit and flat-topped hat, he grins as roly-poly Henry scuttles toward him. He checks his pocket watch. Then he says, "Quickly, lad. Give me your foot."

Without hesitation, Henry deposits his leather ankle boot into the center of the conductor's interwoven fingers. In one exhilarating boost, he is lifted into the air and set upon the engineer's perch. From inside the cab behind the engine, the locomotive driver opens the small hatch and says, "My, my. Who do we have here?"

"I'm Henry! I'm six!"

Grabbing firmly on to Henry's upper arm, the engineer helps him into the cab and out of the rain. He lets him tug on the dangling wooden handle.

*Whoo. Whoo.*

On the platform, the townspeople laugh at Henry's playfulness. As do Eugene and I. Far from disruptive, the train's whistle is such an ordinary part of their daily existence, it simply blends into the clamor of life in the valley. Mother is not as amused. I see that her eyes are white with fright.

"He's fine," I state. "Look at his happiness."

Clearly on top of the world, Henry yanks the handle a third time.

*Whooooo.*

"He's a child," she says, stepping near enough to clutch my arm. "*My* child." Turning her head away, Mother presses her handkerchief to her chest and whispers, "If anything happened to him, I would die."

Her sincerity startles me. I want to hide from the stark vulnerability that has blanched her face. Eugene witnesses it, too. Without a word, he hurries to the conductor.

"Sir, would you be so kind as to help my young friend down?"

The conductor nods and hoists himself onto the steel ledge.

Henry's wide grin fades like the final sliver of a setting sun. Reluctantly, he lets the conductor encircle his waist to secure his footing earthward. Only when Henry's feet touch ground and Eugene returns him to Mother does the desperate look in her eyes abate.

"There, there," I say to her, as if *I* am her mother. "You needn't fret."

My brother is again swallowed into the folds of her skirt. Mother bends down to rain kisses on her son's rosy cheeks before raising her head to thank Mr. Eggar, but he has already disappeared.

## ···⊰❪ CHAPTER 6 ❫⊱···

SOUTHERN CALIFORNIA

*Present*

In the normal order of things, the Parkers and the Adells would never have met. Fifteen miles and a universe apart, they circulated in different orbits. Until their worlds collided in a spectacular explosion of space debris.

"I got in!"

The previous March, Lee Parker skipped into the family kitchen brandishing a letter. Her father was sitting at the table and her mother was standing at the sink. Too excited to utter anything other than "Eeeeeee!," she tapped her finger four times on the insignia. Co-lum-bi-a. Columbia *University*, that is. The Ivy that her three-point-nine GPA and SAT score over twenty-one hundred (first try) got her. One of the achievements Lee wrote about in her admissions essay was the Chamber Music Club. It met three times a week *before* school and it was well established that Lee wasn't a morning person.

Best of all, Lee's parents had the tuition in the bank. By her tenth birthday, Lee knew what a 529 savings plan was.

"One day you'll thank me for having your birthday party in the backyard with a homemade cake," Valerie had said.

For Lee, her college fund was like a fudge brownie wrapped in foil and stashed in a far corner of the freezer. Knowing it was there was delicious.

That day, in their Valley kitchen, with the harvest-yellow refrigerator that didn't match anything, Gil Parker lifted a glass of scotch to his lips. Val stood at the sink with a tissue pressed to her nose. A faint aroma of vomit infused the air.

"What's wrong?" Lee skidded to a stop. The black energy between her parents was so thick it literally smacked her in the face. "Has somebody *died*? Did Scott—?"

"Heavens, no," her dad said, gruffly. Only then did Lee wonder why he was home in the afternoon. "Are you okay?" she asked her father as fear blanched her face. He said nothing. Her mother still hadn't turned around. Lee wobbled in place. Her feet seemed to weigh more than her whole body. She had the sensation of being one of those dashboard figurines, as if she could fall all the way forward on ankles made of springs.

Gulping the remains of his drink, Gil held the glass to his face until the half-moon ice cubes crashed down to his lips. With a grunt, he stood up. Placing one meaty hand on his daughter's back, he stiffly guided her through the kitchen doorway into the living room. Past the piano. He sat his daughter down on the white damask couch that was reserved for company. Valerie followed with her chin on her chest.

In a ripped-off Band-Aid sort of way, Gil blurted the news.

"Your college money is gone."

Lee looked at her parents, still standing in front of her. "Gone?" Her eyes darted left and right. She wondered if "gone" might be some obscure financial term meaning, perhaps, invested offshore? Maybe a foreign word she misheard? *Gund? Kahn?* Blinking, she waited for an explanation or a hidden camera to be revealed. Her father's eyelids hung heavily. He shoved his hands in his pockets and jiggled his keys.

At last her mother spoke. "Your father had been investing it—"

"Yes," Lee interrupted. "In the five twenty-nine."

"Well, there was no five twenty-nine."

"No five twenty-nine?"

"Initially, there was one, yes. But, see—"

Over Lee's head, Valerie said to her husband, "Gil?" She then turned away as if she couldn't bear to look. Though Lee didn't want him to, her father sat next to her on the company couch and took her hands in his. She felt his failure in the sticky dampness of his palms, smelled his acrid breath. Intermittently, he squeezed her fingers so hard it hurt. It felt intentional, though she was sure it wasn't. Was it? Gil muttered something about a broker and bad advice and a housing bubble back in 2008 and Wall Street crooks who made promises they had no right to make.

"The system is rigged," he said. "Where's *my* bailout?"

The 529, he spat out indignantly, was earning a measly 6 percent. "Six percent? That would have been *criminal* when the housing market was on fire."

Lee's brain swam with numbers. Six percent compounded annually. Times seventeen. Plus reinvested dividends. Carry the one. Had her father forgotten how good she was at numbers?

Even with the early withdrawal penalty, Gil Parker droned on, the credit default swaps his broker set up made it look like a no-brainer. He laid it out on a spreadsheet, a *spreadsheet*, for God's sake. Why, the guy at work who turned him onto the broker took his family on vacation to St. Bart's!

"Only a fool would have played it safe, Lee. Don't you see?"

While her father spoke, Lee stared at his lips, marveling at his ability to form words with a tongue and teeth. Stunningly, the man could string entire sentences together with fancy words like "derivatives" and "subprime collateral debt" while she could barely breathe. He said, "I believed our time horizon was sufficient to recoup. But here we are." Gil blathered on about some whale in London and filled the stale air in their living room with the smell of low tide. Not once did Lee hear the two words she was expecting: "I'm sorry." Or better still: Plan B. Instead, Gil gave Lee's hand a one-two pat. He then let go and clapped his knees in a what's-done-is-done sort of way. It seemed to her a period on the discussion, as if he were slapping blood back into his legs, readying them to leap up and trot him out of responsibility.

"There are loans," Valerie said quietly. "And financial aid."

Financial aid? Had Lee known there was no money—had she not been lied to for *years*—she would have applied for financial aid while she had the chance. She never would have let the deadline pass. And school loans? At Columbia University?

Well, at an estimated $64,000 a year, she would graduate with more than a quarter-million dollars in debt. Seriously, had her parents *forgotten* all the math tests she'd aced?

"This is a speed bump in life," Valerie said, attempting to summon a silver lining from the stash of optimism she kept on her person at all times. Still finding it hard to expand her lungs, Lee wanted to spit out, *Hear that ditty from Dr. Phil?* but she knew it would sound mean. Her mother wasn't to blame. Her dad— the man they both believed in—had blindsided her, too.

In a similar yet altogether different way, Esther and Leonard Adell had also been knocked off their feet. It happened one evening in September. They were sitting in the teak-paneled den of their multimillion-dollar home. The one with the moldy pool house.

"Isn't that *Kenneth*?" Esther Adell pointed an arthritic finger at the television screen. Beside her, Leonard ate his dinner on a Lucite tray. Their formal dining room was too large for the two of them. Especially since old age was shriveling them up. Watching Fox News in the den with supper prepared by their maid, Delfina, was an evening ritual. Leonard adored her chicken with rice.

"Look. There." Esther's forefinger resembled a dog-chewed stick. "I'm quite sure that's *Kenneth* in the crowd."

An old friend from law school, Kenneth Derrid had roomed with Leonard Adell their senior term. Over the years, they'd kept in touch. Gold-printed holiday cards. Collegial backslapping at charity events. No question: Kenneth had done well. He had a $7 million mansion on Long Island, a Central Park West pied-à-terre in the city, a beachfront condo in Miami, a blinding Rolex that hung heavily on his wrist. Leonard had done well, too. As an attorney who schooled corporations on tax inversion and other legal ways to avoid paying what they owed to the United States, his business was booming for much of his career. His lifelong passion for modern art and architecture had been an expensive hobby he could well afford.

When Kenneth launched his own hedge fund, he quietly invited Leonard and Esther into his exclusive investment group. They were honored to be regarded so specially. Though Leonard would never be so gauche as to brag, he was heard to remark, "My chum Kenneth is our bank." Eyes cast floorward like a coquette's, Leonard would sip Camus Cognac from an etched Fostoria tumbler, his professionally buffed fingernails gleaming.

For years, the Adells gave the Bank of Kenneth all the cash they didn't spend on art and the construction of their gallery of a home. He invested their money and made them wealthy. The Adells lived in an obscenely large house made almost entirely of glass, designed by an architect with one name. Like Cher. Or Ludacris. The house sat like a fallen asteroid—glowing and otherworldly—above Mulholland Drive. It had taken so long to build, the architect never got around to updating the creaky pool house down the hill.

Investing in Kenneth's fund had been a no-brainer. Only a fool accepted a federally insured interest rate. The Adells' monthly financial statements were like opening a holiday gift. Many happy returns. Until the night they ate chicken and rice while watching the evening news.

Leonard looked up from his plate and stopped chewing. He

tried to swallow the masticated rice, but couldn't. His mouth had gone dry. There, on the television screen—jostled by reporters and jabbed with phallic microphones—was indeed Kenneth Derrid. Their bank. He had the same sappy smile Bernie Madoff had had during his perp walk. Those thin upturned lips made the Adells sick to their stomachs.

"This can't be," Leonard mumbled, mouth full.

"Impossi—" At that moment, both Esther and her husband had no choice but to deposit their bites of supper into their linen napkins.

It couldn't be . . . but it *was*. Kenneth's hedge fund turned out to be a feeder fund to another fund that had been a sham. Like the Madoff scheme, it had been an elaborate way to enrich brokers with fees while the paper profits reported on their investors' monthly statements were exactly that: paper. Unbelievably, Leonard Adell—an expert at hidden assets—hadn't suspected a thing. Frankly, he hadn't even thought to look closely. How could he be swindled by a friend? A roommate, no less. They'd shared late-night secrets in beer-muddled whispers.

Up the hill in North Beverly Park, a partner in Leonard's law firm negotiated a confidential deal: the Adells would be allowed to live in their glass house for the remainder of their lives if they quietly signed over the deed and select works of art to the liquidation trust fund. An original Basquiat paid their legal fees. (*Donated* to his law firm, of course, for the tax deduction.)

The only downside was: when the trustee arrived with the notarized paperwork, Delfina and the Adells' undocumented staff saw the federal logo on his sedan and skittered out the back door.

Down the hill in the San Fernando Valley, the bankruptcy court whipped the Parkers' house out from under them like a magician pulling a tablecloth off a fully set table. *Abrakazam.* It was gone. In a tornado of dust balls, Lee lost her bed and her bedroom and her piano. Everything she owned that couldn't easily hide behind a couch was sold or given to Goodwill. Storage was too expensive. Lee lost college and the corner where Shelby had impatiently waited for her. She lost her dad, too. Gil Parker did something Lee didn't think parents were allowed to do: he ran away from home.

In the aftermath of both disasters, Valerie needed a job and a home; Esther needed a maid who could keep her mouth shut. A deal was struck. Val would help the Adells maintain the illusion that they were still rich. *Be* the help, actually. When the Adells had company, Valerie would wear a maid's uniform and a lacy white cap straight out of the nineteenth century. She would serve cold salmon salads and hot tea. Plates from the left, beverages from the right. She was to be neither seen nor heard.

"A *teenager*?" Mrs. Adell's face blanched when Valerie asked if Lee could live with her.

"She's quiet and studious. It would only be for a little while. She has a job." Unexpectedly, tears welled in Valerie's eyes. It happened. Life's battering had busted her ability to control her tear ducts. A few days before, she'd broken down at the sight of three bobbing balloons in front of a Verizon Wireless store.

Mrs. Adell patted Valerie's arm with her clawlike hand. Unable to conceive children, Esther Adell had always envisioned herself as the type of mother who would tear up at the mere mention of her offspring. It was the sort of fantasy only childless women have. "She'll be discreet?"

"Absolutely."

They made a deal. Valerie and Lee were forbidden to talk to anyone in the main house or tell *anyone* where they lived. It was a rider in their clandestine landlord-tenant contract, subject to immediate eviction with the first infraction. Their "address" was a post office box in the Valley. They parked their car in a vacant strip of dirt down the hill. Friends were not allowed to pick them up even *near* the Adells' electrified gate, or visit them in the pool house, or—heavens, no—ease the Californian heat with a dip in the infinity pool just outside their wall of windows.

Esther Adell held on to the ruse that she was still rich the way a hyena clamps its jaws on a fresh carcass. Nothing could persuade her to loosen her grip. Her luncheons were repetitions of the same dance: bejeweled, crinkled women buzzed about each other with stinging air kisses. "That hairstyle *never* gets old, dear." Reeking of spray gel, they spumed their importance with chatter about giving back.

"To much is given, so much is expected."

All the while treating Valerie as if she had no ears and no feelings.

"Dear me, my coffee has spilled onto my saucer. It's *literally* impossible to find good help."

Each morning when Lee awoke on the moldy sofa bed, she was again struck by the insane setup. The Adells lived in a designer home and pretended to be rich. Below them, the Parkers lived in a pool house and pretended to be homeless.

Crazy.

After her shift ended, Lee sat in her sauna of a car and prayed that it would start. She once read that it takes half a teaspoon of gas to ignite an engine and that's about all she had in the tank.

"C'mon, baby," she whispered, feeling the floral stink of work bake onto her skin. "Just get me to the gas station across the street."

The key clicked to the right. The car started. Lee crumpled in relief. Pressing her foot to the gas pedal as lightly as possible, she backed out of the parking space and drove to the exit in the middle of the shopping center. Luck was with her. The lights were green. She crossed Ventura Boulevard without idling and pulled straight up to the pump. With her last twenty—payday was next week—Lee bought as much gas as she could. Enough, she hoped, to fuel her journey downtown the following day.

After eighteen years of questions, she was about to get some answers. Nothing was going to stop her now. She would *walk* if she had to.

# ·∘❦| CHAPTER 7 |❦∘·

THE SOUTH FORK DAM

*Memorial Day*
*May 30, 1889*

Colonel Unger thoughtfully sent his man from the lake to pick us up at the station. Unfortunately, the large trap carriage is open to the elements in spite of its attached roof. The rain is soft, but steady.

"Here, miss."

Nettie hands me one of the cashmere lap robes Colonel Unger has stored in the back of the carriage. Mother has already wrapped Henry in his like a chrysalis. I shiver slightly. Outside, it *is* unseasonably cool.

My maid climbs to the open perch beside the driver—not her beau, Floyd, I notice—and eases in with Mother's maid, Ella. Maggie, the undercook, sits next to me. We will have to make do with a skeleton staff. The clubhouse dining room will be closed and Father flatly refused to part with the family's butler and primary cook. "Two weeks without Ida's Nesselrode pie?" he said. "Unthinkable!"

"Did you see me up there, Mama? Did you?" Henry is still excited. Sensing his elation, the horses gnaw on their snaffles.

"Settle in, darling."

"But did you *see* me?"

"I saw you." At last, Mother smiles. Her fright at Henry's folly dissolves into the sodden air. Turning to me, she asks the question I have been expecting. "How is it you know a town boy?"

I long to inform Mother that I have a full and intricate life beyond her reach, but of course, it isn't true. I reply, "He was helpful last summer with Ivy Tottinger."

Mother's brows press together in a dubious expression. To quiet her doubts, I add a small untruth.

"He works in the boathouse at the club."

Just then, the carriage lurches forward and Henry claps his hands. He clucks his tongue the way he's heard carriage drivers do. The horses' ears flicker. Nettie and Ella look back at us and smile from beneath their umbrella. Little Henry's exuberance is infectious. My leaden mood has disappeared. Perhaps a few days of solitude will soften the tautness I've noticed around my mouth. With so much to plan and think about in Pittsburgh, the tension of my debut has begun to announce itself in my complexion.

Suddenly a strand of sunlight peers through the wet leaves. The rain lightens to a drizzle as the ominous gray clouds float toward the valley. As we ascend the winding mountain road, the carriage gently sways side to side. The rhythmic clip-clopping of the horses' hooves makes me sleepy. I snuggle beneath the lap robe and settle in for the ride.

Pinnate leaves of the ash trees hang over the road like a dancer's graceful hands. Distant hills are a dusky purple hue. Pops of yellow daffodils delight my eyes. These mountains are magnificent—once one rises above the sooty valley. Even though the air is soggy, it's impossible not to feel stirrings of joy at the promise of warmth. Last winter was abominable. And the Alleghenies cling to winter longer than Upper St. Clair does. Father said they were completely blanketed in deep snow. This season, Colonel Unger may be able to forgo restocking the lake. Fresh bass from the mountain streams are always better tasting than the imported variety from less pristine waters.

"When I'm grown-up, I'm going to drive a train," says Henry, dreamily. "Trains are . . . are *magical*."

Mother grins and tucks the blanket even more tightly around her son's small body. She refrains from correcting him. Why spoil his boyish dreams with the adult knowledge of his certain future? Henry Haberlin will grow into a physician like his father, or a banker or a lawyer. If lucky, perhaps he will one day *own* a railroad.

"Settle in, my love," Mother says to him.

We ride uphill in silence, each to his or her thoughts. As we near the crest of the long, narrow incline, the South Fork dam comes into view. As always, I am struck dumb by the utter *presence* of it. The dam—a massive sloping wall of mud and muck that contains our beautiful lake—seems to be a living, breathing beast. Made of puddle clay, hay, gravel, manure, tree trunks, rocks—anything and everything, really—it smells of the forest floor. Today, that is, as it glistens from the spurts of rain. In the heat of midsummer, the earthen dam is alive with aromatic material that appears to be both growing and decaying before our very eyes.

The carriage driver pulls back on the reins and slows the horses just beyond the first "No Trespassing" sign. Henry squeals, "Whoa!" The driver then makes a sharp right turn and steers us directly atop the flattened breast of the mammoth South Fork dam. Through the wheels, I feel the dam's throbbing. Its *heartbeat.* As other drivers do each summer when Pittsburgh's finest families arrive one by one for their getaway at the mountain retreat, our driver stops in the very center of the crossing to allow us a moment to enjoy the breathtaking—and hair-raising—view. To the left is a sheet of beryl blue as far as the eye can see. From this vantage point, our private lake looks almost like an ocean. To the right: a vertical drop is as deep as Pittsburgh's courthouse tower is high. Or deeper. Far below us, I see pointed treetops and jagged rock. A curving, snaggle-toothed ravine that snakes steeply downhill into darkness. I cannot stare into that black valley without a loss of equilibrium. Even now that we are not as high up as we once were. The club's governors hired workmen from town to lower the top of the earth-packed dam a few feet so that the dirt road would be wider. Crossing the top of the dam is the only convenient way in and out of the club. Naturally, a wider road makes it easier to accommodate the passage of our carriages.

"Progress."

It's the word I overheard Mr. Frick use to describe widening the dam's crossing by lowering its top. So certain is he that motorcars will soon replace horse-drawn carriages, he is pleased that the more forward-thinking members of the South Fork Fishing and Hunting Club had the foresight to create a wide enough road to handle modern transportation.

Not everyone agreed. More than once, men in the clubhouse parlor hotly debated the decision to lower the dam. Enveloped in cigar smoke, they tugged at the satin collars of their dinner jackets.

"The dam should be *higher*," one said.

"Rebuilt entirely," added another.

"Where is the discharge pipe? When is the last time Unger cleared out the debris around the spillway?"

"We're tempting fate."

The opposition was a large chorus with one refrain: "Have you any idea of the *cost*?"

A thoughtful silence most often ensued. Followed by the stroking of chin beards or the curling of wax-tipped mustaches or the flagging down of waiters for more refreshment. Ultimately, four words prevailed.

"Evolve or go extinct."

Was that Mr. Frick's voice I heard utter that persuasive statement? Probably. It was spoken with his usual confidence. Often I overheard those words uttered to end an argument flat. Henry Clay Frick is a man who often gets his way without tedious debate. Father once privately described him as a *capitalist*. He meant it not as a compliment. I have heard that Mr. Frick's steelworkers at the Homestead mill despise him. His reputation is one of a cruel boss who values profit over humanity. A robber baron. When workers in the Johnstown Valley bitterly dubbed our mountain retreat the "Bosses' Club," Mr. Frick laughed and bellowed, "Damn right we're the bosses."

*Why shouldn't he feel proud of his accomplishments?* I thought when I first heard tell of it. Ungrateful workers were forever grumbling about one thing or another. As if they expected the men of the Bosses' Club to give them every dime from their pockets. Cruel? Ridiculous. Whenever the impeccably dressed Mr. Frick saw me, he self-assuredly took my hand and lifted it to his lips in the most graceful manner. "The lovely Miss Haberlin," he said, his eyes twinkling. "How well you look."

What do people expect? A man who is in charge of other men must at times be ruthless. As Mother has taught me, a leopard that is born a leopard and raised a leopard will never be a house cat.

One thing is for certain: with the lake lapping up to the dam's top on the left side, and the vast drop into the valley on the right, it's both a thrilling and terrifying sight. Even Henry is silenced by awe.

On that soft, damp dirt road across the dam top, I listen

to the muted roll of the carriage wheels as we get under way. Contentedly, I sigh as my mind drifts back to that same crossing last summer when my heart was thrumming in anticipation of seeing my friends and winning the summer's competitions.

The biggest competition, of course, was for James Tottinger.

# ·∘꒰ CHAPTER 8 ꒱∘·

## SOUTHERN CALIFORNIA

*Day after Memorial Day*
*Present*

All those women do is *not* eat!"

Valerie shook her fists inside the car. She was frazzled. They were late. Mrs. Adell's luncheon had gone overtime. At the wheel, Lee sat as upright as the obelisk in Griffiths Park, hoping a still posture would calm her. Today was the day. Would they be too late? Would she have to take another afternoon off work?

"For an *hour,* I watched them move food around their plates like they were playing checkers."

Blowing a clump of bangs out of her eyes, Valerie grunted with exasperation. No one could sour her naturally sweet disposition as readily as Esther Adell and her ridiculous "yellow jackets"—the name Valerie gave to Mrs. Adell's luncheon friends. Wearing belted silk dresses or nubby tweed suits in pale lemon—Chanel, Dior, YSL—they crammed their bony old-lady feet into low-heeled pumps with brass piping on the toe. What did they know of genuine need? Fear so insistent it felt like a chronic migraine.

"One yellow jacket had the gall to pat my hand," Valerie railed. "Pat. My. Hand. Like I was the family dog."

Still dressed in her uniform, minus the lacy white cap, Valerie appeared as though she was on her way to a costume party. A lady's maid from *Downton Abbey*. Mrs. Adell insisted Valerie call her "ma'am" and her husband, "sir" and back out of rooms with her head down.

Steadily inhaling and exhaling to quiet her thrumming heart, Lee held her head up. Although she was certain they were doomed, her mother was (of course) unwilling to give up. The barest glimmer of hope was all she needed to fuel her desire to outwit L.A. traffic and make it downtown before the state office closed.

"We'll take the canyon," she said, as if no other driver ever had the very same notion.

They took the canyon. Lee counted mailboxes. She ignored the sound of blood pulsing in her ears. The curves of Beverly Glen were clogged with cars, but moving. Droopy eucalyptus branches shaded empty driveways, their leaves crispy from the drought. From somewhere, a dog yapped. *Small and white,* thought Lee. *With one of those pink rhinestone collars.* All four windows were rolled down. Her armpits were damp. Again, the air conditioner was off to save gas. Twenty dollars had barely moved the gauge. Valerie was broke, too.

"If you ask me," Valerie said, "a little fat looks *good* on an old woman. Who wants to hug a brittle bag of bones?"

Lee glanced at her mother and they both erupted in laughter. Esther Adell was the personification of a brittle bag of bones.

"Not many brake lights on Sunset," Valerie chirped in the blistering car as the canyon drive spilled onto the main artery to the freeway. "Things are looking up!"

## ⌁❧[ CHAPTER 9 ]❧⌁

### SOUTH FORK FISHING AND HUNTING CLUB

*The previous summer*
*1888*

Mother dislikes summer as much as I adore it. The heat seeps through my skin and warms my bones. When I tilt my head back and let the sun bathe my face, all the cares in the world melt away. It's as deliciously forbidden as an extra slice of Battenberg cake.

On this particular day, Lake Conemaugh twinkles in the

late-morning sunlight. There isn't a cloud in the Tiffany-blue sky. At this elevation, high above the grit of Johnstown, the ordinary world and its troubles feel blessedly far away. My friends, Julia and Addie, join me on the clubhouse veranda, pretending to inhale nature.

"Shall we go for a sail?" Addie asks me.

I laugh. We all do. Addie wears her best sporting dress—a burgundy pleated frock of silk and cotton. Despite the warmth of the day, she has buttoned the matching jacket to her neck and placed a satin-edged hat over her painstakingly frazzled fringe. Julia's corseted shirtwaist and ankle skirt are more appropriate for the casual atmosphere of the club, but they are clearly her finest activity clothes. I, too, am wearing my best and newest. The lavender cotton of my underskirt is patterned in paisley swirls; the swag is striped in glorious cobalt. Earlier, I had Nettie take extra care to secure my hair with the amethyst-tipped clips I bought on my last trip to New York. None of us would even consider the risk of soiling today's clothes by venturing onto the lake in a wobbly sailboat. Or worse, a canoe. Last summer, with Julian at oars, the canoe capsized us into the water. Thank heavens we were mere feet from the dock.

"They should arrive any moment," Julia says, excitedly. "I hear their family's bloodline can be traced back to a relative of Countess Augusta Reuss of Ebersdorf, grandmother of Queen Victoria herself."

"I hear their London home has *two* grand staircases in the entry hall, curving upward to the central master suite," Addie says, adding, "*Three* water closets. With a built-in bath. One on the second floor."

My heart is pounding, though I adopt an air of indifference. We have all heard so much about the fetching Mr. James Tottinger from Great Britain. But, fawning over a man is unbecoming. I am nearly a woman. It's time to act like one.

Still.

Before any of us arrived at South Fork for the summer, the whole of Pittsburgh society was abuzz with anticipation at the arrival of our British visitors. The elder Mr. Tottinger had sent Mr. Carnegie a telegram seeking advice on expanding his textile empire to the United States. True to form, Mr. Carnegie invited the entire Tottinger family to Lake Conemaugh. A generous offer, to say the least. But one that anyone who knew Andrew Carnegie would expect. He was renowned as an altruistic man who went out of his way to be helpful. Why, he postponed his own wedding to please his mother! Mr. Carnegie never forgot his modest roots in Scotland, unlike Mr. Vanderhoff, whose bluster was as loud as the machinery at Cambria Iron.

"Nothing fancy," Mr. Carnegie surely said of the clubhouse rooms in our rustic retreat. "Though you'll have all you need."

As soon as word got out that the Tottinger family—the elder Mr. Tottinger and his wife; James, their son; and Ivy, their teenage daughter—accepted Mr. Carnegie's invitation, club members scrambled to reschedule their allotted vacation times to coincide with those two weeks. Particularly families with marriageable daughters. The clubhouse was filled to capacity.

Rising up three stories like a gray whale in the green woods, the clubhouse of the South Fork Fishing and Hunting Club is the size of a fifty-room hotel. Behind its clapboard façade, the dining room is large enough to seat one hundred and fifty. The bedrooms are spare: slender bed, washbasin, bureau. The more prominent members of the club are assigned front rooms with lake views, of course.

Mornings in the dining room are when and where the club members meet to plan the events of the day. Sailing, canoeing, horseback riding, dressing up and posing for tableaux vivants. Evenings are for entertainments. Some of our own invention; others hired from down the hill. Piano recitals, theatricals, dance practice. Every night it's something new and cheerful. I can only imagine the excited whisperings down the narrow clubhouse halls at bedtime, the boasts, the dares.

Most members of the South Fork Fishing and Hunting Club wouldn't dream of owning a cottage like ours—one of only sixteen. They want a carefree rest in the country. "Roughing it" in the woodsy clubhouse with their peers, leaving their personal servants back home in Pittsburgh. As I would prefer, too. But Father built our cottage—with its medical office—when the club first opened.

"My patients expect instant access to me wherever they are," he said.

I would have thought Father overly solicitous had I not seen it for myself the summer before.

It was the middle of the night. There was pounding on the cottage door. "Mind the children," Father called to Mother as he ran down the stairs.

Mother, of course, ran to Little Henry's room first. I dashed to the stair railing. "His pain started about midnight," I overheard a man's baritone tell Father. Then I heard a groan, and my friend Edmond's distressed voice.

"It's my stomach. Muscle cramps."

Panic rose into my chest. Cholera hadn't made its way to our retreat in South Fork, but we all feared it would. Everyone knew the symptoms: diarrhea, vomiting, dehydration, muscle cramps. Anyone rushing to the outhouse was suspect. I nearly crumbled to the floor. Edmond was my age. Would I lose my friend? Were we *all* in danger? Father quickly led Edmond and his father to the back parlor and shut them in his office.

That night, I barely slept. The next morning, I tiptoed downstairs filled with dread. I expected to see pots of water boiling on the cookstove and Edmond's parents weeping in our parlor. Instead, I smelled bacon.

"Is Edmond going to be okay?" My breath was shallow, my lips dry.

"He's fine." Father sat at the head of the dining room table. He reached for a piece of toast.

"Is it—?" I stopped, as if merely mentioning the dreaded disease would bring it into the house.

"An overzealous badminton game is all," Father said.

"What?"

"Pulled muscles in the abdomen."

When I laughed, Father firmly admonished me. "My patients are not to be ridiculed, Elizabeth."

"Yes, Father, but—"

"Never discuss this case, or any other, with your friends. Do you understand me?"

I nodded.

"Say it out loud."

"I understand."

"As far as you are concerned, Edmond and his father were never here. Do you hear me?"

"Yes, Father. I hear you."

"The privacy of my patients is what puts food on our table."

I understood. There were rules. We all had to abide by them.

Edmond never mentioned that night, and neither did I. Ever.

"Goodness, when will they get here?" On the clubhouse porch, Addie has begun to perspire. She sips iced tea to cool herself.

"Here," I say, "let me take your jacket."

Addie looks at me, and I look at her. We both burst out laughing. Only *after* being introduced to James Tottinger would we dare change our outfits.

The loud nicker of a horse causes us to turn our heads toward the entrance road from the dam. But it is a false alarm, only the arrival of Mr. Vanderhoff and his family. Roderick and Albert Vanderhoff hop out of the carriage and head straight for the clubhouse. Oddly, Lily Vanderhoff sits on the open seat like a sack of flour. She stares straight ahead without seeming to see her husband or children at all. She very nearly crumbles to the ground when Mr. Vanderhoff encircles her waist to assist her.

"Oh my." Next to me, Addie notices it, too.

We both register the impatient embarrassment on Mr. Vanderhoff's face and overhear him mumble something about motion sickness. Quite curious since I have traveled in carriages with his wife before and endured only her nonstop chatter.

"Here we go, Georgie." After the Vanderhoffs' luggage is unloaded, the driver clucks his tongue at the club's chestnut Haflinger, a faithful workhorse I have ridden many summers. Though broad in the back, she is nonetheless nimble. And quite beautiful. Named after the fair-haired actress Georgiana Drew—married to handsome stage star Maurice Barrymore—Georgie's mane is long and light. She's always been my favorite horse at the club. "Back down the hill, girl," the driver says. Off they trot. And our anticipation resumes.

Though I wish it were not so, James Tottinger's reputation has occupied my mind for weeks. It is rumored that he once kept company with the stunning Elizabeth Wharton Drexel, daughter of banker Joseph Drexel, of the New York Drexels. Back in London, Mr. Tottinger supposedly had his knicker-bockers tailored to flatter the musculature of his legs. They say the very sight of him on horseback has inspired such intense gasps that proper ladies forget to resume their breathing and faint dead away.

The Tottingers of Great Britain are probably as close as any of us will come to meeting royalty. With the exception of Mr. and Mrs. Carnegie, perhaps. Our American prince of steel and his bride.

Quite honestly, however, the more I hear of Mr. Tottinger, the more he sounds insubstantial. What woman could be interested in a man who thought more of himself than her? Personally, I am most intrigued by a fact I recently learned about him: he was born in the same year as my favorite poet, Rudyard Kipling. Eighteen sixty-five. Add the numbers together—one, eight, six, and five—and you get twenty. The age I plan to be when I marry. Ever since I was a girl, the deeper meaning of numbers has fascinated me.

"Hello, dearests."

Behind me, flitting out from the open clubhouse doors, I hear the avian voice of Francine Larkin. Without turning around, I picture her fluttery entrance. Doubtful such a hummingbird of a woman could summon the lung capacity to yelp for assistance if she fell overboard during a regatta. It was a wonder she could even stand on those miniature feet. She was always lamenting the impossibility of finding button boots so petite.

"Have you tried a shoemaker for *juveniles*?" I once asked when I could no longer stand it.

"No sign of the royals yet?" Francine chirps.

"They're not royals." I glance only briefly behind me, wishing Francine Larkin would flap her winglike arms and fly back indoors. "Not genuine royals, anyway." She's dressed in silly pink. Taffeta, of course, from head to toe. Her hair is so blond it belongs on a child. Or a Haflinger horse.

On the wide waterside porch running the length of the clubhouse, my friends and I gaze at the stunning mountain scenery encircling our sparkling lake. This is the most idyllic spot in all of Pennsylvania. With the gently undulating water stretching to the emerald horizon on the far shore, it's easy to imagine we are the only souls on earth. Our very own Garden of Eden. In the afternoon sunlight, the diamonds in my bracelet reflect the twinkle of the lake. Long ago, Mother insisted that I remove my bracelet for day wear. But, just as long ago, I refused. No matter what I am wearing, I never take this bracelet off. It was a gift from my late grandmother.

"Did you hear?" Francine says. Her voice is like a tic in my ear. Always one for gossip, Addie wheels around. "Hear what?"

"Father took tea with Mr. Carnegie in the city last week and they spoke of the Tottingers."

"That's news?" Admittedly, my tone is as sharp as a shard of broken china. Like nearly everyone at the club, I've known Francine Larkin all my life. From the start, I've found her as shallow as the stream at Graesers Run. My hope at the moment is that she will drop her "news" like a sparrow drops a worm and flit back inside before the Tottingers arrive.

Instead, tiptoeing up to the porch railing, Francine rests her diminutive hand on the balustrade and turns, forcing us all to face her. "Well," she begins, obviously settling in to entrap us for a lengthy period. "Father told me that Mr. Carnegie told the elder Mr. Tottinger that summer weeks at the lake were intended for pleasure and sport. However, since they'd come so far to discuss business, he proposed that the men enjoy *weekends* only at the lake, returning to Pittsburgh on the Monday-morning train."

"So?" I say.

"So—" Her gaze meets mine with brows peaked, a sliver of superiority on her lips. "Supposedly, the elder Mr. Tottinger summoned his son into the grand parlor of their home in London. His son being the eminently eligible gentleman, James Tottinger, a relative of Countess Augusta Reus—"

"We know who he is, Francine." Even mild-tempered Julia found Francine irksome at times.

"Yes. Of course. Back to my *news*." She darts a glance at me. "The elder Mr. Tottinger told his son that he—James—

would *not* be returning to Pittsburgh on the Monday-morning train with the other men. He was to remain here for the full two weeks. Which, I heard, distressed him greatly. According to Father, James Tottinger said, 'Stay in the woods with a bunch of women and children?' Then he asked his father if he'd gone mad."

In spite of myself, I laugh.

"You see," Francine continues, "Mr. Carnegie told the elder Mr. Tottinger that South Fork was more than a club for fishing *bass*. He told him that Pittsburgh's most prominent young ladies summer here and there was no better place for his son to cast his line."

"That's absurd." Swiveling away from Francine, I mentally will her off the veranda and into the lake. "Mr. Carnegie would never say something so crass."

"He would and he did. I trust Father completely."

Addie asks, "How did James Tottinger respond?" Out of the corner of my eye, I see her fuss with the silk flowers atop her hat. Then she presses a handkerchief against the beads of sweat on her upper lip.

"He was pleased."

"Pleased?" Addie echoes.

*"Pleased?"* I feel my heart increase its beating.

Pausing for dramatic effect, Francine Larkin takes one tiny step closer, leans in on her baby feet, and whispers, "He grinned devilishly and said he'd always been an expert *angler*. Clearly, the thought of having unfettered access to us all excited him no end."

My dark eyes grow black. "Is this true?"

"As I said, I trust Father completely." Francine lifts her pointed chin in the air with absolute confidence.

I don't need to hear more. Such impudence. Being compared to a *fish*? Paraded about for a foreigner's selection? Not me. Not *ever*. Just thinking about it brings color to my face. How could a gentleman like Mr. Carnegie even hint at such a thing?

"Shall we?" I say to Addie and Julia. They stare at me, dumbfounded. Julia sputters, "No one has summoned us into the dining room yet."

"Surely you don't intend to stay here and subject yourself to such an insult?"

Again, Addie's fingers fumble about her hat. Julia stares at her feet, mumbling, "I'm quite sure he meant it as a compliment."

"Compliment? Likened to a smelly, scaled, bug-eyed, flapping creature without limbs?"

Immobile, they gape at me with lips parted like . . . like *fish*. Francine's petite shoes suddenly seem permanently attached to the wood planks of the porch floor. Her brows still reach up to the treetops. I can endure no more.

"I will be dining at the cottage today," I say, calmly. "I'm sure Ida will be happy to prepare extra for whoever wishes to join me."

"You mustn't!" Julia says. "The royals!"

"They are no more royal than you or I."

With that, I spin on my heels and descend the side steps that lead to the boardwalk. My shoes percuss the wood slats. My head is held high, my back straight. The blue lake glistens like the tail feathers of an Indigo Bunting. On my way to the far end of the row of cottages, I turn back briefly to catch a glimpse of Francine's beaky grin. She mocks me, but I don't care. The other girls can pother like guppies around the arrogant Mr. Tottinger, lips parted, eager to snag his fishing line.

Not me.

Not ever.

# ·≈[ CHAPTER 10 ]≈·

## SOUTHERN CALIFORNIA

*Day after Memorial Day*
*Present*

### 4:23 P.M.

With seven minutes left before the state office closed, Lee's tires screeched into the parking lot of a cement-and-smoked-glass rectangle that rose out of the asphalt like a gray block of Legos.

"Don't bother locking the car." Valerie swung open the passenger door before Lee had come to a complete stop. Her soft white work shoes hit the ground running. "We have nothing to steal."

State workers were already flooding through the exit doors. Two salmon swimming upstream, Lee and her mother wiggled their way inside.

"Excuse me. Pardon me. Oops. Sorry. Coming through."

Indoors, it was blessedly cool. With its washable wood paneling, vibrating white lighting, and smudged stainless-steel elevator doors, the lobby resembled any government building anywhere. Security waved them over to a metal detector. Valerie groaned. As the guard peered into Lee's cross-body bag and pushed Valerie's used Kleenexes aside with his rubber-gloved hand, she thought, *The terrorists have already won.*

"Who are you here to see?" the guard asked.

"Adoption Unit. Fifth floor," Lee said. After scribbling their names on a sign-in sheet, the guard flagged them through the metal detector and they raced for the elevator bank. Furiously poking the up button, Lee stole a peek at her phone even as she knew it was less than a minute since she'd last looked. Four twenty-four. Six minutes to go before she'd be locked out of her future . . . and her past.

Eyes pressed shut, Val willed the elevator to arrive. "Come on. Come on." Lee stared at the digital readout. *Nine, eight, seven.* Unbearable pauses at each floor.

"Follow me."

Grabbing her mother's hand, Lee pulled her to the stairwell door and swung it open. Together, they dashed up five flights of cement stairs, two steps at a time. By the time they reached the top, both were pink-cheeked and gasping for air. "Here. To see. Adoption counselor." Lee plunged her sweaty hand into her bag and produced the wrinkled letter she'd kept in her underwear drawer for months. "I'm eighteen," she heaved. "I have proof."

A receptionist was just rising up from a scuffed white desk. "Ooh," she said with a pout. "We're closed. It's four thirty."

"Four twenty *eight*." Valerie testily tapped the face of her watch.

"We've driven from—" Lee didn't want to say North Beverly Park, which would convey the wrong message. Though they lived in one of the richest neighborhoods in Los Angeles, they didn't really *live* there. They parked their bodies in the pool house, not even allowed to use the pool. "We've driven from the Valley."

"Sorry." The receptionist's lower lip protruded in mock sorrow.

She seemed like a temp. Barely into her twenties, she appropriated an officious tone that betrayed her inexperience. As if sitting behind that childish desk was her first real job and she was drunk on the power of it. Pushing her rectangular wire-rimmed glasses up the bridge of her nose, she gave Valerie's maid's uniform the once-over. Adjusting her posture, she picked up a pen and pretended to write something important. Lee noticed that her purse was already out of its storage drawer and her desk was neatly organized. Ready for work the next day. Post-it notes were tucked into a corner in a perfect yellow stack.

"Look here, missy." Valerie's ruddy cheeks got even redder.

"Mom—"

"We will spend the night on top of your desk if we have to. I will snore all over your in-box, drool on your keyboa—"

"Is there a problem?"

From around a fabric-covered partition, a woman holding a stack of manila envelopes appeared. She was stunning. Her flawless purple-black skin glistened like a ripe eggplant. The close crop of her copper-colored hair highlighted exotic features: almond-shaped eyes, lips the color of peach flesh. She stood as tall as a windmill, owning her height as if no one had ever advised her to slouch near the short boys.

"Yesterday was my . . . my . . . birthday." Without warning, Lee erupted in tears. They spilled from her eyes like paint from a kicked-over can—all thick and spreading across her cheeks. She slapped one hand over her mouth to stop them, but it was too late. A year's worth of emotions flowed out of her. She cried for her lost future, her old bedroom with the front window that cast slanted shadows on the walls she'd painted herself. She missed Shelby; her brother, Scott; her dad. Beyond any ability to control it, she wept for all the ways life wasn't the way it was.

"I've been wondering when these would appear," Valerie softly said, fishing wads of tissues from her purse.

*"Now?"* Lee blubbered, causing both her mother and the tall goddess to laugh. Valerie shrugged and said, "Tears happen."

Quietly, the young receptionist gripped her handbag and tiptoed for the elevator bank. In the elegant accent of a Somali princess, the woman with the manila folders flagged them inside saying, "I have more tissues at my desk." Then she lightly placed her hand on Lee's forearm and squeezed. "I'm Abiya-tou," she said.

"I don't usually cry in public," Lee cried. "Or at all really, that much."

"It's okay. We see a lot of tears in this office. Happiness. Misery. Premenstrual."

Lee sniffed and smiled. "Thank you, Abitoy—"

"Call me Abby."

"Thank you, Abby," Valerie said as they both followed the beautiful woman into a large air-conditioned space full of cu-

bicles and leaning stacks of files. Around them, computers were
being shut down, chairs were pushed under desks, lamps were
clicked off, totes were swung onto shoulders.

"Say a prayer that my kids haven't been playing video games
with the a/c blasting all day." A middle-aged woman with cot-
tony hair joined her coworkers on their way out. "My DWP bill
was over two hundred dollars."

The sights and sounds of exiting filled the cluttered room.
"See you tomorrow. Same time, same place, same bad coffee.
Ha ha ha."

By the time Lee and Valerie reached Abby's cubicle near the
far window, almost everyone else was gone.

"It's my fault we're late," Valerie confessed. "Lee would have
been here hours ago. I shouldn't have insisted on coming with
her. I know better. Mrs. Adell is *always* careless with the time.
My time. Today, of all days, I should hav—"

Abby silenced Valerie's mea culpa with a pat on her hand.
"You got lucky today. My ride home is delayed. Have a seat."
She put the manila folders in her in-box and dragged one of her
coworkers' chairs to the opening in her cubicle. With a gentle
motion of her slender hand, she invited Lee to sit in the chair
beside her desk. Then she seated herself and faced them both.
"How can I help you?"

"I got this letter," Lee said, wiping her nose with the tissue
and inhaling a hefty breath to recover her composure. "Well,
*we* did. My parents. But it's about me. Sort of. I mean, I think
so. Part of me. Yes, *me*."

Lee bit the inside of her cheek to shut herself up. Abby leaned
forward and took the letter. As she read it quietly, Val and Lee

watched her eyeballs move from side to side like windshield wipers.

"Let's see here." She placed the letter next to her computer and smoothed it flat with her hands. After turning the screen away from Lee and her mother, Abby rested her long fingers on the keyboard. She typed in the case number Lee knew by heart. From their vantage point, all Val and Lee could see was the back of Abby's computer and the rippled harvest moon of her hair. Keyboard clicking was the only sound in the room. In fact, it wasn't until Lee audibly sucked in air that she realized she'd been holding her breath.

"Here we are," Abby said. "You're the Parkers?"

"Yes." Valerie leaned forward. "I'm Valerie and this is my daughter, Lee."

"Elizabeth," Lee blurted. "My original name. The name on the letter."

"Yes. I see."

"I know all about my adoption," Lee added quickly. "It's never been a secret. I mean, you don't have to protect us. My mom wants me to know whatever there is to know."

Abby nodded as Valerie pressed her lips together in a tense smile. When she reached for Lee's hand, Lee understood the gesture was meant to calm her down. *One, two, three* . . . she counted the numbers on Abby's keyboard. "It's been a tough year," Val said.

"These things are always emotional," Abby stated, simply. Then she jotted something on a scrap of paper and hit the escape button on her keyboard. "Can I see your ID?"

Lee pulled out her driver's license and handed it to Abby.

As she held it up to Lee's face, Abby's wheat-colored eyes compared the photo with the real girl. Satisfied, she said, "I'll be right back." Up she stood.

Valerie stood, too, moving her chair aside to let Abby out of her office. In silence, Valerie watched Abby glide over to a bank of lateral filing cabinets and consult her paper. She saw her pull out a drawer overstuffed with files. Each file a person. A life. A family. A mystery. Suddenly her cheeks stung. She felt like crying, too. The letter had stated they had information regarding "medical history." What if they found out that Lee had inherited a disease? Or some kind of defective gene she would pass on to her kids. What if she decided not to have kids as a result? Val would never be a grandmother. Lee would never be a mother. She would die alone with an arthritic cat. Maybe *twenty* cats. All strays. How was it possible she'd never worried about any of this until that very moment? Critical medical information was never *good,* was it? No one sent you an official letter to inform you that your genetics pointed to an ancestry of centenarians who died in their sleep.

"Lee." Valerie wheeled around and looked at her daughter, seeming so small and vulnerable in the state-issued office chair.

Instantly, Lee read her mother's face. "It's going to be okay," she said.

"It's not too late to forget about the whole shebang and go home."

Gripping the vinyl armrests, Lee admitted, "I'm a little scared, too."

That's all Valerie needed to hear. Crouching low before her daughter, she placed both hands on Lee's knees. Softly, she said, "We *can* leave, you know. Abby will understand. We can march straight for the elevator right this second. You needn't ever be more than Lee Parker. My daughter. That has always been—and will always be—enough."

Lee looked into her mother's light green eyes and saw the love she knew would forever be there. She wanted to whisper, *Let's go.* Together, they would thank Abby and she would nod knowingly. They would pass the slow elevators and run for the stairs again—set free—handbags flapping in their wake. Outside, in the broiling downtown parking lot, they would tilt their heads up to the setting sun and clamp one hand on their pounding chests and say, "Whew. We dodged a bullet." On the way home, Valerie would type "ice cream" into Lee's iPhone and say, "Left at the light. Right two blocks ahead." All the lights would be green. Inside Baskin-Robbins, Lee would inhale the smell of frost and order a double scoop of Pralines 'n Cream. "Don't miss that mother lode of caramel," she'd say, joking but serious. As they slid into pink seats attached to a pink table, they would reach their free hands across the sticky surface to grasp each other in solidarity. It wouldn't matter that Lee's fingers were long and thin and her mother's were Jimmy Dean sausage links.

Still.

"If I don't find out now," Lee said, her voice quivering, "I will always wonder. I don't want to always wonder."

"Everything okay?" Abby suddenly materialized at the entrance to her cubicle with a single folder in her hands. Lee was shocked to see how thin it was. As if nothing were in it at all. Her heart began to push its way out of her chest.

"Honey?" Valerie said to her daughter, still squatting.

"I'm fine." Lee sat up straight. "I'm ready."

"You're sure?" her mother asked.

Lee nodded. Not sure she could trust her voice.

As soon as Valerie got up and out of the way, Abby entered the cubicle and sat down. She set the closed file aside. "We're in no rush here," she said. "The information we have for you is yours forever."

"I want to know," Lee blurted. "Now. Whatever it is."

"Some adoptees wait until they're ready to have children," Abby went on. "Others don't feel the need to know medical history at all. You're young, Lee. You have plenty of time to find out about yourself. What's the hurry?"

How could she answer in front of her mother, the woman who didn't give her life, but who gave her *a* life? How could she admit that her need to know who she was had been a shadow standing next to her always?

"I'm ready," she said with a period, silently thinking, *Right now. Not in another eighteen years or eighteen seconds.* Yesterday was her birthday, but that sunny afternoon in Abby's cubicle was the moment of her *birth*.

"What do you have to tell me?" she said.

Abby nodded. "Okay."

For the next several minutes, Abby explained the process. She counseled Lee and her mother on what they might hear, what it might mean. "Genetic predisposition is not fate. It's an elevated risk due to the discovery of a gene mutation. It may, or may not, result in disease."

Valerie squeezed her daughter's hand. Lee swallowed. Both bobbed their heads even though they didn't fully comprehend what Abby was saying. Did Lee have a mutant gene?

After she was done speaking, Abby made a copy of Lee's driver's license. She gave her a form to sign and notarized her signature. In a soothing voice, she asked, "How are you feeling?"

"Nervous as hell," Valerie said.

Abby smiled. "I'm wondering how Lee feels, too."

Lee paused. How did she feel? *Nervous?* Yeah. *Excited?* Yeah. She felt so many different emotions she couldn't put her finger on one alone. Out of the blue, a thought popped into her mind. She said, "I feel like I'm about to meet myself."

At that moment, all doubt vanished like chimney smoke on a cold desert night. "Let 'er rip," she said.

Abby opened the skinny file. Over its top edge, Val and Lee again watched her eyeballs move left and right. "Oh," she spurted. "Interesting."

"Interesting?" Lee and Valerie echoed the same word at the same time.

"Are you familiar with the Ashkenazi tribe?"

"Indians?" Lee asked. "I mean, Native Americans?"

"No. The Ashkenazim are an ancient tribe of Jews."

"I'm Jewish?"

"Yes, actually. On the maternal side of your birth genetics is a direct line back to the Ashkenazim. Probably from Germany. Maybe Palestine."

"Neat," Lee said, grinning.

"The only reason this is potentially important information is because recent genetic testing has revealed that there are some elevated medical risks particular to Ashkenazi women. That's why your file was flagged."

"Risks? Like what?" Valerie leaned forward.

Abby said, "Again, genetic risks can be relatively small. Although, Ashkenazi women who inherit a certain gene mutation do have to be vigilant. The reason we inform adoptees is so they can make sure this information is a part of their medical record. Your doctor will help you decide if genetic testing is appropriate."

"Genetic testing for what?" Lee gripped the armrests again.

"Well, breast and ovarian cancers are the biggest concerns," she said, gently.

"Cancer?" Valerie blanched.

"And some other diseases like—" Abby's fingers returned to the computer keyboard. She read: "Bloom syndrome, Canavan disease, Gaucher disease."

"I've never even *heard* of those. Is my daughter in danger?"

Abby replied, "We advise all adoptees and their families to discuss this information with a licensed genetics physician. I can give you a list of referrals in your area."

"Thanks," Val said, still pale. Lee felt numb. She'd come all this way to find out she might get cancer?

"While I get that for you," Abby said in a bright voice, "there's something in your file you might want to see. I have no idea how we ended up with it. Maybe your birth mother attached it to her paperwork? At any rate, I see no harm in showing you if you want to see it."

"See what?" Lee blurted.

"A photograph of your maternal ancestor."

Lee's mouth flew open. "What?" Valerie scooted to the edge of her seat as Abby pulled an old black-and-white photo out of the manila folder. She handed it to Lee, who was surprised to feel her hands tremble. The photo was a small snapshot of two women—one tall, like her, the other short. Both were regal in their way—staring straight into the camera lens. All around them was dirt and rubble. Leaning in to take a look, Valerie squealed, "Honey! That's you!"

It was true. The tall woman on the right, slightly in the background, looked just like her. She had dark messily upswept hair, wavy bangs that danced across her forehead, intense eyes like espresso beans. Like Lee's. In her placid face, Lee saw her own slightly pointed nose, the heart-shaped curve of her upper lip, the same two valleys just below her cheekbones. Lee felt an instant connection. At last, she'd found her people.

"What's her name?" she asked, excited.

"I'm sorry, I can't tell you that," Abby said. "As you know, yours was a closed adoption. All identifying information is sealed."

"Can I keep the photo?"

"I'm afraid not. It stays with the file. But, go ahead and take a few minutes to look at one of your blood relatives. I'll be right back."

While Abby left to get the physician referrals, Lee gripped the picture tightly in both fists. She lifted it up and held it close to her eyes, examining every millimeter of the tall woman's body. Every fold in her long skirt, the high collar on her puffy white shirt, the wisps of hair bouncing about her pretty face, the way she stood so very erect in the aftermath of what had obviously been some kind of disaster. Just as Lee was reaching into her pocket for her iPhone—what harm could a quick photo do?—Valerie leaned close to her daughter and read the tiny printing on the back of the snapshot: " 'Woman with Clara Barton.' "

Pulling back, she looked at Lee quizzically. "Isn't Clara Barton the woman who started the Red Cross?"

Just then, Abby returned to the cubicle and plucked the photo out of Lee's hands. Turning it over, she read the back and said, "You probably shouldn't have seen that."

"Is Lee related to Clara Barton?" Valerie's eyes were as round and shiny as new quarters.

"For the record, I believe that Clara Barton is the woman on the *left*. Lee's ancestor is the unidentified woman on the right."

"Great, great, great," Lee said, almost to herself.

"Isn't it?" Valerie excitedly cupped her daughter's chin.

Sitting back in her chair, Lee grinned. Judging by the Victorian hair and clothes in the photograph, she figured the photo was taken sometime in the nineteenth century. Which meant five generations ago. Maybe six. At twenty-five years per generation, the unidentified woman on the right—the one who looked just like her—would be her great-great-great-grandmother. At the very least.

Thank goodness she was a whiz at math. She now had a starting point.

# ·❧] CHAPTER 11 [❧·

## SOUTH FORK FISHING AND HUNTING CLUB

*Summer 1888*

A re you unwell, miss?" Nettie's hazel eyes regard me with
concern as I stomp into the cottage and call her to my
room.

"Not in the slightest. Could you please help me out of these
clothes?"

"A royal family is arriving from England today, miss."

"They're *not* royal. Besides, I don't care."

On my way up the stairs, I reach my hand into my upswept hair to pull out the amethyst-tipped clips. To Nettie I say, "I'll wear my brown box-pleat skirt today."

Now she looks alarmed. "Surely the other ladies will be dressed in their best sport finery."

"Surely. And my plain shirtwaist, too."

"Is something wrong with the lavender cotton?"

"Yes. It's too lovely for a day alone in my room."

Scurrying after me, Nettie watches me yank the final clip from my hair to release my bound-up locks. In a tumble of dark curls, my hair falls nearly all the way to the small of my back. Like a wet dog, I shake my head and feel delicious freedom. Today will be my happiest day of the whole summer. Solitude and liberty. Glorious!

Inside my room—decorated in the same heliotrope colors as my bedroom in Upper St. Clair—I stand in front of the pier glass between the windows and wait for Nettie to unbutton me. My cheeks are still flushed with indignation. In the reflection of the mirror I see my maid's freckled hands clasped in front of her. Her body shape is unfortunate. As plump in back as she is in front. Strands of her red hair are stuck to the perspiration on her forehead. Clearly, she fears I've gone mad.

"I'm behind on my correspondence," I say, by way of explanation. Not that I owe her one. "I've decided to stay indoors today. Could you please tell Ida I'll be taking my meals in my room? Mother, Father, and Henry will be dining at the clubhouse, no doubt."

"Are you certain, Miss Elizabeth?"

"I am. Now help me out of this dress."

As Nettie works to extricate me from my corset and layers, I inhale deeply and know that I'm making the right decision. With my debut only a year away, I must focus my efforts solely on gentlemen of *substance*. Not foreign men who think American ladies are his playthings. The nerve of him.

Although, I now sigh, the thought of marrying one of the men—*boys*—from the club depresses me. Julian has the same roly-poly middle as my little brother, Henry. His cheeks are two pomegranates. Roderick—Mr. Vanderhoff's son—has the swagger of his father. His hair appears to have a mind of its own. And his hands, once encircling my own at a ball, felt as rough as a gardener's. Roderick's attempt to grow a mustache and beard like Mr. Carnegie's and Mr. Frick's is laughable. One can clearly see the skin within them. Edmond and Oscar are the opposite: barefaced and as soft as baby thighs. All would bore me into spending my days in bed, weeping.

Mother has already advised me to lower my standards. "You'll never find a *perfect* husband," she said.

"What about Father?"

"No man is perfect."

What I have yet to mention is my desire to find the ideal husband for *me*. I don't care the slightest bit if he's perfect for anyone else.

After Nettie helps me out of my lavender skirt and petticoat, she removes my matching blouse and lays the entire outfit on my bed to prepare it for another day's wear. In my underclothes, I sit at my dressing table and brush my hair. "You needn't fuss over those frocks now," I tell her. "Have Ida pack you a picnic and enjoy a day at the lake."

"What about your hair, miss? Your washbasin—"

"I will take care of myself."

She poorly contains her glee. "You're certain?"

"I am. But first, please open the green hatbox at the back of my wardrobe." Now *I* poorly contain my glee. A giggle escapes through my lips.

As instructed, Nettie trundles over to the corner of my room and opens the wardrobe. Bending over to retrieve the hatbox, she slides it out of its hiding place and opens it. Inside is my favorite summer straw hat.

"*Under* the hat," I chirp.

When Nettie peers beneath the hat, her eyes open as round as ivory buttons. I put my finger to my lips. "Mother needn't know."

"*Bloomers,* Miss Elizabeth?"

"Why corset myself up just to sit alone in my room?"

Nettie reaches into the hatbox and gently removes the scandalous cotton and lace undergarment, holding it aloft.

"Isn't it divine?" I leap up to join her. "Tilly brought it back for me from her holiday in France. There, they have all sorts. See the beautiful stitching."

The world is changing. Why can't I be modern, too?

"Today," I say to my maid, "we are both liberated."

Nettie grins and whispers, "I won't breathe a word."

Before she leaves, Nettie sets out the plain brown clothes I've brought to the lake for solitary walks in the woods. It can get terribly muddy after a rainfall. She helps me out of my ordinary drawers and into my extraordinary new bloomers. Together, we both admire the prettiness of the pink satin ribbon that secures the soft fabric to my knees. The sensation of liberty is almost sinful. I want to skip through the cottage singing.

Let the other girls have the counterfeit royal, Mr. Tottinger. I have something much more desirable: *freedom.*

"Have an enjoyable day, miss," Nettie says, leaving me alone to finish dressing. With only a basic skirt and shirtwaist to slip over my bloomers and camisole, it takes but a minute to dress. I even remove my leather shoes and stockings to let my toes wiggle in bare abandonment. Why haven't I thought of this before? A lady needs occasional solitude to gather her wits about her. Mother has said so often.

"Let James Tottinger impress *himself,*" I say out loud.

The cottage is blessedly silent. As is—it seems—the entire world. From my second-story window, the view is splendid. A vast sparkling sapphire. Our cottage feels as though it's floating on top of the lake itself. A huge houseboat, adrift. I notice the gentle bobbing of our skiff secured to our dock. Father often uses our small rowboat to patrol this far section of Lake Cone-maugh for driftwood and dead foliage that would mar our blue view. The dense woods surrounding our lake are forever shedding branches into the water. Colonel Unger, the club's caretaker, often bemoans the clogged spillway. The heavy mesh fish guards installed to prevent the lake's bounty from swimming downstream into Johnstown is a catchall for every manner of lake debris.

"We can't have townspeople fishing from our stock," he'd exclaimed when someone suggested removing the mesh to let the lake's runoff flow freely into the valley rivers down below.

Of course not. Lake Conemaugh is *our* lake. The "No Trespassing" sign before the dam crossing (and other spots through-out the woods) makes that abundantly clear.

In my room, I place both hands on my torso and feel it rise and fall. With each unfettered inhalation, I rejoice in the eman-cipation of my lungs. Air rushes in and out as nature intended. It's an almost indescribable joy. As if I were sleeping while awake. I feel complete calm.

On a cushioned seat in front of my window, I sit and feel the deliciously forbidden weight of my long swirling hair down my back. To launch my relaxing day, I open the book I've been reading nightly. Thomas Hardy's *Wessex Tales*. I begin to read. Then I stop. Ribbons of yellow sunlight angle through the glass. The glare bounces off the page oddly. It makes me squint. I move away from the window to my settee in the corner, but I can't find a comfortable position. Perhaps I'll read later this afternoon, when a cloud forms.

Feeling the cool of the polished wood floor beneath my bare feet, I skip over to my desk, sit down, and retrieve paper and pen from the top drawer. A thank-you letter to my New York friend, Tilly Hinton, is overdue. Though it requires a bit of sub-terfuge since Mother has recently taken to reading my corre-spondence to ensure my grammar and diction are suitable for a young lady on the verge of her debut.

"Nothing can be the slightest bit amiss," Mother said. "Only if we are extremely careful will *you* be the belle of the ball."

If Mother had suspected I'd returned from my visit with Tilly hiding bloomers in my trunk, well, surely her reins would be pulled ever tighter.

For inspiration, I gaze out my window over the sparkling

lake, its water now as blue as Bristol glassware. "Oh, Tilly, to be strolling through Central Park, deeply inhaling the green scent, on a day such as this," I write. Then, grinning, I add, "On your recent visit to France, were you free to roam the Tuileries unfettered?"

Tilly will know exactly what I mean.

Pen in hand, I find it difficult to compose a third sentence. Especially when Lake Conemaugh seems to extend all the way to the horizon. As yet undisturbed by boats, its surface is as smooth as ironed silk. *Has Colonel Unger cut back on the fish stock?* I wonder. *Is the water warm or cold? When I go for a sail later in the week, will I see fish dart away through the transparent swells?*

Setting Tilly's unfinished note aside, I decide to write a different letter to a friend from school who has moved to a horse farm in Vermont.

"How lovely it must be to look out over a pasture of viridian green." (We both excelled in literature class.) Again, I gaze out my window for inspiration. The lake, I notice, is trimmed all the way around in trees of every possible shade of green. Emerald, olive, sage, and yes, *viridian*. The pines are vibrant beryl where their peaks puncture the sunlight; below the tree line, their needles darkened to moss. At nightfall, when the lake is so black it seems to swallow the jagged mountains surrounding it, the trees are the very definition of forest green. How terribly interesting, I ponder. Nature produces more color variations than humans can devise proper words to describe. Why, there should be *dozens* of words for green. And in fall, how could one ever adequately capture the spectrum of reds alone?

Curiously, the rhythmic ticking of the clock in the far corner of my room suddenly seems to grow both louder and slower. As I sit at my desk, I begin to anticipate the *tick,* then the *tock.* Then the *tick* again. How have I managed to sleep through such noise?

I set my pen aside. I consider walking downstairs to practice the piano, but I'm not in the mood. Instead, I twirl my bracelet around and around my wrist to watch its rose-cut diamonds send flickers of light bouncing about the room. Just looking at the exquisite swirling stones makes me happy.

Soon my thoughts drift back to life in Pittsburgh. It's a plain fact for a woman born into my circumstances: every day is as predictable as a sunrise and sunset. Nettie attempts to wake me with the swooshing of velvet drapes across my shiny bedroom floor. She's never successful. Not even direct sunlight on my face can rouse me. My maid tells me it takes a full minute of shoulder jostling for me just to open my eyes. It's no secret that mornings are my least favorite time of day. All that bustle when I'm barely awake.

"My daughter, the somnambulist."

Without fail, Father greets me in the breakfast room by tipping down the corner of his open newspaper. Mother, in turn, regards him reproachfully. She disapproves of reading at the dining table, considers it the height of bad manners. But Father dismisses her with a smile. "How else can I keep up with my patients?"

At precisely eight o'clock in our Upper St. Clair home— Father insists on early rising, much to my dismay—our butler, Mr. Tilson, enters the breakfast room carrying a platter of freshly fried meats. Unfailingly, Father exclaims, "Splendid."

He then lifts himself up with a grunt and makes his way to the buffet at the end of our long paneled room. That's the moment Mother and Mr. Tilson exchange glances. Theirs are two expressions I know well. My mother's pleading eyes beg our butler, "Can't you please fill our breakfast buffet with healthful foods?"

Of course, Mother doesn't eat pork, nor any organ meats or shellfish, but she insists there are plenty of other delicious options. Mr. Tilson's unspoken reply lets her know he is powerless to defy Dr. Haberlin's wishes. If the doctor asks for bacon or deviled kidneys or plump sausages or all three—which he often does—the staff is obliged to comply. Mother can only sigh— which *she* often does.

Day after day it is the same routine. How many scales and arpeggios can a person practice in an afternoon? How many peacocks and pastoral scenes can one girl needlepoint without noting the pointlessness of it all? I take my seat across from Mother with a slice of toast and milk tea.

"Elizabeth, please eat more than a sparrow."

Forever, Mother is after Father to eat less and me to eat more.

"I ate two eggs, five bits of potato, and half a bowl of porridge," Henry chirps from his perch at Mother's right elbow.

"Fine boy," Father booms, though his attention is fully focused on bacon and the next item of news in the paper.

"Henry, a gentleman never boasts about his abundance," Mother says, sipping her own milk tea.

I yawn behind my hand. As I always do. In Pittsburgh—in spite of my recent intensification in debutante training—life is a series of minutes, gathered into hours, twisted into days, braided into months, and coiled into years. Never have I been able to embrace the monotony. Most often I feel like a race-horse trapped in the starting gate.

Until summer. Oh, how I love summer at the lake.

At that precise moment, a warbler opens its black beak and calls to me. *Swee, swee.* Or is it the eastern bluebird? The chirping begins just outside my window, then grows fainter. Did the bird fly to the opposite shore? Was it silenced by the sight of an animal wandering through the woods?

I rise from my desk and return to the window seat. Opening my window as wide as it will go, I lean out to inhale the fresh mountain air. My lungs lusciously expand to their full capacity. A whispery breeze tickles my loose hair. I decide to compose a poem.

*Water of azure, sky of teal . . .*

Surely there are hundreds of words that rhyme with "teal." In my head, I begin listing all I can recall: zeal, conceal, real, reveal, meal, feel.

When no adequate couplet enters my head, I wander over to my full-length mirror and gaze at myself, turning this way and that, examining every inch of my reflection. My nails, I notice, are imperfectly oval. How careless of Nettie not to remark upon it. Thank goodness I caught it before Mother noticed. Returning to my dressing table, I use the sterling file Mother gave me to slowly shape each fingernail to flawlessness. I massage a touch of rose oil into each cuticle and camphor cream into my elbows. Around and around I rub until the cream disappears. Then I add a dab more for good measure. Around and around and around.

By the time Ida knocks on my bedroom door with a lunch tray, I can stand it no longer.

"Set it anywhere," I say, brusquely, attempting to secure my hair into a top twist. It falls lopsided, the amethyst-tipped clips creating only the barest semblance of a proper bun. How does Nettie do it so expertly every day?

A shocked look flares in Ida's eyes when she sees my state of dress.

"Are you unwel—?"

"Never felt better."

With tendrils springing onto my face and neck, I leap up and grab the stockings I'd worn that morning, rolling them onto my feet. Ida stands there, befuddled, as I hastily step into my boots and haphazardly secure the laces. Dashing past her, down the stairs to the side door, I leave her standing in my room holding a steaming tray of roasted beef and summer squash.

# ·⊰】CHAPTER 12 【⊱·

## SOUTHERN CALIFORNIA

*Present*

As Valerie feared, Lee was instantly obsessed with her new identity. "Maybe the woman in the photo was a *nurse,*" she said in the car as Valerie drove them home from Social Services. "Have you ever known me to, like, faint at the sight of blood?"

In the sludge of rush hour, on the misnamed *free*way, they lurched forward foot by foot. Valerie stared numbly at the scratched bumper on the car in front of her. "What about that genetic Ashkenobi thing?" she asked her daughter. "You know, the reason this whole trip was important?"

"Ashken*azi*. I think Ashkenobi was a character in the original *Star Wars.*"

They both laughed. Val felt a surge of tenderness. She hadn't seen her daughter this animated in months. Not since before her father ripped off her future like a hot wax strip. Lee bent her neck over the iPhone screen in her hand, her thumbs in motion. On the other side of the freeway's cement partition, headlights blinked on like fireflies. Inside the car, a faint glow of green haloed Lee's mass of dark curls.

"Interesting," she said after a minute or two.

"Tell me."

"Ashkenazi comes from the Hebrew word *ashkenaz,* meaning 'Germany.' My peeps are German."

A pinch stung Valerie's chest. She wanted to shout, *Hey!* I'm *your peep.* Her grip tightened around the warm vinyl steering wheel. She felt a sudden urge to snatch Lee's phone and hurl it out the window. "Hmm," she said, instead.

"Ninety percent of American Jews are Ashkenazim," Lee went on. "Seems we may have migrated from Palestine to Europe."

*We.* Valerie pressed her lips together.

"There's some controversy, though." Lee expanded the word size on her iPhone. "The debate is, did Jewish men and women migrate together? Or mostly just men? Like, did the guys arrive with their Jewish wives? Or did they marry European women later and convert them?"

"Why does it matter?"

Lee looked up and grinned. "I'm not sure. I've only been Jewish for twenty minutes."

Her mom exhaled a laugh. She said, "Why don't I treat my Jewish daughter to a Shake Shack burger for an early dinner."

"Aren't we broke?"

"Completely. But I have an emergency twenty for moments like this. Two hungry girls out on the town."

Normally, Lee's eyes would light up. With money so tight,

they rarely went out. Valerie had become a wizard at the microwave meal. "Steamed broccoli à la Cajun turkey breast. With crushed cornflakes for crunch."

From behind her curtain of hair, Lee smiled an acknowledgment of her mother's effort and parried back, "Okay, but no bacon." Grinning, she continued her Internet search. Again, Val felt a twinge in her chest, the spot directly above her heart. The nook where a mother holds love. Front and center. As she inched north on the San Diego Freeway, she pressed her fingers on her chest as if she could pluck out her heartache and crush it in her fist. She cursed her body for threatening tears. She also cursed her husband, Gil, for leaving her to handle this alone. They both knew this day would come . . . somehow. If not by letter, then via an ancestry search or a blood test or a call on a weekend evening while they were watching TV.

*Um, sorry to bother you, but I've been doing some digging . . .*

Of course Valerie was happy for her daughter. Of course. They had joked about Lee's biological roots a hundred times over the years.

"Maybe you're a long-lost relative of Czar Nicolas and Alexandra?"

"Great-great-grandchild of Crazy Horse!"

After the CDSS letter had been pushed through the mail slot in their old front door, their musings became more current.

"Perhaps I am Chaz Bono's secret love child from before she became a he."

Speculation had been fun. Especially in the past months when they both needed to imagine a life different from the one they were living. Fantasizing alternative families was a bright spot in their dismal year.

Still.

In the harsh glare of genuine DNA, Valerie felt something she hadn't expected to feel: *excluded.* Gil was gone. Scott had slipped off the grid. Now Lee was on a journey away from her. How had life become a series of losses?

"C'mon, c'mon," Valerie muttered as she flipped on her blinker in an attempt to cross four lanes before the next exit. "Let me in, *pleeeeease.*"

On a Los Angeles freeway in rush hour—the birthplace of road rage—relinquishing your spot in the herd is considered a weakness. A limping zebra on the African savannah. Allow one commuter to squeeze in ahead of you and the whole freeway will smell your vulnerability. You'll never get home. Valerie's green-light traffic karma was lost in the lanes of bumper-to-bumper.

"Thank you!" Valerie waved to a young colt in a convertible who accidentally allowed a gap while he answered a text.

"Wow," Lee piped up. "My people are a genetically tight group." She read: "Every Ashkenazi Jew is a thirtieth cousin."

Lifting her head, facing her mother, Lee beamed. "I must have family everywhere."

# ·☜❮ CHAPTER 13 ❯☞·

SOUTH FORK FISHING AND HUNTING CLUB

*Summer 1888*

The screened door at the side of our cottage slams on my way out. In the storage space beneath the side stairs are four bicycles. Two for ladies, one for a man, and one for a boy. Grabbing mine, I set off quickly down the dusty access road behind the cottages. Hatless, corsetless, ducking branches, feeling the filtered sun on my face, I roar with delight, as if I'm a lioness let loose from the Philadelphia Zoo. Mother would be horrified. My untethered waistline feels exquisite. Much too free to be proper. Not to mention sun on my face and unruly hair. But it doesn't matter. Not this once. No one will see me. All of Pittsburgh society is already in the clubhouse dining room by now. Lunch, no doubt, is being served. Through the trees, as I cycle past, I spot no one on the boardwalk. Still, I take no chances. The back road is deserted. I will be safely back at the cottage, in my room, before dessert is set out on the buffet. I only need a moment to satisfy my curiosity. One tiny *glimpse*. For some inexplicable reason, I must know: Does James Tottinger's face match his conceit?

The clubhouse draws near.

I hear him before I see him. His accent is unmistakable.

"Do you gents play football?"

Apparently, the boys have yet to enter the clubhouse dining room. I stow my bicycle against a tree several yards back and silently creep up to the rear of the building, hiding myself in a birch thicket. They are gathered on the grass beside the side stairs. What good fortune to be wearing my brown skirt. Though Nettie will have to work her magic on the hem. The dirt behind the clubhouse is wet and muddy.

"*Proper* football," James says. "It's a bit like rugby. And rugby is a bit like your soccer."

His tone of condescension is unmistakable, too. It takes all my strength not to throw a rock at him.

From my shroud of foliage, I raise my head ever so slightly to examine the lofty Mr. James Tottinger of the London Tottingers, relative of Countess Augusta Reuss of Ebersdorf, grandmother of Queen Victoria herself.

That's when I see him.

He is tall and trim. Hatless. His mahogany tweed breeches are tailored to perfection. Not a trace of facial hair softens his angular visage. His maple-colored hair sports the slightest wave—ripples bouncing above the upper folds of his delicate ears. Both brows are as expressive as a dancing bear, though one arches more dramatically than the other, creating a fear-less expression. His narrow lips seem locked in a playful snicker. Though his complexion is pale, it only magnifies the startling blue of his eyes. Quite simply, James Tottinger is the most ex-quisite creature I've ever seen.

Only when my chest burns do I realize I've been holding my breath.

Along with everyone else, I am *mesmerized*. Even as I real-ize the strutting Mr. Tottinger is performing for the crowd's benefit, I can no more pull my gaze away from him than I can move my boots out of the damp muck beneath my feet. Julian, Edmond, Oscar, Roderick—boys I've known all my life—stand on the grassy shore in a semicircle. They, too, are smit-ten. Dressed in their loose-fitting breeches, they look thoughtful with their straw boater's hats tilted to the backs of their heads.

"I know rugby." Stout Julian steps out from the crowd, his chest thrust forward. "My father is a Harvard man."

Roderick scoffs. "Yale is the better team."

Suddenly feminine sounds flicker through the air. My friends—and others—giggle behind their hands. Descending the side clubhouse steps like a flock of geese, they venture into the clearing, feigning a need to stroll off the curried eggs they'd just eaten. Creeping closer to a prickly hedge at the base of the birch coppice, I burrow ever lower. A thorn nicks my cheek.

"Ach," I gasp, slapping my hand over my mouth. Thankfully, James Tottinger is too busy enjoying the sound of his own voice to notice mine. In his throaty tone, he says to Julian, "You, my good man, are now captain of Team Blue. I shall front Team Red."

Julian beams. Standing like Big Ben in the center of the clearing, James Tottinger divides the boys into teams while the girls pretend not to watch.

"Can anyone spot me a soccer ball?"

Captain Julian dispatches Edmond to the sports closet in the clubhouse. "Quickly," Julian says, as if the commanding Mr. Tottinger might tire of the whole business and leave them flat-footed. In an outbreak of activity, the remaining boys scatter to toss errant bits of lake debris back into the water. They scoop up dead leaves with their bare hands. They remove their jackets and hats and tug at the pointed edges of their vests. Huddling ever deeper into the brush, I stare, unblinking, as the magnificent Mr. Tottinger unbuttons the jacket of his linen sack suit.

"Might I impose upon one of you lovely ladies to keep my jacket out of the dirt?" he says, turning to the flock.

Francine Larkin immediately steps forward with her clapper claw hands fluttering in the air.

"With pleasure, sir," she says in that sparrow voice of hers. Within my leafy cover, I roll my eyes. Had I not been a lady in hiding, I would have groaned audibly. With Francine clutching James's jacket to her breast, the arrival of the soccer ball, the peacocking of the man from England, and his accent making every word sound more exotic and important than it is, I finally come to my senses and decide I've seen enough. I've had my glimpse. Though my heart is pumping warm blood through my entire being, the absurdity of my position suddenly strikes me. Standing in shrubbery to watch grown men scamper through the grass like children? Particularly one man who so clearly believes he's the desire of everyone? Well, if my inquisitiveness had not gotten the better of me, this is not a position into which I would ever lower myself. James Tottinger may be handsome, he may be the most superb specimen of a man I've ever set eyes upon, but he's not for me. I prefer men with *real* confidence. Like Mr. Carnegie, who doesn't need pleasing features to gain respect.

Sweeping the unruly hair out of my eyes, no doubt smearing a bit of blood across my cheek in the process, I quietly gather my skirt and lift my muddy feet out of the soil, one by one. As I pull them from the muck, each boot makes a smacking sound. The noise of a mother's lips on her baby's cheeks. *Kiss. Kiss.* Still crouched low—rotating ever so slowly—I tiptoe in the direction of the tree trunk where my bicycle sits. Already I can feel the heavenly sensation of the hot bath I'll ask Nettie to draw as soon as she returns from her picnic. I do hope she hasn't thought I meant she could take the *entire* day off.

"A forest nymph!"

Midstep, I freeze.

"You there. In the bushes. Real or mythical?"

I don't need to turn around to know that James Tottinger has spotted me. Besides his melting accent, the raucous laughter of my so-called friends is confirmation.

"Elizabeth *Haberlin*? Is that possibly *you*?"

One brow shoots up. I recognize the voice instantly. It's Francine's. Of course it is. Her chirpy tone is unmistakable. I want to leap over the hedge and fill Francine Larkin's avian mouth with mud. But, of course, a lady mustn't act on every errant thought. Instead, I take a deep breath into the expandable elastic of my bloomers and extend myself to my full height, aligning my spine just so. With the countenance of Queen Victoria herself, I slowly turn around.

"Why, hello, Francine. Hello, everyone. Lovely day."

I then blow a clump of unruly hair off my bloodied face and turn my back on the laughing group to trudge my muddy shoes to the bicycle waiting in the woods. Only once do I glance over my shoulder to see that James Tottinger is silently mocking me and Francine Larkin is grinning at him with her bird lips.

Summer at South Fork. Let the games begin.

# ❊| CHAPTER 14 |❊

## SOUTHERN CALIFORNIA

*Present*

Shortly after her life imploded, Lee's laptop crashed, too. Looking back, she viewed its incremental disintegration as a metaphor for all the life signs she'd ignored, too. Like that *whirring* beneath the keyboard. Wasn't that similar to the distraction she'd heard—but overlooked—in Shelby's voice as she packed for Malawi?

"Um, yeah, don't worry, I'll FaceTime you."

And Shelby's last text from Malawi: "There's this boy. A carpenter for Habitat. Yum!"

Shouldn't she have seen that coming? The same way all those frozen Web pages foreshadowed the Blue Screen of Death? If she'd been paying attention, she wouldn't have felt so run over when Shelby changed her relationship status on Facebook. How could her best friend since *middle school* change her relationship status without telling her?

When Lee spent the night of her eighteenth birthday eating microwave popcorn in front of the TV with her mom, she realized she should have made more friends. You know, as backup. In case her very *best* friend left the country to have a yummy boyfriend without bothering to mention it. In case her brother decided to *vanish* into the woods and her dad ran away from home, leaving her mother feeling all clutchy, as if Lee were the only person left in the world.

There were lots of other signs that things were awry, too. Like, for months, Lee's computer had been super slow. Constantly buffering. An endlessly rotating color wheel in the center of her screen reminding her that she was going nowhere. Wasn't that spinning symbol of impending disaster just like the foreboding of her dad's drinking? Its downward spiral? Like the way she noticed, but didn't fully note, that his glass of wine with dinner became two, then it included a cocktail while her mom was cooking, then scotch in a tumbler the moment he got home from work with his breath already ignitable. Hadn't he been disappearing in plain sight for years? And taking her future with him?

If her eyes had been open, she would have noticed that her computer was infected by something malicious; she would have begged her dad to get help before he dragged them all down with him. Had she been paying attention to all the ways her father had become little more than a prop around the house, she wouldn't have been so knocked off her feet when he called several months after he packed up and left.

"It's me," he'd said.

"Dad?"

"Yep."

"Where are you?"

Gil sighed and muttered something about an inability to cope. Life, he said, had gotten the best of him. "I'm a human being, Lee. With flaws."

His speech was slow. The word "flaws" had two syllables: *fill-aws*. It was barely four o'clock and he was already drunk.

Lee said, "Lots of fathers have flaws."

Gil Parker sighed spitily into the phone. In a confessional sort of way, he unburdened himself. "See, that's the thing, Lee. I've never been father material. I realize that now."

"Um, *what*?"

"Not all adults are meant to be parents. I'm sorry. Truly."
*Tur-ew-lee.*

Lee sat there blinking. Like a pulsing blob, she felt her blood *ba-blump, ba-blump* through her aorta. Had she really heard what she thought she heard? Had her father *quit*? Were dads allowed to do that? All this time, had he only been faking fatherhood? Pretending to love her? Was it because she wasn't genetically his? Was he father material to her brother, Scott?

It wasn't remotely close to the conversation she had imagined having when her father finally called. She'd pictured tears and apologies. *His.* She'd envisioned herself taking the high road.

"Come home, Dad," she would say, nonjudgmentally. "We'll forget about the past. Let's start over."

Maturely, she wouldn't mention how they'd had to cancel cable and the landline because creditors kept calling during dinner—which was now usually beans and rice. Or how her mother had lied to her father's boss when it became clear that he'd quit his job, too.

"I'm afraid he's too ill to come to the phone," she said for as long as she believably could. Finally, she had to come clean.

"Gone?" his boss had asked. "Gone where?"

"I haven't a clue."

"When will he be back?"

"I'm afraid he's left us."

Nothing is more pathetic than *silence* after you admit something like that. That's what Valerie said after she hung up. And nothing is more terrifying than the abrupt disappearance of automatic paycheck deposits.

In the gazillion times Lee had rehearsed their phone conversation in her mind, she never told her dad that Shelby's parents gave them money for a mortgage that was already way past due. Not a word about the bankruptcy lawyer that her mom had to hire even though she had no money. And she certainly never let it slip that there were lots of days when she came home from school to find the curtains drawn, the house dark, and her mother hastily dressed in clothes from the floor—her hair flat on one side, crust in the corners of her eyes, and pillow wrinkles fresh on her face.

Gil had ended the call with a resigned "Okay, then."

Lee's cell felt like a brick in her hand. Before her father hung up, she quickly asked, "Have you heard from Scott? Do you, um, know how we might be able to reach him?"

Shouldn't *somebody* inform her brother that his family had disintegrated like cotton candy left in the sun?

Snorting a sad laugh, Gil said, "Apparently, he takes after his dad."

Then the phone went dead.

Nothing but pathetic silence.

Just like the day her laptop crashed for the last time. She felt the same panicked loneliness when she stared at the dead machine that once contained her whole entire life.

So, now, Lee Parker's eyes were wide open. No longer would she look the other way. Now she *noticed* the gray shadow that flickered past Valerie's sunny disposition each time Lee searched her iPhone for any possible information about the woman in the photo. True, in her initial excitement, she'd been a clod. Totally insensitive in the car on the way home from Social Services. All that stuff about her peeps. But now she was keenly attuned.

"Come watch TV with me." Valerie patted the sofa cushion. "Here. With your *mom*."

Now Lee was aware of the way Val kept identifying herself.

"How 'bout a good-night kiss for your *mom*?"

As if Lee would somehow forget.

Lee noticed. She got it. No way was she going to hurt the only person who hadn't left her to fend for herself.

Still.

No way could Lee let it go either. As any adoptee knows. The tiny pebble of information she now knew only expanded the ripples of her desire to know more. Where was she born? How had she come to be? Where had her birth mother drowned? Why the name Elizabeth? Did she have siblings? A father? Had he been looking for her all her life? Who made her tall, dark, and broody? And, the most pressing question of all: Who was the woman in the photo? The genetic relative whose blood pumped through Lee's veins. After eighteen years of wondering, she now had a name and a clue: Clara Barton and a pileful of rubble. Could the woman who founded the American Red Cross lead Lee to the dark-haired woman who stood next to Clara so many years ago? And, in turn, could the dark-haired woman lead Lee to the birth mother who had once pressed her palm onto her distended stomach to feel her child's stretching arms, her flexing legs, her impatience to get out and meet her? Could the woman in the photo lead Lee to the identity of the woman who gave her life?

For Lee, that simple question was the biggest ache and *pain* of her life. The mystery of her history. The elephant in the living room she'd been tiptoeing around ever since she saw the photo. Of course she wanted to know. Who wouldn't? But the distressing truth was: uncovering the identity of her birth mother would bruise the only mother she'd ever known.

There was only one solution: going forward, Lee would secretly search for her mother without her mom finding out.

# ·⇥[ CHAPTER 15 ]⇤·

SOUTH FORK FISHING AND HUNTING CLUB

*Courtesy of the Johnstown Flood Museum Archives, Johnstown Area Heritage Association*

*Summer 1888*

Fresh from my mortification in the bushes behind the club-house, I hop on my bicycle and pedal. Past the clubhouse, past our cottage, as far as the dirt path will allow. I search every clearing for Nettie and her picnic. My shoes are caked with mud, as is the hem of my skirt. If not for the breeze caused by my haste, I would scarcely be able to see through the errant fronds of hair that fall onto my face like drooping leaves of a weeping willow. My heart thrashes inside my chest. In part, the pounding is due to the exertion of exercise, but also it's a result of the wild anticipation of what I'm about to do. If I could only find Nettie.

At the path's end, I lean my bicycle against a gnarled tree stump and scramble forward on foot. Dead leaves and lake sand crunch beneath my feet. The scent of rich, damp earth envelops me like an opera cloak. I feel like a Scotland Yard sleuth. My eyes are fixed to the occasional footprints in the path. For the next several minutes, I stoop under low-hanging branches, clamber over fallen saplings, extricate myself from mud hollows, and snag my skirt on every jagged twig. I follow any shoe-sized indentation I can find. My own shoes are a fright. Mother will be cross beyond words.

At long last, I hear laughter coming from a clearing in the woods. As I draw myself closer to the familiar sound, I notice a flash of fabric.

"Nettie!" I call out.

Silence.

"Nettie. It's Elizabeth."

A great rustling ensues. Rewrapping her picnic fare, I assume. Marching straight toward the sound, I am startled to see Nettie with a horseman I recognize from the clubhouse stable. He scrabbles to his feet. Heaven knows what I might have interrupted.

"Ma'am," he mumbles, adjusting his grubby cap.

"Miss Elizabeth," Nettie sputters. Clearly, she is disconcerted to see me outdoors without a corset.

"Forgive my intrusion, Nettie," I say. "I hope you won't mind cutting your picnic short. I've changed my plan for the day. I now need your help."

Perhaps there is the faintest flicker of annoyance in Nettie's expression, but it fades too quickly for me to formally note it. And the gentleman with her stares at his feet. Almost certainly he spotted my natural waistline and unruly hair. To his credit, he doesn't embarrass me by staring at my state of undress. Not once does he look up.

"We must move quickly," I say, turning. "I'll be back at the cottage waiting for you." Without wasting another moment, I hurry back to the path. My bicycle, with its muck-encrusted tires, is nearly impossible to pedal. Yet I somehow manage. Such is the force of my determination.

Early afternoon has settled in by the time Nettie makes her way back to the cottage and to me. No one is there, thank goodness. Ida, our cook, and Ella, Mother's maid, are working teatime at the clubhouse for the day. Extra hands were required to ensure the Tottingers wanted for nothing. I shut my eyes for a moment in exasperation. The only thing that Tottinger fellow needs is an ample serving of humble pie.

We don't have much time. Surely Mother will come looking for me once she hears of my folly in the birch thicket behind the clubhouse. If she hasn't heard gossip about it already. I will be reprimanded severely, I'm sure. Which is why I am willing to do what I plan to do next. The rules have already been broken.

Why fret over breaking a few more? If we move hastily, I will make it before teatime *and* before Mother returns to thwart me.

"What happened to your face, miss?" Nettie asks, alarmed. We meet in the cottage hallway. In the mirror behind the coatrack, I see a smear of dried blood directly in the center of my cheek. There is also mud on my forehead and brambles in my hair. Mother would lock me away if she saw such a sight. The very last thing a proper lady would ever do is allow her face to get so dangerously close to a hedgeful of bristles.

"I had a mishap," I say. "But you and I will undo it."

The preparations begin in earnest. Nettie races to the kitchen to heat water. Then she returns to the parlor and sits me down on a sturdy chair. Squatting in front of me, she works her magic with a buttonhook. The laces on my leather boots are rigid with mud.

"You decided to go out after all, then," she says with a wry smile.

"Indeed."

"Did you see the royals?"

Sighing with exasperation, I repeat, "The Tottingers are *not* royal." Then I sigh in an altogether different manner. "But James may as well be."

Nettie grins. At last, she is able to release my feet from their muddy bondage. "Mercy," she says. "I'll have to use saddle cleaner to restore any use of these."

"Perhaps your stable-hand friend has some to spare?"

Now she blushes. Hoisting herself up, my maid dangles my dirty shoes away from her dress. In a commotion of fabric, she is out of the parlor and on her way to the kitchen where my bathwater is hopefully near a boil.

"Hurry!" I call after her as I race up the stairs to my bedroom. "We don't have a moment to waste."

If this were any normal day, I would accept Nettie's help in undressing. But, today is far from ordinary. Thankfully, my clothes are easy to remove. The shirtwaist has but five buttons down the front; the simple skirt but one in the back. And my hair is already tumbled from any semblance of containment. By the time the bathtub is full and sufficiently warmed, I am stripped down to my scandalous bloomers and camisole. Since we are alone in the cottage, I have no worry of anyone seeing my near nakedness. Though, of course, Little Henry would no more notice underclothes than I would notice the manner of steam propulsion on a train.

"Here." I meet Nettie in the bathroom and hand her the bottle of lavender oil I purchased on a recent trip into Pittsburgh. "I am told that two drops will scent an entire bath."

It's true. The room soon fills with the sweet aroma of purple flowers.

Unlike the large bathroom next to my bedroom in our Upper St. Clair home, the cottage bath at South Fork is scaled down but serviceable. There is a washing stand near the curtained window, a rolled-top bathtub next to it, and a commode against the facing wall. Admittedly, the commode is the one luxury that makes staying in our cottage worth it. The clubhouse has only an *out*house—though it is a two-story structure, and more modern than one might expect so far into the woods. In our cottage bathroom, there is no need for a fireplace since we are rarely here once summer has passed. Still, Nettie warms my linen towel in the kitchen oven.

"Shall I wash your hair, too, miss?" she asks, helping me out of my undergarments and into the warm, floral water.

"Not today," I say. "I must be ready by teatime."

After quickly plucking bits of scrub from my hair and pinning it atop my head to keep it dry, my maid commences scrubbing my back and arms with carbolic soap and a hand-sized cut of cotton fabric. Next come my feet and legs, which she washes with both diligence and care. I cleanse my private areas while Nettie rushes back to my bedroom to retrieve my traveling satin robe. Before she exits, I say, "I'll be wearing my *best* corset this afternoon. And the white silk stockings in my second trunk."

Stopping, Nettie wheels around with a furrowed brow. "White silk?"

"Yes." Then I shift my back to forestall further discussion.

Unlike my usual half-hour soak, today's bath takes less than ten minutes. The moment I step out of the water, Nettie is there to wrap me like an Egyptian mummy in a length of absorbent cotton. The warm fabric feels glorious on my washed and scented skin. Nonetheless, I welcome the unfurling. I am nearly completely dry when Nettie hands me my robe and we both dash back to my bedroom.

With the clamor of the clubhouse a good half mile away, it is silent in my bedroom. Even with the window open, I hear only the chatter of birds. Still, I can almost hear snippets of gossip about me.

"Ah yes, Elizabeth Haberlin has always been a bit of a rebel." (Francine.)

"I heard she once betrayed a confidence." (Untrue.)

"She once refused to apologize for unladylike behavior." (True.)

From my second-floor window, I see that the sun is orange. Afternoon is fast slipping away.

"We must move swiftly," I tell Nettie, "or all will be for naught."

With expert movements, Nettie opens my wardrobe and mines for my finest set of drawers and prettiest silk chemise. On my direction, she retrieves the crinoline cage and pink satin corset I bought on my last trip to visit Tilly in New York. Mother adores this corset. Its boning is so stiff my waist is a full three inches slimmer than normal. If it weren't an emergency situation, I would never subject myself to such torture. But, today, I can endure pain and suffocation for the greater good. Thank heavens I had the foresight to pack an extra trunk with such finery.

"All this for tea at the clubhouse, miss?"

I answer with a question of my own: "Are there still fresh wildflowers behind the cottage?"

"I believe so."

"Good. Please bring me several cuttings of baby snapdragons. Heliotrope, if possible. The best you can find."

Nettie nods and scampers off. While she is gone, I dash into the kitchen for a lemon. My fingernails are a horror. My bath wasn't nearly long enough to coax out the mud beneath my nails. After cutting the lemon in half, I return to my bedroom and sit before my vanity mirror. Inserting each finger into the lemon's center, one by one, I twist and squeeze until the citrus juice has cleansed each nail and bleached away any discoloration, leaving only the scent of sunshine.

"We had a good crop," Nettie says, returning with an apronful of purple snapdragons. "For your hair, I assume?"

"Yes. Work your magic."

Deftly, Nettie sets the flowers on my dressing table and proceeds to brush my unruly hair with speed and expertise. Once it is smooth, she coils it into a tight French twist. Holding the style in place with her left hand, she inserts pins with her right. Then, with fingers waggling like an upended centipede's feet, she frazzles my forehead fringe in exactly the manner I prefer. A light waterfall of tendrils in uniform density above my eyes, barely brushing my brows. Nothing as old-fashioned as finger waves or ringlets. Heavens, no. In a matter of minutes, I am transformed from forest nymph to debutante. Perfect. After Nettie tucks baby snapdragons down the length of the coil, I swivel my head left and right to note the swinging of their bell-like shapes.

"Stunning, miss," Nettie says, admiring her work.

"I agree." I clap my hands like a child.

Turning me away from the pier glass, Nettie commences work on my face. First, she smooths on a jasmine pomade I had sent all the way from the Orient. Its milky hue, infused with the faintest hint of glimmer, is an excellent canvas for the restrained application of beet juice on my cheeks and lips. With her smallest finger, Nettie dips into the ground charcoal I brought from Pittsburgh. Ever so lightly she brushes it across my lashes. Finally, I see her hurry over to the open window and lean all the way out. Just as I'm about to grab her foot, she pops back in the room holding a tiny feather. "There is *always* one about," she says, dipping the quill end into my basin water, then twirling it in the charcoal. "Look up, miss."

I look up. With the precision of Gustave Courbet, Nettie touches my cheek once with the charcoal-tipped quill. Then she turns me to the mirror. I gasp at the sight of me. The jasmine pomade has created the most beautiful white sheen. And the charcoal dot conceals my thorn wound with a thoroughly modern beauty mark. "Oh, Nettie!" I squeal. Behind me, she smiles and squeezes my shoulder. Then we quickly get back to work.

With the nimbleness of a cotillion waltzer, Nettie stands me up and inserts me into my white silk stockings, petticoat, chemise, corset, and bustle. "Hold still," she says, circling around to my spine. Bracing herself against my bedpost, she rears back and draws the laces of my corset into her chest as if attempting to stop a team of runaway stallions. I groan.

"Apologies," she says.

"Harder," I gasp.

Grunting and wheezing herself, Nettie uses her considerable heft to pull mightily. As if escaping a torture chamber by the only available exit, my breasts heave upward, nearly brushing my chin.

"Well done," I say, feeling faint.

At last, we are ready for the final layer. My crowning glory.

"Are you sure you want to do this, Miss Elizabeth?"

"Absolutely," I say, without so much as a glimmer of doubt.

With that, my maid takes pains not to ruin my hair as she dresses my body in the finest silk and lace. She fastens the satin-covered buttons down the length of my spine and slips my stockinged feet into delicate silk shoes. Onto each hand, she carefully slides lace gloves from Paris. The gloves I have been saving for my debut. No matter. I'm quite sure no one will be noticing my hands. Nettie encircles my neck with a pearl choker and adorns my earlobes with fire opals. Of course I wear Grandmother's bracelet. My lavender bath has made the diamonds gleam. Assisting me down the cottage stairs, Nettie follows me out the back door to the formerly muddy access road that has, thankfully, dried to dust.

"Allow me, miss."

Trundling ahead of me, Nettie clears the path of fallen branches and large stones. She points to shallow puddles and directs me around them. It's warm out, but not too terribly hot for a late summer's afternoon. The earlier sun has softened. We make our way to the clubhouse. As we get closer, I hear laughter and bluster. Teatime is upon us. The boys will have buttoned their sports jackets; the girls will have fluffed the sleeves of their shirtwaists or dusted off their jackets.

A cooling breeze stirs over the lake. By the time I reach the clubhouse's rear entrance, it is half past four. "Perfect timing," I whisper to myself. Tea will be in full swing. By now, my family and friends will have assumed I'd taken a nap instead of joining them. Perhaps Mother had heard about my foolishness in the foliage. Maybe she's glad I have chosen to stay at the cottage after such a spectacle. Little does she suspect the scene that awaits her now.

"I can manage on my own from here," I tell Nettie. She nods and stands back with her hands again clasped at her waist and a worried expression on her face. I take a step toward the open clubhouse door, then quickly wheel around and scamper back to my maid.

"I couldn't have done this without you," I whisper, throwing my arms around her neck.

"Promise you'll tell me all about it?"

"Every detail."

Nettie squeezes my shoulders and says, "Good luck." Inhaling deeply to steady my nerves, I turn to face the clubhouse. Through the open threshold of the back door, I hear a jumble of conversations merging into one.

" . . . archery competition? Wondrous ide—"

"Another round, old sport?"

" . . . as was last year's debu—"

"Will you be sailing to Southampton?"

Extending my neck to its full length, with not even a *hint* of a slouch, I gather my wits and confidently march through the doorway. As expected, all conversation stops short.

"Elizabeth," I hear Mother sputter. There is also an audible gasp or two. I smile serenely. With my head erect, I slowly walk past the clubhouse bar in the lounge feeling my gown brush against the men's trouser cuffs. Mr. Phipps, Mr. Frick, Father, Mr. Vanderhoff, and several other men hold crystal glasses of amber liquid in their hands. Father seems to be frozen in place. Mother is seated with Mrs. Mellon, across the room near the window. Her porcelain teacup is also perched midair. It's as if time has stopped and turned everyone to stone.

My calm smile remains affixed. My heart beats as fast as a jackrabbit's. Inside my head, I squeal. But my exterior betrays no such immaturity. Floating through the entire length of the room, making certain *everyone* sees me, I ask a passing server if I might trouble him for tea. "Please forgive my tardiness," I say.

"Right away, miss."

He bows awkwardly and backs away from me as if I am royalty. This pleases me enormously, though I don't let it show in my countenance. I continue my sashay about the room with unshakable confidence. It's an attitude befitting my gown. A Charles Frederick Worth original. The fawn lace collar hugs the back of my neck, tumbling down in front to the bodice. The sleeves are long and tight to my wrists, with a spray of lace kissing my gloved fingers. Made from cream-colored satin— imported from Istanbul—the gown reflects all the light in the room. Embroidered rosettes skip down the front and sides in floral vines. Inserted within each satin pleat are more rose embellishments—some a complementary yellow to the violet blossoms in my hair, others a muted bisque. The modern bustle is augmented with a large blush-colored bow; the hem an accordion strip of hand-sewn ribbon just long enough to cover the satin tie on my buttery silk shoes. In such a gown, I surely scandalized Mother with my flushed cheeks and charcoal lashes. Not to mention the shamelessly Parisian addition of my beauty mark. Nettie's inspired touch. In this dress, one cannot help but feel extraordinary.

"You look stunning, my dear," Mr. Vanderhoff says as I pass him. "Is there a ball tonight on the sand?"

Twitters sprinkle throughout the crowd. I dare not look Mother's way again, though I do spot my sweet brother, Henry, near the dessert table, clapping his hands with delight.

"What could be more special than summer at the club?" I ask with supreme confidence.

"Here, here," says Mr. Frick, raising his glass, clearly attempting to defuse the awkwardness. One of the more prominent members of the Bosses' Club, Mr. Frick offers his blessing to relax the others. Not that I'm concerned in the slightest. I'm not here for his approval.

As soon as the waiter reappears with my tea, I thank him graciously, take the cup and saucer in my gloved hand, stop, sip it daintily, then set it aside on a table to continue my elegant promenade down the length of the clubhouse dining room. Having all eyes upon me is a thrill beyond measure. In the silence, I fear the whole crowd can hear my pounding heart.

As I make my way outside to the veranda, Roderick Vanderhoff is the first of my friends to speak to me.

"Have you gone batty, Elizabeth?" he asks, overheated in a slightly drunk sort of way.

"If I have, would I know it?" I say, grinning slyly.

The chatter level resumes behind me in the dining room—no doubt spiced with whispers about my scandalous exhibition. On her teeny mouse feet, Francine Larkin totters over. "Whatever are you thinking?" she asks, softly enough to appear as though she is speaking to me in confidence, yet loud enough for all on the porch to hear. With one raised brow, I glance at her girlish pink dress.

"One can feel so very homespun out here in the summer," I reply. "Don't you agree?"

Without waiting for an answer, I continue my stroll to the far end of the patio, past Lilly and Vivian, past Oscar and Julian.

Past shy Ivy Tottinger, who blushes crimson at the very sight of me and grips her lemonade glass with both hands. There isn't a moment that I don't feel her brother's gaze on me. The heat of James Tottinger's stare has propelled my feet. The entirety of his focus is upon me still.

At the end of the long patio, I gently place my hand on the wide railing. The diamonds in Grandmother's bracelet catch the orange sunlight. With a luxuriant sigh, I take in the beauty of our stunning lake. In the fading sun, the water is the color of mercury. Its soft ripples are folds of fresh bed linen. I can almost feel the undulation of the water in the rise and fall of my breasts. Even the trees on the far shore seem to sway with each inhalation.

"I think I'll rest before dinner," I say to no one in particular.

Then I swivel on my silk shoes and make my way back through the far end of the parlor lounge. As abruptly as I'd entered, I exit. Without a further word to anyone. On my way out the door, back to the cottage, I have but one thought for the cocky Mr. James Tottinger of Great Britain.

*Who is the fisherman now, and who is the fish?*

# ·∘》[ CHAPTER 16 ]《∘·

## SOUTHERN CALIFORNIA

*Present*

For such a small woman—barely five feet—Clara Barton had a large life. Quickly, Lee realized it was impossible to adequately research her on a petite iPhone screen. Valerie had been right to tell Lee she'd go blind staring at that small screen.

"Can I use the car today?" It was Lee's first full day off since she'd turned eighteen. Unbelievably, she was awake and alert by nine.

"Sure, honey. What's up?" Ready for work, Val was spot-cleaning a smudge on her uniform. Esther Adell hated her maid to look mussed while she cleaned the toilets.

"I want to research more about the Ashkenazi genetics. You know, make sure I know all I need to know, medically. So, I thought I'd go to the library."

Like any good lie, Lee's story skirted the edges of truth. As a point of fact, the medical genetics of her newly uncovered DNA barely made a dent in her consciousness. Yeah, she'd feel for lumps in the shower, have her baseline mammogram at forty, a Pap smear at twenty-one. Blah, blah, blah. At *eighteen*, however, another matter was on her mind: Identifying her dead birth mother without upsetting her living mom. And Clara Barton—the woman who founded the American Red Cross—was going to help.

"Library?" Val said. "How retro."

"I hear they have these rectangular objects inside them? I think they're called *buks*?"

Valerie laughed. "Don't forget to sunscreen the backs of your hands." She followed Lee out the pool-house door. After seeing the mottled claws of the yellow jackets each time they dabbed linen napkins at the corners of their scrunchie lips, Valerie slathered sunscreen on her hands—and neck and face—365 days a year.

"Already done." Car keys in hand, Lee waggled her fingers midair. "I'll be home for dinner."

"Dinner? Good heavens. How much is there to know?"

She had no idea.

"Maybe I'll pick up Baja Fresh?"

Yesterday was payday. Things were looking up.

MULHOLLAND DRIVE SNAKED over the Santa Monica Mountains. It squiggled along thirsty brown cliffs and crispy ravines spiked with olive-green succulents. Even with the air conditioner on full blast—Lee had filled the tank—heat baked the windshield and sent waves of warmth onto her chest. She held the steering wheel at its base. On top of it, her hands would have been fried like two bugs beneath a magnifying glass. Sunscreen or not.

Driving her tatty car past the mottled gray trunks of eucalyptus trees, hills polka-dotted with pine scrub, overgrown hippie houses, and millionaires' curved driveways, Lee deliberately shut her mind off from all thoughts of her friend Shelby, her dad, her brother burrowed into the Idaho woods. It was time to let them go. Especially since they were already gone. Beneath the solar blast of the Southern Californian sun, she focused on the road ahead. Everything else was a sad rearview.

After crossing Sunset Boulevard at the light, Lee steered into a residential neighborhood. Down palm-lined streets. Past old-money Spanish mansions and new-moncy cubic fortresses of glass and white stucco. Straight through the heart of Beverly Hills. Today, Lee Parker would mingle with the one percent.

The landmark library was gorgeous. Tucked into the historic City Hall complex—with its robin's-egg-blue-and-yellow Castilian tiled dome and Gothic arches—it was everything a research structure should be. Quiet, imposing, illuminated by natural light, and both modern and reeking of history. Merely standing inside it made Lee feel like she could accomplish anything. The very air in Beverly Hills was scented with success. Its sunlight was more golden than the Valley's harsh white-hot glare.

Beneath one of the high arched windows, Lee sat at a vacant computer. Across from her, a middle-aged woman with carp lips smiled fakely. *Why would a woman inject stuff into her lips?* Lee wondered. *Who wants to look like a fish?* Lee had never understood Southern California's obsession with plastic surgery, the way so many women chose to erase all individuality from their faces. Crazy.

Wearing Levi's and an Old Navy T-shirt, Lee knotted her bushel of hair atop her head. Unlike most girls her age, she steadfastly refused to succumb to fashion's whims. All that fuss over frills. Didn't women know they were *pawns*? Manipulated to change styles each season only to enrich designers and keep money flowing into stores. Wasn't there a better use of funds? Like, what Shelby told her in her last text: "A single pair of Balmain jeans can feed and house a Malawian for more than two years."

It made you think. Particularly if you didn't have enough money to buy jeans at Target.

Lee's one concession to bling was the vintage Hollycraft bracelet her grandmother gave her before she died. Lee never took it off. Its pastel rhinestones twirled around her wrist in tiny daisies. She loved the way the rock crystals caught the light, flickering freckles of color into the air.

Setting her backpack on the floor at her feet, Lee got busy. She wiggled the mouse to wake the computer and typed "Clara Barton" into the search engine. The screen filled with links. As she had frustratingly attempted on her iPhone, Lee rolled the cursor up to the "images" icon to—hopefully—find the photo from her adoption file. Wasn't *everything* online if you dug deeply enough? Down she scrolled. Down, down, down. Pages of black-and-white portrait photos appeared. Young Clara Barton and old. Round, smooth cheeks and lined eyes. Serene smiles. Crinoline dresses buttoned up the neck. Red Cross brooches. Battlefield illustrations. Images of wounded soldiers. On and on and on. But no woman with dark hair standing with Clara Barton in rubble.

Bending down, Lee reached into her pack for the thermos of green tea she'd brought with her. A Starbucks Trenta Teavana was more than five bucks! Absurd. After pouring herself a cup of tea and taking a sip, she returned her long fingers to the keyboard and left the images link to launch a Web search. If she couldn't find the photo, she was determined to figure out where it was taken. And when. Even if it took all day, she would unearth what she needed to know about the one person who could lead her to her roots. Clara Barton, the founder of the American Red Cross, had somehow met her great-great-great-grandmother, at some time, in the aftermath of some calamity. Before the day was done, Lee was going to find out what it was.

Again, she fortified herself with a sip of tea and a deep inhalation. Judging by the vast amount of links on the screen before her, digging into Clara Barton's life would be an *excavation*.

"Here we go," Lee whispered under her breath.

*Click.*

Right away, Lee Parker learned that Clara Barton was not only a woman of her time, but one *ahead* of her time, too. Both lonely places for a nineteenth-century woman to be.

## ⋅⋅◦❊[ CHAPTER 17 ]❊◦⋅⋅

Courtesy of the Johnstown Flood Museum Archives, Johnstown Area Heritage Association

**SOUTH FORK FISHING AND HUNTING CLUB**

*Summer 1888*

The thumping of Mother's footfalls up the stairs rattles the entire cottage. Nettie is rattled, too; her hands quiver as she rushes to remove my gown.

"Leave us, please," Mother says when she sweeps into my room without so much as a tap on the door. Tucking her chin,

Nettie pivots and silently disappears, turning the knob all the way to the right to soundlessly give us privacy. With the back of my dress only half unbuttoned, I nonetheless take a deep breath and turn to face my punishment with my head held high. "I acted purposefully, Mother," I say, attempting to camouflage my nerves in haughtiness. "My sanity, and my reputation, are intact."

Mother says, "Here." Brusquely, she spins me around to continue what Nettie had started. "You mustn't soil your gown. Whatever possessed you to bring it to the lake?"

Truthfully, I haven't a proper answer. The honest reply would be a single word: *love.*

On my last trip to New York, traveling with Father, I'd seen the gown on a mannequin in a dressmaker's shop window along Sixth Avenue. At first sight, I lost my breath. Such fine detailing. What exquisite color combinations. Cream, blush, butter. The pleating, the rosettes. Perfection. Quite simply, it *called* to me.

"Father, I must loo—"

"Go," he'd said. As the fates would have it, there was a cigar shop a few doors down with its own smoking room. Father had regarded it covetously as we strolled past. Brilliant location on the Ladies' Mile. How many other fashionable women had deposited their fathers and husbands there? My father was all too happy to escort me into the dress shop with the promise that he would return in half an hour or so. Smelling, no doubt, of Brazilian tobacco—his favorite.

Oh, what a joy that dress shop was. Running my hand over the silks was like stroking the belly of a kitten. The gown in the window was French (of course), from the House of Worth. Charles Frederick Worth was expanding his ready-to-wear line beyond Paris. No stylish American lady could boast a proper wardrobe without at least one of his creations. Not that the dress in the window was factory-made. Heavens no. It was a Charles Worth *original,* intended to do exactly what it did: entice women into the shop.

"I see you in *bisque,*" one of the gentlemen on the sales floor cooed in my ear as he draped a swatch of sinfully luxurious lace over my shoulder. "See how it complements your raven hair?"

Clearly he believed I was older than my seventeen years. A fact that flattered me no end. I smiled regally as I noted the elegant way he wore his foppishly billowing ascot. Was that clear varnish on his nails?

"The proportions of your figure are exquisite, my dear," he went on. "Mr. Worth would be honored to personally design a gown for you that would be the talk of New York."

"I live in Pittsburgh," I said, adding, "Upper St. Clair."

"Even better. Have you any special events upcoming?"

Disclosing my debut the following year would reveal my youth. Plus, the gentleman would most certainly conclude that Father couldn't afford such a splendid couture dress if he believed I would purchase a debut gown a full year before the ball—one that wouldn't be the very *latest* style.

"Wouldn't wearing a Charles Worth original make *any* event special?" I asked with a twinkle in my voice, pleased at my quick wit.

Throwing his head back in a hearty laugh, the salesman

steered me over to the pier glass and said, "Let me fetch Miss Callaghan to take your measurements."

I asked, "Might the dress in the *window* fit me?"

One brow cocked like a pixie's. "Let's see."

How could I say no?

I could not. Though Father could. After Miss Callaghan took me into the dressing room to assist me into the gown, Father returned to the store to find that his daughter was passionately in love.

"It's divine," I said, swooning, twirling so that the lace overlay fluttered like a butterfly's wings. "The only alterations needed are minor. The cuffs and the hem and perhaps the tiniest tuck in the waist."

"Do you have any idea of the cost, Elizabeth?" he said quietly in my ear. It wasn't a question seeking an answer. More, it was a statement that I'd gone mad.

"Priceless, I should think," I whispered in return. "I'll wear it at my debut. You'll have the most beautiful daughter in all of Pittsburgh."

At that moment, it wasn't a complete untruth. In my mind I told myself that I *would* wear that stunning gown if I were able to resist showing it off before my coming-out ball. *If.* Dizzy amid so many fine textiles, how could I be blamed for lacking the clarity I needed to tell the absolute truth? Besides, Father would never remember what I promised a full year earlier. He wouldn't even remember Mother's birthday if our butler didn't prod him with the gift he bought for her. Using household funds, of course.

"I already have the most beautiful daughter in Pittsburgh," Father said.

Extending my neck to kiss his cheek, I told him quite honestly, "I shall expire at this very moment if I cannot call a Charles Worth original my own."

Silently, the salesman appeared behind us. Almost to himself he said, "Nothing makes a woman feel more prized than a touch of glimmer to bounce the light."

How extraordinarily true.

How could Father say no?

He did not.

When we returned home to Pittsburgh on the evening train, with a large tissue-wrapped package, Father told Mother he'd been unable to resist. Mother sighed. "I knew it was dangerous leaving you alone with her."

It took a few weeks for my grandfather's talented apprentice to fine-tune the alterations. By the time he was done, we were nearly set to summer at Lake Conemaugh. The mere thought of leaving such a masterpiece alone in an Upper St. Clair cupboard for three months was unbearable. I had to have it with me. To stroke it and admire it and try it on from time to time. So I brought an extra trunk.

Who knew I might need it so soon?

In my cottage bedroom, with Mother's help, I step out of the glorious gown. She also unfastens my petticoat and releases my rib cage from its corseted vise, carefully laying the items flat on my bed for Nettie. Then she turns to me—still in my underclothes—and says, "Sit."

I sit. My earlier confidence has all but drained away. I feel tears approaching. My head dangles forward on my neck. A purple snapdragon tumbles onto my lap.

"Do you have any idea what you've done?" Mother says.

Lips trembling, I nod. "Discretion and propriety are as important to Father's practice as a proper diagnosis." I echo Mother's frequent admonition. She sits beside me and takes my hands in her soft grip.

"My brilliant daughter," she says.

"But, I—*pardon?*" Looking up, I can do little else but blink.

"Unless you do something irreversible in the coming year, you'll have your pick of Pittsburgh's *best* after your debut. Even the handsome Mr. Tottinger, if you want him. I saw the telltale expression in his eyes."

"Expression?"

"Awe, my darling. That very rarest of emotions."

Rising, Mother catches her reflection in my dressing-table mirror. She reaches her hands up to smooth her hair into shape. Before leaving me alone to my thoughts, she says, "We have much work to do. You are not to leave the cottage today. But tomorrow, wear the lavender cotton."

## ·•ᴉ[ CHAPTER 18 ]ᴉ•·

OXFORD, MASSACHUSETTS

*Christmas Day*
*December 25, 1821*

C hristmas morning in eastern Massachusetts is stunning.
Pristine snowfall blankets the fields like cake frosting; ice
sheets slide down the French River. The morning Clara Barton
came into the world was no different. Except, perhaps, for the
scandal of her birth.

"Whatever was Sarah thinking?"

"Clearly there was no thought at all." The ladies of the village snickered behind their gloved hands as they descended
the church steps. Word had spread quickly that forty-year-old
Sarah Barton had delivered a daughter that morning. But the
women in town had been gossiping about it for months.

"I, for one, feel sorry for the poor dear. To be married to a
husband with such an appetite. No wonder Sarah spends so
much time cleaning her home. It's her only rest."

After an eruption of laughter, the ladies of Oxford hurried into the warmth of the nearest home to resume the more decorous discussion of the proper baby gift for a child who was so clearly an accident.

Honestly, few women in town were close to Sarah Barton. All those eccentricities! Her family was well off, but she had been seen rummaging through produce bins in search of *spoiling* fruits and vegetables. It was said she preferred to buy unfresh goods only to cut away the darkened bits. Good heavens. And there was that furious housekeeping. Often, she scrubbed the stairs in her home so vigorously her knuckles bled. Once, she dismantled—piece by piece—the iron stove her husband gave her and threw it in the pond on their property. Its function was subpar, she exclaimed, her cheeks ruddy with fury. Her old fireplace oven worked more efficiently. How could she run an immaculate household with an inferior cookstove?

"It's not as if baby Clara can wear her sister's infant clothes or play with her baby toys," one of the townswomen said. "Dorothea is *seventeen*."

At the mention of Clara's troubled eldest sister, the women fell silent. Dorothea Barton was well known in town. A wild child from the start, she had grown more unmanageable as the years passed. At the most inopportune times, she would chatter nonstop. Other days, her mood was as dark as a thundercloud. Rousing her from bed was not for the faint of heart. Rebellious and disobedient as she was, it was feared Dorothea would never entice a suitable husband. Who would take on such a handful? The best the family could do was lock her in her room in an attempt to alter her nature. With solitary reflection, they prayed she would remember that she was a *lady* and act accordingly: passive, compliant, dutiful, beholden to men.

No such blessing. When confined, Dorothea only went mad. So furiously did she pitch back and forth in her rocking chair her father was eventually forced to saw off its legs.

"Did you hear?" One bleak morning, whispers circulated around the village square like wasps the honeypot. "Dorothea Barton got out."

"Out?"

"Climbed through her bedroom window."

"Dear me, no."

"Her father found her in the backwoods at midnight. Muddy, incoherent. Her hair untended and full of brambles."

"Is she bound for the asylum?"

"In a manner of speaking, yes. Mr. Barton has now installed *bars* on her window. They are at their wits' end."

Such was the chaos into which Clara Barton was born. A bipolar sister, obsessive-compulsive mother, and, later, a suicidal brother who scandalized the family by succeeding in taking his own life. Clara, herself, would battle bouts of melancholy, occasionally suffering so severely she found it impossible to pull herself out of bed.

From childhood, Clara Barton learned to navigate the bedlam in her family by steering clear of her tempestuous mother, attempting to calm Dorothea's manic tirades, and doing her best to fit into a family of adults. All the while fighting a crippling shyness that often rendered her unable to speak.

As Lee Parker discovered that afternoon in the tawny sunlight of the Beverly Hills Library, Clara Barton spent much of her childhood feeling lost and lonely. As if her mere presence were an inconvenience. As though she were always in the *way*.

Until one late afternoon in 1833 when everything changed.

It was a typically striking day in New England. Maple and birch trees were ablaze in flaming orange. In preparation for winter, the Bartons were raising a new barn. As was customary, several men from the village were there to assist. It didn't matter that the Bartons were odd. When a fellow farmer needed help building a new barn, all able men were on hand to help. Such was the New England way.

The rafters were already up. The long wood slats of the sides had been nailed together on the ground. All that was left to do was raise the sides and affix them to the sturdy frame.

Suddenly eleven-year-old Clara heard shouting through the open window of her bedroom in the house.

"Summon the doctor!" Panic was clear in the baritone voice. Like spatter from a puddle, the family scattered. Mr. Barton raced to the village for the town physician, his wife ran to the cabinet where she kept rudimentary medical supplies. Dorothea pounded her fists against her locked bedroom door. Little Clara dashed outside to the barn. There, she saw a sight she would never forget: the twisted, bloody body of her twenty-five-year-old brother, David. He lay on the ground, writhing in pain.

"He fell from the rafters. One moment he was straddling the center beam, the next . . ." The man's voice trailed off in despair. Clara dove to her brother's side.

A throng of men huddled around the injured David Barton. Several tried to shield young Clara from the awful sight of her brother's broken body, but she refused to leave him until the doctor arrived. Not even when her mother scuttled through the crowd with clean bandages and wringing hands. Only when professional help appeared did Clara stand and melt into the crush of neighbors. Yet, she remained and watched. She saw the doctor calmly assess the damage, gently squeezing the bones in David's legs and arms. The doctor's relaxed breathing was a soothing tonic, soon quieting her brother's moans. Clara noticed the way the doctor firmly hushed everyone when he pressed the ear trumpet to her brother's chest for auscultation. She saw him take a fold of clean gauze from her mother's hand and press it to the bloody wound on David's forehead. Utterly composed. Completely in control. Calling for a stretcher, the physician directed the men to lift David onto the transport so gently the motion would not injure him further. Clara insisted on joining her parents on their way to the hospital. For the first time in her life, she felt unconcerned about herself and her shyness. Her brother's well-being was all that mattered.

That awful day altered the trajectory of Clara Barton's life. Her brother would survive, but his injuries would disable him for two years. During that time, he needed around-the-clock care. Little Clara volunteered. Her parents refused. But their young daughter was not to be dissuaded. With care and calm beyond her years, she proved that she was up to the challenge. At *eleven*, she changed soiled bandages, administered medicine, even applied and removed leeches when doctors suggested "bleeding" David to health. She demonstrated that she could care for her brother as well as any professional nurse. No longer would she be in the way. Clara Barton had found a purpose. At last, she felt *useful*.

# ·⊰I CHAPTER 19 I⊱·

SOUTH FORK FISHING AND HUNTING CLUB

*Summer 1888*

In any semblance of honesty, I cannot claim that I don't notice the moment James Tottinger enters the clubhouse. Even as my gaze never leaves the book I'm pretending to read. Dressed in my lavender cotton skirt and freshly pressed shirtwaist, with my hair in a flattering frazzle about my face, I've positioned myself on a red velvet settee in the clubhouse parlor. The color combination of red and purple is striking. Sunlight from the front window highlights the shine in my dark hair. I feel Mr. Tottinger's scrutiny upon me in the tingle of my forearms and the flush in my cheeks. My right hand reaches up to turn the page, my neck swivels slowly. Steadying the book's spine at an appropriate reading distance, I float my gaze from left to right at the speed of reading. In the background I hear chatter through the open windows from women who've gathered to visit on the porch.

" . . . oranges all the way from California. By *train*."

"What could be more delightful than fresh marmalade in winter?"

Far behind me, on the opposite end of the lakefront veranda, male voices are faintly audible. Not that I need to hear them clearly to know what they are talking about: money. It's all society men ever talk about when they are assembled with cigars and drink.

"Another careless Hunky burned his hand at the mill, costing me more than a hundred in underproduction."

The volume of Mr. Tottinger's presence raises the temperature in the room. I struggle to modulate the rise and fall of my chest. He struts closer to the corner where I sit, posed to perfection. The haylike aroma of his riding tweeds conjures the image of an accomplished equestrian. One who effortlessly leaps onto a steed and communicates his directives with a commanding squeeze of his thighs. Unlike Julian and Oscar, who are scared of a horse's teeth.

"Is it always so frightfully warm?" James Tottinger asks me.

The sound of his voice startles me for a moment, though my bearing betrays nothing save the pink tint on my cheeks and the slight sheen of nervous perspiration along the edge of my temples. Doubtful Mr. Tottinger will notice. He is a man accustomed to people noticing *him*.

"Pardon me?" I look up with a quizzical expression. My chest burns for want of air.

"The mountains in Europe are almost always cool."

"Ah. Well. You're certainly not in Europe now." Without further comment, I cast my eyes downward and return to the pages of my book. Rude, I know. But following Mother's strict instructions, I resolve not to engage Mr. Tottinger in conversation until we have been properly introduced. Let Francine Larkin march up to him with her arms outstretched. I will show the audacious man from England that I am no ordinary girl. Even as I couldn't help but instantly notice his splendid velvet-edged sack coat and the derby bowler atop those playful golden-brown curls. He now stands near enough for me to inhale his ambergris scent.

At that moment, I silently pray that Mr. Tottinger will pivot on the heels of his shiny riding boots and join the men on the veranda so that I might breathe fully. My lungs are screaming for oxygen. Instead, I hear the sounds of *his* calm respiration. He doesn't move an inch. With supreme effort, I quiet the quiver in my hand and deliberately turn the page.

Yesterday afternoon at the cottage, Mother sat me down to educate me on matters of the heart. Not that I ever requested such instruction.

"You must give Mr. Tottinger very little, so he will want very much," she began.

"I have no interest in giving that conceited man anything."

"My beautiful Elizabeth," she said, cupping my cheek in the same way she caresses my little brother. "One day you will understand men as I do. They are in constant competition with *each other*. Remember that reality always. Right now the handsome Mr. Tottinger is not only the desire of your friends, he's the envy of every young man at the club. And he's been enticed by *you*. My darling, if you are able to maintain his interest while he's here, every other man of means will want you, too."

Noting the serene smile on Mother's lips, I asked, "Is that how Father chose you?"

"It is indeed. Now, our goal is a lofty one but I believe you have positioned yourself brilliantly to achieve it."

"What goal is that, Mother?" I was feeling nettled. I'd had my fun with James Tottinger. Putting him in his place. Though, true, he was blessed with the most pleasing features and a worldly way about him that inspired confidence at first sight. Such magnetism! It emanated from his being and instantly captivated us all. Still, I had no desire to pursue a further acquaintance. He lived an ocean away, for goodness' sake. Wouldn't my future be better served by beguiling a suitor closer to home?

"It's all about *choice*," Mother had stated. "Mr. Tottinger must definitively choose you so every other man of his standing will want you as well. There is no better way to secure your place in society."

I groaned at the ridiculousness of it all. Mother's disapproving look silenced me. "You are too old to be naive," she said.

Sadly, that was true as well.

"Before young Mr. Tottinger returns to England in two weeks, he must declare his desire to return for your debutante ball."

"Mother!" I was aghast. My debut was still a year away. I had only begun the barest musings about whose hand I wanted to feel on my back as it steered me around the dance floor on the biggest night of my life. Since, of course, I already knew all the boys at the club—and had since birth—I was hoping for a newcomer. Every girl does. But an arrogant European? Hardly. I was praying for a New York financier. One whose head was full of numbers instead of the endless squabbles of millworkers or the secret medical woes of their bosses. How lovely to be whisked away from Pittsburgh's blackened smokestacks for a life filled with daily strolls through the walkways of Central Park.

"We've been given an opportunity, Elizabeth, and we mustn't squander it. Please don't test my patience with your resistance."

"But, I simpl—"

"Hush, now." Mother held up her hand. "Tomorrow you must follow my guidance without question."

"But—"

"*Without* question."

Pouting was useless. On these matters, Mother was resolute. A locomotive steaming its way to the next station. There was no steering her off course. Reluctantly, I agreed.

So, here I sit, staring blindly at the paragraphs in my book, moving my eyes in the speed of reading, fearful that I shall soon expire for lack of sufficient air. Unbelievably, Mr. Tottinger refuses to move away. I sense his amusement. I believe I hear him chuckle. Mother never mentioned how to handle this. My chest is on fire. It takes all my strength to maintain the modulated up-and-down motion of natural respiration. If left to their own devices, my lungs would be pumping air like a fireplace bellows.

Just as I am plotting my escape—a graceful rise to my feet, polite nod to Mr. Tottinger, and elegant exit out the rear clubhouse door to scurry behind the nearest tree and gasp for air behind it—I hear Father's voice.

"There you are, my dear."

I raise my head. Father is looming over me with the elder Mr. Tottinger at his side. His stout and sour-faced wife and their bashful daughter stand in his shadow. As Mother arranged, no doubt. James Tottinger takes a small step back to make room for his family. I note the barest wisp of a grin on his nicely plump lips.

"May I present my daughter, Elizabeth," Father says, extending his hand to assist me to my feet. Setting my book aside, I use the exertion of standing to inhale and exhale as deeply as possible within my corset. As I feared, it isn't nearly enough oxygen to extinguish the fire in my lungs.

"Elizabeth," Father continues, "I'd like you to meet the Tottinger family from Great Britain. Mr. and Mrs. Tottinger, their daughter, Ivy, and their son, Mr. Jam—"

"We met yesterday." James interrupts Father to move forward and extract my palm from Father's grip. I'm shocked.

Taken aback by his insolence, I let my hand go as limp as a stocking left hanging over a chairback. Surely he can't have the ill manners to consider my fashionable sashay through the clubhouse an *introduction*. A gentleman would never even mention it. I simply stare as James Tottinger removes his hat, bows, and presses his lips upon my hand. I use the brief moment to inhale and exhale deeply. Once he has lifted his head, I boldly meet his piercing gaze.

"Forgive me, Mr. Tottinger," I calmly state. "I don't recall being introduced to you before this moment. But it is a pleasure to meet your family."

Turning ever so slightly away from him, I pluck my hand from his grip and transfer it to the elder Tottinger and his wife, who appears unable to erase the prunish look on her face. It feels as though my chest will soon ignite.

*Observe how a lady displays discomfort.* Hearing Mother's voice in my head, I extend each vertebra in my spine. I ignore the torment my too-shallow breathing continues to cause me. With deliberate dignity, I bow my head to the Tottinger clan.

"I do hope you enjoy your stay in our little mountain retreat," I say, inhaling. "Ivy, are you fond of croquet?"

The little mouse in the fussy dress blushes and mutters something I can't comprehend. Her mother's husky voice reprimands her. "Lift your chin and enunciate, dear. Miss Haberlin asked you a question."

"I don't know how to play," Ivy stammers. Her eyes dart to the door, clearly desiring escape. Seizing the opportunity to escape myself, I gently reach for her hand and give it a soft squeeze. "I shall take it upon myself to teach you personally."

Ivy beams. I suck in a hearty breath in the guise of my happiness at our upcoming recreation.

Of course, it was Mother's suggestion that I befriend the shy sister. With her prissy ringlets and ankle-baring skirt, it's clear that Mrs. Tottinger desires to retain Ivy's childhood long past its natural demise. Poor little possum. She must be fourteen or fifteen. On the very cusp of womanhood. My heart *is* warmed by her awkwardness. I've always wanted a younger sister to groom in the ways of the world. First, I shall start with her unattractive hair.

"Was it not *you* in the bushes yesterday, Miss Haberlin?" James persists. I want to grind my heel into the top of his boot.

Father looks alarmed. "The bushes?"

"I'm quite sure we met then." James Tottinger is obviously enjoying himself. "Although I do concede that it's unlikely you would consider crouching in the mud a formal introduction."

"Mud?" Father turns his wide eyes to me as I release Ivy's hand and set my gaze squarely upon her brother.

"Once again, forgive me, sir. Was that *you* playing on the sand while I gathered specimens for my botany studies? I was far too absorbed in my educational endeavors to properly notice men at play."

James Tottinger flings back his head and laughs with abandon. Quite unrequested, he gives us a clear view of his perfectly even molars. Yesterday, as I crouched in the birch thicket, I was too far away to note the alluring creases in his cheeks. Nothing as juvenile as dimples, but certainly far from a wrinkle. The best way to describe the animation in his expression is to say that his smile extends well beyond the limit of his lips to include the whole of his face and head. Even his hair seems amused. His green-blue eyes—not unlike Mother's—join in the festivities of his enjoyment. They are the color of Lake Conemaugh on the coolest day of summer. James Tottinger's eyes appear lit from within. At the moment, I can barely breathe at all.

"Might we start our croquet lessons today, Miss Haberlin?" Stunning us all, Ivy speaks.

I smile broadly. "Only if you call me Elizabeth." Retaking her hand, I say to the group, "If you will be so kind as to excuse us, Ivy and I have a rendezvous at the sports closet."

Grinning like a child, Ivy allows me to lead her out of the clubhouse parlor. On our way out, I note Mrs. Tottinger's initial protest, but her husband silences her with a grip on her arm. Out we go, all smiles. I feel the heat of Ivy's brother's approving eyes on me. I purposefully slow my gait and maintain a neck so elongated I sense the proximity of the ceiling. Never before have I been so impressed by Mother's wisdom. The power surging through my veins supplants the pain in my depleted lungs.

As soon as we are safely behind the closed clubhouse door, I double over and violently suck air into my chest. "Forgive me," I rasp. "My corset was fastened too tightly this morning."

"It's James," Ivy says, simply.

"Who?" My eyes avert.

"My brother always causes women to lose their air."

Allowing myself a full minute to regain the cadence of normal breathing, I rise up and smooth my skirt. I smile softly and place one hand on the frilly fabric covering Ivy's shoulder. "Innocent flower, your brother has no such effect on me."

"You find him unbecoming?"

Perhaps Miss Ivy is less timid than one assumes.

"Certainly his features are well proportioned. And his carriage is the personification of confidence. And his eyes sparkle like moss agate and—" I stop, abruptly aware of yet another quickening in my breath. I take moment to inhale and exhale fully. "Dearest girl, I prefer a man who would rather gaze at *me* than his own reflection."

Erupting in giggles, Ivy scoops up my hand and says, "I believe I shall like you enormously!"

## ⋅∘⟨ CHAPTER 20 ⟩∘⋅

WASHINGTON, D.C.

*March 4, 1861*

Little Clara Barton had come a long way. In spite of her insecurities—or, more likely, *because* of them—she barreled into adulthood determined to matter. Now forty, she lived in Washington, D.C., and worked at the U.S. Patent Office.

"Doesn't that spinster have a father?" Her coworkers often whispered behind her back. All male, they resented her presence. Not only had she taken a fine job away from a man, she was an unmarried woman interloping in a married man's domain. How could they be themselves around her? Since she'd obviously been unable to entice a husband, wasn't it her *father's* responsibility to put a roof over her head? Maintain his daughter's respectability by putting her to work around the *house*? Or, at the very least, if Miss Barton insisted on employment outside her father's home, why didn't she do something feminine, like teach school?

Clara *had* taught school and hadn't liked it. Why did every man assume every woman wanted to spend her days with children?

That day, March 4, 1861, Clara stood shoulder to shoulder with nearly everyone in Washington, D.C. Gray clouds threatened rain. Winter's frost had barely receded. Yet Clara was happy to join the crowds in the cool air outside. As she waited along Pennsylvania Avenue, in front of the Smithsonian, her heart beat as fast as a thoroughbred's. The day she had prayed for had finally arrived.

"The carriage has left the Willard," someone shouted.

Earlier that morning, Mr. Lincoln's heart had pounded, too. He could scarcely intake proper breath. Delivering his inaugural address was the nerve-jangling first step in the long and pitted road he had ahead of him. The country was in deep trouble. North and South were entrenched in their disparate positions. America had been built on the backs of slaves; now slavery might well be her undoing. South Carolina had already declared its secession from the Union. A fate he simply could not allow.

When he folded himself into the carriage waiting at the Willard Hotel, settling in alongside outgoing President Buchanan, he asked, "Any final words of advice, James?"

James Buchanan grunted. "Good luck."

The carriage clip-clopped down the cobblestoned thoroughfare to the Capitol. Clara Barton held her position in front of the crowd. Upon seeing the presidential convoy, she waved enthusiastically. Always opposed to the barbarism of slavery, she felt a surge of hope. The wise and thoughtful Mr. Lincoln would calm the raging passions in her country and set things right.

Order out of chaos. That's what Clara Barton lived for. And meaningful work was the fuel that fed her self-worth. Without a useful occupation, she felt the same way she had as a child: in the way.

On the day of Abraham Lincoln's inauguration, Clara was filled with the effervescence of optimism. She had written countless letters of praise to any congressman or senator who decried the abomination of slavery. Thank goodness Mr. Lincoln had been elected. At last, humanity could prevail.

The crowd amassed behind the presidential carriage. Clara again wriggled her way to the front so that she might be in a fine position to hear Mr. Lincoln address the country once he arrived at the Capitol.

She was. Right up front, beaming.

"Fellow citizens of the United States," Mr. Lincoln began, standing tall and gangly at a podium on the Capitol steps. He dove directly into the anxiety of the day. "I have no purpose, directly or indirectly, to interfere with the institution of slavery in the states where it exists."

Applause broke out. Clara felt her heart pump blood into her ears. The new president had clearly chosen his words carefully. For the next several minutes he spoke at length about maintaining states' rights and upholding the Constitution. He acknowledged the differing points of view between southerners and northerners. In the end, however, he vowed to maintain the Union, at all cost.

"We are not enemies, but friends. We must not be enemies.

Though passion may have strained, it must not break our bonds of affection. The mystic chords of memory, stretching from every battlefield and patriot grave to every living heart and hearthstone all over this broad land, will yet swell the chorus of the Union, when again touched, as surely they will be, by the better angels of our nature."

As Abraham Lincoln stepped away from the podium, Clara—and hundreds of other Americans who crowded around her—had tears in her eyes. Theirs was an imperfect union, though a *union* it would remain.

Clara Barton returned home that day with a full heart.

Thirty-nine days later, in the dark hours before dawn, a single mortar shot exploded over South Carolina's Fort Sumter. There, a garrison of Union soldiers was awakened by terror. Already, they had been riddled with anxiety. Food and supplies were low. If they were not replenished soon, the men would starve to death. And now Confederate boats filled the Charleston Harbor. With seacoast mortars pointed at the fort and plentiful ammunition.

There was no way out. The worst had happened.

Civil war had begun.

When Clara Barton heard the news, she was devastated. How could this occur in the *United* States?

For the next four years, the country would fight its most vile war: Us against Us. Americans killing Americans. Ugly, face-to-face combat. Terrified young men bayoneting, stabbing, clubbing, shooting other terrified young men who would otherwise be their friends. Soldiers—on both sides—perished in fields of mud, their open wounds untended, their hands unheld.

Field hospitals were a shambles. The stench from rotting piles of severed limbs made breathing unbearable. Men died from ghastly infections simply because no one was there to clean a wound.

As soon as word spread about the dire conditions on the battlefield, Clara felt the same way she had many years earlier when her brother suffered his fall: compelled to help. To be *useful*. So, at forty, she did the unthinkable. Single and childless, she used her own money to arrange for a horse-drawn cart full of supplies—clean bandages, books, favorite treats—to ferry her through the muck and blood to the moaning, screaming, bleeding, dying soldiers on the front lines.

At first, she tried to get permission. When consent was not forthcoming, she went anyway. The field commanders were furious. Who the hell was this woman? An unmarried do-gooder wandering among burly, sweaty, bloody men? Barely five feet tall. Who did she think she was? At best, she'd pass out at the first sight of an armless soldier; at worst, she'd be hit by a bullet. How could they explain that to the secretary of state?

Clara Barton ignored them all. As if to compensate for the chronic shyness that tormented her all her life, she marched onto the battlefield without a thought for her own safety. She bullied her way into the war, ignoring the generals who tried to stop her.

In a rickety open carriage pulled by a plodding horse, she rode straight into harm's way. As every other civilian fled or hid, Clara Barton moved forward. Into the bloody battle. The air was choked with musket smoke and the wretched smell of death. Between mortar blasts, commanders shrieked orders. "Forward to that ridge!"

Bullets whirred past. Cannons bellowed. Fear was as thick as artillery residue. The unseeing eyes of the dead reflected yellow sunlight and silver moonlight. Their arched backs and open mouths resembled those of suffocated fish. Lifeless gazes stared up from the battlefield like a thousand strewn marbles. Clara was horrified. Yet, she continued on.

Upon hearing a soldier's moan, Clara stopped the horse. Amid the whistle of rifle shot, she climbed down from her cart and wove among the corpses to the sound of despair.

"Hello, sir," she said, finding him, affixing a gentle expression to mask the gruesome sight of his injuries. "I'm Clara. Where are you from?"

Union or Confederate, it didn't matter. The "Angel of the Battlefield" believed every soldier deserved respect and care.

Throughout the war, Clara Barton walked among corpses that lay crumpled in ditches or flat in rows where they'd stood. She passed the scattered remains of human life: arms, torsos, severed heads. On the front lines and back, Clara waded onto blood-soaked battlefields to wrap clean bandages around wounds as purple-red as horsemeat. She held the trembling hands of dying men, soothed the panic in their eyes. She made sure they didn't die alone in the mud.

Death's acrid smell was barely endurable. Clara was petrified. Yet, she maintained a serene expression. As she'd seen the doctor do those many years ago when he tended her broken brother, she projected a calm demeanor so that others would trust her competence. She tucked her fears inside so that she might soothe the frightened men around her.

Clara witnessed grisly sights she would never forget. Often, the hem of her skirt was so stained with blood she struggled to scrub it clean each night. In the field hospitals, she read aloud to soldiers too sick or wounded to do anything but keen. Her ears were filled with the terrifying sounds of men screaming in agony. The sickening smell of rotting flesh never left her nostrils. But, she didn't blink. Instead, she proved that a woman could be as strong as a man. Even stronger. One small woman could make a big difference. She could *matter*.

# ·∘❧ CHAPTER 21 ❧∘·

### SOUTHERN CALIFORNIA

*Present*

Lee Parker was impressed. In the afternoon glow of the Beverly Hills Library, she sat back in her chair. As the dipping sun bounced orange light off the stones in her bracelet, she reflected upon the woman she'd been researching all day—a woman born at a time when doctors believed that being scholarly damaged a woman's *uterus*. Lee marveled at Clara Barton's guts. She wasn't born to greatness; she created it. Her heartbreaking experiences in the Civil War inspired her to continue helping soldiers and others displaced by disaster by founding a humanitarian organization that would continue to flourish more than a hundred and forty years later. One horrible morning in September, the American Red Cross would be on the front lines of a war Clara Barton couldn't even fathom: passenger planes intentionally flown into the World Trade Center and the Pentagon, still another—on its way to Washington, D.C.—crashed into a field near Shanksville, Pennsylvania.

*If Clara were alive today,* Lee thought, *reality would kill her.* People murdered one another in the name of God. Bad police officers shot unarmed citizens in the back or the face. Young people who felt like they didn't matter—people like Clara herself—brought assault weapons into schools and opened fire. *If Clara were alive today, she'd never get out of bed.*

For a moment, Lee sat still in the quiet of the library. She felt frustrated. Though it had been interesting learning about a trailblazer like Clara Barton, Lee was no closer to identifying her great-great-great-grandmother than she had been when she'd first arrived. The woman in the photo from her adoption file could be *anyone.* A battlefield nurse, the wife of a soldier searching for her slain husband, a passerby who got caught in a snapshot of history.

Plus, Lee was hungry. Her thermos was empty. Soon there would be traffic back over the canyon. The L.A. challenge: getting on the road before everyone else does.

Once more, Lee grabbed the mouse and jiggled it to revive the computer screen. She again typed "Clara Barton" into the search engine, clicked on the "images" link. A screenful of small, square, black-and-white portrait photos appeared. A pageful of passport shots. Clara Barton's face in all its ages—youthful plump cheeks, eyes lidded by middle-aged wisdom, elderly sagging on both sides of her chin. Leaning close to the screen, Lee examined each photo. One by one. They all had the same serene smile. Gently upturned lips, no display of teeth. The outward expression of calm and competence.

Clara's shiny crinoline dresses were all long-sleeved. Dark. Their white collars, buttoned to the neck, were adorned with round brooches.

"Talk to me," Lee whispered to the many faces on-screen. "Where did you meet my relative?"

Lee's gaze moved from left to right across the screen. *Tick, tick, tick.* Like a loud clock in her head. She stared at each photo before moving on to the next. And the next, and the nex—

"Hey, wait a minute."

Beside her, another woman with carp lips looked up from her laptop and said, "Shhh."

"Sorry," Lee mouthed.

In silence, Lee examined each photograph. One by one. Clearly, Clara Barton had aged from a young woman to an elderly one, yet two things remained the same in each photo: her tranquil smile and her *hairstyle*. Incredibly, Clara never updated her hairstyle from youth to old age. It was always parted down the middle in a hatchet-straight line, with each side rolled backward into a tight, tidy bun at the nape of her neck.

Hairstyles *must* have changed. Clara Barton lived into her nineties. When she was born, women spent their entire lives inside the home; by the time of her death, Harriet Quimby had flown herself over the English Channel. Corseted waists were set free, bustles disappeared, hairstyles softened. As Lee remembered it, the woman in the photo next to Clara Barton had a less buttoned-up look than Clara did. Her hair was somewhat haphazard: loosely upswept in a pouf, with wispy *bangs*. A softer appearance. Was it possible that Lee's great-great-great-grandmother was in style and Clara was not?

Feeling a surge of energy, Lee Googled "Victorian hair-styles" and watched an array of fussy hairdos fill the screen. Corkscrew tendrils, back braids, billowy topknots, and . . . *bangs*. Ringlet bangs, finger waves, frazzles. There was noth-ing simple or static about any of the women's looks. *Sheesh,* she thought, *the amount of time those women put into their hair. No wonder the rich needed maids.*

She examined each photo until she spotted one that most resembled the hairstyle her great-great-great-grandmother had sported. Long hair knotted loosely on top of her head, soft wisps about her face. Bangs frizzed across her forehead. Not overly coiffed. A hairstyle definitely *un*like Clara Barton's rigid center part and bun. When Lee clicked on it, she was linked to a Pinterest page with several hairstyle drawings from that same era. As it turned out, they were all from the *end* of the Victo-rian era. Closer to the beginning of the Edwardian years when styles loosened up.

One photograph in particular caught Lee's eye. It was a pic-ture of a woman in a white shirtwaist, a ruffle of lace down the front. Her skirt was dark and unbustled. Falling unfet-tered to the floor. Her waist was tiny, secured by a plain black band. One hand held a tiny beaded handbag, the other rested gently atop the back of a carved wood chair. Rings adorned neither hand, yet it was clear she was a woman above the work-ing class. A teacher, perhaps? The way she posed her delicate fingers spoke of breeding. But what struck Lee most was her *hair.* Exactly the same style as the woman's in the adoption file photo, it was loosely bound on top of her head. Dancing across her forehead were bangs that were frazzled just so.

Lee checked the year: 1889.

She gave it a try. Back up to the search engine, she typed: "Clara Barton 1889." The screen immediately filled with links about a place she had never heard of before.

Johnstown, Pennsylvania.

# ·⊰[ CHAPTER 22 ]⊱·

## SOUTH FORK FISHING AND HUNTING CLUB

*Summer 1888*

Almost instantly, croquet bores us both. On her turns as striker, Ivy grips the mallet too tightly, foolishly uses the side face despite patient instructions not to, crookedly aims, and carelessly takes her shots. The first falls far short of the hoop, the second veers off in a spinning wiggle. The third—

walloped in frustration—flies past two wickets straight into the underbrush.

"Is there more to it?" she asks me.

I camouflage my peevishness with a smile. Did she not ask me to teach her the game? "It's more fun once you're able to sharpen your aim," I say. For a brief moment I am tempted to display my expertise by knocking my yellow ball through all six wickets so that I might hear the satisfying *thunk* of a win. But I contain myself. Ivy would surely report back to her brother that I am as conceited as he.

"Know what I'd *really* like to do?" Ivy drops the mallet in the dirt.

Silently, I pray that she does not wish to attempt badminton. "The clubhouse has draughts and dominoes," I say.

"Certainly not," she replies. "Now that I am free, I plan to stay outside. Mother treats me like a toddler. She's afraid I'll mature and marry and leave her. Which, of course, I desperately want to do. But am I not entitled?"

"Surely she wants you to have a life of your own one day."

"No." Ivy's ringlets bounce childishly when she shakes her head. "Raising me is Mother's only purpose. Once I am on my own, she will cease to be useful. She has told me so herself."

My heart softens as I picture my own mother. Without Henry to fret over, how would she fill her days? I, too, have bristled under the chafe of a mother's grip on my spirit. The longing to be set *loose*. Feeling more kindly toward this girl who is so clearly a different person away from her suffocating mother, I say, "Okay, then. Today we are both free. How shall we make the most of it?"

Ivy's green eyes go round. They are lit by a fire within her. Like her brother's. Both contain the soul of a rapscallion. "Please, Miss Haberlin," she says with a pixie's grin, "will you take me *sailing*? Mother won't allow me on the water. She frets over every possible moment of my fun."

I glance at the discarded croquet mallet. As smart as a whippet, Ivy adds, "*Real* fun."

Now I laugh. I remember my delight when Mother allowed me to race in last summer's clubhouse regatta. Who am I to squash the same?

"Come," I say, reaching up to cup Ivy's chin the way Mother does mine from time to time. "We'll row across the lake in our private skiff. No one needs to know about our *real* fun except you and me."

Clapping her hands like a toddler, Ivy grins with her whole face.

"But you must promise me one thing," I say.

"Anything."

"You will call me *Elizabeth* from this moment on."

"Yes, Elizabeth. Most certainly, yes!"

"Good. Now, follow me. We have one stop to make first."

Wending along the shaded path behind the boardwalk, Ivy and I both feel the cool kiss of low-hanging trees. The dirt is soft beneath our feet and the silence of the woods is glorious. It speaks of the freedom to be ourselves. To *breathe*. To shake off the shackles of propriety. Everyone is at the clubhouse. No doubt preening around Ivy's family like squawking mallards diving for bread crusts thrown on the lake. For the moment, I am utterly content to leave all that nonsense behind. My spirit is renewed by glimpses of twinkling sunlight and the melodic warble of water thrush.

"Our cottage is up ahead," I say.

"Oh, joy!" Ivy replies. "May I see it?"

"Of course. I want to change my skirt."

"Not the cottage. The *dress*."

I smile. She reminds me of a younger me. As I did earlier at the clubhouse, I take her hand and squeeze it. A bit shyly, Ivy asks, "What possessed you to do it?"

"Do what?" Not that I don't know.

"Walk through the clubhouse in that gown?"

Between the thick groupings of hemlock trees, with their glossy spinach-green needles and ammonia-like scent, I stop and turn toward the impressionable young girl. "Sometimes a woman must stir the pot." Then I turn away and walk on. Over my shoulder, I add, "If my maid is there to help, I'll let you try it on."

Never before have I seen a happier girl.

"NETTIE!" IVY AND I are pink-cheeked by the time we reach the cottage at the far end of the access road. I call out to the back of the house as we scurry up the stairs to my room.

"Coming, miss!"

Inside my room, Ivy rushes over to the window seat to marvel at the lake view. Only from this height can one see the full breadth of Lake Conemaugh. From up here, its beauty and serenity can't help but melt other cares away. Nettie thumps up the stairway. In my open doorway, she dries her wet hands on her apron and says, "I didn't expect to see you before it was time to dress for supper."

"Change of plans. Could you please help me out of these clothes and into something suitable for a row across the lake?"

"Certainly, miss."

"And my young friend here would like to try on my Charles Worth."

Nettie stops. "The *gown?*"

"Whatever else?" I stand before the vanity mirror and smooth the thick waves in my braided bun. "Plus we must do something about her ringlets. Can you do a quick French twist?"

Ivy squeals and leaps up. "Might you frazzle my bangs, too, Nettie?"

Upon hearing Ivy's British accent, Nettie darts a knowing look at my reflection in the mirror. Perhaps I had mentioned that James Tottinger had a sister; perhaps Nettie had heard Mother speak of it from the other side of my closed bedroom door. "What hairstyles do proper ladies wear in England, then?" she asks.

Frowning, Ivy says, "We are hopelessly behind you Americans. Absolutely *everything* in London is old, old, old. But I shall watch carefully, Nettie, so that I can teach my maid something new."

"Let's get to it, then." With expertise born from years of dressing and undressing me, Nettie quickly has me out of my lavender cotton and into a suitable white linen ensemble that will look splendid against the beryl backdrop of Lake Conemaugh. While I search for a matching sunbonnet, she bustles over to my wardrobe to gently remove my Charles Frederick Worth original from its linen covering. Upon first glimpse, Ivy gasps. "I only dreamed of feeling the softness of this satin!"

"Yes," I say, with a hint of superiority, "Mr. Worth dresses royalty."

With Nettie's help, young Ivy steps out of her frilly girl's dress and into the luxury I felt against my skin a mere day ago. When Nettie turns Ivy toward the pier glass, she squeals with delight at the sight of herself. Poor girl, she has yet to develop breasts worthy of such a gown. Still, in watching her swing left and right in front of the mirror, I feel a flush of pride at how lovely I must have looked with my powdered bosom rising up from that spiderweb of lace. What a thrill to feel everyone's attention on me alone!

"I doubt I'll ever be as beautiful as you, Elizabeth." Ivy sighs.

I hug her in a sisterly way. "You'll be your own kind of beauty. Which is the only kind of beauty to be."

In her grateful smile I feel a twinge of regret that Mother and Father never provided me with a sister to shape and school. I'm quite sure I would have been spectacular.

"Nettie?" I say, quietly, as Ivy is still riveted by her reflection. "Can I speak to you for a moment?"

"Yes, miss."

We excuse ourselves and leave the room. As soon as we are beyond Ivy's hearing, I say, "When it's time to pack my things at the end of the summer, I want you to leave my Charles Worth gown here, at the cottage."

"Here? Whatever for? Won't you be wearing it to the ball?"

"That's just it," I whisper. "Now that everyone has seen it, and Miss Tottinger has *worn* it, I can't possibly appear in it again. Father will squawk at the cost of a new gown, but what can I do? My Charles Worth was left at the cottage—during damp winter—it will be too ruined to properly present."

Nettie presses her lips together.

"Don't worry," I say. "I'll make sure to tell Father that you left it here by accident. You won't be blamed."

Swirling around, I sweep back into my bedroom and light-heartedly tell Ivy Tottinger, "Time to give me back my gown and let Nettie fix your hair. Our adventure awaits."

# CHAPTER 23

NORTH BEVERLY PARK

*Present*

M om!" When Lee got home at dinnertime, with a Baja
Fresh burrito for her mom and three soft corn tacos for
her, she could barely contain herself. She'd found it. The field
of rubble where her maternal ancestor had stood with Clara
Barton. Disaster had struck a small town at the foot of the Allegheny Mountains. Clara's Red Cross had swooped in to help.
Lee's great-great-great-grandmother had been there, too. At
least, she was fairly certain of it. Though Lee hadn't found the
exact adoption file photo online, she'd seen many others like it.
Same time, same place, same rubble, same hairstyle.

"You won't believe all the interesting things I found out," she
chirped while unpacking the takeout bags. The steamy aroma
of cilantro and lime infused the air. "We're talking holy days
up the *wazoo*."

Of course, Lee had decided not to tell her mom about her

birth-mother search. Valerie didn't deserve another emotional blow. So Lee came home prepared. At the library, after she'd unearthed information about the disaster in Johnstown, she Googled something else: what it meant to be Jewish.

"Talk to me," Valerie said. Still dressed in her maid's uniform, she poured herself a glass of wine and shimmied onto a stool in front of the kitchenette counter.

"Tisha B'Av is coming up and I don't have the faintest idea how to pronounce it."

IT HAD BEEN enlightening, to say the least. Lee's brief research into Judaistic divinity had highlighted how lax her parents' religious cherry picking had been. She faintly remembered attending a church of some kind (the vibration of the organ music in her chest was thrilling), but her mother told her they stopped going to services when the family decided to "replace organized religion with spirituality."

"Can you just *do* that?" young Lee had asked. "I mean, is God *okay* with that?"

Valerie had replied, "God is everywhere, honey. It says so in the Bible." Then she tucked an errant clump of hair behind her daughter's ear and asked if she wanted pancakes.

At the time, Lee had loved sleeping in on Sundays and eating pancakes in the shape of Mickey Mouse and hanging out with Shelby, whose parents were heathens, too. Now, with her life in upheaval, the thought of a loving father figure keeping his eyes on her eternal soul was a comfort. Living was hard when you had to do it by yourself. Even with a mom as caring as Valerie. She had her own issues.

Lee was excited to try Judaism on for size. Not that it would be easy.

First, there were all those unpronounceable holidays. Tu B'Shevat, Yom Ha-Atzma'ut, Shavuot. Even Hanukkah had thirteen different spellings. And, no matter what Hallmark would have you believe, Hanukkah was *not* a Jewish Christmas. As far as Lee could tell, that whole gifting thing was merely a way to make Jewish kids not feel left out at the end of December.

Second, she was shocked to discover that the religious service was on *Friday* night. Which felt plain wrong. Friday night was movie night. No way could she stream movies with her mom on Sunday mornings. The sun blared through their wall of windows, for one thing.

Lee decided to do more research to see if there was wiggle room on that rule. Like, the way midnight mass on Christmas Eve exempted you from church on Christmas morning. Perhaps she could swing by the synagogue after her late shift on Thursday?

For now, Lee was busy wrapping her head around the weird food rituals. Vegetables dipped in salt water, hidden matzo, bitter herbs, a roasted egg. How, exactly, does one *roast* an egg? Particularly tricky since she only had a microwave. During a holiday called Sukkot, Lee was supposed to eat all her meals outside, beneath a thatched roof. Since Mrs. Adell would go berserk if Lee constructed a little hut by the pool, could she sneak a sandwich into the outside shower while wearing a straw hat?

Lee had loads of questions.

At some point she would have to schedule an appointment with a rabbi, though she feared he would insist she have a Bat Mitzvah and she read that they cost as much as a wedding.

"Any new info about your genes?" Valerie asked, lifting the wineglass to her lips.

"Nothing we need to worry about."

"That's a relief." Valerie took a bite of her burrito, chewed, swallowed. Then she pasted a smile on her face and asked, "What about that woman in the photo? Did you search any archives in the library? Find a copy of the photo buried in the depths of the Internet?"

Lee hopped off the stool and leaned over to circle both arms around her mother. Softly, she said, "You are the only mother I'll ever need. Who cares about a woman in a photo who is long dead and gone?"

Yom Kippur—the Jewish day of atonement—was a few weeks away. She'd confess her white lie then.

# ·◦·❉|CHAPTER 24|❉·◦·

## SOUTH FORK FISHING AND HUNTING CLUB

*Summer 1888*

It is nearly noon by the time we are dressed and coiffed and prancing to the end of our dock where Father has tethered the family's skiff. Off-season, he stores it in the boathouse with the others. But now it's bobbing gently on the surface of our stunning lake. The clear blue water is rippled with fish swimming below its surface. More than enough for the clubhouse men *and* the dining room chefs to catch and fry.

Feeling mature with her perfectly frazzled bangs and stylish French twist, Ivy has immaturely refused to cover Nettie's handiwork with a sunbonnet. In spite of my best efforts to warn her against the dangers of direct sunlight, she has refused to cover up. What can I do? In our few hours together, I have noticed that Ivy Tottinger has a fully formed will of her own. Perhaps it's a family trait? One born of too much privilege?

Gathering my skirt with one hand and gripping the dock with the other, I lower myself into the small boat first, admittedly not my most graceful effort. In an alarming fashion, the skiff rocks frighteningly from side to side, nearly spilling me into the drink. But I sit in the center of the plank seat and quickly regain my equilibrium and a modicum of dignity.

"Hand me the picnic basket, will you?" I say to Ivy, smoothing my hair. Nettie hastily packed food for our journey. In the cottage, when she placed the basket in my hands, she whispered, "Shall I fetch one of the boys at the clubhouse to accompany you?"

"Whatever for?" I'd asked, indignant. I'd watched Father and several male club friends propel me around the lake many times. How hard could it be to row a boat?

"The basket, Ivy. Please."

Suddenly fearful, Ivy Tottinger stands on the dock like a pine tree. In spite of her grown-up hairstyle, she is every bit a child. Stubbornly, she refuses to move. It's as if she just now realizes that boating requires being on unstable *water*. Lake Conemaugh is quite deep, indeed. I'm sure my clumsy entrance into the skiff did nothing to inspire her confidence. Still, I'm not about to clamber out now that I've regained my bearing. I look up at the girl. Having once been the same willful adolescent who now stands like a post on the pier, I know it's best to say nothing and wait her out. Affixing a pleasant smile on my face, I do just that. I wait. Thank goodness it doesn't take Ivy long to realize I'm not getting out. She must get in.

Gingerly bending over the edge of the dock, Ivy hands me the picnic basket. After setting it on the floor of the skiff, I plow onward. "Good," I state. "Now untie the mooring line and toss it to me." My voice mimics an authority I don't remotely feel. Again, Ivy imitates a tree.

"That rope *there*, Ivy. See it? Looped over the piling. Could you please untie it and hand it to me?"

With the utter incompetence of a pampered girl who has never even laced a boot—not that I have properly, of course, though I'm quite sure I could—she creeps over to the piling and fumbles with the line.

"Loosen the knot. Yes. A bit *looser*. Good. Now pull the free end out through the knot. Yes, that's the free end. Good girl."

My fingertips are white with the effort of steadying the swaying skiff against the weathered wood of our pier. The lake looked so still before I got in the boat! Why does the gentlest lap of water cause such undulation? It's nearly impossible to neatly coil the freed line at the bottom of the boat with one hand. Yet I do. Rapidly losing my patience, I say, "Now step in and sit."

Only then do I realize I should have untied the *boat* side of the line and tossed the rope within reach on the pier. Oh, dear. How will we secure ourselves upon our return?

I decide to worry about that later. At the moment, Ivy's timid side has resurfaced and she shrinks into her fussy dress. I feel heat rise to my cheeks. Was it not Ivy herself who suggested our outing? With a deep inhalation, I calm myself.

"I'll hold the boat steady while you step in." I enunciate the last two words distinctly. *Step. In.*

At last, clutching the piling with her right hand, Ivy gingerly sets her left foot on the plank seat in the boat and, stunningly, leaves her other foot on our dock. Instantly, the skiff darts away. I feel the rough decking pop from my grip. Panic flares on Ivy's face as her legs float apart. It's only by divine miracle that I'm able to grab her forearm and snatch her into the boat before she tumbles into the water.

"Did I need to instruct you to step *both* feet in?" In the heat of the moment, impatience flares.

"I . . . I . . ." Tears begin to rise up.

"No matter. We are under way now." Inhaling deeply again, I gather my wits enough to reassure her. "Off we go," I say cheerfully. In wobbly style, we set off. As I have seen Father— and other men—do, I clutch the grip end of the oars and dip both paddles into the lake. Then I pull them through the water. "Nothing to it," I say, wincing slightly.

While it's true I underestimated the difficulty of rowing the vast girth of the lake, we soon settle into a gentle rhythm. The steady glide of the skiff soothes us both. From the clubhouse in the distance, faint sounds of music float on the air. Colonel Unger hired a band to entertain our overseas guests. Their horns send low notes on the breeze. The only other sound is the lapping of my oars as they loop in a lazy circle. From this vantage point—water level—Lake Conemaugh feels even larger. The trees on the far shore are tiny peaks on the horizon. We are but a speck in this vast tableau of nature.

"I knew it would be lovely," Ivy says, her previous fear vanished into the sunlight. She tilts her face up to the cloudless sky. "There is nothing like this in gray and rainy London."

Already, I note the pinkness of her nose. Freckles pop up before my eyes. I also feel an ache in my upper arms and shoulders. Our dock is a distant sliver of cedar behind us. In my head I hear Mother's reprimand: "You took a *child* out in a *boat* without a *hat*?" Suddenly our trip across the lake feels impossibly foolhardy. My stomach is making all sorts of unhappy noises. My normal lunchtime passed while we were fussing with the line. In an attempt to change course, I lift one oar out of the water and row with the other as I have seen father do.

"You're not turning back, are you?" Ivy looks cross.

"Certainly not," I reply. "I'm heading for a cove so we can have our lunch." My sensible maid had known how long a short outing could take.

"A picnic in the woods!" Ivy again claps her hands like a child on Christmas morning. "How divine." Reaching her pale dimpled hands to the back of her head, she pats the French twist to make sure that it is still secure. A sinking feeling descends upon me as I realize this is probably the first time this girl's virginal neck has seen sunlight.

Enduring my sore limbs, I row straight for the first shady cove.

It's rare for me—or anyone—to be on the other side of the lake. Wisely, the builders of our mountain retreat kept us all together. After crossing the dam, there are but a few cottages before the clubhouse. Then the rest are within walking distance beyond it. Our cottage, though last in the line, is still close enough to the clubhouse to take our meals there if we so desire. As far as I know, the only person to live on the north side of the dam is the club's caretaker, Colonel Unger. I suppose he wants to be far enough away from his employer to feel autonomy, yet near enough to maintain the South Fork Fishing and Hunting Club both off and on season.

Come to think of it, whenever Father or Julian or Roderick took me out in the skiff, they were rowing us to the clubhouse—absolutely in the opposite direction. This side of the lake feels wild, untamed. Fallen branches and hollowed tree trunks litter the shoreline. Why, it's almost as thick as the lake debris that gathers around the spillway by the dam. Our little boat bumps and scrapes into all manner of nature's shedding as I try to maneuver our way to the darkened shore. It's difficult to see exactly where the water ends and the land begins. Only when the skiff hits sand do I realize we're onshore.

"There," I say, as if I meant to come aground. "Now, let me stand up fir—" Before I can finish my sentence, Ivy is on her feet and the boat is again wobbling horribly beneath us. The very action of her standing has pushed us out into the water.

"Dear me." Stupidly, I rise to steady the lurching back and forth. At that same moment, Ivy sits down hard and destabilizes us further. Once the boat starts rocking, it's impossible to stop it. The more I try to balance us, the more violently we roll from side to side.

"Elizabeth!" In her panic, Ivy rises again. She screeches and grabs my arm. The jolt of it tips us even more. Left, right, left, right. The two of us stand, clutching each other, as the boat threatens to capsize. My knees have turned to flummery. Water sloshes in; the skiff floats farther out. It's inevitable—we are going to tip over into the lake.

"Hold on to me," I shout into the whites of Ivy's terrified eyes. At that instant, the rocking stops short. Incredibly, the boat seems to be on land again. I'm so stunned I don't feel the tight grip on my upper arm.

Then I do.

"Unhand me, sir."

Startled, I glare up at a man—a town boy—balanced on a large fallen log that is jutting into the lake. His left arm is looped across an overhanging branch; his right hand grips me tightly. We three are a chain, with me in the center. Ivy clutches my left arm as tightly as he clutches my right. "This is private property," I state haughtily, my cheeks aflame.

About my age—perhaps slightly older—the town boy wears dungarees, a broadcloth vest, and beige cotton shirt with the sleeves rolled past his veined forearms. A wool cap sits atop his charcoal curls. He stands so sturdily he seems almost a tree trunk himself. Were I not able to locate his station in life by his clothes, the cracked and callused skin on his strong hands would tell me he is a workingman. Probably one of the mill-workers from Johnstown.

The boy laughs. "You want me to let you go?"

"This instant."

He lets go. Ivy screams as the boat once again rocks violently and my arms flail like a broken windmill. Just as we are about to tip into the lake, the town boy grabs my upper arm again. This time, he takes charge.

"First, still yourselves." He speaks with quiet command. "You must regain *your* equilibrium so the boat will regain hers."

I note that he uses the feminine pronoun to label the boat. *Is he mocking me?* I wonder. *The boat is as unbalanced as these silly women?*

"Good," he continues. "Now lock arms with each other so closely as to be one person."

Shakily, Ivy slides over to my side and clutches me for dear life.

"Good. When I count to three, I shall pull you onto this log."

"But—"

"One, two—"

Before the third number, we are yanked onto the fallen log with him. Close enough to smell the pleasantly horsey aroma in his clothes.

"Three," he says, grinning. Then he expertly guides us off the log and onto the dry shore. Overcome with gratitude, Ivy gushes, "Thank you, sir. I'm ever so grateful. I can't swim."

My eyes flash with annoyance as I smooth the front of my skirt. She thought not to mention that morsel before we went out on a *lake*?

"Yes, thank you, Mister—"

"Eugene Eggar." Mr. Eggar lifts his cap and bows his head in my direction.

"Please don't let us keep you any longer from your journey through our property."

Boldly, Mr. Eggar smiles as he says, "As luck would have it, I worked the dawn shift this morning and have the whole afternoon off to fish." I note his surprisingly even teeth and the cleanliness of his skin. Not as grubby as one might expect from a workingman.

"Fish?"

"The wiggling flashes of silver beneath the surface of the lake."

Ivy giggles. I ignore her to inform Mr. Eggar, "Those flashes of silver belong to the club. The *private* club."

"Ah yes," he says, still relaxed and confident, without the slightest hint of deference. "The Bosses' Club. Down in the valley we often look up to see your white sailboats crisscrossing the sky."

"How divine!"

Silently, I resolve to remove the word "divine" from my vocabulary. Especially when uttered in an English accent, it sounds so abominably big-headed. Ivy skips about the shore-line kicking leaves and twigs to the side, making room for our picnic. I stand on the sand with Mr. Eggar and subtly rub my aching arms. Obviously enjoying himself, Mr. Eggar says, "Do not trees in a forest and fish in a lake belong to God alone?"

I will not be bowed. "Not when one thousand black bass are purchased from Lake Erie and transported via rail to the lake that *we* created and own." I had heard Father speak of this amazing feat many times. He was disappointed to have missed the spectacle of a railcar full of squirming bass being dumped into the lake.

"Your lake," Mr. Eggar says, suddenly serious, "will one day be a murderer."

Ivy gasps. I scoff, "Ridiculous. Our caretaker, Colonel Unger, has assured us all that the dam is perfectly safe."

I knew exactly what Mr. Eggar was talking about. The previous year I overheard Father and other club members discussing the concerns of Johnstown. Residents who lived a full *fifteen* miles down a long canyon below us. The town that I could see on my way up to the club from the train station was full of smokestacks and sooty air. Its iron mills churned out steel rails and barbed wire and black plumes of smoke day and night. Clearly envious of our idyll in the mountains above them, the townspeople frequently complained of the earthen dam's "poor maintenance" and its ever-springing leaks. As if it might one day simply burst open and send tons of water onto their heads. As if the club's caretaker and its prominent members would allow such a thing.

As a matter of course, the concerns of the townspeople were dismissed. It was well known to us that Mr. Benjamin Ruff, president of our club and a respected railroad executive, had settled the matter once and for all. After one of Johnstown's leading citizens—Mr. Morrell, manager of Cambria Iron and a member of the South Fork Fishing and Hunting Club himself—discussed his worries about the dam's reliability with Mr. Ruff, a formal letter was sent down the hill. In it, Mr. Ruff stated unequivocally: "You and your people are in no danger from our enterprise." What could be clearer than that?

Sadly, Mr. Morrell passed away a few years ago. Still, complaints popped up from time to time. Mostly from young men like Mr. Eggar who wanted the spillway unclogged so fish could escape down the mountain into the streams below and provide them with easy access to food.

"Look *down* the next time you cross the dam," Mr. Eggar says to me. "Note the center of the dam top, where it sags and dips. Tell me that you do not see the leakage, the height of the lake now that your so-called experts lowered the breast of the dam to accommodate your fancy carriages. Tell me you do not feel the strain of that muddy beast in your own gut when you stand upon it."

I turn away. Of course I had seen and felt all that he mentioned. We all had. But Colonel Unger had men there to repair every leak. It wasn't as if the club simply turned its back and let the dam crumble. Why, the previous summer I had seen a team of workers from Johnstown and Cambria shoving an entire *tree trunk* into one of those leaks.

"You will excuse us, sir, while we enjoy a private picnic."

"Our lunch!" Ivy yelps as she notices that the skiff—with our picnic basket inside it—has floated away from shore. It bobs among the buoyant fragments of forest like a shipwreck. Without a word, Mr. Eggar leaps into action. He scrabbles back onto the jutting log, secure in his footing, snapping off a long, skinny branch along the way. Grabbing on to a broken stump at the end of the overhanging limb, he leans far enough out to snag our little boat with the end of his long stick. The muscles in his bare forearms quiver with the effort. Admittedly, I am impressed with his competence. I cannot imagine Roderick or one of the clubhouse boys even attempting this. Surely they would toss their hands in the air and berate me for my carelessness at depriving them of lunch. Even James Tottinger with his store of inborn confidence would probably look around as if to summon a servant.

"Lunch is served," Mr. Eggar says as soon as he has pulled the skiff safely ashore. Ivy, of course, claps her hands in glee. Her excessive youth is wearing on my already frayed nerves.

"Please accept our sincerest thanks." I nod once to politely dismiss Mr. Eggar before yet another mishap befalls us and this town boy concludes that we are utterly useless.

"And join us for lunch." Like a forest sprite, Ivy skips over to the picnic basket and peers inside, exclaiming over every morsel. "Cheese sandwiches, smoked herring . . . are these deviled kidneys?"

The aromas of smoked fish and soft cheese blend lusciously with the smell of damp earth and bark. I silently curse Nettie for packing such abundance. Clearly there is ample food for several people. Had she thought we would feed the bears?

"An apple tart. How divine!"

It takes all my will not to groan out loud.

"He cannot stay," I state. Kindly, but with a period. Then, softening, I add, "We must let the gentleman enjoy his day off."

Mr. Eggar is not unwise to the ways of the world. Surely, he notes the impropriety of a workingman sharing a secluded picnic with two society ladies he happened upon in the woods. Young Miss Tottinger has been overly sheltered, indeed. Her suggestion is beyond scandalous. Gratefully, Mr. Eggar recognizes it as thus. With grace, he says, "Thank you for your kind invitation, but I must respectfully decline."

As Ivy extends her lower lip in a pout, I extend my hand. Once again, I thank Mr. Eggar for his assistance.

"Would an hour be sufficient?" he asks.

My hand drops. "Sufficient for what?"

"My return."

In response to my startled expression, he calmly states, "You will need someone to row you back across the lake and help you moor that skiff. I noted the line at the bottom of the boat."

I open my mouth to protest, then close it as quickly. Of course, what he says is true. My arms still pain me from the journey there. Who knew oaring was so taxing on one's muscles? And my stupidity at untying the mooring rope is beyond comprehension. What had I been thinking? My quandary is clear. I cannot possibly row all the way back to our dock and somehow anchor the bobbing boat long enough for Ivy to climb out and secure the line to the piling. Not when she so inexpertly *untied* the line and nearly tumbled into the lake merely getting into the boat. Heavens, we might be floating helplessly until a search party is dispatched to find us. Come to think of it, Mrs. Tottinger believes her beloved Ivy is playing croquet with me. I'm sure she'll soon wonder how long a game of croquet can possibly take. I wouldn't be surprised if she's fretting already.

What if she's sent her husband to the cottage to look for us? Or worse, James Tottinger himself. What if the whole family is waiting, frantic, on our shore? The very last thing I need is for the Tottingers to see Ivy and me, alone, in a shaky rowboat that is unable to land. Mother would be apoplectic.

"We will be in your debt, sir," I say, chastened.

Mr. Eggar tips his cap to both of us and retrieves his fishing pole from behind a tree. He then drapes his traveling sack over his strong shoulder. I note that it is bulging with fish. Before disappearing into the woods, he says, "See you in one hour."

Before I can rethink my rudeness at not offering a portion of our lunch to take with him, he is gone.

# CHAPTER 25

## NORTH BEVERLY PARK

*Present*

Gone Hollywood!" Valerie left Lee a Post-it note. It was stuck on top of the counter above the minifridge that rattled laboriously in the thick heat of midday. Mrs. Adell forbade them to run the window air conditioner in the back room while they were at work. Not even on low. And no way could they leave the French doors open. Not when someone up at the house could see it and ask, "Is someone in there?" As a result, it took twice as long to cool the pool house to a livable temperature in summer. Crazy.

"Mrs. A's charity lunch!" Valerie's note continued. "Back by dinner!" Lee chuckled over her mother's signature exclamation points. Her leaden mood disappeared. Val's cheer was infectious.

Ever since that day at the Beverly Hills Library, Lee used every quiet moment at work to scuttle to the break room—or burrow into the shower-curtain display—to troll the Internet for information about Johnstown, Pennsylvania. But there were so many links, and so much information, her iPhone was too small and too slow to do anything but frustrate her. She *almost* had enough saved for a new laptop. Well, not *new*, exactly. Thank God for eBay.

As soon as she had a new computer, she would resume her clandestine search for the Victorian/Edwardian woman who would lead her to her birth mother. Until then, life ambled on. She drove down the hill to Bed Bath & Beyond, and up the hill to the pool house, enduring the suffocating heat of summer both ways.

On that particularly stifling afternoon, Lee had worked the early shift. Before the store opened, she stocked shelves and ran the microduster along overhead ledges that few saw up close. Once the manager unlocked the doors, a surprising amount of time was spent helping customers find as-seen-on-TV junk.

"You know, it's a *pillow*. Made of gel or something? It doesn't get hot under your head? I saw it on TV in the middle of the night."

"It's this fold-up thingie. You unfold it and slide it under your sofa cushions so they don't sag? I just happened to see some commercial for it during a late-night movie."

"I forget what it's called, but it's a metal tray that defrosts meat in half the time? I was wide-awake in a hotel room when I saw it on television."

Before Lee worked at BB&B, she had no idea how many insomniacs lived in the Valley. She was stunned, too, to see the number of gullible women in posh Encino. As if some made-in-China gadget would solve every annoyance in their lives. I mean, couldn't they pull the grass-fed beef out of the freezer an hour earlier? Or have the housekeeper do it?

Dead tired when she got home, Lee flipped on the air conditioner and kicked off her shoes. She then peeled off her hippie-smelling clothes and grabbed a towel from the hook in the bathroom. A quick, cool shower was just what she needed to wash off her day. By the time she was done, the pool house would be chilled enough for a nap. Already, she could feel the nubby couch fabric beneath her back; the cool press of the Egyptian satin pillowcase she'd coveted since she first saw it at work. The initial sensation of burrowing her face into that shiny smooth pillowcase would be as luscious as a first spoonful of gelato. If so many BB&B customers hadn't returned that gel pillow ("It popped!"), Lee would have bought one for sure.

Naked, wrapped in her towel, Lee headed for the outside shower. The heat instantly pushed against her face and bare shoulders like the blast from an open oven on Thanksgiving. The sunbaked terra-cotta tiles burned her bare feet. Wasn't it supposed to be breezy up here? Isn't that why the rich fled from the Valley to the hills?

On impulse, she skittered to the shallow end of the infinity pool and set her bare feet on the top step. No one was around to see her violation of the rules. *Gone Hollywood!* The cool water felt heavenly on her hot feet.

"Ah," she moaned, stepping down one more level to feel the water chill both calves. Overhead, the star-shaped leaves of the sycamore pointed their fingers at her. White rays of sunlight flashed through the branches. Ripples on the pool's surface spread to the side and disappeared over the infinity edge. Lee glanced up the hill. The glass mansion appeared just as the architect intended: a sparkling diamond in a forest-green setting. It was both beautiful and completely out of key. Perhaps that was his intent? Why blend in when you can stand out?

Faintly, Lee heard the hum of a distant leaf blower at a house down the hill. In the pool, the battery-operated skimmer propelled itself around the water with a *pfft pfft* noise, pushing dead leaves around and scooping up flailing, leggy bugs into its net. Still gripping the towel to her chest, Lee glanced up at the mansion once more. Her heartbeat quickened. In a rush of defiance, she flung her towel to the terra-cotta tile and dove in. Underwater, she squealed with the first chill. The water swirled around her naked body as she swam to the far side, popping up only to suck in air before sinking beneath the surface again. It took three and a half lengths to acclimate to the cold water. But Lee kept swimming. Beneath the dead leaves. Under the drowning bugs. She felt giddy. A captive dolphin released into the ocean. Twirling, gliding, rising only for air. Mrs. Adell and her mother wouldn't be back for hours. *Back by dinner!* Clearly, Mr. Adell hadn't shuffled down to clean the pool in weeks. Why would he choose a hot day like this to tidy a pool that no one used?

"Marco!" Lee yelped in the deep end. Then she swam underwater and popped up near the shallow steps. "Polo!" she called out, breathless. The tensions of her day, her customers, her *life*, sloughed off in a rush of chlorinated water. Underwater, bare, she felt scandalous and free. She swam beneath the surface until her lungs burned. "Marco," she sang out.

"Polo."

A male voice.

Lee's head whipped around. A guy about her age stood near the pool steps, head down, staring at his neon Nikes. Lee shrieked and lurched to the side of the pool to press her nakedness against it. "This is private property!"

He looked like a college boy. Or a character from *The Great Gatsby*. Dressed in tennis whites, he wore pristine socks that hugged his ropy, tanned calves. Both hands were tucked into the pockets of his shorts. Top-heavy dark curls tumbled onto his flushed face. He shook them back, but they fell forward again. Lee was agog that he didn't move.

"Can I *help* you?" she asked, testily.

He released a short laugh. Still not looking up, he said, "My friend lives halfway down the hill. I'm visiting from New York. He's an ass. We were playing tennis in his backyard. He hurled my racket into the bushes up here. Sore loser."

Lee stared and blinked.

"I heard you in the pool," he said. "Marco Polo."

Admittedly, he was cute. The part she could see, anyway. He still wouldn't look up, which Lee appreciated even though she was pretty sure he couldn't make out an actual body part. Other than her arms, of course, and her head. Both of which she hoped looked sporty. Amazingly, she didn't feel afraid at all. Nor embarrassed. The pool water felt like clothes. And there was something about this boy that relaxed her. Unlike other boys who made her brain feel like scrambled eggs.

"I see my racket over there," he said, flicking his head. "I didn't mean to intrude. I'm an idiot."

Suddenly channeling her mother, Lee trilled, "Okay! Thanks

for stopping by!" Then she pressed her eyes shut and fought the urge to sink her head below the surface of the water and stay there. It was the word "intrude." Most boys she knew wouldn't use it. They'd say "bother," maybe, or "bug." "Intrude" was an SAT word. An AP English word. A word used in North Beverly Park. It caught her off guard.

Swiveling on his new tennis shoes—miraculously clean from the slog uphill—the boy took a step toward the downhill slope before stopping. His neck cocked. "You live here, right?"

Lee side-glanced at the pool house. "Yes. I live here."

"There's this party."

She opened her mouth, then closed it, not sure how to respond.

"You probably know about it already," he said.

"Probably," she replied, though she hadn't a clue.

"Maybe you want to come down?" he said. "Like, after ten?"

A rich college boy standing in the vicinity of her bare body was inviting her to a party? Had he decided to invite her when he first came up the hill and saw her naked? Before she covered up with the side of the pool? Did he think she often swam like this, that she was rich, too? Of course he did. No one walking into that scene would ever dream she was the daughter of the *help*. Lee inhaled. Her exhalation made little ripples on the surface of the water.

"Tonight?" she asked as nonchalantly as possible.

"Yeah. If you want. Down the hill." He pointed. "The house with the tennis court. Can't miss it."

"Maybe," Lee said, careful *not* to add, "I have to check with my mom, the maid."

The boy nodded. A gentleman, not once did he look directly at her. Except, probably, when he first climbed the hill and entered the yard. While she was pretending to be a mermaid dolphin-kicking under water. Lee felt her cheeks flush.

"Again," he said, "sorry to infringe." With that, he quietly exited the way he entered: down the hill, into the brush.

Amazingly, Lee didn't feel dead tired anymore.

## ·◦]I CHAPTER 26 I[◦·

SOUTH FORK FISHING AND HUNTING CLUB

*Courtesy of the Johnstown Flood Museum Archives, Johnstown Area Heritage Association*

*Summer 1888*

A distinct snorting catches my attention.

"What's that?" Ivy fearfully shifts her weight to my side of the picnic blanket. Once again, I am agog at her utter lack of common sense. Has the girl never heard the sound of a horse complaining against its snaffle? Has she never noticed the live beings that transport her family's carriage?

"It's a—"

"Horse!" Ivy leaps up.

Appearing out of the dark woods, Mr. Eggar strides into our clearing atop a shiny black steed. It is, admittedly, a startling sight. One might easily conclude Mr. Eggar was born an equestrian. His enormous horse seems an extension of his own muscled workingman's legs. With his perch high and his back straight, Mr. Eggar resembles a medieval knight on his stallion. Albeit one in dungarees on his working animal.

"Shire?" I ask, standing, noting the height of his mare, the white feathering on her feet, and her long, lean head. Though her muscular back is built for work, she is nonetheless a beauty.

Mr. Eggar's eyebrows peak. "You know your horses."

"I ride a Haflinger at the stable here." *Quite well,* I am tempted to add. Back in Upper St. Clair, I've won blue ribbons in several equestrian events. When Father is able to convince Mother to allow me to participate, that is. Feeling the flex of a steed's back muscles beneath my thighs is a sensation of power unlike any other. I feel *fused* to the horse's back, as if we are one. "The club also has a Murgese and a Percheron with the most extraordinary blue-black coat."

Ivy steps closer to the horse and asks, "May I touch her?" As I open my mouth to caution against it, Mr. Eggar says, "She loves to be stroked on her nose." Without a hint of trepidation, Ivy marches up to the horse's mouth and runs the palm of her hand up and down the horse's long, flat muzzle. Ivy coos, "There, my pet, that feels lovely, no?"

Truly, the girl is a puzzle to me. Terrified at the *sound* of an approaching horse, yet fearless in the face of a beast that could easily mistake her hand for lunch. Young Miss Tottinger's brain is a labyrinth.

As I quickly gather our lunch remnants and return them to the basket, Mr. Eggar dismounts with athletic ease. "Mady is as reliable as the sun and the moon." He lovingly pats her haunches. "She's fast, too, and surefooted. My girl knows every twist and curve of the mountain. At speed, she can get me down to Johnstown in five minutes."

Straightening my posture, I frown at the town boy. "Obviously you and your horse climb the mountain regularly."

Meeting my gaze squarely, he replies with a devilish grin. "This cove is my favorite fishing spot."

In one elegant motion, Mr. Eggar swoops down and sweeps our picnic blanket into his arms. He steps around Ivy to the shoreline, where he shakes the dirt off the blanket with a determined snap.

"Mady's eyelashes are simply *divine*," says Ivy. "Elizabeth, you must come close and see how long and curled they are."

"Shall I pack your blanket inside the basket, Elizabeth?" Mr. Eggar asks. "Or might you want it as a wrap? The lake can get chilly."

I stop, stunned. "Please forgive me for not properly introducing myself, sir," I say, swallowing the icy edges of my voice. "I'm Miss Haberlin and my companion is Miss Tottinger."

Mr. Eggar regards me with amusement before politely doffing his cap.

Still stroking the horse's snout, Ivy pipes up, "Do call me Ivy, won't you, Eugene?"

I scarcely know where to look.

In a matter of moments, Mr. Eggar has neatly folded the blanket, stowed it in the picnic basket, and placed the basket in the bow of the skiff. He then secures Mady to the trunk of a dogwood tree, where she instantly stretches her neck up to reach the tastiest leaves.

"Shall we?" he says, one foot firmly on shore, the other even more firmly stabilizing the boat.

"How I would love to stay here longer and explore the woods on Mady's back." Ivy leans languorously against Mady's satiny coat as the horse lazily chomps the sweet dogwood leaves.

"But you cannot."

After I secure my sunbonnet, I take a firm step in the direction of our skiff and allow Mr. Eggar's strong hand to completely encircle my upper arm. In his grip, as he guides me into the boat, I feel not one bit wobbly.

"Miss Haberlin," he says with the merest glimmer of a smile.

"Mr. Eggar," I reply, nodding my appreciation as any lady of breeding would. Once inside the rowboat, I position myself in the center of the farthest plank and smooth my skirt. I tighten my bonnet satins and sigh with relief that my dignity has remained intact. Ivy, I'm afraid, does not follow my lead. As I watch, helpless, she allows her youth to overtake propriety. When Mr. Egger attempts to guide her into the boat in the same manner he escorted me, Ivy Tottinger yelps and executes a tiny hop into the air, flinging both arms about his neck. Poor Mr. Eggar is forced to grip her entire body in one arm while he maintains his balance as well as the boat's. Quite stunningly, he does just that. Without complaint or obvious effort, he effectively carries her—one-armed—into the boat. It is a feat of astounding strength on his part, and unimaginable hubris on hers. I am rendered speechless by both.

"Where shall Mady sit?" Ivy asks in a silly, flirty voice. Her nose, I now see clearly, is freckled from nostril to bridge. As are the apples of both cheeks. Someone will have hell to pay. Right then and there, I decide it will not be me.

"Mady will happily wait for my return on foot," Mr. Eggar says. With that, he steps into the center of the skiff, steadies himself, then grabs an oar and pushes us off the sand. Ivy squeals the moment we are afloat.

"How long to the other side, sir?" I ask.

Grinning, he replies, "There is only one proper answer to that. As long as it *takes*."

## ❄❫ CHAPTER 27 ❪❄

NORTH BEVERLY PARK

*Present*

The moon was nearly full, sufficiently bright to highlight a pathway down the hill, yet not penetrating enough to illuminate the underbrush. In the clear black sky, the stars were out in force, winking overhead. What possessed her, she hadn't a clue. Lee knew there were skunks and God knows *what* burrowed beneath the scrub, yet she tiptoed out of the pool house after ten wearing sandals, bare legs, and a flared ModCloth minidress she'd bought used on eBay. What's more, Lee had decided not to mention the party to her mom. Exhausted from an entire afternoon with the yellow jackets, Valerie had arrived home late with the weary pronouncement: "If I never smell Chanel No. 5 again, I'll die happy." Then she headed straight for the shower and to bed early. Why stress her further with worry that their cover would be blown? Lee knew how to keep her mouth shut. Besides, she was *eighteen*. Too old to need a mother's permission.

"Here we go." Lee crept to the edge of the yard where the Adells' infinity pool dropped out of sight. Then she began her descent.

California's chronic drought, interrupted by blasts of rain, had left the ground on the hill rock hard and dusted by a fine layer of slippery dirt. Lee stepped carefully, hearing the crunch of dead needles beneath the thin soles of her sandals. Her bare toes would be filthy by the time she made her way to the party. But she had a plan.

The Mediterranean-style mansion midway down the hill was enormous. It was the type of house that needed intercoms. Thumping music vibrated from the inky interior of the ground floor while Creamsicle-colored light spewed from every arched window above. Red clay tiles rippled down the multi-angled roof, swirly wrought-iron railings contained the mini balconies beyond each window, slate tiles lay in a stone pattern around the lagoon-inspired pool. It was a picture straight out of *Architectural Digest*.

Lee's heartbeat soon fell in sync with the *whomp, whomp* of the audible bass. Her sandals slid backward as she zigzagged around the low bushes, focusing only on the dirt path beneath her feet. Why invite trouble by scanning the hill for movement? Let the rodents hear her and hide themselves. "A rat is only a squirrel with a bald tail," she said, brightly, attempting to calm herself. "A skunk will only spray if you scare it."

More than once she asked herself, "What the hell am I doing?" Sneaking out to a rich boy's party wasn't like her at

all. Then again, everything that *was* like her—college; her best
friend, Shelby; a future—had been snatched away. Maybe it
was time to reinvent.

Not surprisingly, the only enclosure around the backside
of the Mediterranean estate was a squat retaining wall around
the pool area and a chain-link fence around the tennis court.
The rest of the yard was wide open. An access peculiarity of the
wealthy. While it was most certainly gated from the front—as
was the Adells' home—the back of this gazillion-dollar mansion was open to its neighbors. The hill connected everyone
who lived on it. Outsiders were forbidden in. But if you were
already *in*, admission was free. If you braved the hill, that is.
Which, of course, no one with other options would even consider after dark.

Lee's other options—driving the old Toyota around to the
front or walking around on the sidewalk—were out of the question. Either way was a dead giveaway that she didn't belong at
that party. Nobody in L.A. walked anywhere unless her car
was broken down. And nobody invited to an *Architectural Digest*
sort of house would have a car on its last legs. Plus, Lee never
did get the name of the boy who had invited her, and he didn't
know hers. What could be more humiliating than standing
before a gate speaker sputtering, "Um, he had dark hair? And,
um, neon Nikes?" No way would they buzz her through. Her
only choice was to enter the party the way the boy had entered
the Adells' yard. If she didn't slip on her ass or encounter a crit-
ter that sent her screaming down the hill. A stealthy entrance
to the pool was critical.

The temperature had fallen, as it always did after dark. It

was a breezy fifty degrees. Still, Lee knew everyone at the party would be wearing summery outfits—as she was—the memory of the hot day still fresh in their minds. It was the Southern California way. A minisweater over a stretch cami was the most girls were willing to surrender to the chill. And the only way to tell if a Californian boy was cold was to note how deeply his hands were shoved into his front pockets. At least, that's how it was in the Valley. Up here, in North Beverly Park, the rules could be completely different. *God,* she thought, *I hope no one wears* fur.

Feeling a rush of bravery, Lee quickened her step. Her dangly earrings kissed her neck, the coconut essence in her shampoo brought to mind a tropical beach. (Not that she'd ever been to Hawaii, or even Santa Barbara.) It excited her to think that no one at the party would know who she was. Lee Parker could be anybody she wanted. She could adopt a British accent. *Cheers, gov!* Or claim that her parents were expatriates from a "stan." Turkmenistan, perhaps? Or the one that starts with a UZ? If the boy with the curly dark hair wondered why she'd had no accent earlier when they met at the Adells' pool, she could simply state that she'd been faking an American accent then. Actors did it all the time.

For one night, Lee wanted to forget that her father squandered her college money and ran off, her brother was also gone with the wind, her best friend had moved on without her, her parents had split up, and her mother worked as a maid. Tonight, she would be anyone but a broke girl who secretly lived in a pool house. With germs all over her toothbrush.

"What's the worst that could happen?" She chuckled to herself.

At that moment, as if ferried on a surge of adrenaline, a panic list shot through her mind. *What's the worst that could happen?* Hundreds of bad things could happen! The son of a Turkmenistan diplomat could be there. What language did they speak there, anyway? Certainly not Turkish. Was it Russian? Would she insult him if she answered *"nyet"* to every question? The girl who sold her dress on eBay could be there. She could march up to Lee and coyly say, *"Love* the dress. Where did you get it?" When Lee lied (of course), the girl would move in for the kill. "Funny, I had a dress just like it. There was the tiniest raspberry stain on the hem. Oh. There it is." Lee knew girls like her; she had avoided their wrath all through high school. There was no stopping a girl like her.

"I'm curious . . . how does it feel to wear someone's old clothes? I was shocked when it sold. You did wash it, right? God, I hope so. That dress and I went to a *lot* of wild parties. I'd hate to have it scanned with a UV light. Ha ha. Of course, that was ages ago. Who would ever want to wear my old dress now? Oops. Sorry. *You.*"

Truth be told, Lee hadn't washed the dress. It looked—and smelled—perfectly clean. She'd never even considered a forensic examination. Suddenly her legs felt like two tree trunks lumbering down the hill. She stopped to catch her breath while her mind continued to race.

What if the cute boy from the pool didn't recognize her?

"You're *who*? From *where*?"

What if someone recognized her from Bed Bath & Beyond?

"Hey, didn't I see you yesterday? You helped me find that pillow? You know, the one that doesn't get hot?"

The nearest BB&B was at the Beverly Center, on San Vicente. Technically, it was closer than the Encino branch, but everyone knew that San Vicente Boulevard was a traffic nightmare. It had taken Lee forty minutes just to get to the Beverly Center on the day she applied for a job there; parking in that sperm whale of a mall, plus finding the store entrance from within the garage maze, took another fifteen. When she was hired to work down the hill in Encino, she was glad. The Encino store had a parking lot right in *front*. If you got there early enough, there were spots in the shade. From Mulholland Drive, it was a winding road directly into the Valley. A short hop on Ventura Boulevard. Who *wouldn't* shop at the Encino branch?

Despite the chill of the night, Lee felt her armpits go damp. Her stomach felt leaden. "What the hell am I doing?" she asked herself out loud.

Grandchildren of the gossipy yellow jackets would most certainly be at the party. Didn't the rich hang out in cliques? Hadn't everyone known each other from birth? They went to the same boarding schools. They shared the same private tutor. How simple would it be for word to get back to the Adells that Lee had been swimming in their pool, naked, when a neighbor's friend spotted her? Such a juicy tidbit would be the *first* topic of conversation at a supper prepared by their private chefs.

Lee took a few more tentative steps. Again, she stopped.

With sickening clarity, she realized that—far from her secrets being safe—her cover could be blown *easily*. Worse, she risked endangering her mother. One breach of their contract and they were both out on the street.

Nearly down the hill—close enough to spot a boy and two girls chatting by the tennis court—Lee listened to her breathing. A whoosh of oxygen filled both lungs, a rush of carbon dioxide exited both nostrils. The boy held a brown beer bottle by its neck; the girls flipped their sheets of creamy-blond hair. He mumbled something; they overlaughed. Dust settled around Lee's bare toes. The vibrating, glowing villa suddenly looked as forbidding as Buckingham Palace. Tears rose to her eyes. Her heart sank. She knew.

*I can't go.*

She shrank into herself. The cute boy she'd met earlier had said he was from New York, right? He'd be going home soon, right? If she never saw him again, he'd forget all about her. Even if he told his friends, they would soon dismiss it. "You met a naked girl in a pool? Yeah, right. A mermaid?"

If Lee turned around that very minute, it would soon feel as if nothing had happened at all. Her old life could resume. Work. Home. Repeat.

Crushed, she swiveled on her dusty sandals and made her way back up the hill. A prickled stem in the scrub nicked the skin on her calf. She cursed her father for ruining her life. She could be at *Columbia* right now. Summer prep courses. Or in Malawi with Shelby. Instead—

In the darkness between two mansions, Lee saw the trajectory of her life. Community college, a job in health care—nursing informatics? MRI technician?—married to a balding man in middle management who fell into his recliner the moment he

got home from work. Budweiser in hand, he burped luxuri-
antly and griped about his lazy boss during every commercial.
He dreamed of entering an Ironman competition, though it
had been years since his last push-up. With their entire savings,
they bought a foreclosed ranch-style house in Tarzana. The
lawn was dirt and the dishwasher didn't work. Neither was ever
replaced or revived. She brought McDonald's home from work.
"Use the paper as a plate." Of their two kids, one hated school,
the other rarely attended. His baggy clothes always smelled of
weed. *God, Mom, stop sniffing me.*

Life, once filled with such promise, would feel extraordinarily long.

Lee pressed her hand to her chest and felt her racing heart.
She stopped and tilted her head to the night sky. Its vastness
made her feel like a speck of humanity. As never before, she
felt like she didn't belong anywhere. Who was she? Her ancestry was a question mark. Her recent past was a mess. And
Gil Parker—the man who was supposed to protect her—had
derailed her future and kidnapped her present.

"Stop," she said, abruptly. "Enough." Exhaling frustration
into the sky, Lee took several more fortifying breaths. Until she
stopped wanting to cry. Until she felt her footing again.

"Lee Parker," she announced, "your future is *yours*. Take it."

Adding one last word: "Now." She fluffed her hair and ran
her ring fingers beneath both lower lashes to remove any mascara smudges. Then she turned around and marched down
the hill.

## ❧ CHAPTER 28 ❧

SOUTH FORK FISHING AND HUNTING CLUB

*Summer 1888*

U nder Mr. Eggar's expert command, the return trip is considerably more enjoyable. The sun has darkened to the color
of a fresh egg yolk, the water is as deep blue as a field of violets.
With my back against the front of the boat, I note the beauty of
where we've been. Lake Conemaugh is a sight to behold. Our

sparkling gem. Mr. Eggar, too, has his back to the front of the boat. In essence, he rows us home *backward*. His steady, circular strokes only highlight the inadequacy of my own oarsmanship. However did I manage to get us to the cove!

" . . . *begged* Mother to let me swim in the pond at Hampstead Heath . . ."

The only blight on our beautiful journey back to the club is Ivy's incessant chatter.

" 'Too *murky*,' she said. Which is exactly the point. Those dreadful spa waters at Friedrichsbad are so . . . so *clinical*."

I cannot help but wonder if I was ever as immature. Only a few years separate us, though Ivy Tottinger seems closer to Henry's age. Has she no sense that Mr. Eggar might not want to hear every mundane detail of a life he can only imagine?

"I was very nearly forbidden to take this trip to America. Mother feared seasickness across the Atlantic, but I never felt the slightest hint of—"

"Have you lived in the area long, Mr. Eggar?" I interrupt, steering the conversation into a more appropriate arena.

"All my life," he says, turning his neck so that I might see his profile.

"Your family lives in Johnstown?"

"They do. My father was one of the last puddlers at Cambria Iron. I'm now the youngest blacksmith." His expansive shoulders straighten as he returns his focus to the shrinking woods behind us. As he expertly glides us through the water, he speaks with the same pride I have heard in Mr. Frick's voice when he boasts of profits at the mill. Says Mr. Eggar loudly into the air, "My family and my neighbors make the steel that builds America."

"Goodness!" Ivy exclaims.

I, too, am impressed. It strikes me that none of the men in my social circle have made anything other than money. And most, not even that. Theirs is inherited wealth, not the result of a learned skill.

"Is that *Father*?" Ivy suddenly leans to the right of me to see the shore. Mr. Eggar and I both twist around to look at the front of our cottage. My lips part. I cannot believe my eyes.

"Oh, dear," I whisper.

Our narrow dock is packed with people. Father and Mr. Tottinger lead the throng. Behind them, I see Colonel Unger, Mr. Ruff, Mr. Frick, Mr. Vanderhoff, and Mr. Mellon. Roderick, Oscar, Albert, and Edmond are there, too, wildly waving their arms, as is James Tottinger. Lining the sand at water's edge are Julia, Addie, and their younger siblings. Mother stands stoically alone while (of course) Francine Larkin makes a show out of comforting a clearly distraught Mrs. Tottinger. She appears to be weeping behind a large white handkerchief.

"A welcoming committee!" Ivy squeals.

Mr. Eggar and I exchange looks as he continues to row us into our fate. Clearly the Tottinger girl is barely beyond an imbecile.

"Did you tell anyone you were going out in the boat?" Mr. Eggar quietly asks me.

I shake my head. "In retrospect," I say, "that was ill-advised."

After an astonished moment of silence, he laughs. I cannot

help but laugh with him. Even as I notice the unmistakable chin-strapped hats of the Johnstown Metropolitan Police.

In a cacophony of shouts, orders, and exclamations, we float up to the dock and land against it with a thunk.

"Ivy, dearest, you're alive!"

"Give me your hand."

"Quickly. A blanket."

"If you'd drowned, we never would have found you!"

"Who is this man, Elizabeth?"

"Ivy." *Gasp.* "You're covered in *freckles.*"

In a multitude of flapping hands, Ivy and I are practically lifted out of the skiff. We're both instantly swaddled in blankets and hustled off the dock as if being rescued from a shipwreck.

"We're fine," I say to deaf ears. "Perfectly warm and dry."

" . . . fallen croquet mallets . . . we feared the most dire . . ."

"Not the slightest clue!"

"Unforgivable."

"My precious! What has she done to your ringlets?"

" . . . visions of waterlogged bodies . . ."

"We're *fine*, truly. Ivy—" I look up to see a blanketed Ivy Tottinger burrowed against her mother's voluminous skirt and whisked away. Her brother, James, scurries after the two of them. But not before he glances back at me with the most peculiar look on his face. Is it *amusement*?

"All's well that ends well," one of the police officers says, corralling the crowd on the shore. "Nothing more to see here."

Along with the other officers, he turns to take the boardwalk path back to the clubhouse and the stables beyond, where their horses are waiting.

At the steps up to our cottage, Mother's stern expression chills me more than the breeze on the lake. "What possessed you, Elizabeth?"

I have no satisfactory answer. To avoid her accusatory stare, I turn to thank the town boy who rowed us safely back to the family dock.

"Mr. Eggar?"

He is gone. The skiff is secured to the dock piling, the excess line is coiled in a neat circle. The picnic basket sits primly on the pier. Shaking off the blanket in which I am ridiculously wrapped, I turn all the way around and search for that rugged face.

In the midst of the entire hubbub, Eugene Eggar has vanished into the woods he probably knows better than anyone else.

# ·∘≥[ CHAPTER 29 ]∘·

## NORTH BEVERLY PARK

*Present*

The lagoon pool was lit lime green. Its free-form shape wound around little palm tree islands like the lines on a topographical map. Robotically wiggling through the water were large, brightly colored mechanical fish. They swam around each other like a party scene in a cool, downtown aquarium. The effect was magical. In the deep end, instead of a diving board, a slide curved out of a rocky structure to spit its riders into the water. This was a pool built for *fun*. Completely opposite to the Adells' pristine infinity rectangle. As Lee furtively hopped over the stucco retaining wall in the dark, she heard the trickle of a water feature from somewhere behind the slide. A Jacuzzi, no doubt, tucked into a private cove.

Quietly, she made her way to the shallow end of the pool. Across the crew-cut lawn, the downstairs windows of the house seemed to bulge with the mass of dancing bodies within. A hip-hop beat was all bass. The trio by the tennis court had gone inside, or gone somewhere. No one was in sight, just writhing shadows barely visible through the windows. Kicking off her dirty sandals, Lee stepped into the chilly water and swished her feet around, thinking how fun it would be to play Marco Polo in a pool with so many hiding nooks.

"The heat's off." From the shadows near the house, a familiar voice startled her. When the boy stepped into the light, Lee saw that it was *him*.

"I—" she blurted, unsure what to say next.

"I get it," he said, ambling toward her. "You were a fish in a former life. You can't resist water. Your secret is safe with me."

Lee laughed. The boy said, "I've been waiting for you. I saw you walk down the hill. Then back up. Then back down."

Unnerved, Lee froze. Then she removed both feet from the cold water, blushing, grateful for the darkness. With his chin on his chest the way she'd seen him earlier, the boy said, "That sounded *way* creepier than I intended. Honestly, I haven't been standing here all night watching your movements. Well, not *all* night."

Again, Lee laughed. She bent over to pick up her sandals. After clapping the soles together to shake off the dirt, she tossed them beneath a nearby chaise. Her cold toes were ten perfectly shaped digits. Her best feature.

"I'm George," the boy said, standing in front of Lee with his hand extended. He was gangly and shy. But it was the type of shyness that had confidence at its core. George's demeanor bespoke a boy who was raised to believe that all doors were open to him. All he needed to do was grab the handle and turn it.

*"George?"* It slipped out. Lee pressed her eyelids shut. "That sounded *way* meaner than I intended."

When George grinned, Lee noted three divots on his face: two dimples and a cleft in his chin. Her heart hip-hopped, too. They shook hands.

"I would have named myself Bubba," he said.

"Bubba?"

"Or something like that. But I come from a family of Georges. It was preordained. I'm the fifth."

"George the Fifth? How regal."

"My friends call me 'York.'"

"Ouch. Duke of York. Sorry about the demotion."

He laughed. "It's much lower than that. They call me York because I live in New York. Among the commoners."

Lee's toes were frozen. Not that she cared.

"That's a relief," she said. "I've let my royal etiquette training lapse. Not sure if I bow to a duke. But, as I recall, with a New Yorker, the protocol is giving you the finger, right?"

York laughed full out. In the now-chilly air, Lee felt warm all over. His very essence relaxed her. She felt like someone else. A *clever* girl, reeking of confidence. Even as she discovered that York's face—now on full view—was perfectly pleasing in every way. His eyes were as dark as his hair. His nose was straight and large enough to look masculine. Black stubble on the verge of beard appeared in patches on either side of those massive dimples. Plus his lips, wow, they were down cushions the color of mulberries. Lips that looked as if they always tasted sweet.

York was *way* out of her league. If he knew who she really was, he'd politely excuse himself. If he knew.

"Do you have a name?" York asked. "Nemo, perhaps? Or Ariel?"

Grinning, Lee said, "I'm . . . *Elizabeth*."

"Like Queen Elizabeth?"

"Exactly."

He bowed. As she had seen earlier in the Adells' pool, York's loose ringlets fell onto his forehead. He wore light-colored khakis and an ironed white oxford shirt, the sleeves rolled up. On his feet, a pristine pair of black-and-white Air Jordans.

"We are amused," Lee said, feeling flirty. She drank in York's effortless style and resolved to remove her chandelier earrings as soon as he wasn't looking. Dangly, fake-gold evidence that she was trying too hard. The rest of her ensemble, she reasoned, could pass. Her hair, dark and curly like his, fell nicely down her back with the help of the deep-conditioning shea butter masque she'd applied that afternoon after her swim.

"Want to meet my friends?" York asked.

Lee fought the urge to say, *No. I want to stay out here by this amazing pool and trace the shadows of the water ripple along your chin line.*

"Sure," she said, instead.

Inside, a blast of music assaulted her senses. It was hard not to gawk. The ceiling in the huge room overlooking the pool rose up two stories. Beamed in dark wood, it was a sharp contrast to the white walls and cobalt-blue, green, and sun-yellow floor tiles. The tiles felt cool on her bare feet. Even without shoes, Lee was an inch or two taller than George. Not that he seemed to notice.

There must have been speakers tucked into walls all over the house because the pulsing music seemed to come from the air itself. The dance floor—really just the center of the enormous room—resembled a giant sea anemone. Bare arms bobbing in the air, bodies undulating in sync. Lee felt her confidence quiver as she spotted one gorgeous blonde after another. Those who weren't dancing were draped decoratively on white furniture along the edges of the massive room. Couches, easy chairs, upholstered chaises were sprinkled in conversational clusters throughout the open space, with a quieter alcove at the far end of the room. How did all that light fabric stay clean? The girls wore skinny jeans and bejeweled high-heeled sandals. They drank pink cocktails and vaped at each other. Real gold and silver spangles decorated their wrists. Lee made a mental note: You really *can* tell the difference between real jewelry and fake. No matter what the Home Shopping Network would have you believe. Thank God she left her cheap sandals outside! As she'd expected, the girls were dressed for the warmth of daylight. Their tight sleeveless tees revealed serious tanning commitments and trainer-led workouts. Lee quickly removed her earrings and tucked them in the pocket of her dress.

"York, my man! Whom do we have here?"

A boy who resembled every other boy at the party marched over to Lee. Like York, he wore light pants and a dress shirt open at the neck with rolled-up sleeves. His excessive brown hair was perfectly tousled and his features were, well, *perfect*. The genetics in that room were mind-blowing.

"Elizabeth, meet Drake," York yelled over the music.

*Of course his name is Drake*, Lee thought, her pulse pumping blood into her face. *No Bubbas in this crowd*.

"Hey, Drake," she yelled back, wondering if she should shake his hand the way York had shaken hers by the pool. To test the waters, she flopped it in front of her waist in a semiwave. Had he wanted to, Drake could have grabbed it. But his right hand was holding a craft beer bottle and his left was casually tucked in his front pocket. Shaking her hand might have ruined his *GQ* look.

"Elizabeth lives up the hill," York said.

Lee's heart clutched.

"The Adells' house?"

She swallowed. "Actually," she hollered, "York found me wandering in the brush."

Drake laughed. "You know, there are skunks in that hill."

"Aren't there skunks everywhere? I mean, we *are* in L.A."

Again, he laughed. York did, too. Drake shouted, "What's your drink?"

"How 'bout something pink?"

"I like her," he said to York, before turning around to flag a roving waiter. Lee couldn't believe there was a *waiter* at a college party. The last party she went to was in a Northridge garage. When they weren't completely contaminating the keg's spout with their slobbery lips, everyone gulped cheap beer out of red plastic cups. The food was a giant bowl of Doritos.

To the waiter—as handsome as every other male in the room—Drake ordered, "Two Naughty Sauce Stouts and something *pink* for the lady."

*The lady.* Lee liked that.

In a gentlemanly way, Drake put his hand on Lee's back and guided her to the quieter end of the room. York followed.

"Unencrypted biometrics . . . 6TB SSD . . . islands of serrated wrack . . . degaussed cop cams." Sporadic words poked through the primal beat. They made no sense at all. *The rich even have their own language,* Lee thought. As the threesome snaked their way through the wriggling bodies, Lee mentally calmed herself with the knowledge that no one at the party knew her and no one would ever see her again. The freedom of it felt exhilarating.

In the back alcove, there was more white fabric and dark wood and stunning coeds perched on every surface. It looked like a Tommy Hilfiger ad. With the music now muted, Drake asked, "How is it we've never met?"

Again, Lee's heart lurched. Her gazed quickly flicked over to the corner of the room. "Bösendorfer Imperial?"

Drake's brows shot up. "The lady knows her pianos."

"A pilot could land a small plane on that soundboard."

"You play?"

Lee nodded. "Unfortunately, that's exactly right. I *play.* I never got good enough to do more than that."

York looked perplexed. "What's stopping you?"

What could she say? There wasn't room in the pool house for a *shower,* much less a piano. Not even her secondhand Baldwin.

Thankfully, the waiter appeared. On his tray was a skinny-stemmed, triangular glass full of frosty pink liquid and two brown bottles of beer. Drake gulped the last of his old beer before taking a fresh one. Lee held her glass by the stem.

"To new friends and old money." Drake raised his beer bottle.

"And pink drinks." Lee felt suddenly brash. She liked being somebody nobody knew. Someone else entirely.

At that moment, another handsome waiter appeared with a silver tray full of sushi. Lee had never had sushi before. Raw fish at the mall's food court had never seemed like a wise nutritional choice. And she'd once read that cooked rice left at room temperature too long can breed spores of *Bacillus cereus*.

Lee politely declined. York lifted his beer bottle up to his berry-colored lips. Drake leaned in and kissed Lee on the cheek. "Now that you're properly hydrated, I must continue my duties as host. Fabulous meeting you, Elizabeth. Come down anytime to play our Bösendorfer. Or tennis."

"Will do," she said, sounding mortifyingly like her mother. Lee brought the pink drink to her lips and took a swig. Instantly, she realized how dangerous the fruity, tart liquid was. It went down much too easily. One gulp too many and she'd be stumbling back up that hill. The only other alcohol she'd ever tasted was beer and she didn't like it. Especially when it came from a germy keg.

*No more gulps, girl*, she said silently. *Sip, sip, sip.*

With easygoing Drake gone and the distraction of dancing and thumping music off in the distance, awkwardness bubbled up between Lee and York. Suddenly it felt like York was stuck with her whether he wanted to be or not. After all, he did invite her. How could he now cut her loose to roam among strangers?

"I see someone I know," Lee lied, saving him, pointing her drink at a group of girls gathered in a hallway leading to the mansion's southern wing.

"Oh," York said. "Okay." Then he looked so crestfallen Lee changed course. "Know what? Who cares?" she said. "I can see her anytime."

"No, go ahead. Have a good time." He swiped a clump of curls off his face and swallowed a gulp of beer from the bottle. "I'm fine." York looked so vulnerable Lee wanted to gobble back her words and swallow them with a sip of her pink drink. "I've never been keen on parties," he mumbled.

*Keen.* Lee smiled. "Aren't these your friends, too?"

York shook his head. "Most are from Drake's UCLA fraternity and their sister sorority."

The moment he said it, Lee knew that it was true. They had the *look.* Girls: flat-ironed hair, eyebrows peaked in a professional pluck, salon tans, nail art, jeans that could support a Malawian family. Boys: sockless, deliberately disheveled, shaded with studied stubble, chinos or Brooks Brothers trousers. Smooth, clear, genetically posh skin. No one, Lee noticed, wore a dress. No one let her dark curls tumble down her back.

As if on cue, a Sienna Miller clone walked past and flicked her hair in Lee's direction. She smiled fakely. Lee felt outed. Rich girls could *smell* an interloper in their midst.

"There's only one thing to do," she said, quickly. "Create our own *fratority.*"

York grinned.

"Eighteen hundred SAT score, or above."

"Three-point-five GPA."

"Or above."

"*Preferably* above."

Lee laughed and sipped her drink. "No fake nails."

"No spray tans."

"No ionic hair irons." (They were big at BB&B.)

"No vaping."

"God, no. Who would want to put germy metal in their mouth?"

Lee couldn't help but stare at York's hands. His fingers were long like hers. Only they looked as strong as a basketball center's. His hands were both smooth and muscled, as well manicured as a girl's yet not at all prissy. Lee couldn't believe that a boy with those hands would ever be interested in a girl like her. A girl whose cuticles were usually trimmed with her teeth. *Pffft.*

"We need a Greek name for our *fratority*," he said, his dark eyes flashing. "How about E'na, Di'o, Tri'a?"

*Of course he could count in Greek.*

"I'm thinking something more accessible," Lee said. "Like Eeeny, Meeny, Mynee."

York laughed. A waiter walked past. "Second round, Elizabeth?"

"I'm good." Her pink drink was still half full. York said, "I could go with Manny, Moe, and Jack."

"Jacqueline. It's a frat*ority*, remember?"

Together, they laughed. York's teeth were flawless. Years of orthodontia, no doubt. Flush with solidarity, Lee said, "I'm not keen on parties either."

When York grinned, she felt like she was already in love.

*Is this how the rich get together?* she wondered. *No games, no drama? I like you, you like me, let's banter in a quiet alcove?* Or was it just him—George—the Duke of New York?

Lee didn't care. For that night—one night—she would be

Queen Elizabeth from North Beverly Park and everything would be possible. Tomorrow, York would fly home and she'd turn back into Cinderella.

Pink drink in hand, she suggested they sit outside, by the amazing pool, and watch the fake fish.

"If it's not too chilly," she said.

They snaked through the crowd to the back door. Outside, it *was* too chilly. For Lee, anyway. Beneath the stars over the house on the hill, the warm air rising up from the valley had cooled to the midfifties. Lee tried not to shiver as she reclined on a teak chaise facing the pool. She didn't want the night to end; she didn't want to go back in the house.

"Here." Reaching into a fat wicker basket behind the lounges, York pulled out three huge towels. He handed Lee two, then spread the other one over himself. "All the comforts of home," he said.

Grateful, she unfolded her billowy towels and snuggled under them. Together, side by side, they stared up at the twinkling sky and down at the undulating fish in comfortable silence. From inside the house, the party showed no sign of slowing down.

"How long have you lived up the hill?" York asked, turning his head.

"Feels like forever."

"Do you go to UCLA? USC?"

She swallowed. "I'm taking a break. Columbia is my dream school."

"I'm a sophomore at Columbia!"

*Of course he was.* She quickly buried her jealousy. "What are you studying?"

"Premed. You? When you're off your break, that is."

Lee pulled her arm out from under the warm towel and reached down for her pink lady drink. "At the moment I'm into textiles." She omitted, *And as-seen-on-TV junk.*

"Are you considering Parsons in the fashion district?"

"No." She took a dainty sip. Tuition at Parsons School of Design, she happened to know, was $50,000 a year. Which didn't include an apartment in New York City and enough money for subway fare and ramen noodles from Costco. Not that Columbia was any cheaper. "Honestly, I'm not sure where I'll end up going."

"Did either of your parents go to Columbia?" York asked.

Lee stifled a snort. "I can't imagine them leaving California."

"My parents are that way about New York. To them, no other city exists. But I'm lucky, I guess, that my dad graduated from Columbia. I got in on a Legacy Admission."

It didn't escape Lee's notice that York assumed her only hurdle would be admission instead of tuition.

"Not that I had a choice," he mumbled.

"What does that mean?"

"My life has been planned from birth. Trinity, Choate, Columbia, Harvard postgrad. If I don't cure cancer, my parents will consider me an ignominious failure."

*There he goes with the SAT words*, Lee thought. Though she said, "I'm sure that's not true."

"It is. Drake and I went to Choate together. He is my parents' ideal of the perfect son. Totally driven. They send me out here for a couple of weeks every summer hoping he'll rub off on me."

"Has he?"

York swivels his head to gaze up at the black sky. "I'll never be who they want me to be. My dad is obsessed with making money and my mom is obsessed with spending it. Theirs is a match made on Madison Avenue."

"So, who do *you* want to be?"

"Still to be determined. Just not that."

Sighing, Lee said, "I know what you mean. I love my parents, but I don't want to end up like them."

"What do they do?"

Lee again sipped her pink drink. "Mom, well, it seems like her whole life has been a mission to help the helpless. And Dad, well, Daddy is a free spirit. He's currently looking for his muse somewhere in Topanga Canyon."

Last she heard, anyway. Lee downed the rest of her cocktail. Did she just say "Daddy"?

"My father would disown me if I became a free spirit."

"Isn't that what a free spirit is? Someone disowned?"

For a long time, York said nothing. Then he twisted onto his side and whispered, "You're not like other girls, are you?"

He had no idea.

"Around you," she said, softly, "I'm more like me."

# ·≈[ CHAPTER 30 ]≈·

*Courtesy of the Johnstown Flood Museum Archives, Johnstown Area Heritage Association*

SOUTH FORK FISHING AND HUNTING CLUB

*Summer 1888*

Like a wasp's nest hit with a stick, the clubhouse is abuzz with what is quickly dubbed my *escapade*. As if I spirited away Ivy Tottinger against her will. As if I am some sort of hooligan. Preposterous. Yet chatty Miss Tottinger is suddenly mute. Francine Larkin flits back and forth between the clubhouse and our cottage to apprise me of every last detail.

"They are preparing to leave this very afternoon." Her cheeks are aflame as she describes the accusatory grumbling of Ivy's parents and the flurry to muster enough clubhouse staff to pack them quickly. "The poor dear girl cannot speak for the trauma."

"What trauma?"

"Why, the trauma of nearly drowning, of course."

Only Francine's eyes would gleam like polished silver at the mention of another's distress. Even if it's a fabricated one. Excitedly, she tells me that the elder Mr. Tottinger was heard by all to shout, "Ready the carriage!" as if he were Napoleon mustering the French cavalry.

"They cannot bear to stay a moment longer," Francine chirps.

"Was it the fresh air in Miss Tottinger's lungs?" I ask in mock horror. "Or perhaps the pink kiss of sun on her neck? Shall I have Father summon an ambulance?"

Francine purses her lips in a reprimanding manner. "While you scorn, Elizabeth, that poor dear girl suffers." She then wheels around and scurries back to the clubhouse for more news.

Poor dear girl? Ivy Tottinger? It's so utterly ridiculous. I cannot but laugh. Oh, would it be so that Father and Mother

---

felt the same. Both are quite cross with me. As I climb the cottage stairs for a much-needed rest in my room, Mother follows on my heels.

"How it is possible you let a *child* dictate your common sense?"

I stop and sigh. When I swivel around to face her, I notice that Mother's lips are pinched into a bone button. Her nostrils flare like a Percheron's.

"It happened spontaneously," I say. Once the words leave my throat, I realize how inadequate they sound. "What I mean to say is—"

"And such a delicate child at that?"

"Delicate? Hardly. *Sheltered*, most assuredl—"

"Did you not once think to offer the poor dear girl a sunbonnet at the very least?"

As I cannot endure those three words again—"poor," "dear," and "girl"—I silently wheel around and continue up the stairs to escape them. "Nettie," I call out. "Could you please help me with my boots?"

"Or a parasol? Heavens, Elizabeth, what were you thinking?" Mother follows me into my room.

"Nettie!" I yelp even as I hear the rustle of her skirt up the stairs. She enters my room with her head down.

"Right away, miss," she mutters.

Exhausted, I fall into my vanity chair and extend my muddy boots for my maid to lift into her lap. She pulls a buttonhook out of a front pocket in her apron and sits on a stool before me. Beyond my open window, the warbler's *chirp, chirp* harmonizes with the throaty whistle of the meadowlark. It's as if Mother

Nature herself is commiserating with me. She was there; she knows how little choice I had in the unfolding of events. In the increasingly orange light slanting through the cottage window-panes, I see that sunset is approaching. Abruptly, I feel very sleepy.

"No need to fetch my satins, Nettie. I believe I shall rest before supper."

"I could fetch your slippers, 'Lizbeth."

Little Henry hovers near the open door, one foot on top of the other. The button-up side flap of one brown boot is undone. He stares with the frightened eyes of a chital.

"It's *E*lizabeth, Henry. How many times must I tell you?"

Mother's harsh tone startles him to near tears. She alarms me by positioning herself firmly on my corner settee. Far from waning, our conversation appears to be barely ignited. Dear me, it's nearly impossible to keep my eyelids from drooping shut.

"Certainly you are aware of Mr. Tottinger's importance."

Out of nowhere, Father appears. He, too, enters my room, now as crowded as a train station. Nervously, he fingers the curl of his mustache. "It was incumbent upon all of us at the club to put our best foot forward. Mr. Mellon was counting on us. His bank has yet to secure the financing commitment for Mr. Tottinger's enterprise here in the States."

"Father, I did nothing wron—"

"Not to mention securing the interest of his son."

"Mother!" I say, shocked.

Her tight face bears the veneer of impatience. "Your naïveté is unbecoming, Elizabeth," she says, flatly.

I blush. Nettie glances up at me as she pulls both boots off and quietly carries them downstairs to the anteroom off the kitchen.

"I believe an apology will go a long way to repair the damage."

The flare of anger awakens me. "Certainly, Father, you speak of an apology from Miss Tottinger to *me*. It is *she* who—"

"This is no time for impudence, Elizabeth." Mother's chin juts forward. "Do as your father says."

"But—"

"Nettie!" Mother calls down the stairs. "Elizabeth needs freshening. And clean shoes."

"I'll go with you, 'Lizb—*E*lizabeth," says Henry, looking as if he might soon dissolve into sobs. It's a rare event when both parents scold me. "I'll hold your hand."

My heart softens at my little brother's kindness. Though it immediately hardens when Father states, "This is something Elizabeth must do by herself. And quickly. The Tottingers will be leaving on the next train out of South Fork."

"But—"

Mother extends one hand to silence me.

It's all so unbearably unfair.

In a flurry of activity, Nettie sweeps into my room again. This time, a new pair of freshly polished shoes dangles from her fingertips. Mother stands and steps aside. She loudly sighs her disappointment before making her way to her son, encircling him in the folds of her skirt. She then leads him away from his felonious sister. While Nettie inserts my tired feet into shoes I do not wish to wear, Father stands tall before me and announces, "Additionally, Mother and I have decided to cut summer short this year."

"*What.* Why?"

He flashes a piqued expression. "Come Monday morning," he says, "we will all return to Upper St. Clair on the early-morning train. For the rest of the summer, you will work in the clinic with me."

My jaw drops. "The clinic? I have no medical experience whatsoever. What will I do?"

Before leaving me alone to refresh my appearance and affix a properly contrite expression on my face, Father simply states: "Whatever needs to be done." Upon his exit he adds, "Do not tarry, Elizabeth."

Never have I felt so utterly misaligned and misjudged.


IN THE LIFE of every girl my age and circumstance comes a moment when she realizes propriety and justice are at odds. My such moment occurs on the access road behind the clubhouse. As I approach from the cottage path, my stomach is a swirl of disquiet. Before I see a soul, I hear the murmur of nearly everyone I know coming from the clubhouse's front veranda. It sounds as if all of Pittsburgh society is milling around outside with overexpressive eyebrows and warming glasses of iced tea that they will nurse to the final drop. No one wants to miss the event of the summer. The Tottingers leaving in a huff as a result of Elizabeth Haberlin's escapade. What could be more delicious? They will dine on the gossip for weeks.

I inhale deeply into my corset. I fluff the sleeves of my shirtwaist. With my back erect and my neck elongated, I march forward.

Colonel Unger has ordered the stable hands to hitch up the large carriage for the Tottinger family and their tower of traveling trunks. I see that the club's Percheron and Murgese are already in their breast collars with the driving halters secured to the carriage shaft. Nettie's friend from the stable is seated in the perch. Ungraciously, I wonder, *Will delicate Miss Tottinger march up to these horses' snouts and plant kisses?*

"Poor dear Ivy." From the direction of the populated porch, I hear the unmistakable warble of Francine Larkin. No doubt her cheeks are still flushed with the thrill of my downfall.

As I approach, the last of the trunks is being secured to the back of the carriage. The moment I fully emerge from the shadows of the clubhouse, a thick silence blankets our mountain paradise. Even Francine has swallowed her animated concern. Though I do not dare look, I feel all eyes tracking my every footfall. Just as they had during my sashay along the length of the porch in my Charles Worth gown. The irony of this does not escape me.

"Good afternoon, Colonel," I say.

"Miss Haberlin," he replies, nodding hello.

At that very moment, the Tottinger family descends the side clubhouse steps. With dour expressions, they make their way to the waiting carriage. Mrs. Tottinger wears black, from head to toe. As if she is in mourning, for heaven's sake. Does she *travel* with bereavement attire? Ready at any moment for disaster? I inhale fully to summon the strength not to groan. Ivy's French twist has been hastily dismantled; sad ringlets tumble onto her shoulders. Her face is shiny, slathered in a thick cream. The childish bow securing the hair at the crown of her head is even more comically large than it was when I first met her. For a brief moment, she darts her eyes in my direction. In them, I see the mischievous expression of a pixie. As if this is all a game. I look away. She will not have the satisfaction of my pleading— silent or otherwise—for her to honorably reveal the truth. Let her live with the trouble she has wrought.

"Mr. Tottinger, sir," I say to the elder, stepping forward. "Please accept my sincerest apologies for my lack of sound judgment. Your lovely daughter is so mature I mistook her for a peer."

Beside him, his obdurate wife looks away and *humphs*. The club members are still silent on the veranda. It's a wonder the porch doesn't collapse under the weight of them. With the focus of an eagle on its prey, I affix my gaze on the Tottinger patriarch. "My family is distraught by my behavior as well, sir. I respectfully ask you not to hold them accountable for my indiscretions. I am old enough to know better."

He smiles and begins to accept my apology when Mrs. Tottinger intercepts the hand he extends in absolution. "Very well, then," she says curtly. "We must be getting on."

With that, she uses the support of her husband's outstretched hand to hustle herself and her daughter into the open carriage. After settling with an exaggerated display of discomfort, she stares straight ahead. As does Ivy. My blood simmers. On the ground, the elder Mr. Tottinger glances at me with an apologetic look. In his expression I understand it all: Mrs. Tottinger brought the wealth into their union. Probably the land and estates as well. Far from allowing their marriage to blend monetary assets with social graces, she chose to daily remind her husband of his dependence on her. I feel for him. In a flash of compassion, I sympathize with young Ivy as well. As I well know, it's not easy living with a mother who would prefer you stay a child.

"Safe travels, Mrs. Tottinger," I call into the carriage. "And to you, poor, dear Ivy."

Ivy steals a smile at me. Before her mother can contain her hand, she wiggles her fingers in an apologetic good-bye.

"This *is* a most beautiful retreat," Mr. Tottinger says before climbing into the seat beside his wife and daughter.

"It is," I concur. "Your family is always most welcome."

Behind me, I note the disappointed nodding of several friends. They, too, are annoyed by my decision to take Ivy Tottinger on our lake outing. Because of me, our esteemed guests are taking an early leave. With them departs the fetching son. The arrival of James Tottinger brought a froth of excitement. His early exit flattens the spirits of every eligible woman.

As if summoned by heaven itself, James Tottinger suddenly appears at the back of the carriage. I do not meet his gaze. To see my disgrace reflected in his lovely blue irises is too much to bear. Though my flirting had been fun, it was only amusing when I felt myself in charge of the situati—

"Elizabeth."

In the shadow of the stack of trunks, he whispers my name. I look up. Quickly, he hands me a folded note, small enough to conceal in my hands.

"Shall we be off?" he then says loudly, leaping around to the carriage step, where he hoists himself onto the seat next to his father.

"To the station!" old Mr. Tottinger shouts, overdramatically.

"Godspeed," Francine Larkin yells from clubhouse steps.

The Murgese flips his mane as the driver shakes the reins. Off they trot, leaving a wake of dust that settles on my skirt and the folded note tucked secretly into the palm of my hand.

# ·ᐣᑲ CHAPTER 31 ᑲᐣ·

NORTH BEVERLY PARK

*Present*

Like Cinderella, Lee awoke feeling the shabbiness of her real life. Sunlight blared through the French windows of the pool house. The night before, she hadn't bothered to tape a towel over the windows. It would have fallen anyway. Valerie, she could hear through the wall, was in the outside shower. Lee ran her fingers lightly across her mouth. She could still feel it. The spiky stubble above his upper lip, the slight give when his mouth met hers. It had been the perfect kiss: intentional, insistent, landing squarely out of the blue.

"Why didn't I meet you earlier?" York asked as they sat by the pool, his voice barely above a whisper.

"I'm here now," Lee replied.

In one fluid motion, the boy from New York reached across the chaise to encircle Lee's neck with his hand. At the same moment, he leaned into her lips. Lee stretched her body toward him. They met in the middle space with their noses at the ideal tilt, their lips mildly moist, their eyelids half fallen. With the softness of a feather bed, his lips landed on hers. No tongue gymnastics. Not at first, anyway. In a playfully sexy way, he planted baby kisses all over her mouth, her cheeks, the tip of her nose, the flat space between her closed eyes. He circled back to her lips, gently parting them with a tongue that explored the inside of her mouth like an angelfish zigzagging through a live coral reef. His breath had the inexplicably delicious scent of beer and wet grass. Lee, unlike any Lee she'd ever been before, relaxed into his touch. Her mind didn't flash on what might happen next, on whether her breath was sweet, her kiss experienced enough. For once, forever, she felt the present pleasure of York's mouth on hers. As kisses go, it was epic.

"Morning, sunshine!" Wrapped in a towel, her hair wet, Valerie slapped her bare feet into the pool house. "Nothing like a solid ten hours to revive the mind and spirit!"

Lee rolled over and groaned. With her face tucked beneath the blanket, she licked both lips to taste York one last time.

It was past eight thirty.

His plane was on its way back to the East Coast. Her castle was a pool house again. Her life was in a pumpkin carriage going nowhere. Though they had exchanged cell numbers, Lee knew it was over. If he texted her, she wouldn't respond. One night was flirty *pretending;* any longer was outright lying. How could she lie to a boy like York? He didn't deserve it. Best to cut it off cleanly before her feelings flowered into expectations of something real. Like a rosebud on Valentine's Day. Flawless and contained. But, in reality, already dead.

Lee sighed. Whom was she kidding? Real life was nowhere near a fairy tale. If York lived in North Beverly Park, he'd quickly discover her true Cinderella status. He'd roll his eyes when she said, "Technically, I didn't lie to you. Like, when you asked if I lived at the Adells'? My eyes darted to the *pool house* when I said I did."

Now Lee rolled her eyes. Even to herself she sounded like a loser.

He was a rich boy, she was a poor girl. Their fantasy night was just that: a *fantasy*. Time to wake up.

"What time does your shift start?" Val skittered into the kitchenette to make tea.

Words still jumbled inside her sleepy head, Lee muffled, "Mofftay."

"Come again?"

She rubbed the blood into her face. "I'm off today."

"Lucky you. I'll be up at the house helping Mrs. Adell clean out her closets. She wants to donate to Dress for Success for the tax deduction, but who else but a yellow jacket could fit into those tiny clothes?"

"So I can use the car?"

Valerie nodded. "Exciting plans?"

Lee dragged herself into a sitting position on the sofa bed. In the corner of the room, draped over a kitchenette stool, she spotted her party dress. On the floor beside it lay her sparkly sandals coated in brown mountain dirt. For a brief moment she felt so hollow she slumped into herself like a crushed toilet paper roll. The electric kettle shot steam into the air. Valerie unplugged it and filled two mugs with boiling water. Lee commanded her lungs to expand and contract. *Repeat.* She willed herself into the new day.

Now that she knew her great-great-great-grandmother was with Clara Barton in Johnstown, Pennsylvania, in 1889, Lee had an idea.

"Same old, same old," she fibbed, padding into the bathroom and shutting the door.

# ·•ঃ[ CHAPTER 32 ]ঃ•·

### SOUTH FORK FISHING AND HUNTING CLUB

*Summer 1888*

Now the *cottage* is in a tizzy. After Father's announcement that I must return to Pittsburgh with him on Monday morning's train, Nettie is scurrying about packing my things and readying herself for the journey home. Though she won't say it directly, I sense that she is cross with me. As is everyone else. Nettie's dalliance with one of the club's stable hands appeared to be in its initial flush when I came upon them in the woods. She probably believed she had all summer to enjoy his companionship. But is it *my* fault that Father is being so unfair?

"I'll set out the pleated plaid for the train," Nettie says to me, gruffly.

I silently nod my approval and swallow an apology. "It's Nettie's *job* to do as you ask," Mother says whenever she hears me apologize to my maid. "Never forget you are a Haberlin."

Sighing loudly, I once again feel the pinch of my family's circumstances. While Nettie packs me, I fall facedown onto my bed. Ivy Tottinger has ruined everything.

SUNLIGHT WAKES ME the following morning. It's Sunday. When I pad over to the cottage window, my heart sinks. Of course, it's the most stunning day of the whole summer. Lake Conemaugh is a jewel. Already, sailboats are slicing through the turquoise water. The Tottingers left yesterday. We will be leaving tomorrow morning. It's so terribly unfair. The rest of my summer will be filled with Father's hypochondriac patients and the snotty noses of their children.

James Tottinger is but a memory. And, of course, a note.

It pains me to admit it, but a flash of electricity surged through my forearm when he placed that note in my hand. In the shadow of the carriage, the touch of his fingertips felt like a forbidden kiss. At first, I was too startled to do anything but feel my cheeks flush. After Mr. Tottinger leaped onto the carriage and the horses clip-clopped toward the dam crossing, I stood like a tree stump.

"Anyone feel like rowing me across the lake?" Roderick said, loudly, from the clubhouse porch. Francine's shrill laughter rose above everyone else's. I returned to my senses. Without even looking at my friends, I marched with my head up to the access road behind the clubhouse to make my way home. I pressed my thumb into the note to secure it in my palm. I didn't dare read it before I was safely in my room at the cottage with the door closed. Already I was fodder for tongue-waggers. Why give them more ammunition?

At the cottage, while Nettie and Ella packed supplies in the kitchen, I tiptoed up the stairs and closed myself in my bedroom. I stood away from the window. By now, the note had absorbed my body temperature. My hand tingled with the feel of it. First, I felt the thick paper with my fingertips. Then I lifted the folded note to my face and inhaled. It smelled as sweet as fresh cream, though there was also the faintest hint of horse. Blood pulsed into my chest. I tried to moisten my lips but my tongue was as dry as the endpiece of last night's roast tossed into the woods for the raccoons. Holding the note between my fingers, I opened the first fold, then the second. Then I unfurled it completely and held it up to my eyes.

"I must see you again."

James Tottinger's words were simple—five in all—yet his intent was clear. He did not say how or when, but it scarcely mattered. In his five words I fully read his desire. I knew he would make the trip across the Atlantic again with the sole

purpose of seeing me. If not sooner, then definitely for my debutante ball. A man like James Tottinger would never allow another suitor to usurp him. I smiled. The choice was now *mine*.
Mother would be pleased.

Refolding the note into a tight square, I walked over to my
wardrobe and opened its door. Lifting out the satin shoes I'd
worn with my Charles Worth gown, I slipped the note far into
the tip of one of the toes. No one would find it there. Which is
exactly what I wanted. In the aftermath of Mother's reprimand
for doing *nothing* but attempting to satisfy the mercurial wishes
of an indulged Ivy Tottinger, I decided not to share the note
with her. It was my note, after all, and it would be *my* secret to
have and to hold for as long as I wanted.

Now, this Sunday morning as I stand at the cottage window,
I have a thought. I realize what I must do. Something important and overlooked.

"Nettie!"

She doesn't answer. I open my bedroom door and call her
again. More insistently this time. Finally, she trudges up the
stair and stands in my doorway with her eyes cast down. Still
upset with me, she refuses to make eye contact.

"I need your assistance and discretion."

My maid inhales into the snug fit of her work skirt. Normally, the suggestion of a clandestine escapade would ignite a
mischievous light in her eyes. At this moment, she barely covers
her ire. I ask, "Have you packed all the Sunday outfits?"

"I set out the pleated pla—"

"For *you*, I mean."

"Me?"

"We are going to church."

"Church?" Nettie's eyes now register surprise. At last, she looks at me. Very nearly, she scoffs. Though my family attends Father's church in the city—Pittsburgh's finest Presbyterian— summer at the club is a time to reflect in *nature*. Such is Father's decree. There's no church on the club grounds, of course. Not even a chapel. And no one would dream of venturing downtown. A few of the more devout members leave early on Sunday to make it home in time for the late service, but most agree that God would grant them the dispensation of two weeks to pray under his powder-blue sky. Certainly, it's a bit scandalous that the Haberlin family spends *all* summer here without attending an official church, but Mother silences naysayers by stating matter-of-factly, "Where is God if not in the glory of trees?"

Mother attends Father's church for appearance's sake, anyway. It's an ill-kept secret that Mother refused to formally abandon her own faith in exchange for Father's. She agreed to attend Sunday service. That's all. Within the privacy of our home, Friday night's Sabbath is sacred. And Mother often spends Saturday morning at her synagogue.

Also, Father treats the entire clergy of our church in Pittsburgh without compensation. Everything from gout to influenza. No one would dare proclaim that we are not the holiest of families.

"Leave the rest of the packing until later," I tell Nettie. "Get yourself dressed in the best you've brought with you."

"But, why—?"

"No questions," I say brusquely. I am a Haberlin. No need

to explain to the maid. "We're heading to the stable to arrange for a ride into town."

At the mention of the club's stable and—no doubt—thoughts of seeing her paramour one more time, Nettie at last looks excited. Though she doesn't know it, her expression befits the adventure upon which we are about to embark. As does mine. My eyes sparkle like two firecrackers.

"Right away, miss!" she says. And off she scampers down the stairs.

THE SUN IS high and white. Wearing my very favorite day dress and matching hat, I descend the cottage stairs to the front parlor. The cerulean shade of my subtly ruffled underskirt is the perfect complement to the lighter-hued bodice, its three-quarter sleeves allowing full view of grandmother's diamond bracelet. The silk African violets lining the rim on my bonnet offset my pale skin. If I may be so brazen as to think such a thought, I am a vision.

Nettie joins me at the door. She has refashioned her hair to tame the rust-colored curls that tend to pop out like old bedsprings. Her work apron is off; she wears her very best black cotton. Poor soul, it's not her station to wear vibrant color. A practical advantage, I should think, since dyed silks are so difficult to keep clean.

"Wherever are you going?" Mother asks, alarmed, when she spots us in the foyer.

I am prepared.

"Oh, Mother." I attempt to summon a glistening in my eyes.

"This morning as I dressed, Nettie and I discussed how very awful we both feel at my folly on the lake."

Nettie quickly glances at me. With no change in my contrite expression, I push on. "For me, at least," I say, "I suspect my head has been filled with the trifles of summer instead of my duty to set a proper example for poor, dear girls like Ivy Tottinger."

Noting a trace of suspicion creep into Mother's facial expression, I hurriedly add, "So I have asked Nettie to pray with me."

"*Pray?*"

"We both feel in need of divine guidance."

Mother cocks her head.

"Nettie tells me of a church service in town that is most inspirational. She came across it several days ago when I gave her the afternoon off."

"Town?" Mother's eyes become as round as tea tarts.

Johnstown is a murky mystery to us at the club. With the exception of the late Mr. Morrell, who actually *lived* there, South Fork club members typically regard the town below us as a smoky working-class enclave that we pass by with little thought on our way up the hill from the train station. Johnstown has nothing to do with our way of life. Some of its citizens are employed in service to the club, of course, but our interaction with them is barely more than a nod and a polite "thank you" when they serve our meals or tether our skiffs. We have all we need at the club. Who wants to venture off our beautiful mountain into a choking shantytown built around a belching steel mill?

"If there were any house of God *here,* of course, we would not need to venture elsewhere."

With a visible lift of her brow, Mother darts a look in my direction. Though she would never admit it in front of my maid—or to anyone at the club—I know that our lack of formal worship all summer irks her. In spite of her public protests to the contrary.

"What about packing for our departure tomorrow?" she asks.

"Nettie has finished," I lie.

"How do you propose to get downtown?"

"One of the stable boys will escort us down the mountain in a carriage and wait for us in front of the church," I say. "We will be gone for two hours at most."

Sensing an oncoming challenge, I augment my statement with: "Time enough for me to repent and properly reflect upon my carelessness."

Standing behind me, Nettie nods ruefully. Her hands are clasped in a penitent manner just above her waist. Admittedly, I am impressed.

"Mother, *please.* I am no longer a child. Am I not free to commune with my own God?"

The alarm on her face is clear. Why, it seems as if that very moment she notes that I have grown into a woman. It is a struggle to contain my exhilaration. Yet, I do. For I am a woman now.

"You'll be back by supper?" Mother's hand rests lightly on her throat.

"Of course."

She pauses, then relents. How could she say no to God himself?

"Take care of yourselves," she says, before turning to join Father in the front parlor. He has no patients today. His examining room at the back of the cottage has already been locked up. Nettie and I don't wait for Mother to rethink her permission. Together, we hurry outside to the boardwalk leading to the club's stable. As soon as we are beyond overhearing, Nettie asks, "Why are we really going to church?"

I erupt in giggles. "Church? Hardly. We are on a much more Christian mission. I intend to find the man who very possibly saved two lives."

# ❧❦ CHAPTER 33 ❦❧

JOHNSTOWN, PENNSYLVANIA

*Summer 1888*

The carriage ride across the dam is as thrilling—and terrifying—as ever. I don't dare look down into the abyss. But once we are on the other side, I settle in for a lovely ride. The mountain road that winds downhill into the Johnstown valley is shaded by the overhang of trees bursting in green. An aroma of mud and horse fills me with a sensation of wildness.

*Seven, eight, nine.* As is my inclination, I count each tree trunk as we clip-clop past it. *Ten, eleven, twelve.*

Once we are out of sight of all club members, Nettie tucks her chin and bashfully asks me, "Might I ride up front with the driver?" She is no longer cross with me. As good fortune would have it, her beau, Floyd, was on duty at the stable. He leaped at the chance to escort us into town.

"Of course," I say, feeling very mature and magnanimous. Perhaps it's actually true: I have entered womanhood. Today, out on my own, I feel extremely grown-up.

"This outing is as much for you as me," I say, graciously. "Enjoy your time together."

Floyd pulls the carriage over to the side of the road and Nettie scrambles up to his perch. I note the subtle way she nestles herself next to him and wonder if their relationship is more advanced than I thought.

In his midtwenties, as is Nettie, Floyd has the roughhewn handsomeness of a workingman who's spent his youth outdoors. A thatch of hay-colored hair prongs out from his worn wool cap; his tanned hands are tipped with ridged fingernails. The cuticles are thick and craggy yellow. Squat and sturdy, Floyd appears as though his meals are built around biscuits. Breakfast begins with biscuits and gravy, lunch is a hardy

supply of biscuits with slabs of ham, supper is stew with halved
biscuits lining the bottom of the bowl. Perhaps this is how
he met Nettie. Ida's buttery sour-milk biscuits are legendary
around Upper St. Clair. When Father doesn't devour them—a
rarity—I've seen her offer day-old batches to needy families
sent to Father for charity medical treatment. It is certainly possible she gave Nettie some old biscuits to distribute to workers
at the club during summer.

*Does Floyd think Nettie can cook like Ida? Dear me.*

Such are my mindless musings on this most pleasant summer
Sunday.

On the way down the hill, with the carriage gently rocking
me side to side, I am surprised to see several plumes of white
smoke spiraling into the sky. "The mills are active on Sunday?"
I ask Floyd.

"Yes, miss," he says over his shoulder. "They run twenty-
fours hours a day, seven days a week."

"But what about rest? Family time? Worship?"

"Most millworkers pull a six-day week, ten to twelve hours a
day, unless it's a long turn."

"Long turn?"

"Full Sunday into Monday shift."

"Goodness," I say. "I had no idea."

"The blast furnaces are too hot to shut down and reheat. So
the bosses run them nonstop. Besides, the whole country needs
the rails and barbed wire we make. They buy 'em as fast as we
can make 'em."

It doesn't escape my notice that Floyd uses the pronoun "we" even though he works all summer in the club's stable, not at Cambria Iron or the Gautier mill in Woodvale. I also hear satisfaction in his voice in spite of a millworker's grueling hours. Apparently, in the Johnstown valley, everyone feels proudly connected to the mills.

All of a sudden the smell of raw meat left too long outside the icebox rises into my nose. I try not to look obvious as I cover the bottom half of my face with my gloved hand.

"Burning sulfur and oil," Floyd states, without even looking at me. "Oil is used to grease the machinery and the rails."

"Ah," I say. Nettie turns and offers a clean handkerchief from her pocket. It's extremely kind of her, yet I refuse it. I have my own fresh square of embroidered cotton in my purse, but I won't use that either. As soon as we enter Johnstown it will be clear enough by my silk dress that I am an outsider. I won't offend these hardworking people with a rude announcement of my delicate sense of smell. Besides, as we near the outskirts of town, the smell oddly grows both more intense and more bearable. Soon enough, I can't smell it at all, though the air is as dense as fog.

Just before the final bend in the road into town, I brace myself for what I am about to see: coal-stained immigrant faces, tattered clothes, filthy bare feet, urchin children running as wild as mongrels in the streets. Of course, Mr. Eggar was clean and well nourished when I first met him in the woods, but he is surely an anomaly. Though I have never actually set foot in Johnstown—only seen it smoking in the distance from the South Fork train station—my long-held vision is akin to an anteroom in the underworld. Dark, ominous, packed with foul-smelling wretches. Silently, I applaud my bravery and charity for even attempting to plumb such depths.

"Oh."

Immediately I am startled by the number of church steeples. I count six as we cross over the Stonycreek River that flows through downtown. Beautiful limestone churches are under the Gothic steeples, with pointed arches and leaded windows. Dare I say it, they are houses of worship befitting the best of families.

In town, the streets are paved in cobblestone. Goodness, there are pedestrian sidewalks. I had expected hard-packed dirt. I am stunned to see respectable two-story homes lining the wide thoroughfares. Gable pediments adorn the windows like perfectly arched brows. We pass a school—a real *school,* not a ramshackle schoolhouse—a hardware store, a grocer with his wares so abundant they spill out on display racks on the sidewalk. There is even an imposing library made of brick. I am speechless.

"Our biggest meeting hall is down there," Floyd says, pointing. "And our dry-goods store, plus a tavern with billiards and music."

Floyd clearly has no desire to drop me off anywhere. Instead, he steers the carriage around the vibrant downtown to show me—and Nettie—the distinctions of his home city. At ground level in the valley, the gray air is above us. While I cannot claim that Johnstown is anywhere near as lovely as Upper St. Clair—I do spot plain company homes in the distance near the mill's riverbank—it's nothing like I imagined. Mature elm trees line the side streets. *Fourteen, fifteen, sixteen* . . . too many to properly count. A railroad track runs along one of the two rivers that encircle this compact enclave tucked into the bottom of the Allegheny Valley. The mountains on every side of us are as imposing as they are lush with summer vegetation. In their shadow, one can't help but feel small. When I look back toward the South Fork Fishing and Hunting Club, I now see what Mr. Eggar was referencing when he said he saw our sailboats crisscross among the clouds. Our magnificent lake is practically overhead. What curious geography. A lake in the *sky*.

Strolling women are dressed almost as well as I am. They hold the hands of their little girls in blouse dresses and bonnets, their boys in Sunday knickerbocker suits. True, many of the pedestrians resemble Nettie with their aprons over their plain black skirts, or men with worsted vests over rolled shirtsleeves, but no one is gaunt and stained by sulfer residue. On Main Street, I see an opera house! I am dumbfounded. Johnstown is a *real* town that functions as such. What made me think everyone worked in the mill? There is so much more here. I see a clothing store that sells everything from boots to hats. And, softly, at first, I hear—

"Is that a . . . *drum*?" I ask Floyd.

He grins. "Probably the Hunkie marching band practicing for the Independence Day parade down Main Street."

"Hunkie?" I have overheard men at the club use the term before, but don't know what it means.

"Hungarians. Johnstown is filled with working people from all over. Hunkies, Germans, Irish, Welsh. And they all have their own bands and their own social clubs. Just like yours, miss."

My cheeks redden. How arrogant of us at South Fork to assume that *we* are the only sophisticates in the area.

"Over there is the police department," Floyd continues, "behind there is the town jail. The Quicksteps play baseball on the field yonder."

"Johnstown has its own *baseball* team?" Again, I am astonished to the point of staring, agog.

"We may be from everywhere, miss, but we are as American as steel. Our team lost to McKeesport—a heartbreak, to be sure—but we trounced Altoona. What a game that was. Rumor has it our pitcher is headed to the majors. His knuckleball rivals Toad Ramsey's, and his speed is—"

Nettie touches Floyd's thigh in the same wifely way I've seen Mother tap Father's knee when a third glass of amber liquid fills him with bluster. I feel a surge of heartbreak. Am I to lose my maid to love? Joy for her; sadness for me. Breaking in someone new is always so tedious.

"Over there is our new train station. And way down by the river, near the mill, is the company hospital." Floyd continues his tour. "Most of the newer houses have indoor plumbing."

My cheeks again flush. Though our cottage has indoor plumbing, the clubhouse does not. How many times have I heard Mr. Unger boast about the innovation of the club's two-story outhouse? As if the club had, quite literally, the *height* in modern privies. Only recently was the clubhouse itself wired for electricity. The main carriageways of Johnstown, I see, are dotted with streetlamps as large as those in Pittsburgh. I am humbled to view myself through the lens of reality instead of the blurred vision of privilege.

Floyd steers our carriage past the lovely Lutheran church where, he tells us, the Harmonie Singing Society meets, past beautiful Turner Hall, where the Germania Quartette sharpens their choral arrangements. In the very center of town, we pass a park with a starfish-shaped pathway in the grass. All points lead to the central fountain with its gurgling water tumbling over a watchful sentry of swans. It's the ideal place to wile away an afternoon, as many residents now do.

"I had no idea there was such a thriving town here," I say, almost to myself.

Perhaps impertinently, Floyd replies, "South Fork Club members live in their *own* world."

I can't fault him for such a statement because it's absolutely true. By design, our club is a refuge from the cares and woes of modern life. I have heard it often: on the shores of Lake Conemaugh, one feels alone in the splendor of nature. With society, of course.

Thank goodness I have ventured out on my own. Beyond the shelter of my upbringing. It's so very educational.

"Excuse me, Floyd, do you know how I might find a specific person who lives in Johnstown?"

"I've lived here all my life. I know almost everyone. Do you have a name?"

"Yes. Eggar. Mr. Eugene Eggar."

He pulls back on the reins to stop the horse. Twisting around to face me, he says, "I know the family well. They live on Washington Street."

"Splendid. Will you be so kind as to take me there?"

Hesitation briefly darkens Floyd's face like the first thunderclap in an oncoming storm. I meet his gaze with calm—and silent—reserve. I owe him no explanation. Nor am I inclined to offer one. Again Nettie rests the palm of her hand on his leg like a fallen feather. Floyd darts a glance her way, she nods almost unperceptively, and away we go.

## ·›❦‹ CHAPTER 34 ›❦‹·

JOHNSTOWN, PENNSYLVANIA

*Courtesy of the Johnstown Flood Museum Archives, Johnstown Area Heritage Association*

*Summer 1888*

The Eggar home is one in a tidy line of well-kept clapboard colonials. Two stories high, its façade is similar to that of its neighbors. The exterior is painted the palest of yellow. Three multipaned windows sit in a row on the second floor; two windows and a door define the simple ground-floor design. Each window is shuttered in glossy black. It is a perfectly serviceable, perfectly lovely home. On my request, Floyd and Nettie wait in the carriage while I approach the front door and knock.

"Yes?" A woman of Mother's age opens the door and dries her hands on her apron. She is plain of face, though not at all unpleasantly. Her cheeks are plump and bronzed by the sun. The slight downturn to her narrow lips is balanced by the bounce of dark curls pinned atop her head. It is clear she is Eugene Eggar's mother; they have the same midnight hazel eyes.

As it's my first time visiting on my own, I am careful to maintain the maturity of my mother. She would never forgive me if I sullied the Haberlin name with the frivolity of youth.

"Please forgive my intrusion," I begin, swallowing my nervousness. "I'm looking for Mr. Eugene Eggar. Might he reside here?"

She cocks her head and looks puzzled. I quickly add, "Allow me to introduce myself. I'm Elizabeth Haberlin of Pittsburgh. My family summers at the South Fork Club. I've come to thank Mr. Egga—"

"Miss Haberlin! Yes. My son told me about you."

Admittedly, I am flattered, though I try to contain my smile.

"What a delightful surprise. Please come in. Eugene is at the stable. I'll send my husband for him."

"I couldn't possibly interrupt your family's Sunda—"

"Interrupt? Nonsense. We would be honored to have you and your companions join us for lunch."

She steps back to usher me inside.

"Forgive me, Mrs. Eggar—you are Mr. Eggar's mother, is that so?"

"I am."

"Your offer of lunch is terribly kind, but I must get back up the mountain soon. My own mother is waiting for me."

At the mention of another mother, she nods knowingly. "Certainly you'll have time for tea?"

To refuse would be rude, indeed. And I think, *Tea downtown? What an adventure.* I want to leap through the door. But I contain myself. "That would be lovely," I say with impeccable propriety. "If it's no . . . imposition."

My brain searches for words Mother might use.

"No imposition at all. Do come in. And invite your companions inside as well."

I turn to see Nettie and Floyd staring expectantly. "Mrs. Eggar has kindly invited us for tea," I call out. "Nettie, will you please bring my box?"

She clambers down from the perch. Floyd searches for a post upon which to secure the horse and carriage. I don't wait for them. Instead, I follow Eugene Eggar's mother into his family's home.

The parlor to the right of the front entrance is clean, but simply furnished. A settee in front of the window is large enough for two. Its faded herringbone upholstery is a testament to frequent use. Two matching chairs sit on either side of the fireplace. A club chair of worn green velvet sits opposite. On its seat is the indentation of the previous user. A pale red Oriental rug covers the wide-plank wood floor. It, too, shows signs of wear. No doubt a result of tending the fire during Pennsylvania's snowy winters and frequently dusting the family photographs that decorate the mantel.

Mrs. Eggar dashes into the parlor ahead of me to scoop up the pages of a newspaper that have fallen to the floor in tented triangles. Her ruddy cheeks show no embarrassment—nor should they, since *I* breached etiquette by brazenly knocking on her door—but the exasperation of living with messy men. An annoyance of which I'm familiar. How many times have I heard Mother exclaim, "Must you leave a trail of clutter everywhere you go, Stafford? Don't the maids have enough to do?"

Clearly, the Eggars' parlor is a functional hub of family life. A pair of men's slippers sits at the foot of the club chair. Two crusts of bread and a sprinkle of crumbs are forgotten on a small plate beside it. A tiny pool of milk coffee stains the interior of a teacup. As she scurries past them, Mrs. Eggar slides the slippers beneath the chair with her feet and gathers the dirty dishes. She wears a working dress: black, cotton, basic. Her curly hair, I note, was hastily pinned up herself that morning. In the bright sunlight that illuminates the Eggars' frayed parlor, I feel foolish in my blue frippery. What possessed me to wear robin's-egg-blue satin gloves? Without fanfare, I yank them off my hands.

"Please. Sit." Holding a jumble of newspaper pages in the crook of one elbow, and the used dishes in her hands, Mrs. Eggar tilts her head as if to invite me to select any seat. I turn to find Nettie in the doorway. She holds a ribbon-tied box I have brought from our cottage.

"My family's cook makes the most scrumptious biscuits." I

take the box from my maid and give her my gloves. "Made fresh this morning."

Thank goodness I remembered to circle back and sneak through the back door of our kitchen to ask Ida for her extra biscuits. Otherwise, I would have arrived empty-handed. If Mother ever caught wind of that, she would never forgive such an etiquette blunder.

I want to present the box to Eugene's mother, but she hasn't a free hand. Plus, she seems flustered, as if unsure what my gift might require of her. I hastily add, "We are unexpectedly returning to Pittsburgh on the early train tomorrow. Ida will be pleased to know that her biscuits are being enjoyed."

Deliberately, I refuse to meet Floyd's gaze in case he has the ill manners to protest, "What about me?"

"Why, thank you, Miss Haberlin," says Mrs. Eggar, readjusting the bits and pieces in her grip to take the box. "I'll set them out for tea."

"I've included a jar of jam made from the blackberries in our garden back in Upper St. Clair. It's in the box."

"Oh," she says, "how lovely."

A moment of awkwardness follows in which I remember my own manners. With a rapturous smile, I march into the parlor. "Your home is as warm and inviting as an afternoon at the lake!"

Mrs. Eggar curves her lips up. My maid and driver examine their feet. I select the chair by the fireplace to avoid any discomfort over who might settle in next to me on the settee. Nettie and Floyd follow.

We sit.

I must confess: it did not occur to me until this very minute that my endeavor to thank Mr. Eggar might be a source of anxiety. While his mother scrambles into the kitchen, then upstairs to rouse her husband ("Hurry, Oscar! They are waiting!"), I notice a faint look of panic on Nettie's face. Her back is unnaturally rigid and she keeps fussing with her hair. Floyd, next to her on the settee, leans forward with his elbows on his knees. He holds his cap in his hands and twists it as if wringing water.

"Such a lovely room." I attempt to ease the tension that has suddenly descended like a coating of coal ash. Then I scan my brain. What else would Mother say?

"Yes, miss," Nettie replies. Her hand reaches up again to tidy her hair. My satin gloves are rolled into a robin's-egg-blue coil in her lap. Overhead, we hear the thunk, thunk of heavy boots. Then the swishing of a petticoat down the stairs.

My brain is suddenly a jumble of fluff. Until this very moment I hadn't realized how utterly full of poppycock it is. Cotillion gowns and satin shoes. Did I ever talk to Nettie about *her* life, apart from mine? Does she dream of living in a home such as this?

"Have you a residence nearby?" I ask Floyd, with a slight stammer.

His eyes briefly cast downward before he replies, "My family lives on Franklin Street. Close to downtown."

"How very convenient."

"Yes, miss."

"Do you travel to Pittsburgh much?"

"No, miss."

"I suppose you have all that you need right here."

He nods. Now I feel panic rising. So chatty in the carriage, Floyd is now nearly mute. Nettie looks ready to leap for the door. Silence passes like the tick-tock of a clock.

"I imagine you secure employment in Johnstown during the club's off-season?" I prod, nervously.

"Yes, miss. I work at the mill."

"Dear me, I hope you don't work the long turn."

He smiles. Relief floods my being. Floyd says, "Sometimes I do, miss. Sometimes I do."

We have, at last, connected. My confidence is buoyed.

Suddenly a girl about Ivy Tottinger's age appears in the parlor holding a tray with teacups and saucers on it. She has Mrs. Eggar's tight curls and her fullness of cheek. With great concentration, she lowers the tray onto a small round table to the side of the settee. The porcelain teacups clatter with the vibration of her nerves.

"Goodness," I say, "you must be Mr. Eggar's sister. I see the resemblance in your face."

"I am, miss," she says, blushing to near purple.

"Please forgive my ghastly manners at showing up unannounced. I hadn't intended to cause such a stir."

The girl stands with the look of a possum upon her face. Her hands grip one another at the front of her blue striped skirt. My area of expertise, I say brightly, "What a fetching frock. Blue is my favorite color. Yours, too?"

Before she can answer, her mother bustles in with a plate piled high with Ida's biscuits—I count nearly a dozen—our homemade jam, a butter bell, and a pot of tea covered in a hand-knit cozy. Its top is a round bauble of red yarn.

"The water was already hot," she says. "As luck would have it."

"Lovely," I reply. Floyd eyes the biscuits lustily as I say, "Is there anything Nettie can do to help you?"

As if awakened from a hypnotist's trance, Nettie's head pops up. "Certainly!" She jumps to her feet.

"Sit. Sit. You are *all* our guests."

At Mrs. Eggar's urging, Nettie lowers herself to the settee and reaches a hand up to tame her hair. Mrs. Eggar says, "Elsie, you come with me."

"Elsie," I say, "it's a pleasure to make your acquaintance."

In all the commotion, we were never properly introduced. No one seems to notice as Elsie curtsies clumsily and scuttles out of the parlor in her mother's wake. Never before have I been so keenly aware how handy it is to have help. The teacups sit unfilled. Are we to reach over and grab a biscuit ourselves? With our bare hands? Floyd does exactly that.

"Mmmm," he moans, nearly devouring half a biscuit in one bite. Nettie glances at me with a stricken expression.

"Biscuit?" I say to her, sweeping my open hand in the air as if to free all permission.

She asks, "Might I prepare one for you, Miss Elizabeth?"

Before I can reply in the negative, the front door opens and a billow of warm air wafts into the parlor. All heads turn to see Mr. Eugene Eggar walk into the room ahead of his father. Momentarily, I am struck dumb. Perhaps it's due to the low ceiling, but the younger Mr. Eggar appears considerably larger than I remember. His shirt is unbuttoned to the chest and his vest is unsecured entirely. Both show evidence of perspiration and the fine, damp dirt of a stable floor. Obviously, he'd been hard at work. The horsey aroma that precedes him is not at all unpleasant. I feel heat rise to my cheeks.

"Miss Haberlin?" He pulls his cap off, as does his father behind him. "Are you all right?"

The elder Mr. Eggar—his former handsomeness camouflaged beneath deep crevices in both cheeks—appears to have a problem with his leg. Even standing still, he leans noticeably to the left.

"Splendid." My voice is an unnaturally high octave. I swallow and take a controlling breath to regain my composure. "Forgive this imposition, Mr. Eggar, but the other day you disappeared before I could properly thank you. My family is returning to Pittsburgh tomorrow, so I wanted to tell you how very much I appreciated your help at the lake."

As I speak I feel the weight of my ridiculous hat. Silk African violets? With fluted viridian leaves? What had possessed me? And why hadn't I removed it instantly when it became clear that no one else wore a hat? Even Nettie left her bonnet in the carriage.

"Quite unnecessary," Mr. Eggar says. "But a pleasant surprise for all of us. You've met Mother and Elsie?"

"Yes. They have been lovely."

"This is my father, Oscar."

I stand as Oscar Eggar proudly limps toward me. Extending my hand, I feel the calluses in his grip as he shakes it with suitable firmness and tempo. This is not a man unfamiliar with the ways of proper society. He says, "Welcome to my home." His green eyes reflect kindness and knowing. Instantly, I feel his confidence. He wears it as easily as one might swing a cape over one's shoulders on a chilly night.

"It's clear, sir, where your son gets his graciousness. Your entire family has made us feel utterly comfortable."

Silently, I congratulate *myself* for the maturity of my remark. It's exactly what Mother would say whether she believed it to be true or not.

Oscar Eggar smiles and glances beyond me to Nettie and Floyd, still perched on the settee. Goodness, am I to formally introduce my maid and driver? I turn to see that I was correct in my assumption about Floyd's diet. He now swallows the final bite of his second biscuit.

Nettie, sweet Nettie, comes to my aid as she has so many times before. Standing, she inspires Floyd to rise to his feet as well. I note the bobbing of his Adam's apple as the chewed dough makes its way down his throat. Both step toward Mr. Eggar with hands outstretched. Nettie bows slightly as she says, "I believe you already know Mr. Capelli. Permit me to introduce myself. I'm Nettie MacAuley."

"Hello, Floyd," Mr. Eggar says. "It's a pleasure, Miss MacAuley."

"Oscar," Floyd says, looking as though he'd like to leave.

Eugene steps forward to shake Nettie's hand. Like his father, he addresses Floyd by his first name. "How are you this fine afternoon, Floyd?"

Obviously, there is something amiss between the two men, but I have no idea what it is. Saving us all from discomfort, Mrs. Eggar flutters in with another tray bearing an opened tin of corned beef. I feel both honored and embarrassed that she has served such a delicacy. Surely they were saving the corned beef for a special occasion.

"You two wash up," she says to her husband and son. "Miss Haberlin, please sit and let me pour you a cup of tea."

Without further fuss, the men disappear and I return to the chair next to the fireplace. But not before I reach up and remove my blue, blue, blue hat.

ONCE WE SETTLE in, tea at the Eggar home could not be more enjoyable. After the initial disturbance of my unannounced arrival dissipates, the most amiable conversation I've had all summer effervesces like bubbles of champagne.

"The sight of two women bobbing along in the skiff was quite hilarious," Eugene Eggar says, beaming. "Mady and I watched them attempt to come ashore with great amusement."

"And yet you remained in your hiding place," I parry back.

"What else could I do? You had to get close enough for me to help you. It would have done you no good to see me and be too fearful to row onward."

"True enough. I would have paddled right back into the center of the lake!" My cheeks are aflush with laughter. I imagine they are the shade of a Persian rose. A fact that pleases me, since my skin can appear so pale.

"Another biscuit, Floyd?" Mrs. Eggar asks.

Brazenly, Eugene quips, "That would make it half a dozen."

Everyone laughs heartily. Even Floyd. *Especially* Floyd. Whatever had been awry between the club's stable boy and the Eggar family is now buried beneath an avalanche of good cheer.

"Your son told me that you work in the mill, Mr. Eggar." I turn my attention to the patriarch of the family. He has been sitting quietly—though attentively—in the club chair in the far corner of the room. *His* chair, quite obviously, with his slippers stashed beneath.

"Worked. I was a puddler."

"The *best* puddler at Cambria Iron," Eugene adds with obvious pride.

"Please forgive my ignorance, sir. Does a puddler make train rails?"

A brief shadow veils Mr. Eggar's eyes. "We were once the backbone of the mill." He uses his hand to reposition his left leg. "A puddler works—*worked*—the furnace. We heated the pig iron to molten metal, stirring it over and over in the fire until the carbon burned off. Only the most experienced puddlers could make steel. If you didn't get it just right, the steel was no good. It went brittle."

He falls silent. Outside, metal wheels of a wagon are audible as they roll over cobblestone. I also hear horses chuffing and children squealing as they trundle hoops in the street. Elsie Eggar sees me notice her longing glance toward the window and smiles shyly.

"I was replaced by a machine," Mr. Eggar says, quietly, "but not before—"

He stops. He runs his left hand over his thigh.

"My husband had an accident at the mill, Miss Haberlin. A spit of fire from the open furnace ignited his trousers. Before they could extinguish it, his leg was badly burned."

"Dear me," I gasp, my hand to my chest.

"That *mill*," says Mrs. Eggar, her jaw tight.

"That mill fed this family." Mr. Eggar's tone silences his wife. "It put a roof over our heads. The mill hospital saved my life. There will be no blaming the mill. I knew the dangers of the job."

I reach for my teacup, lift it to my lips, and take a sip. Around me, all do the same.

"It's safer now," Eugene says, softly. "The only accidents we have in the blacksmith shop are unplanned children."

"Eugene!"

His father and Floyd laugh. Elsie and Nettie blush. Eugene grins at me.

"Miss Haberlin is tougher than you think, Mother. How else could she row clear across a lake?"

"Indeed," I say. Surprisingly, I am undisturbed by Eugene Eggar's indelicate remark. His comfortable home, his proud family, his sweet sister, his gracious mother all conspire to show me how sheltered I'd been. Beyond the pretense of "roughing it" in our pristine mountain retreat, free from the restraints of Pittsburgh society, apart from all that is expected and required of a girl born into the Haberlin family, I now see a glimpse of the real world.

*Now that my eyes have been opened,* I say to myself on that warm summer Sunday in the cozy parlor of the Eggar family home, *they will never again be closed.*

# ···❦[ CHAPTER 35 ]❦···

NORTH BEVERLY PARK

*Present*

Lee had been downtown twice. Once at the Department of Social Services to uncover who she really was; this second time to find out what that really meant. With the late-morning sun still high in the sky, she drove west on Sunset Boulevard to the San Diego Freeway, taking in the brown scenery along the way. If it didn't rain soon, Los Angeles would turn to dust.

The low, wide white building sat squarely in a crispy yellow field. On its face was a familiar symbol: the crimson "plus sign" of the American Red Cross. As Lee pushed through the glass doors into the lobby, she felt her blood pumping throughout her body.

"Um, hi," she said to the receptionist. Sitting at a utilitarian desk in the sun-flooded lobby, the receptionist looked up and smiled. Her expectant expression caused Lee's face to flush. Suddenly she was tongue-tied. Instead of mooning over York in the car on the way downtown, why hadn't she figured out what she was going to say?

"I'm Lee Parker," she spluttered. Then she swallowed and dove in. "I'm trying to identify a woman in an old photograph with Clara Barton. The photo was taken in 1889." She cleared her throat. "The woman with Clara Barton is, um, my great-great-great-grandmother. I mean, I think so. That's what I'm trying to find out. See, I'm adopted—"

Lee stopped herself from blathering by biting the inside of her lip.

"Okay," the receptionist said, stretching the vowel. *Okaaaaay.* "I'll show your photo to my boss."

Something between a cough and a nervous laugh escaped Lee's throat. "Funny thing is," she said, "I don't actually have the photo. Before I was able to take a picture of it with my phone, it was taken away."

"*Okaaaaay.*" The receptionist's brow creased in a furrow of confusion.

"Of course, I've *seen* it," Lee added, quickly. "It *exists.* I just don't have it in my, you know, physical possession. It's up here."

She tapped her forehead. Her face grew redder.

"Have a seat." The girl behind the desk swept her open palm to the waiting area as if she were a model at a car show. Lee swiveled on her heels and trudged across the gleaming travertine floor, berating herself for being such a troll. Perhaps she should have come later in the day, when her brain was operating on all cylinders.

"Miss Parker?"

After a few minutes, a young woman about Lee's age appeared next to the armless settee where Lee sat, slumped. The girl looked like she was nice. Orange freckles, black-rimmed glasses, a tranquil smile, biggish ears. Hers was the type of open face that could comfort a person in the throes of a disaster. She wore an ironed white shirt, navy-blue pants, and a red suit-type jacket that sagged slightly in the shoulders. *Uniform?* Lee wondered. She stood up.

"I'm Hannah." The girl extended her hand. "Please have a seat."

Feeling a little silly, Lee shook her peer's hand. It was doubtful that Hannah was over twenty. Her knuckles were dimpled. She had clear polish and fingernails filed into perfectly rounded peaks. Like Lee's, her long hair was profuse. Only Hannah's mane was reddish brown and pulled into a tight, high pony, secured with a red rubber band. Her black leather loafers were as shiny as her glossed lips.

Lee sat. Hannah pulled up a chair next to the settee.

"I'm an intern here," she said. "How can I help?"

Gulping a mouthful of air, Lee exhaled the whole story. "Here's the thing," she began. In a flood of words, she spilled all. Bathed in the radiance of Hannah's warmhearted gaze, she ceased to care if she sounded dopey or inexact. Wasn't life full of muddy emotions?

" . . . so then my computer crashed . . . share a car with my mom . . ."

Out it all flowed. Something about the way Hannah perched on the edge of her chair, both hands on her lap, fingers entwined, inspired Lee to talk until she had nothing more to say.

" . . . didn't think I would find anything . . . felt so hope-less . . ."

"Ah. Ooh." Hannah responded in all the right places.

"No way would I ever hurt my mom." Lee heard her voice waver. "It's not her fault that I need to know where I came from."

Hannah whispered, "My best friend is adopted. She feels the same way."

"I thought I was okay with everything. You know, with *not* knowing. My family is my family. For better and worse. But when I saw the photograph in the adoption file—" Another deep breath. "It became so *real*. A living, breathing ancestor. An actual relative of the woman who carried me inside her for nine months. She had a life, a family. A *history.* Unlike mine that pretty much starts with me. The moment I saw the woman in that photo—my *blood*—I realized how much I'd needed to know all along. It was here—" Lee pressed the tips of her fingers onto her chest. "Buried, but always inside me."

Hannah bobbed her head and pressed her lips together. Lee added, "I was finally able to trace the photo back to Johnstown, Pennsylvania. Around Memorial Day, 1889."

"Oh."

"You know about what happened there?"

"A little."

"My God, when I think about those poor people . . ."

Nodding, Hannah sighed. They both paused to imagine the unimaginable.

"For some reason," Lee said, "my great-great-great-grandmother stood with Clara Barton in the aftermath of the Johnstown nightmare. A photo was taken of the two of them. Standing in rubble. I'm hoping to find it. Maybe identify the woman in it?"

"Ah." Again, Hannah nodded. With her serene smile affixed to her face, she released an audible outbreath. Then she reached out and rested her palm on the back of Lee Parker's hand. She gave it a one-two pat. Lee crumpled. A hand pat was never a good sign. It's what veterinarians did before they told you your dog didn't make it. It's what Gil did before he ripped the future out from under his daughter's feet. Bracing herself to hear, "Gee, Miss Parker, I wish there was something I could do," Lee let her chin dip down to her chest.

"Do you have time today?" Hannah asked.

*Time?* Lee lifted her head, momentarily confused. *Today?*

"Clara Barton was somewhat of a pack rat for documents and photos. There's an archive of her diary and letters in Washington, D.C. Memorabilia, too. Cool drawings and stuff. It's all in the Library of Congress. If you have time, I can do an archive search of her collection. We have access to some of the documents that the general public doesn't."

"Wait. What? Today? Yes I have time. All day. I've been waiting eighteen years. Wow! Great! Thank you!" Lee felt like Valerie. The maven of exclamation points.

Hannah laughed and stood up. With her eyebrows arched up to her hairline, she said, conspiratorially, "Who doesn't love a good mystery?"

# ·∘I CHAPTER 36 I∘·

SOUTH FORK FISHING AND HUNTING CLUB

*Memorial Day*
*May 30, 1889*

*10:43 P.M.*

The sun set hours ago amid rain that intensified with each passing hour. When we arrived at the train station earlier, and made our way to the cottage, I noticed some bursts of sunlight through the gray clouds. I felt a flicker of hope that the heavens would tire of pelting Lake Conemaugh with its tears. No such luck.

Inside the cottage, Nettie and Ella lit every fireplace to dry the dampness and warm the chill. Maggie prepared a pot of Purée Mongole with the turnips, leeks, and peas she brought with her on the train. While we ate supper, no one spoke as we all listened to the rain hammer the cottage roof.

Suddenly there was a knock on the cottage door. Nettie hurried from the kitchen to answer it. "Excuse the interruption," we heard from the front entryway. Mother and I both left the table to see who would call on such a stormy night. Colonel Unger, the club's caretaker, stood dripping on our Oriental rug.

"Goodness, Colonel," said Mother, "you're soaked to the bone." Water streamed off his black rain slicker in rivulets.

"Forgive me, Mrs. Haberlin."

"Nettie," Mother said, "please help Mr. Unger with his coat."

As my maid stepped forward, Colonel Unger raised his hand. "I can't stay. I've come by only to make sure your family is okay."

"Why, yes. Fine, fine," Mother trilled, smiling falsely as if to convince herself. "Warm and dry."

"Good." He turned to leave, then paused. "If anything should happen—"

"Like what?" I asked. Mother glared at me for my want of manners. Yet I didn't back down. I remembered Eugene Eggar's words the day we first met in the woods: "Your lake will one day be a murderer."

Colonel Unger's gaze, I noted, darted about the room. Everywhere but into my eyes or Mother's. Henry suddenly appeared from around the balustrade. "It's raining cats and dogs!"

"That it is, son."

"What might happen, sir?" I took a decisive step toward him.

"A roof leak, high water, thunder strike, *anything*." He turned and reached for the doorknob, his head down. "Please stay put. I am aware that you are here alone. Don't worry. You are safe. I'll come for you as soon as I can if anything—Just a precaution, Miss Haberlin. I'm sure you'll be fine. We all will."

With that, he pulled open the cottage door and the whooshing sound of rain filled our ears. Mother, Henry, Nettie, and I watched him disappear into the silvery darkness.

After I retired to my bedroom for the night, I couldn't sleep. Now my clock says a quarter to eleven. It's no use lying in bed listening to my heart thump as loudly as the rain on the roof. Peeling back my quilt, I get up and make my way to the window in the eerie darkness. The downpour is still so loud I hear it in my chest. When I slide the curtain aside, I see needles of rain angrily pelting our lake. The water roils and spits in the violet moonlight.

Fear swallows me up. In the corner, the clock tick-tocks. My being grows cold. "Is tonight the night?" I whisper in horror.

Will the monstrous beast that contains our lake open its mouth and release its fury onto the heads of the sleeping citizens of Johnstown? If so, what can I possibly do?

Standing at my window, staring at our churning sea of a lake, I do the only thing I am able to do: I lower my head and pray.

"Dear God, please save us all."

DAWN CREEPS INTO my bedroom as silently as a jewel thief. Perhaps I *had* slept an hour or two, for I awake beneath the covers of my bed and don't remember how I got there. It's as silent as a graveyard. In the timid light of earliest morning, the stillness makes my heart thud. Is the lake . . . our beautiful plaything . . . *gone*? Has it slipped away in the night?

A lack of breath burns my chest. With dread overtaking me, I roll back the covers and tiptoe to the window terrified of what I might see. What I might *not* see. Utter quiet engulfs the cottage. My eyelids press shut before the curtains. I force air in and out of my lungs. Inhaling to fortify myself, I reach out a hand. I grip the curtain panel. Ever so slowly, I peel it back. Then I lean forward and look. And I see it. Our lake! A flat sheet of tin glistens in the faint light. It's the most beautiful sight I have ever seen. We are saved! My breath returns. We have made it. The dam held. Johnstown, and the club, are intact.

Relief exits my chest in a giddy whistle. Mr. Ruff was right: Johnstown was in no danger from our enterprise. The worst is over. We are safe. Weak with happiness, I skip back to my bed and sleep until a deafening clap of thunder wakes me just before noon.

# ·◦❧ CHAPTER 37 ❧◦·

Courtesy of the Johnstown Flood Museum Archives, Johnstown Area Heritage Association

SOUTH FORK FISHING AND HUNTING CLUB

*May 31, 1889*

*11:58 A.M.*

D ear me. The rain has resumed. Again, it pelts our lake.
Why is God testing us? Dressed for the day, I descend the
cottage stairs for breakfast. My spirit feels weighted. Though
it is barely noon, Maggie, the undercook, has lit all the lamps.
Such darkness in daytime only magnifies my foreboding.

"'They came to the castle of a giant who had three heads,'"
Mother reads to Henry in a whispery voice. "'He trembled so
that his heads began to knock one another very hard.'"

"'Three heads, but no brains!'" *Jack the Giant Killer* is Henry's
favorite book. Though he knows all the words by heart, he never
tires of it.

"That's right, my darling," Mother coos. In her murmur of
love, I hear a sliver of apprehension. As I pass by, she looks up
at me with anxiety creases in her forehead. I smile to soothe
them, and my own.

"'He mostly stood—I know you'll laugh—about as high as
a giraffe.'" Henry eggs his mother on. In spite of our disquiet,
Mother and I both laugh. Oh, to be six years old and free of
worry!

Nettie and Mother's maid, Ella, are in the cottage basement
moving everything of value off the floor. Mother fears the lake
may rise to the height of our foundation.

"Best to be safe instead of sorry," she told them.

Maggie has baked breakfast rolls. The kitchen aroma is en-
ticing, but I can only eat one or two bites. My stomach is a
mass of knots. With a cup of hot tea, I climb the stairs to my
room. Again, I stand before the window and gaze out at the
rain. The sky is as gray as steel. What I wouldn't give to see the
color blue. Rain tap-dances upon the cottage roof. Thunder

rumbles in the distance and lightning cuts jagged scars in the overcast sky.

I do note, with a slight surge of hope, that the rainfall doesn't feel as violent as it did the night before. In spite of the addition of thunder. To be honest, I cannot tell if I was overly wrought last night or am *under*estimating the danger now. When I look out at our vast lake, I am reminded how many times we have endured rainfall during our summer stays. The dam has always held. Certainly Colonel Unger would fetch us immediately if it were about to burst. How many times have the men of the club debated the safety of the dam only to resolve to leave it as it is? It was absurd to think they would arrive at such a decision lightly.

I'm being silly. More than that, if I'm harshly truthful with myself, I must admit that I'm leaning upon my fretfulness to postpone a dreaded task.

A letter.

One that I must compose to perfection. Today. Now. Whether it is tempestuous outside or not. Though I'd very much like to, I can no longer delay it. I must write the man who has promised to escort me to the cotillion. The escort who will be the envy of every debutante at the ball.

James Tottinger.

The very thought of his name makes me uneasy.

Since Mr. Tottinger so suddenly left the club with his family last summer, he has written to me often. And I to him. Though not as often. As Mother expertly instructed me, men prefer a *chase*.

"Like hounds after a fox?" I asked, haughtily.

"Precisely."

Initially, I asked our postal carrier for discretion when he delivered the mail to our home in Upper St. Clair. After my parents so unfairly made me leave the club last summer, I was not inclined to tell Mother about the note James slipped into my hand before he left.

*I must see you again.*

Plus, I didn't feel like telling Mother about the many letters James had written to me since. At first, I thought them too vain to take seriously.

"Have you thought about me at all, Miss Haberlin? When you stroll the thoroughfares of Pittsburgh, do you imagine doing so on my arm?"

Then Mr. Tottinger's letters became increasingly ardent. In his last communication with me, he wrote, "I awoke to a cloudy London sky this morning and realized that the sun will not come out for me again until I have the pleasure of gazing into your fiery brown eyes."

Admittedly, I was impressed that he accurately noted the color of my eyes. Previously, I would have thought he looked into them merely to catch his own reflection. More letters arrived with flattering prose.

"Miss Haberlin, you are as unique as a winter rose." Splendid.

Almost without my noticing, I began to feel a . . . a . . . *stirring*. Now, after reading several clandestine letters, I confess Mr. James Tottinger has captured my fancy. And when he offered to cross the Atlantic Ocean to escort me to the debutante ball, well, I confess I felt the slightest bit *superior*. Entering the cotillion hall on the arm of dashing James Tottinger from Great Britain, a relative of Countess Augusta Reuss of Ebersdorf, grandmother of Queen Victoria herself (so they say), was every girl's dream. We would make the most fetching couple, if I may be so bold. It was in that mood that I accepted. Only then did I share the letters with Mother.

"My darling girl!" she exclaimed. "How coy you have been!"

"Before this moment, I wasn't sure I liked him."

"Not sure? Dearest, he's related to a *countess*."

From that hour until the present one, Mother has suffocated me with reminders about etiquette, dress, posture, manners. As if I'd been born in a brothel. Did she not trust that I was properly raised?

And when I quietly suggested needing a new gown, saying, sheepishly, "Nettie accidentally left my Charles Worth at the musty old *cottage*," Mother didn't hesitate.

"Of course you'll need the very latest," she said. "A trumpet skirt, I should think. We'll take a trip to New York."

Mother was alive with purpose. A successful union with the Tottinger family would elevate my family's place in society and secure our future. Which is why I've been dreading telling her the truth. I haven't heard from Mr. Tottinger in weeks. My last *two* letters have gone unanswered. At first, of course, I blamed the post. Perhaps his letter is floating in the Atlantic? But the silence following my second letter to him is more ominous. I feel it in my marrow. Something is amiss. He had plenty of time to write me before I left for the cottage. And the cotillion fast approaches. Our shopping trip to New York is scheduled for mid-June. I've begun to regret letting it slip to Francine Larkin that Mr. Tottinger was to be my escort at the ball. Most certainly she has told everyone by now. If Mr. Tottinger changes his mind, Francine will delight in inflaming my humiliation. I'll be lucky to be escorted by a stable hand.

And so, today, in the gray light of a storm that matches my own agitation, I must compose the most clement letter of my life. Its tone must reflect breezy independence, a flutter of desire and a gentle—but unmistakable—resolve to uncover what is afoot. Is something bothering him? Is he to rescind his offer to escort me to the ball?

Am I to be disgraced?

Sitting at my desk, I hold my fountain pen above a clean sheet of paper. Then I wait for inspiration to strike like a thunderclap over the lake.

# ❧❦ CHAPTER 38 ❦❧

SOUTH FORK FISHING AND HUNTING CLUB

*May 31, 1889*

*1:46 P.M.*

My tea has grown cold. As, it feels, has my blood. I rise from the spill of light on my desk and leave my unfinished letter to make my way down the dark cottage stairs. It's barely

afternoon, yet it seems like coming night. The air has an odd
*yellow* tint. It's as thick as pie dough. My heart falls to my feet.
The storm has swelled and is quickly swallowing us up. In a
matter of seconds, all signs of daylight vanish into the gloom.

The moment my shoe hits the bottom step of the cottage
stairs, a thunderclap shakes the walls. It's the sound of shatter-
ing glass. My hands fly up to my ears. Raindrops pummel the
cottage roof like falling pinecones.

"Mommy!" Henry leaps into Mother's arms. His moon face
is shadowed in fear.

"There, there," she says, her lips white. "It's only a storm."
With Henry clinging to her skirt, Mother takes him upstairs as
Nettie emerges from the kitchen, gripping her apron with both
fists.

"We're gathering candles," she says, on her way to the cottage basement. "Just in case."

I nod. Then I race to the front window. The sky is the color
of charcoal. All light is lost. Though I cannot clearly see the surface of the lake, I *hear* it. Raindrops smack the water. Another
thunder roll passes through my chest like an angry phantom.
Outside, it looks like midnight. And the rain—the vengeful
rain—is clearly just getting started.

As it did the night before, a shiver envelops me. One that I
cannot deny. Without hesitation, I know what I must do. Ignoring Colonel Unger's advice, I will *not* stay put.

# ·∘⟨I CHAPTER 39 I⟩∘·

Courtesy of the Johnstown Flood Museum Archives, Johnstown Area Heritage Association

SOUTH FORK DAM

*May 31, 1889*

*2:12 P.M.*

M y coat and bonnet are instantly soaked. I grabbed them off the front rack as I scurried out the cottage door. No one saw me leave. As necessity requires. Mother will dissolve in panic when she notices I'm gone. Yet, God help me, I must do what I must do. Some duties are larger than a responsibility to family.

Lake water sloshes up through the slats of the boardwalk. The smooth soles of my leather shoes slip on the slick surface as I run toward the clubhouse. Never before have I seen the lake so far ashore. Last summer, we sunned ourselves on a patch of *beach* here. Ivy Tottinger and I played croquet here. Now our playground is underwater; our placid lake is a churning tempest. As I race past dark and deserted cottages, I hear shutters banging and piers groaning on their pilings. *Thank heavens the skiffs are stowed in the boathouse*, I think. In this swirling wind, they would be smashed to splinters.

Onward I run. If not for the weight of water, my skirt would blow over my petticoat. As it is, the wind presses me sideways. It takes enormous effort to retain my footing. My heart pounds so ferociously I fear it will burst through my chest. Ahead, I can barely make out the club's stable through the silver sheet of rain. The smell of soggy hay and manure is carried on the spitting wind. When I reach the stable, my body sags. The stall doors are open and flapping, the horses gone. The trap carriage sits abandoned and dripping. Where is Georgie? The muscular Percheron? The sturdy Murgese?

"Help!" I yell into the roar of rain even as I see the futility of it. "Colonel Unger!" My voice barely carries beyond my mouth.

Suddenly a jagged line of lightning illuminates the sky. Before its thunder rumbles, I notice movement in the distance, beyond the clubhouse, atop the dam. Horses and men. Propelled by hope and fear, I run toward them. I must see for myself if the dam will hold. I must *convince* myself that it will. My soaked and muddy skirt tugs me to the ground. My stockings are wet through; my shoes sodden. Still, I do not stop. I cannot stop.

Beyond the clubhouse, the path to the dam is the consistency of custard. My shoes make sucking sounds with each step. My lungs burn. Still, I slog forward. Sludge covers my ankles.

"Ach!"

Without warning, I am down. Slipped and fallen into the muck. A rock digs painfully into my thigh. Both hands are black with mud. Tears rise into my eyes, but I bite my lip to contain them. What good would it do? Sobbing into rain will only make me wetter.

"Strength, Elizabeth."

Surprisingly, the sound of my quivering voice is a comfort. Amid the crush of rain, it's an echo of humanity.

"Get up."

I get up. My arms ache with the effort of pulling myself out of the mud. I wipe my hands on my skirt and rub my painful upper leg. In a surge of emotion, I yank at the ribbon on my bonnet. My hat is now so heavy it pains my neck. What possessed me to wear a sunbonnet in this downpour? With a frilly row of silk red asters, no less? I am ridiculous. Tossing my ruined bonnet into the underbrush, I continue on. In spite of my exhaustion and discomfort, I force my legs forward. Around a curve in the path, up a slight incline. Beyond the sparse maple grove where we lazily sway in hammocks each summer. To the dam. The scene of our crime.

"Over here. Quickly!"

I hear him before I see him. Colonel Unger is shouting.

"Another breach! Quickly, men!"

Even as both legs scream for rest, I rush ahead. Waterlogged pine branches droop low in my way. Hurriedly, I sweep them aside with my bare hands. My skin will be scratched and blood-ied, but what do I care?

"Hurry, men!"

In the next clearing, I see him. On horseback, Colonel Unger gallops back and forth along the breast of the dam, frantically shouting orders down into the murk. Drenched workmen— Hunkies from town?—scramble along the front face of the earthen beast with shovels, pickaxes, their bare hands. Des-perately, they attempt to shore up the bloated, muddy mon-ster by shoving rock, shale, hay—*anything*—into the rivulets that appear like tears in a crowd of mourners. Once one leak is plugged, another springs forth. Fissures open everywhere in dripping clefts.

Lakeside, the water level is so high it laps onto the top of the dam—the only road leading to our club—the road that was lowered to make room for our carriages. Using my arms and legs like a crab, I clamber onto a rocky ledge opposite the spill-way. As always, the runoff exit is clogged by lake debris. How could we have been so arrogant? We allowed the club's manag-ers to install wire mesh over the mouths of the runoff pipes to prevent fish from swimming downstream into town? For the sake of a few lost fish, we let a *spillway* clog? As I stand in sight of it, shuddering in the cold, I am shamed to my core. How many times have my friends and I picnicked up here only to remark, "There are so many logs clogging the spillway you can walk on water." We *laughed* about it. Dear God, had we no sense? No regard for those who might be harmed by our carelessness?

Darkness seeps into my soul. Amid the blinding rain, I nonetheless see the futility of the men's frenzied efforts. One workman falls to his knees, exhausted, on top of the dam. He clasps his palms together and shouts, "God, save us all." Rain washes the dirt off his upturned face. Only then do I recognize Floyd, the stable hand who was Nettie's beau last summer. Does she still see him? Is she still in love? My eyelids press shut. I am ashamed to not know the answer.

"Floyd!" I call to him. The wet wind that carried his voice to me now blows my voice *behind* me. I barely hear my own plea. Still, I try again. Does he know that Nettie is here, at the cottage?

"Floyd!"

Scrambling to his feet, Floyd never looks my way. Instead, he rejoins the other workers on the face of the dam, hurriedly patching holes in silence, their heads bowed. Their bravery breaks my heart.

Beneath the soles of my shoes, I feel a juddering. I have felt it before on this very spot. We all have. The *heaving* of our deadly dam. Only now it seems to grit its teeth and groan. It swells and contracts with growing intensity. Against one side—pushing, pushing, pushing—is our massive lake. Its immense weight fills me with terror. I am unable to move even as I shake from head to toe. Our shimmering blue plaything is now a swollen black brute straining at its confinement. A beast in captivity, raging to bust free and devour its captors. As if it had secretly despised us all along. We privileged club members with our silly parasols and canoes. As if it had only been biding its time, waiting for the perfect moment of revenge.

Unable to control my tears any more than I can harness the rain, I feel sobs rise up from my chest and join the water sheeting down my face. Fear renders me immobile. I am a weeping, trembling statue, able only to tilt my head to the wrathful heavens and surrender.

"Forgive our sins, O Lord."

In reply, the sky again ignites in a jagged line. Thunder rumbles through my body. Somehow it revives me. From nowhere, a surge of energy shoots through my veins. Like a blessed ray of sunlight, I feel a rush of purpose. A resolve within me is lit. My sobbing stops. Ignoring the pain in my leg, I leap off the ledge and race to the familiar chestnut shape I see tied to the trunk of a dripping maple. The Haflinger. The workhorse I've ridden so many summers at the club. She glistens in the punishing rain like freshly made caramel.

"Georgie," I coo. Though the rain is deafening, and my heart is pounding, I attempt a soothing tone. Her dark eyes are white-rimmed in fear. She rears her head, tugging at the leather reins that secure her to the tree. "You remember me, don't you, Georgie? I'm Elizabeth. We've strolled around this very lake together. Last summer. Remember?"

Her terrified stare never once leaves my face. I circle around to her flared nostrils and gently reach one wet hand up to stroke the tuft of wet blond hair between her eyes. Gathering all the calm I can muster, I press my forehead to her snout and rhythmically breathe. "We are both cold and soaked to the skin," I say, softly. "Shall we get out of here?"

As I continuously stroke her nose, her forehead, her mane, I breathe in and out. Shallowly, at first, for it's all my hammering heart will allow. But soon Georgie's breathing and my own are synchronized *In, out. In, out.* I blow warm air into her nostrils. Together, we relax each other. I feel her soften beneath my touch. The burning in my chest eases.

"That's my girl," I whisper, my nose still resting on her muzzle. "We will take care of each other."

*In, out. In, out.*

Slowly, I reach my free hand around Georgie's chest to the tree trunk. The leather knot that is securing her to the tree is tight and wet. My fingers fumble to loosen it. As I feel tension again rise in my chest, I tamp it down with monotone reassurances into this animal's erect ears.

"We're going to be fine. A nice canter down the mountain is just what the doctor ordered."

The moment the horse is untied, she lurches forward, then rears back onto her haunches. Gripping the reins, I know I must move quickly and decisively.

"Hang on, girl." I speak as much to myself as to her.

In a motion made possible only by the force of determination, my foot is in the stirrup and I am upon her, astride in the man's saddle. I have never ridden in such an immodest manner, yet it feels absolutely right for this purpose. Still spooked, Georgie crouches on her back legs, then takes off like a shot from a pistol.

We are in flight. Back toward the stable. The wrong way.

I panic.

Ignoring my training, I lean over Georgie's neck and hang

on. My left hand seizes the leather straps as my right grabs the pommel on the saddle. In my too-tight hold on the reins, Georgie stiffens her neck. She pulls her head forward as I yank it back. In our tug-of-war, she wins easily. I had intended to race down the mountain road in front of the dam. But Georgie has other ideas. Apparently, she is madly galloping *home,* to the club's stable. I can do nothing but hold on. My mind races.

All of a sudden I remember: *There is a back way down the mountain.* Mr. Eggar said as much. Beyond the stable. Farther than our cottage. On the other side of the lake.

If only I can control this runaway steed.

Summoning all my strength, I attempt the most difficult task of all. I try to relax myself. I inhale wet air into my lungs and blow it out through my lips. I lower my hunched shoulders. This much I know for sure: Georgie will never feel secure with a frightened rider atop her. Already we only narrowly missed several jutting branches. The rain has not let up. To my utter dismay, it appears to be falling *harder,* straight down in stinging nettles from heaven. Daylight still eludes us even as the hour is barely past two thirty. Ahead, through the gray sheet of rain, I see the clearing behind the clubhouse. Georgie gallops blindly for it, as terrorized horses do.

I am nearly prone on her back, my thighs screaming with the effort of not getting thrown. Still, I know what I must do. Harnessing my own fear, I force myself to sit upright, below her withers. I burrow into the saddle, pressing my backside down. I push both stirrups toward the sodden earth. And I *loosen* the reins.

Georgie's ears perk up.

"There you go, girl." I deliberately modulate my voice to mask my fright. Doubtful she can hear me in the storm, but it's clear that she *feels* my shift from terror to command. Beneath the saddle, I sense the slight slackening of her massive shoulder muscles. The thunderous pounding of her hooves quiets somewhat. Though every muscle in my body screams to return to the fetal position—curled over the saddle, clutching Georgie's strong neck—I resist. I sit as tall as a blue-ribbon rider. "That's my girl," I murmur. "Slow it down."

My heart pounds so hard it hurts.

As we pass the clubhouse and near the darkened stable, Georgie's frenetic gallop slows. Steamy exhalations shoot from both her nostrils. White foam bubbles up from the gullet of the saddle. I see my opportunity. Feigning the air of mastery I felt last summer on horseback, I align my head with Georgie's upright ears and tighten the slack in the reins.

"I know you want to go home," I say, calmly exerting the force of my will. "And you shall. But first—"

As Georgie veers left to the stable, I pull the reins to the right. I press my left thigh into her flank. Her ears fly backward. She flicks her long mane. I hold firm. "You were in charge before," I say. "My turn now."

Determinedly in control, I use my waning strength to hold the reins taut. My arms tremble, but I do not let up. Georgie presses me, and I press her back. I feel her resistance, yet I overpower it with my resolve. In a war of wills, I shall win. I *must* win. With a kick of my heels, I quicken her slowed pace. Again, she rears her head. She gnaws at her bit. I hold firm. Past the stable. Beyond her earthy scents of home.

"That's my girl," I say, feeling her surrender. The moment we are under way again, I reach down and pat her neck. "There you go. We are together in this journey."

First we trot, albeit reluctantly, on the access road parallel to the slippery boardwalk. Then we canter along the muddy path behind the cottages. By the time we reach the backside of our summer home, Georgie is *my* horse. She gallops at a manageable pace. For a moment, I consider stopping to let Mother know I am fine. Surely she is worried to the point of illness. It pains me to think of her distress, but I cannot in good conscience put my family's needs first. Not when we have been party to the horror that is about to happen. Mother will experience the joy of seeing me again. But, if I don't act *now*, how many mothers in the valley will be able to say the same about their own children?

Following my firm direction, Georgie gallops past our cottage to the woods behind the bend in the lake. I don't know exactly how we will wend our way down the mountain to Johnstown, but I *do* know there is a way. A shortcut. Eugene Eggar said so himself.

*At speed, Mady can get me down to Johnstown in five minutes.*

"We can do this, Georgie," I state without so much as a *wobble* in my voice. Atop the broad back of the Haflinger, I maintain proper equestrian form. "We *must*."

And down we go. Into a clammy black forest above a town full of decent working people who must be warned about the disaster that is about to engulf them.

# ··›‹[ CHAPTER 40 ]›‹··

*Courtesy of the Johnstown Flood Museum Archives, Johnstown Area Heritage Association*

JOHNSTOWN, PENNSYLVANIA

*May 31, 1889*

*2:49 P.M.*

This side of the Alleghenies is thick with new growth and old evergreens. It is vastly wilder than the sedate landscaping around the club. Immediately Georgie and I are swallowed in wet forest. Scaly pitch-pine trunks impede forward movement. Their gnarled branches sprout resinous needles that jab me as Georgie and I descend the steep hill in a zigzag fashion.

"C'mon, girl," I shout, over and over. "C'mon!"

Georgie moves as fast as she can.

As yet we are unable to locate a path down the mountain to Johnstown. I thank God for Georgie's hardiness. A less sturdy horse would lose footing on the slick compost that carpets the forest floor. Fallen pinecones crack beneath her hooves like discarded walnut shells. I'm proud of this horse. I feel her struggle to conquer her fear. Though she began jigging at the outset, I circled her completely around to stop it. Now, with rain crackling around us like crumpling newsprint, she tilts her snout down, points her ears forward, puffs breath from her nose, and somehow transports us quickly downhill. Surrounded by forest, I can do little else but hold on and lean back and support Georgie's progress with a calm demeanor. Soaked to the skin, I lock my thighs just behind her shoulders and sit as tall as I can beneath the rain-heavy treetops. Their pointed heads droop like penitents at Sunday mass. In the muted world of the forest, I almost believe that all will be okay. The bloated dam feels days away. How could the water reach all the way to Johnstown, anyway? Why, it must be fifteen miles downhill. Won't the trees stop it? The Portage Railroad Viaduct? Surely the water wouldn't surge past Mineral Point?

The hour nears three o'clock by my estimation. Brief glimpses of the sky reveal clouds as thick as a stable blanket. Amid the density of trees, I feel only a smattering of rain. Occasionally, a pine branch will catapult its water onto me as my sodden shirtwaist sleeve snags a hanging cone. It doesn't matter. At this point, I could be no more drenched than if I were submerged in a steaming lavender tub.

"Ach!" A stiff pine needle nicks my cheek. At that same moment, Georgie slips sideways. Her right croup slams against a tree. She snorts and rears her head. A flurry of agitation follows. Her ears flatten; her tail flicks. I see a flash of yellow teeth as her feet stamp and she flexes her haunches.

"It's okay," I say firmly. My thighs hold tight. "Relax, girl."

When I reach down to pat her flank, my hand comes back red. The sharp tree bark has opened her skin.

"You're okay," I say even as I choke back tears. "Onward."

Not surprisingly, my workhorse gets back to work. With renewed purpose, Georgie regains her footing and surges forward. Through the tangle of trees she finds a way down. I bend forward and rub the area above her cut flesh. For the hundredth time that afternoon, I coo, "That's my girl."

Suddenly we both hear a noise. Our two heads jerk in the same direction. Impossibly, it's the rhythmic gait of another horse, the muffled thumps of hooves on dirt. Georgie lifts her head and chuffs at the reins.

"Hello!" I call out. "Hello!"

My horse quickens her pace. She climbs *up* the mountain, toward the sound. I continue to call out. "Hello? Who's there?" Georgie lifts her head and neighs loudly. I release my grip on the reins and allow her to go where she wants to go. Up we climb in a diagonal line until—in a sudden splash of rainfall—we emerge from the thicket of pine trees into a clearing. A path! And there, like a forest phantom, a black horse gallops into view.

"Mady?" Am I hallucinating?

"Miss Haberlin?"

Eugene Eggar's voice startles me. He sits tall and drenched astride his panting horse. His shirt is a second skin. His thick hair is flattened by sweat and rain. He shouts, "It's not safe. The dam—"

"I know," I yell through the rain. "I've come to warn your family. Bring them up to our cottage."

"Is *your* family out of danger?" Clearly, Mr. Eggar has raced up the mountain to make sure *we* are okay.

"We're safe, sir, but the valley is not."

Mady weaves her head back and forth. She stamps her feet. Georgie is agitated, too. She snorts and bobs her snout.

"Can you ride?" Eugene shouts.

"Yes."

"Follow me." His jaw is set with resolve.

Under Mr. Eggar's expert command, Mady wheels around and rears up before she takes off down the hill. Georgie gallops after Mady, in her muddy wake. The path is narrow, but well worn. There are no slippery leaves or sharp pinecones. It's a gentler—though much faster—slope downhill than the direct descent we were attempting through the woods. I feel Georgie's hooves digging into the soft wet dirt. Her ears point the way. I sense her confidence; it rises into my body and inspires poise in the saddle even as we race downhill faster than I have ever gone before. Though I am careful to hold the reins taut, not tight, my fists clench the leather straps so tightly my fingernails draw blood.

Down we fly as if on a ribbon of brown satin snaking from

the mountaintop into the valley. Errant branches jut forth. I duck beneath them handily. My thighs cling to Georgie's ribs. Our hearts pound together. In the distance, a train whistle shrills. A warning? Mr. Eggar does not look back. He needn't. The thunderous sound of horsepower reassures him that I am close behind. Rain pummels our backs. I no longer feel its wetness. I am immune. Now nature's relentless weeping is a mere backdrop to our mission.

In glimpses through the woodlands, I see the Conemaugh Valley below us. Johnstown sits in its pit like a pile of charred logs. Though it's afternoon, the lack of sunlight creates the illusion that it is dusk. A dreary twilight in winter, not the day after Memorial Day. The smokestacks are oddly quiet now. They stand in the granite sky like silent sentries. As we descend, I spot the two rivers that encircle Johnstown in the same way our three rivers hug the tip of Pittsburgh. So docile when I last saw them, they now rage like lunatics. Restlessly overflowing their banks. White-tipped rapids flick up from the brown water.

In my side vision I am heartened by distant motion. The swishing of skirts, swinging of arms. Like an army of ants, townspeople scurry up the far hills. Their streets, I see, are already flooded. They fear the worst.

*Please hurry their feet.* Silently, I beg God to quickly lead everyone to the highest ground. Certainly change the mind of any family who might decide to ride out the storm inside their home. *Oh, God, please.*

At that moment, I hear a shift of sound. It's far off, but loud enough to be audible over the whooshing of rain and thumping footfalls of our horses. Georgie's ears stand straight up. Eugene

Eggar hears it, too. I see it in the tension in his back. Its muscles tighten against his soaked shirt. The horses slow slightly. Still darting down the mountain, Mr. Eggar manages to swivel around far enough to catch my eye. We lock gazes. My stomach feels as wretched and weighted as a ship's barnacled anchor. I haven't the strength to save my despair from sinking to the depths of the ocean.

"Is that—?" I shout even as I know I cannot be heard. It scarcely matters. Mr. Eggar and I both know the source of that beastly growl.

The dam has broken.

Ahead, in a small clearing, Eugene yanks Mady to a stop. Breathless with fear, I somehow manage to stop Georgie, too. The growl, far up the valley, is now a sickening throaty moan. Mr. Eggar says, desperately, "The portage viaduct may stop it."

Even as the words leave his lips, I know he does not believe them. His shoulders slump as he exhales. He shifts his gaze away. He cannot look at me. I recoil in guilt. The slender portage railroad crossing, with its elegant central arch, is no match for *millions* of tons of water let loose from our massive lake. At best, it will only slow the destruction.

*Your lake will one day be a murderer.*

Eugene Eggar's words pierce my soul. In one moment, I age into adulthood. No longer am I a frivolous girl. Never will I be again.

"The stone bridge." He looks up. "It's our only chance of crossing the rivers. Know of it?"

"No," I say, desperate.

"It's at the farthest end of town. Where the rivers meet."

With no further explanation, he takes off. Mady leaps into action with Georgie on her heels. Behind us, the unearthly moaning deepens to the resonance of thunder. Thunder that does not stop. I hear it in my whole being. A horrid rumbling of earth and water and human anguish so ungodly it rises up from hell itself. Its discord is so profoundly desperate I know at that instant it will forever be the noise of my nightmares. My body is swallowed in its profane bellow. I am unable to hear anything else. The sound shakes the very ground beneath Georgie's feet. Human screams impale the gray light. A baby wails. Mothers shriek. My heart clutches. A ghastly chill runs the length of my spine. How many souls are already dead?

Dear God, what have we done?

TIME, ODDLY, STANDS still. It's as though the earth is spinning around me, but I am fixed in place. My body rises and falls with Georgie's powerful locomotion, yet my mind dulls. I am hypnotized by the moss-green hue that flickers past my side vision in a blur. The stirrups press into the bottom of my soles, yet I feel only a phantom pressure. My thigh aches where I tumbled onto the rock, yet it is someone else's pain. A pain remembered or heard about, not one fully felt. Even my long hair, freed from its daily bondage, seems to flow from another's head. So recently it was weighted with water; now it is lighter than air. Has it all blown away?

Behind us, the devil's wail grows louder. There is no escaping it.

Suddenly—or perhaps it happens slowly?—the foliage thins and a long stone bridge comes into view. With its seven grand arches, it spans the full length of a raging river. A river at the far edge of Johnstown, where the Little Conemaugh and the Stonycreek rivers meet. The commanding rail bridge connects the forest to the end of town. It forms Johnstown's western edge. Eugene Eggar rides straight for it. I follow, without the will to do otherwise.

It's a mystery to me how we manage to climb onto the top of the railroad bridge. Mady seems to know a pathway up, and Georgie follows. In the sheeting rain, an oncoming train would devour us all. But I don't care. Exhaustion has dulled my emotions. It's all I can do to hold on to my horse.

Abruptly, in the center of the bridge, Mady stops. Georgie slows and stops beside her. My head suddenly feels too weighted for my neck. It lolls forward. My bloody hands still grip the reins.

"Elizabeth."

Eugene's voice is strange. Its peculiar tone is devoid of life. Low. Thick. Vaguely, I sense his entreaty. *Look up.* But I am unable to manage such a feat. That's when the horrid clamor following us down the mountain enters my veins.

It is a cacophony of terror: the pounding hooves of bleeding horses, the shriek of terrified hyenas, the howl of a coyote mother who's lost her young, the thunder of a buffalo stampede, the guttural roar of a thousand lions in pursuit of as many fleeing, doomed elephants. It's inhuman and so deafening I am certain I will never again hear another sound, feel no other feeling save its thunderous vibration. The roar has grown ever louder with each curve down the steep mountain road, every bend in the river. Buried deep within the hideous noise is screaming. So much screaming! Surely hell itself has cracked open and released its torment.

I look up. I cannot believe my eyes.

I haven't time to beg God to save my soul. I am already dead.

A massive ball of brown water, uprooted tree trunks, sheared rooftops, bloated horses, stiff dogs and cats, shattered church windows, broken pews, sodden Bibles, Memorial Day flags, busted brick walls, twisted train cars, splintered rail lines, bowed streetlamps, upturned carriages, naked dolls, bent tin soldiers, dented red wagons, books, black stoves, beds, tables, armchairs, mantels, photographs, love letters, wedding dresses, baby booties, and masses of drowned humanity careens straight for us. Neither Eugene Eggar nor I can move. In silent horror, we watch the monster rage into the valley. It's as if a *mountain* has unearthed itself and rampaged downhill—gaining speed as it tumbles uncontrollably. Snarling everything in its path. It swallows churches, the school, meeting halls, taverns, the dry-goods store, the opera house, the company hospital by the mill. Instantly, the roiling ball of destruction is as high as a church's eave, far wider than the Conemaugh River. A black spew of oil and tar spits up from the bottom of it. The ragged sides engorge everything in its path. It seems a solid mass. More debris than water. As if every object—living or dead—has been sucked into the gullet of the beast. Before our eyes is a masticating, gnarling, snarling, crunching, drooling, cackling, bloodthirsty demon. Furious and bursting with bile. Soon to devour the lot of us.

Even as every muscle in my body is locked, I cannot stop

shaking. Mr. Eggar screams something at me. I see his mouth move. His hands flail. Yet all I hear is the desperate wailing of hundreds—*thousands?*—of souls trapped in the jaws of the devil. The *fortunate* are drowned instantly. My heart crushes under the weight of such a thought. From atop the stone bridge, I see thrashing arms and writhing bare bodies and the frantic clutching of empty hands that moments ago held a child, a baby, a husband, a wife. The poor wretches who are sucked— alive—into the turbulence and thrust downhill in the rolling ball of water and wreckage are gasping for air. Grasping at anything to pull them out of the beast's belly. It is an unbearable image. The screams are inhuman. Guttural explosions that erupt from a place beyond any torture humankind can comprehend. I can bear to hear no more. Yet I am powerless to do anything but listen, look, and feel the dark shroud of despair entomb my being. Rain falls upon my head. Beneath me, Georgie rears backward. But I am unable to dismount or even hang on to my horse. If she throws me, so be it. I am already gone. Soon to be consumed by the monster I have allowed out of its cage.

"Elizabeth!"

Mr. Eggar screams again. Faintly, I hear my name and look at him.

"We must go. The bridge is not safe."

Unable to speak, I shake my head. I will not leave my post. I am here with the helpless souls of Johnstown. We will perish together. Turning away from him, I release Georgie's reins and tilt my face up to the black sky. My arms fall limply to my sides. My jaw slackens. Rain spatters my tongue. Soon my mouth will fill with water. I will be swallowed by the demon. I care not. I am drowned. I am dead. I am ready to meet my maker.

*God forgive me my si—*

In a sickening crunch of wood and flesh, the ghastly ball of annihilation strikes the stone bridge. Georgie stumbles. I flop over, but do not fall off. Another wave smashes against the face of the bridge, then another. The stone arches convulse with each assault. Georgie dances, but she does not bolt. She, too, has surrendered. Together, we stare at the rising mound of human debris and await the inevitable tumble into the raging river. The crumbling of stone. Falling, falling, falling into the bitter-cold rapids behind us. My heart, it seems, has already stopped. I hear nothing. Even the thunderous roar is silenced. The wailing of mothers is but the shush of quiet before sleep. Overhead, the clouds gather in ripples of black and gray. They swirl above me in the most beautiful manner. I'm quite sure it is the loveliest pattern I've ever seen. Such artistry! A single ray of sunlight pierces the thunderclouds and lands on my forehead. I am touched. Called. I answer with a body as pliant as pudding. I feel peaceful. My eyes roll into my head. Warmth radiates into my chest. I am ready.

Another impact jars me alert. My eyes refocus. Around me is an eerie orange glow. The sky above is *red*. Am I in hell?

"Elizabeth."

Someone calls my name. It is so faint I can easily ignore it. Which I do. My jaw hurts. Why do my teeth clatter so? Their insistent tapping is an annoyance. I try to reach my hands up to clasp my face but they do not obey me. It is no matter. Soon my wings will sprout. Won't they?

"Elizabeth!"

The sound strengthens. It is accompanied by sobbing. Is that screaming, too? I don't recognize such a terrible noise. It's not one I have heard before. It is a low wail, as if surfacing from the depths of the ocean. A primal bellow expressing unimaginable torment. The very sound of it makes me weep. Tears join the rain on my face.

Mr. Eggar startles me. He is off his horse, at my side. He reaches up to encircle my waist. Georgie stills herself. Suddenly I remember the blood on her flank. I try to say, "We must get her a doctor," but my teeth won't stop rattling. They will not let words pass my lips.

With the gentleness of a mother lifting her baby from his nap, Eugene Eggar slides me off my horse and into his arms. The abrupt warmth of his body reminds me how cold the babies in the water must be. Is theirs the wailing I hear? I imagine my little brother weeping in that ball of torture. Clutching his favorite book, his elfin cap swept off his feathery hair, his small leather boots ripped off his soft feet as he tumbles downhill. My heart fractures in pieces. I must save him. Mother will be frantic. As I try to wriggle free, Eugene holds ever tighter.

"You're safe now," he whispers in my ear. In his strong arms, I believe him. I release myself into his body. I hear galloping. Have Georgie and Mady run off? I bury my face in the hollow of Eugene's wet neck and feel so tired it's as if I haven't slept in months. My teeth quiet their clattering; my jaw rests. Curled into Eugene Eggar's arms, I relax into the motion of his body. Swaying. Jostling. He is carrying me across the bridge.

The *bridge*? Is it still standing?

On a sharp inhalation, my eyes fly open. My ears hear again. I jerk my face away from Mr. Eggar's warm skin and squirm out of his arms. He struggles to hold on to me, but he cannot. I will not be contained. My shoes land on top of the stone bridge with a dull thunk. The firmness of my foothold surprises me. I am alive. The bridge has not crumbled!

Rubble is spattered over the span of the long stone structure. The bridge shudders beneath my feet. Wood fragments are everywhere. Broken branches and torn bits of fabric are snagged on tumbleweeds of barbed wire. *Barbed wire?* In the far reaches of my memory I recall mention of the Gautier plant near the steel works in Johnstown that makes the flesh-tearing wires of steel and spikes. A chill runs down the length of my spine. Was the plant swept away in the tidal wave along with its killing contents?

When I look out on the sea of debris, I see that this is true. Oh, the horror! Twisted snarls of barbed wire snake throughout the massive wreckage. A loud sob lurches from my throat. Yet I push forward. The downpour has eased. A strong odor infuses the thick, moist air. Is it *oil?*

On wobbling legs, I scramble back to the center of the bridge. Eugene races after me. I stumble. Mr. Eggar lurches to grab me. In his grip, I regain my equilibrium.

"Come now, Elizabeth." His voice is deliberately calm. I feel the powerful pounding of his heart. With his large hand on the back of my head, he tries to return my face into the warm crevice beneath his chin. I will not let him. "No."

I break free. I must face the terror of what we have wrought. And I do.

In the middle of the stone bridge, on the upstream side—toward our club and its former lake—I stand and stare. I cannot believe my eyes. The field of wreckage is nearly as high as the bridge, as wide as the river, and as vast as Lake Conemaugh once was. The gruesome sight renders me speechless. Each heartbeat stabs my chest like a bloody dagger. It is beyond comprehension. If we are not already in hell, we might as well be. Hell could be no worse than this. The entire town lies in tatters at my feet.

"Grrrlgh!" Inhuman sounds jab at the air. At first, I don't recognize the godforsaken noise. Demons? The devil himself? Slowly, like the unveiling of a velvet drape, my brain begins to fathom the scene before me.

Human beings are trapped—alive—in the immense pile of rubble.

After surviving the raging wall of water, the battering of trees and homes that were violently ripped from the earth, the grisly sights of mangled, bloated humanity drowned all around them, the damned wail from the depths of the wreckage. Water is now visible only in a mild splash or two. The last remnants of our lake have passed through the arches of the formidable stone bridge and continued on their path, calmer now. Their rage spent. In their wake is a field of utter ruin. Triangles of jagged glass, fractured beams, drowned animals, mutilated limbs of every description. The huge pile pulses. Heaving up and down like an exhausted beast.

The worst is yet to come.

Quiet descends for the briefest moment. The monster's horrendous roar has ceased. Then, in place of the tidal wave's deafening growl, a sound more horrifying than any other pierces the air. It is accompanied by an odor I will forever smell, when my eyes are closed, my world is quiet.

Trapped souls are being *burned* alive.

*How is this even possible?* I think, in terror. *Burned* in water? Yet here it is before me. Pockets of angry red flames erupt and swirl through the wreckage. Far out into the sea of debris, I spot the possible culprit. A derailed tank car is twisted and cracked. Its oil has leaked and coated much of the rubble in black ooze. Fueled by an endless supply of lumber from the destroyed town—drying in the receding flood—it ignites somehow and tortures the life out of every wretched soul trapped within. Entombed beneath coils of mangled barbed wire from the destroyed Gautier plant, and tons of debris, they are beyond any hope of rescue. Their panic pierces the ghostly silence.

"God save us!"

I leap into action. As does Mr. Eggar. Ignoring our own ripped flesh, we grab at anything we can reach. Pieces of broken wood, bricks, shards of glass, toys, torn clothing. Yet a single glance into Eugene's eyes reveals that he knows what I know: it is futile.

Shrieks rise up from the black depths of wreckage that is almost as high as the bridge itself.

"We are here!" I shout, swallowing my tears. "Hold on."

Even as I say this, I pray for God to take them quickly. Theirs is a fate worse than death.

With each seized piece of debris, another falls into its place. The mammoth mound shifts and sways as if to purposely contain the beings within it. Many of the cries are so deep within the belly of the beast they are barely audible. Faint pleas of the wretched.

I do not give up. I dig. I pray. I bleed with everyone around me.

"Please help me." The anguished cries are endless. "Dear God, *please*."

Suddenly, in the misty haze, I notice a bloody and shredded hand reaching up through a loop of barbed wire. It is a woman's hand. I see her wedding band even as the knuckles above it are so stripped of skin they shine like pearls. My stomach lurches. But I will not look away. Peering down into the dark netting of the tangled wreckage, I see a flash of white. Terrorized eyes beseech me. "Help, me. *Please*."

"I'm here." Then I call out, "Eugene!"

Mr. Eggar runs to my side. Together, we dig with all the energy we can muster. Eugene pulls his shirt over his head and wraps it around his hand so that he might pull back the gnarled loops of barbed wire. He bleeds anyway. Soon the shirt is soaked in red. I am cut, too. But I feel no pain. My diamond bracelet— Grandmother's bracelet—is dulled by muck and gore.

"My name is Elizabeth," I call into the darkness, swallowing my own fear in an attempt to calm the woman. "And this is my friend Eugene."

The woman blinks. The whites of her eyes flash on and off. She says nothing.

"What's your name?" I ask, breathlessly tearing through the pile even as she sinks farther away from us.

"Jennie." Her voice quivers in the cold.

"Breathe, Jennie," I say. "Look at my face and breathe."

I force a smile into the blackness. Faintly, I make out Jennie's features. Her nose is flattened and bloody, broken by any number of objects. Her hair is matted with mud. As I reach for anything I can to free her, I gently touch her hand. She curls her bleeding fingers over mine. "I have three children," she says, desperate. "My little one is only two."

I bite at my lip. My heart stabs my chest. I do not dare tell her that her babies are almost certainly dead.

"My clothes," she adds, desperately. "The water ripped them from me. I am not decent. I cannot—"

"No need to worry. I have clean, warm clothes waiting for you," I lie. "Your modesty will be protected."

She sighs. "God bless you." The hopeful look in her eyes brings instant tears to my own. Quickly, I turn my head away and cough to halt my weeping.

With renewed effort, I lean as far over the bridge as I can to reach anything I can dislodge. Eugene struggles to untangle the length of barbed wire over Jennie's head. Blood from his previously cut palms soaks through the shirt wrapped around them. Without realizing it, I cry out. But my anguish is inaudible amid the desperate wailing all around us. The horrendous smell of burning flesh has replaced the scent of ignited oil.

"Hurry, please." Jennie, too, smells certain death.

Frantic, I seize as much debris as I can fit into my own bleeding hands. I throw it onto the bridge top behind me. My shirtwaist is shredded. The long tendrils of my loose hair snag on bent nails and twists of barbed wire. It is yanked out by the root. The pain feels good. Justified.

The deeper I dig into the pile, the deeper it seems to become.

So many people are trapped. So much screaming. Even as we near Jennie, she sinks farther from us. Much of the wreckage is still floating below. There is too much of it. The fire spreads too quickly.

It may be an hour or a minute or an entire day. I know not how long Eugene Eggar and I desperately try to dig through debris as impenetrable as a wall of steel. Every surviving man, woman, and child from Johnstown race to the bridge to join us in the excavation. We all dig. We pray. We bleed along with the trapped. In vain, we claw at the wreckage. We promise salvation that never comes.

At one point, a sudden shift of sound occurs. I don't hear it as much as I *feel* it. A tiny hush. No more than the period at the end of a sentence. In my heart, I know what that small quiet is: Jennie has perished. I can no longer see any sign of her. Her blood drained through the wreckage into the lake water below her. Silently, she slipped into eternity.

"Jennie," I call out.

No one replies.

Tears run down my cheeks. I am unable to stop them.

Still, even as I mourn her passing—and our utter helplessness to save her—I cannot help but thank God for taking her quickly. Jennie, I will soon see, is a lucky one. She did not survive long enough to feel the heat growing ever closer, the unimaginable horror of flames encroaching so near they burned off your eyelashes before devouring your life.

Humans are being cremated alive.

The ghastly cost of our club's folly.

The horror of it will never leave me. I shall never have peace.

# ·≍𝄃 CHAPTER 41 𝄃≍·

JOHNSTOWN, PENNSYLVANIA

*Courtesy of the Johnstown Flood Museum Archives, Johnstown Area Heritage Association*

*June 5, 1889*

Clara Barton had never seen anything so ghastly. At sixty-seven, she had witnessed all manner of man's inhumanity. But the destruction in Johnstown, Pennsylvania, nearly broke her. Five days after Lake Conemaugh emptied itself over their heads—the soonest any relief effort could get to the disaster site—survivors staggered about the ruin of their town. They looked as dumbstruck as Clara felt when she first set foot in the muck. An entire town, and its inhabitants, were smashed into bits.

"I cannot lose the memory of that first walk on that first day," she wrote in her diary. "The wading in mud, the climbing over broken engines, cars, heaps of iron rollers, broken timbers, wrecks of houses, bent railway tracks, tangled with piles of iron wire, bands of workmen, squads of military—the getting around bodies of dead animals, and often people being borne away. The smoldering fires and drizzling rain."

Still, as she had done amid the rotting corpses of the Civil War, Clara channeled her despair into work. She made herself *useful*.

"This will do," she said, coming upon a clearing near a railcar that was upended like a dead rodent. Along with five nurses who arrived with her, and volunteers from Altoona and Pittsburgh and beyond, Miss Barton set up a command post beneath the pitch of a canvas tent. She fashioned a desk from a packing crate and assessed the greatest need.

"Gather as many blankets and clothes as you can find to help these pour souls get dry," she told her workers. As if the citizens of Johnstown hadn't suffered enough, the rain didn't let up for days.

Most critically, they needed shelter, sanitation, and medical care. Food and water donations had begun to pour in from everywhere. As had undertakers and coffins. But few of the survivors had a home that wasn't obliterated or crushed. No one had anywhere to go. And typhoid—the deadly fever feared more than cholera—surfaced on day six. Its bacteria flourished in the decay-filled sludge all around them. The mud beneath the splintered timber that was once a thriving town was so impenetrable, no one knew how many dead souls were buried beneath their feet.

"And you are?" General Hastings—the Pennsylvania militia officer in charge of the chaos—eyed Clara Barton and her tent office with suspicion. The American Red Cross, though officially founded in 1881, was still a little-known organization. And Clara was a *woman*. Single, childless, diminutive, elderly! What was she doing other than getting in the way?

"It's a pleasure to make your acquaintance," she said to the general, introducing herself. Clara's serene smile never left her face. "Might I impose upon you to step aside for a moment, sir? Our trucks must get through."

Responding to her pleas for help, the state of Iowa had sent truckloads of fresh lumber to build housing. They arrived shortly after Clara did. Mere days after the disaster. An incredible feat. As Clara had requested, the scarlet symbol of the American Red Cross was emblazoned on the sides of the lumber trucks. General Hastings—still attempting to organize the chaos—took one look at the supplies and said no more.

As ever, Clara Barton silenced her critics with competence. From her packing-crate desk, she sent for doctors, more nurses, supplies, builders, workers of all kinds. She organized donations and established feeding stations and a Red Cross hospital to cope with the variety of deadly diseases that were now sprouting in the muck like poisonous mushrooms. She directed her workers to quickly erect temporary housing for the homeless, still too dazed by the disaster to even fully understand that their families—their lives—were gone for good.

More than anyone, Clara Barton had the experience to know what disaster survivors needed most: the structure of daily life. *Purpose.*

Using the donated lumber, she arranged for the immediate construction of three Red Cross hotels. In the center of each structure would be a long communal table where residents could mingle and eat meals together and resume a normal semblance of life. A woman of breeding, Ms. Barton understood the healing power of civility. As soon as possible, afternoon tea was served daily. On white cotton tablecloths.

Shortly after Clara arrived, a woman of breeding like herself showed up near the command post, amid the rubble all around them, and said, "I worked in my father's medical office last summer. My name is Elizabeth Haberlin. How can I help?"

## ··❧| CHAPTER 42 |❧··

SOUTHERN CALIFORNIA

*Present*

Hannah's ponytail flicked back and forth as she marched down the long hall to her cubicle. Behind her, Lee's heart-beat synced with the clonking of her shoes on the shiny tile. Overhead, large round fixtures sent spikes of light onto the ceiling. A hint of hand lotion scented the air.

"The Johnstown disaster was important for the American Red Cross," Hannah tossed over her shoulder. "Its first peace-time relief effort. It put us on the map."

Lee made an "oh, wow" face and followed Hannah to her tidy desk. Pushpinned to a corkboard beside her computer screen was a photo of a beagle wearing pink rabbit ears. "That's Nigel Barker," Hannah said. "He hates when I dress him up."

Graciously, Hannah offered coffee, tea, water, soda. Lee politely declined. This close to answering "Who am I?" no way was she going to delay with refreshments.

"Okay, then." Hannah settled in at her computer keyboard. Lee sat in the chair next to the desk. As if steeling herself for the rigors of a Chopin étude, Hannah straightened her back and rested both hands lightly on the keys. Then her fingers flew. In a matter of seconds, she had entered the Red Cross password and clicked through several outer layers to the inner core of Clara Barton's archives. Until she felt her chest burn, Lee didn't realize she was holding her breath.

"Diary pages . . . letters . . . pamphlets . . ." Hannah scrolled through thumbnails of documents Clara Barton left behind. "Lecture notes, passport. Oh, this is interesting."

Lee leaned forward. Hannah tilted the screen toward her.

"Look at all these drawings of different bandaging techniques," she said. "Gosh, I guess a lot of soldiers lost an eye."

*Bandaging techniques?* To be polite, Lee oohed and aahed with Hannah over the various crisscrossing methods, the illustrations of ways to construct a stretcher, the proper technique for carrying a wounded soldier. After an appropriate interval she said, "Gee, I wonder if they still used those methods in 1889." Hopefully, Hannah would get the hint. She did.

"Back to the photo search," she said. Her fingers again took flight over the computer keys.

As Lee had seen on her iPhone and the Internet in the Beverly Hills Library, there was no lack of Clara Barton portraits. For a shy woman, she certainly wasn't *camera* shy. Posed photos of every age were readily available. Even "candid" shots appeared staged. Clara at a bucolic picnic, draped on a twig bench before her household staff, spoon-feeding soup to wounded soldiers. The woman was an expert at self-promotion. In all, the same serene smile, same razor-straight center part. But no younger woman with poufy hair and dark eyes. Like hers. No one with the same square jaw. After several unsuccessful searches, Lee began to lose heart.

"Let me try something else." Hannah readjusted the screen in front of her face. She closed out the archive and entered another in-house Red Cross reference site. To give her breathing room, Lee sat back in her chair. Sounds of the busy office floated over Hannah's cubicle partition. Muted phone conversations, the spitting out of paper from the copy machine, nonstop clicking of computer keys. Lives being saved, disasters relieved. An office clock on the wall clicked off the seconds. Forty-six, forty-seven, forty-eight.

*Clara would be proud to see the continuation of what she started so many years ago,* Lee said to herself. *Or would she be depressed to live in a world with suicide bombers?*

Lee watched Hannah's eyeballs flit left and right the same way she had watched the metronome of Abby's gaze with her mom at Social Services. She saw the same reflection of the computer screen in Hannah's intense eyes.

It was nearing lunchtime. York would be almost home by now, three thousand miles away. Soon their evening together would be a distant memory. His kiss . . . a phantom imprint on her li—

"Here we go." Hannah stopped typing. "Is this her?"

Hannah turned the screen. Lee again leaned forward. Her eyebrows shot skyward. Her hand flew up to her chest. "That's her," she gasped. There it was. The photo of Clara Barton standing beside the woman with her face, her voluminous mane, her determined chin. Was Lee seeing what she was seeing? It felt surreal.

After clicking a few more keys, Hannah said excitedly, "She has a name. Elizabeth Haberlin."

Lee's eyes went white. "Are you kidding me? Her name is *Elizabeth*?"

"It says here she worked with Clara Barton in the aftermath of the Johnstown disaster."

"Elizabeth is *my* name. My original name. I can't believe it!"

Wiggling the mouse over the pad on her desktop, Hannah revved up her search. Now that she had a name, high hopes lit a fire in her chest. Lee's, too. Blinking away her emotion, she leaned in. She watched links fill the screen. Hannah scrolled, clicked, read. Soon, however, their spirits were flattened.

"I don't see more about her. She must have been one of the volunteers."

"Did she live in Johnstown?" Lee asked. "Is there any mention of that?"

Hannah bit her bottom lip. As her gaze roved around the screen, she frowned. "Nope. Rats." Her mouse scrolled down again. "Oh, wait—"

"What?"

"I think I found something."

"*What?*"

She clicked opened a scanned document. Silently, she read. Lee again held her breath. Then she saw Hannah's face light up like a kid seeing a birthday cake for the first time.

"I have no idea how this ended up in the archive, but take a look." With a little squeal, she said, "A *letter*. Written by Elizabeth Haberlin."

"No way."

Hannah's head bobbed up and down. Lee leaned so far forward she teetered on the very edge of her chair. With her heart beating like a hummingbird's, she silently read: "Johnstown, Pennsylvania. June 6, 1889."

"Read it out loud!"

In a quiet voice, she read.

*Dearest Mother and Father,*

*I am alive and well. My heart aches when I imagine how torturous these past few days have been for you, not knowing what became of me. Please forgive me for running out into that storm, but I felt duty bound to warn the good people of Johnstown. Alas, I was too late. Forever I will bear that guilt.*

*I've written as soon as possible. The horrid flood—a tidal wave, really—knocked out the telegraph and made communication all but impossible. I gave this letter to General Hastings, the officer now in charge. He assures me that my communication will be delivered to you. I am writing from a tented shelter near the makeshift hospital in Johnstown that is doing all it can to care for the hundreds of wounded and ill. It is six days past the disaster. The suffering is inconceivable. I pray that Mother and Henry were able to escape the club alive. I could not bear to think otherwise.*

*Father, I am working alongside a most extraordinary woman.*

*Miss Clara Barton of Oxford, Massachusetts, daughter of Captain Stephen Barton. Her organization, the American Red Cross, is here to ease the indescribable misery. I told her you are a physician and would surely come immediately to help the poor wretches here. We are in dire need of medical supplies, food, clothing, anything and everything needed to sustain life. Typhoid is of particular concern. I am securing transportation up to the cottage as soon as possible so that I might retrieve any medicine we have there, as well as clothing and other items of use.*

Lee looked up. "Cottage?"

Hannah shrugged. Lee continued.

*Here among the ruins, Father, I have been looking for Colonel Unger, Mr. Ruff, Mr. Frick, or any of the club's managers who must be eager to make amends for what we have done to these poor people. As yet, I have not seen them, though I am sure they are here somewhere. If you are in communication with anyone from the club, please tell them to find me here, for I was witness to the destruction. Miss Barton will always know where I am, usually working in the hospital, where the need is most desperate.*

*The train into town is now functioning, Father. Though barely. I will watch for your arrival with eagerness.*

*Devotedly yours,*
*Elizabeth*

When Lee finished reading, she asked the obvious question. "We?"

"We what?"

"It says here, 'make amends for what *we* have done.'"

"Hmm." Hannah's able fingers returned to the computer keys. "Let's see. She said her father was a doctor, right?"

"Right."

Hannah typed "Dr. Haberlin" into the search engine. Modern faces of Haberlin physicians appeared on-screen. A surgeon in Charlotte, North Carolina, an internist in Tacoma, Washington. When she added "1889" to the search, more doctors' names popped up. But none that fit the profile of a nineteenth-century father. Then Hannah added "Johnstown, Pennsylvania" and dug deeper than the first few Google pages. Still, nothing. Finally, she deleted "Johnstown" and searched "Dr. Haberlin, 1889, Pennsylvania."

Then her jaw fell open.

"Stafford Haberlin, a physician from Upper St. Clair, Pennsylvania, is listed as—wait for it . . ." Hannah's eyes popped opened as wide as her mouth. "A member of the South Fork Fishing and Hunting Club."

"No way."

"Yes way. He must have owned one of the cottages at the lake. As it says here, 'South Fork was the private lakeside retreat for the wealthy and powerful of Pittsburgh's elite.' Maybe Elizabeth's father was their personal physician. Oh my God, Lee, your great-great-great-grandmother was *rich*."

Lee laughed out loud. Of all the scenarios she had fantasized over the years, being a descendant of the *one percent* never once entered her mind.

# ··❊❘ CHAPTER 43 ❘❊··

Courtesy of the Johnstown Flood Museum Archives, Johnstown Area Heritage Association

JOHNSTOWN, PENNSYLVANIA

*June 9, 1889*

There is so much to do. From sunup to sundown, Mr. Eggar and I work alongside Miss Barton, easing the immense suffering any way we can.

It pains me that I wasted last summer reading *Harper's Bazaar* in Father's medical office instead of learning how to dress wounds or ease fevers. My empty-headedness is beyond comprehension. Before nightfall, I'm hoping to secure transportation up the mountain to the cottage for supplies. The road in that direction has been buried beneath piles of death and destruction.

Eugene has yet to locate even one member of his family. He never mentions his heartbreak, though sadness darkens his eyes like a tarnished coin. Each day, it grows blacker. It's impossible to buoy his hopes.

"Is that the best use of my friendship?" I ask Clara. "Bolstering his hope?" By now, any survivors beneath the rubble have certainly perished.

As always, Clara speaks in a soft, calming voice. "It's been my experience that presence and silence are most helpful," she says. "Be there without judgment or advice to listen when he is ready to talk."

I nod. That's what I'll do. Wait until he's ready, and be there when he is.

On this day, I am given the task of updating our inventory list. So many supplies have come by train and truck, it's imperative that we track them all. "If we don't know what we have," Clara says, "we won't know how to use everything to its best advantage."

I get to work. Mr. Eggar has grabbed a donated shovel to join the other able men digging through the dirt and debris.

Clara Barton is the most extraordinary woman I've ever met. Four times my age, she has twice my energy. Wise, caring, and competent, she has never needed a husband to make her feel important. Working with her makes me feel as though my schooling thus far has been worthless. In the span of a few days,

Miss Barton has taught me the one lesson I never learned: nothing matters as much as *service* to others. No riches—or positions
in society—can replace the precious feeling of being useful.

"Miss Haberlin?"

While I stand inside the supply tent with an inventory list
in my hand, one of General Hastings's men appears at the
door flap. He holds out a letter. My heart flutters when I see
it. I've been so anxious for word about my family. Each day,
as the train spews out more volunteers, more passengers, I
scan the crowd for Father. His failure to appear worries me
greatly. Has something happened to him? Are Mother and
Henry safe?

"Thank you, sir," I say as I take the thick letter in my hand
and sit on a canvas chair near the light. Mother's elegant script
is unmistakable. When I open the envelope, I see that she has
inserted another letter inside. I will open that in a moment.
First, from Mother:

> *Oh, my cherished daughter,* she begins. *How joyous we are
> to hear from you. God has blessed us that you are safe. After being
> forced to leave the club without you, I was inconsolable. Were
> it not for the protection of Henry, I never would have departed
> without knowing what had become of you. My heart can rest now
> that I know you have survived nature's fury.*
>
> *Why have you not come home? You say that you are well, but
> are you ill? Your father has sent a courier with this letter. As soon
> as we receive word that you are able to travel, he will dispatch
> Mr. Tilson to escort you home. We are all so very eager to see
> you again.*

*Rest assured, my darling Elizabeth, that your brother and I are safe. One of Colonel Unger's men knew of a small path on the north side of the lake and he escorted us out via carriage shortly after the accident. Such a dreadful business. We were soaked to the skin. Henry was in bed for nearly a week. It is only by God's grace that we were able to escape.*

*I beg you, dearest, stay away from that horrid hospital. Mr. Tilson will bring all the medical supplies your father can spare. Of course, your father cannot venture into a typhoid zone. Too many of his patients here rely on him. But Mr. Tilson will deliver the supplies to your Miss Barton and rescue you from danger. The generous members of the club have also pooled their resources to send one thousand blankets for the survivors. Warmth is on its way very soon.*

*I am heartened to hear that you are fleeing back to the cottage. Father says this is best. You must stay away from the pestilence. Worry not, Mr. Tilson will find you up the mountain.*

*Once you are home, my daughter, we will put this unpleasantness behind us. Mr. Ruff has already spoken to several club members and all have agreed to forfeit their memberships. How could anyone bear to summer at a lake that is gone? We shall find another place to restore our tranquility. Please don't fret. Once you have returned to Upper St. Clair, you need never think about South Fork again.*

*Oh! In all the apprehension over Henry's well-being, and yours, I nearly forgot to tell you the good news. You have received a letter from Mr. Tottinger. We can relax. It is within an acceptable time period for him to confirm his intentions to escort you to your debut. Barely. I cannot imagine why he waited so*

*long. Perhaps the post was delayed in England? No matter. All
is well now. I have inserted Mr. Tottinger's sealed letter in this
correspondence. Of course, I knew you would not want me to read
it before you did. But, when you return home, dear daughter, we
shall pore over every word together.*

*Yours affectionately,*
*Mother*

For a moment, I hold Mother's letter in my hand. I experience a strange sensation. It's as if the last remains of my youth
just now drained away. I feel the girl I once was vanish into the
foggy air. Oddly, I see my mother—and my family—from *afar*.
The way someone outside our social circle sees us. The way
they have seen us with clarity for years. My vision is almost
more than I can bear. I had always believed us to be kind and
charitable. Did we not let Nettie and Ella and our other servants freely eat our food?

Now profound anguish darkens my heart. From my current perspective down the hill—in the aftermath of what we so
carelessly wrought—I see how blind we've been. For everyone
up the mountain at the club, *our* needs were the only needs that
truly mattered. Though we pretended to care about those in
our employ, it was always exactly that: a feint. Never once did
I imagine that my maid might not *want* to care for me. Or that
Ida might prefer to cook for her own family. Even when I had
the impulse to apologize to Nettie, it was only to make *myself*
feel better. Like everyone else in my position, we enacted a pretense of kindness to satisfy the code of our class: *propriety* at all
cost. Manners. The mask behind which we hide our selfishness.

Now that I am able to see beyond the fog of privilege, I feel no other emotion but shame.

That is, until I read my *second* letter.

The familiar penmanship on the envelope is more flowery than Mother's. And the return address is known to me, too.

*London, United Kingdom of Great Britain.*

With my heart pounding, I open the letter I have been eager to read for weeks. At last, Mr. Tottinger has made contact.

The correspondence begins with the date: May 30, 1889. One day before the disaster. He writes from his home in London, clearly unaware of the tragedy that will transpire the following day.

> *Dear Miss Haberlin,* he begins. *My deepest apologies for this delay in writing to you. You have been much on my mind, as I have been troubled greatly by the news I must impart.*
>
> *Several weeks after my family returned to England, after my many letters to you, I spoke to Father about my increasingly warm feelings toward you. I thought it unwise to declare my feelings to my family until I, myself, was sure of them. Which I was, indeed.*
>
> *After Father and I spoke, he naturally had his man inquire more deeply into your family. Had we spent more time together, I am sure you would have revealed the information Father uncovered. I fault you not for my ignorance.*
>
> *As I am certain you are aware, I am duty bound to keep my bloodline pure. Before our journey to your lovely club, I was assured that all the ladies there had impeccable pedigree. It was, therefore, quite shocking for me to discover that your grandfather and grandmother on your maternal side were born in Safed, Gali-*

*lee. As I am sure you know, before immigrating to Pittsburgh, they fled to Germany following the pogrom in their country of origin. I believe your mother's brother, Avrum, perished in that massacre? My sincerest condolences to her family.*

*Naturally, given the tragedy with her son, it is understandable that your grandmother would end her life in the manner that she did. Still, as I trust you will understand, my solemn obligation to my family is to keep scandal and other impurities from dishonoring our line.*

*It is, therefore, with a heavy heart that I must sever all contact with you. I hope that I have not dishonored myself by leading you to believe we might enjoy a future together.*

*I delighted in our limited time at your beautiful and tranquil lake. Forever, it will be a pleasant memory.*

*Ever your acquaintance,*
*James Tottinger*

After reading this letter, I can scarcely breathe.

# ·◦] CHAPTER 44 [◦·

JOHNSTOWN, PENNSYLVANIA

*June 10, 1889*

M y fury knows no bounds. The impudence! First, to con-
done a stranger ferreting through the tragic history of my
poor grandparents. Then, to disparage my grandmother for
her inability to endure the memory of the mass murder that

took her only son? What an outrage. I am beyond grateful that I learned of Mr. Tottinger's petty character before I was fooled into thinking him a suitable husband. Let him *drown* in his pure blood.

If not for the calming influence of my new friend, Clara, I would have used that despicable letter as fuel to keep us warm in the encampment.

"You may want to respond at a later date," Clara said, resting her warm hand on my shoulder the way I have seen her do for so many others. Her very presence is a tonic. I have much to learn from her about serenity. "I will keep it for you in my desk," she said, "along with your other letter." Then she reminded me, "We have too much to accomplish here to occupy our minds with nonsense."

Nothing could be truer. I get back to work.

Ever since the horror of the flood, my days have been a blur of fatigue, crushing sorrow, and purpose. At first, along with every other able body, I didn't leave the stone bridge until the last cries stopped. In vain, we dug through rubble so vast and deep I have heard it will take more than a year to clear it out. My arms were bloody, my dress shredded. I didn't care. No one did. We ate scraps of food anyone handed us, drank precious sips of water. We slept only when we fell over, unconscious. After three days of fire—such howling as could not possibly come from a human—the torture of the damned was tragically silenced. It was the only blessing left for those poor souls. The stench of burning flesh melded onto my skin. By the third day, I felt nothing. I was numb. Even my anguish had dried up. That day, some kind gentleman with hands like leather gingerly led me to a makeshift tent. There, on top of a blanket spread out on the hard earth, I fell into a sleep so deep I did not awake until two days later. That's when I met Miss Barton. She stood before me like an angel, cleaning the mud off my face.

Today, Johnstown is oddly alive. Reporters are buzzing about, inflating the already dire numbers of dead. More undertakers have arrived from all over the East Coast, as have coffins and volunteers of all sorts. Even, it soon becomes evident, *nefarious* sorts. Gawkers, hobos looking for free food, ghoulish thieves intent on looting corpses. In the aftermath, I see both the best and worst of humankind.

This afternoon, I have an emotional task. Mr. Eggar is escorting me up the mountain. He has been able to repair a large wagon he found amid the rubble. Incredibly, Georgie and Mady were discovered peacefully grazing on a far piece of green. As if hell had not been burning all around them. Other workers cleared enough debris to create a dirt road that will lead us to the mountain road. Though I dread what I might see up at the club, I am eager to retrieve medicine from Father's examining room in our cottage, plus clothes and anything else I can find that will help the destitute here.

With the sun blazing as if summer had merrily skipped in, Mr. Eggar hooks up both horses and tosses coils of rope into the wagon. I tidy up by pinning my hair atop my head with the few fasteners I have left. Clara found me a clean shirtwaist somewhere. And, though Mr. Eggar's home entirely was swept away, he has secured unsoiled clothing somehow, too. I dare not imagine what became of the poor souls who owned our garments.

"Here." Eugene extends his hand to help me onto the wagon's perch. His forearms and hands are covered in cuts, yet he does not complain.

"Are you all right?" I ask.

He says, "I'm alive."

Between us is our unspoken grief. We are both without our families, though for vastly different reasons. Only today do I see Mr. Eggar's hope wither to despair. Even if someone were still alive beneath the rubble, he now silently accepts that they would certainly perish of exposure before rescue was possible. The destruction is simply too vast. The only promise of salvation lies in the prayer that a loved one was at the *front* of the ball of debris that thundered down the mountain. *Before* it was stopped at the stone bridge. It hurts my heart to hear survivors pray that a family member was swept downriver. The Conemaugh River flows for miles. Perhaps a floating log knocked them unconscious, saved from drowning by a tangle of shoreline bramble? Perhaps a broken limb has forestalled their journey home? Such are the desperate longings of the families.

As Clara advised me, I strive to be a silent presence at Eugene's side, ready to listen when he is ready to talk.

At first, Mr. Eggar leads the horses on foot. Slowly, we slog through the thick mud. I try to jump down to help, but he will not have it. "I am still a gentleman," he says. A fact I cannot deny. He has shown me thus many times over. With the weight of the wagon's four large wheels, it is slow progress.

Once we near Cambria City, we see a viable road. There, Eugene cleans off the wheels with his bare hands and sets us upon an uphill journey that passes through South Fork. Like an eerie dream, the town of South Fork is nearly completely intact. The houses, tucked into the hill, stand as they have always stood. Clapboard façades, sagging porches. It's clear that the rushing water ran in a violent river *below* them. As we slowly roll past, residents emerge from their homes to wave forlornly and stare with ghostly faces. Even though they survived the destruction, they, too, have peered into the depths of hell.

Shame reddens my cheeks. How many times had I passed these very homes on my way to the club? Not once had I so much as *noticed* them before. Now I return their waves and nod. Now we share a silent bond.

As we near the top of the hill, I see the most incongruent sight. It's as if the landscape here has been scrubbed *clean*. Trees have been uprooted and swept away; there are no wildflowers to sprinkle color on the foliage beside the road. All that is left is a flat sheen of dirt, now dried in the sun.

And then I see it. The dam. Or, what is left of it.

My stomach lurches. It is a repulsive sight. Jutting out from the right and the left are remnants of the original beastly structure. But the center is completely gone. A huge chunk has vanished. Washed down the mountain. It's a startling gap, like front teeth punched through in a bloody bar brawl. It looks wrong—angry, defiant, wounded. The smell of dead fish and sunbaked manure is putrid. My hand flies up to my mouth. I cry out, "Dear God, what have we done?"

Silent beside me, Eugene Eggar steers the horses around the dam—there is no crossing it—and together we see a sight even worse than the busted-through dam. Stretching as far as the eye can see is an enormous *hole*. It resembles a massive excavated pit. In puddles here and there, muddy water glistens. The air is thick with the stink of dead fish. They lie, arched and openmouthed, on the muddy lake bottom. Choked to death. It looks exactly the way it is: an immense lake that has been drained of all life.

"Eugene," I plead, "will you ever forgive us?"

His face is expressionless. "I know my neighbors well enough," he says softly. "Johnstown will eventually forgive the Bosses' Club because it is the Christian thing to do." He need not add more. I hear his unspoken words, as well: *But we shall never forget.*

In soundless shock, we circle around to the north side of the empty lake. The rattle of the carriage is the only noise to pierce the eerie quiet. Even birds have stayed away. The sun mocks us. I tilt my bare face to the cloudless sky and feel the punishment of its burning rays.

Suddenly there is movement ahead. A man on horseback passes the only house on the north side of the former lake: Colonel Unger's farmhouse. It sits near the now-dry spillway on the very edge of the stinking pit. The spillway he refused to unclog. Once a lakefront home, the house is now—and forever will be—a daily reminder of his incompetence. The cavernous hole of murder on a massive scale.

"This is private property!" the man shouts as we near.

I nearly laugh. "Colonel Unger. It's Elizabeth Haberlin."

He gallops up to us, breathless. "Miss Haberlin! I am so relieved to see that you are alive. I found your bonnet by the clubhouse. I feared the worst."

He looks away for a moment, guilty, then says, "I was able to get your mother and brother safely to Altoona."

"Yes. I was told." My voice is icy.

"Your servants are safe, too."

Mr. Eggar grips the reins.

"I'm here to get the last of my things," Mr. Unger says. "Are you on your way to Pittsburgh? I know a pathway out."

"Pittsburgh?" Eugene says. "Is that where you're headed?"

Colonel Unger swallows and falls silent.

"I've come with Mr. Eggar to retrieve supplies from the cottage," I say.

I note a pulsing muscle in Eugene's jaw. Mr. Unger sees it, too. He reaches a hand up to nervously smooth his white beard and mustache—both stained by tobacco or perhaps that morning's coffee. His horse rears its head, chewing on its snaffle. To me, Mr. Unger says, "Surely you're not going back to Johnstown?"

"*You* are not, sir?"

Perhaps it is my imagining, but I see redness flare in Mr. Unger's cheeks. He will not meet my gaze. His pained expression does nothing to soften my countenance. "I was there," he says, haltingly. "I saw—"

He stops. I expect no further words. How can vowels and consonants describe what Mr. Unger saw? Eugene and I know this better than anyone. As Eugene tugs on the reins to direct the horses to move, Mr. Unger confesses, "I am in fear for my life. Several men from town have already been here looking for me."

"Can you blame them?" Eugene asks, staring. I stare, too, without a shred of deference. He deserves none.

Mr. Unger does not reply. Instead, he quietly says, "The back doors of the cottages are always left unlocked. No one will return here to retrieve their things, meager as they are this time of year. You'll find bedding and soap, at the very least. Rudimentary medical supplies. More in your father's office, of course. Some canned and preserved goods. Summer clothes left behind. Please take it all."

With that, the club's caretaker kicks the haunches of his horse.

"God bless both of you," he says as he gallops into the woods surrounding what was once his beloved lake.

# ·❧[ CHAPTER 45 ]❧·

SOUTH FORK FISHING AND HUNTING CLUB

*June 10, 1889*

I stand on the access road behind our cottage and stare at the destroyed shoreline below. If I had tears left, I would crumple to the ground, weeping. As it is, I can only feel the emptiness that I see. Most of the boardwalk is washed away, but our cottage sits, undisturbed, overlooking the ghastly hole. When I see—and smell—the multitude of rotting fish that lie on the sand beneath our summer home, I am sickened anew. Screening the spillway so that fish couldn't escape downriver? It's unfathomable. Had our precious fish been left to swim freely, the rising *water* would have had a means of escape, too. Had the men of the Bosses' Club been truly generous, instead of pretending to be humanitarians, thousands of souls might not have perished.

Forever, they must live with that knowledge. As do I with my haughty inaction. Mr. Eggar warned me that our lake would one day be a murderer. How could I have so easily disregarded his pronouncement? He knew those mountains better than anyone. Until I die, I will bear that guilt. It pains me with each breath.

Together, Eugene and I circle around to the front cottage door. I know it's unlocked. In our idyllic retreat, no one ever felt the slightest hint of danger. Why would we? I now know *we* were the danger.

Reaching for the knob, I curl my fingers around it. I rotate my wrist and open the door. Mr. Eggar follows me inside.

Unbelievably, everything remains exactly as it was. I see the red Oriental rug in our front parlor, my piano, the velvet settees, our carved mantel, and the gold-filigreed embellishments on the chairbacks. One of Mother's velvet frock coats is still hanging on the mahogany hall tree. Mocking me are four umbrellas in the stand.

I am ashamed to walk through the cottage. I cannot look Mr. Eggar in the eye. Before, I never gave a moment's thought to our abundance. Of course Mother had *several* coats. As did

I. We wore whatever suited our fancy. Now my head hangs on my neck. Around me, I cannot bear to see so many unnecessary ornaments gilding our home. Our *second* home. The one of supposed simplicity. "Roughing it" in the woods. How foolish we have been. How terribly ignorant of the struggles of others.

"We must take everything," I whisper, embarrassed to have Mr. Eggar see me as I truly am. Or, I should say, as I *was*. After all I witnessed—all that I now understand—how can I ever return to blindness?

"There isn't room in the wagon for all of it," Eugene says.

With that, he circles around me to find Father's medical office. I gather my wits and hurry up the stairs.

# ·›I CHAPTER 46 I‹·

Courtesy of the Johnstown Flood Museum Archives, Johnstown Area Heritage Association

JOHNSTOWN, PENNSYLVANIA

*June 11, 1889*

It's morning. A new day. Miss Barton has assigned me a corner of the lower works of Cambria Iron—one of the few buildings to withstand the flood. The blast furnaces have been fired up. White smoke billows from the chimneys. It's a blessing to the workers. Most resumed their jobs almost immediately after the water receded. The exhaustion of physical labor took their minds off the tragedies beyond the plant's doors.

Inside is no place for a lady, yet I endeavor to make it so. In my out-of-the-way nook, I sweep out the layers of dirt accumulated by the machinery's exhaust and the neglect of men. Using clean sheets Mr. Eggar and I carted down the hill from the cottage, volunteers help me construct privacy curtains with rope tied around steel beams. We secure the pier glass from my bedroom to a stanchion near the wall. I fill several of my porcelain pitchers with fresh water. Behind each curtain is a basin. Thankfully, the water lines in town have been restored.

Admittedly, Eugene eyed me askance yesterday when I dragged my dress form down the cottage stairs.

"Only the essentials, Miss Haberlin," he had said.

"This is essential," I replied. "You'll see." Then I added, "And I insist you call me Elizabeth from here on in."

He smiled. An expression of warmth that nearly drew tears.

"Only if you call me Eugene."

And so it was. From that moment on.

All told, my corner of the mill is a fine setup. Perfectly situated for the task at hand. Miss Barton wisely chose the plant for my enterprise so that workingmen could escort their wives and sisters and mothers through the door on their way to work. Otherwise, the town women might have been too shy to approach me, a stranger. Most heartening is the way everyone makes a point of bringing widows and orphans to my corner. Without the insistence of their neighbors, they would most certainly sit in the mud and weep.

"Welcome," I say, smiling.

The first woman through the door is petite. She stands barely five feet. Her hands seem made of bird bones. I notice a patch of mud still matted in her hair. Her eyes retain the terror of the afternoon none of us will ever forget. In as unobtrusive a manner as possible, I run my gaze up and down the length of her tiny body.

"I have just the thing," I say.

Turning to the cart where I have sorted all the clothing I found in my wardrobe at the cottage, plus everyone else's, I select a dress from the pile of the smallest. Thankfully, I find a lovely summer cotton, striped in a muted green. The matching bodice has a fetching stripe of lemon-yellow satin.

"This will offset your complexion in a most flattering way," I say, handing the tiny woman the dress. She looks at it as if she has never seen a dress before. Her small fingers trace circles over the softness of the fabric.

"This way." Gently, I guide her behind the first curtain. There, we have established a cleaning station. Soap, fresh water, squares of bathing cotton. A coatrack on which to hang her new dress while she freshens up. Volunteer women are there to assist. From my side of the curtain, I hear the gentle trickle of water. And I *feel* the renewal of her battered spirit.

"Welcome," I say as my next customer comes through the door.

Word spreads quickly. By next morning, there is a line and lively chatter outside the warehouse doors. Miss Barton sends over new clothing as it arrives by donation. I encourage the women to take fresh trousers and vests for their husbands, sons, and brothers, too. We all know men will not stand in line with a bunch of women to try on clothes.

For the first time since the flood, I feel hopeful. Never would

I have imagined the joy of hearing women banter with one another. And to see them emerge from behind the dressing curtain in a new frock? Well, I have many times come near sobbing with happiness. I now understand Miss Barton's insistence on a life of purpose. Helping the women of Johnstown is the most gratifying feeling I have ever experienced.

Later that day, when an urgent letter arrives from Mother asking why I have not summoned Mr. Tilson to escort me home to Upper St. Clair, I reply, "For what? A life of frippery?" I add that I am well—and sane—and will visit as soon as I can. Then I get back to work so that I may help the next woman in line find a new dress and shoes and corset and petticoat that will make her feel alive again.

Never have I felt more fulfilled.

The most satisfying part of my mission, however, is an idea I had while gathering my things at the cottage.

When my first customer—the petite woman in the striped green cotton—emerged from the dressing curtain, I stood back and said, "Let me look at you." Her face was pink from scrubbing. The matted mud, I noticed, no longer flattened her hair.

"Goodness, how lovely," I said, quite honestly, even as the dress could use the attentions of my grandfather, the tailor.

"I've never seen a dress so beautiful," she sputtered, looking at her skirt with awe. "I cannot thank you enough."

I beamed. "From now on, you must remember that moss green is your color. Though the dress is missing one final touch."

At the farthest corner of my station was my old dress form. On it, a dress. I picked up the scissors I brought from the cottage and marched over to snip off a small square.

"You mustn't!" the woman yelped.

*Snip, snip.* I did.

"Every woman should feel the pleasure of wearing—at least *part* of—a Charles Worth original."

I handed her a square from the bottom of my beaded and laced Charles Worth gown. The buttery gown I once considered wearing to my debutante ball, the mere thought of which now strikes me as absurd. Silently, I thanked God for instilling in me the thought to ask Nettie to "forget" the gown at the club. Only *he* would have known then how truly valuable my gown would become.

"There are sewing supplies just outside, beyond the front entrance," I said. "I'm eager to see how you might use your embellishment."

Some women made a small brooch out of their square of beaded fabric. Others cut it in two strips to enhance the cuffs. Still others shyly requested a piece of the underskirt's creamy satin so that they might tuck it into their bodices to feel its luxury against their skin as they set about excavating—and rebuilding—their lives.

Never before have I felt so useful. Never have I understood the life-affirming value of *true* simplicity: soap, water, a dress in a color that is just so. And, of course, a touch of glimmer to bounce the light.

What else could any woman want?

# ·❦[ CHAPTER 47 ]❦·

SOUTHERN CALIFORNIA

*Present*

She'd tried not to. Honestly, she had. York's first text went unacknowledged. His second—sent twice—was answered with a curt "Sorry. Busy." Lee felt like throwing up after she tapped send. But York wasn't fazed. Perhaps he was so accustomed to being treated well he didn't recognize a brush-off when it came sweeping his way.

He replied, "I'll wait."

In the meantime, he sent silly New York photos with funny captions.

"Mommy, why do you hate me?" A dachshund in a sun hat.

"NYC birdbath." Pigeons in a puddle.

Even as she tried to resist, Lee was constantly tucking herself into a corner of Bed Bath & Beyond and sending smiley emojis to York's witty messages. After work, after class, they would chat on the phone. York was taking two summer classes at Columbia. Lee was working double shifts. Incredibly, they had a lot in common. Both felt trapped in their lives. Both were outsiders. Theirs was a relationship that grew so naturally it felt like they'd known each other all their lives.

Lee tried not to fall in love. Honestly, she did.

"How long before you know who you are meant to be?" she asked him late one night—the *middle* of the night in New York.

"Is it creepy to admit I'm turned on by your proper use of 'who'?" he replied.

Lee laughed out loud. She couldn't believe a guy like that liked a girl like her. But, of course, he didn't know who she really was. That night at the lagoon pool, she'd been a rich girl who lived in a glass mansion, not the daughter of a maid who showered among the skunks. Somehow, she'd never gotten around to telling him the truth. She'd tried to. Honestly, she had.

"York, I—"

Words always lodged in her throat after that.

"When are you coming to NYC?" York texted one day.

A rush of excitement flooded her body, followed by a blackened ball of dread. Lee's heart sank even as she longed to see him again. York deserved better than a liar.

"Someday," she texted back.

"WHEN??? Weekend?"

It never occurred to him that money, not time, was her biggest obstacle.

York persisted. When he proposed flying out to Los Angeles instead, she knew the time had come. She had only one choice: cut it off cleanly, or *come* clean. She'd already waited too long. The more time that passed, the worse it would be.

"Will you be up after eight my time?" It was late summer. She was working the second shift.

"Definitely."

"I'll call you tonight."

"I await with appetency."

Lee's heart fluttered. What girl didn't dream of a boy with a stellar vocabulary?

By seven forty-five that night, Lee's pulse was pounding. She could barely finish her shift. She was on the verge of losing the only boyfriend she almost had. Lee liked York. A lot. She didn't want him to hate her for not being the rich girl up the hill. For leading him astray. As the clock ticked toward eight, she felt the descending gloom of impending disaster. Her feet could hardly carry her to the employees' locker room to grab her stuff. Still, in the parking lot on the way to her car, she forced herself to *face* herself.

"What's up?" York asked, sleepily. It was eleven P.M. in New York. Summer was winding down. Worries over the new school year were revving up. For York, at least. Already he was stressing over sophomore calculus.

Lee licked her dry lips. Her phone felt as heavy as a brick.

"York, I—"

What could she say? *York, I am a liar?* Her head fell forward.

"What is it?"

In the same Band-Aid sort of way her father had delivered his bad news, she blurted, "I'm not who you think I am."

York paused. "You're a dude?"

Lee let loose a jumpy laugh.

"A Rakhari who escaped the Bajoran wormhole?"

"You're demented," Lee said.

"Are *you* demented? Is that what you're trying to tell me? 'Cause I've been wondering."

Lee laughed again. Then she got serious. "York, I—" Again, words vacated her mind.

"What's going on, Elizabeth?"

*Elizabeth.*

That's where she should start. Her original name. The name her birth mother had given her. The one she'd decided to give back to herself. She'd read online that Ashkenazi Jews had a tradition of naming children after a deceased relative. Since she'd faltered on every other tradition—like, did "fasting" mean total abstinence, or were smoothies okay?—she'd talked to her mom about restoring her birth name.

"Elizabeth is the long version of 'Lee' anyway, Mom," she'd said. "Now that I'm older, I want a more complex name."

She didn't mention that Elizabeth was the name of her genetic great-great-great-grandmother—the woman in the photo.

Valerie had rolled her eyes. "A long name does not make a person complex. Look at Arnold Schwarzenegger."

Lee drew her mother close and hugged her hard. "You can always call me Lee, but I want the world to call me Elizabeth."

"Watch out, world," Valerie bellowed. "Multisyllabic woman coming through."

From that day on, Lee called herself Elizabeth even as everyone who'd known her up to that moment never stopped calling her Lee.

Over the phone, York got quiet. He said, "How bad could it

be? You know *my* darkest shame. I secretly watch singing competitions."

Elizabeth—Lee Parker—laughed again. She unlocked the door of her car and got in. Then she pressed her eyes shut and flattened her palm against her chest to calm her heart.

"I don't want you to hate me," she whispered.

"Inconceivable."

After a deep breath, she let go. In a jumble of sentences, she opened her mouth and allowed it all to tumble out. She told York about the pool house, about her mother (the maid), and her father (the disappearing act). She confessed that her college money was gone. Her brother had vanished, too, and her once best friend, Shelby, had moved on without her.

"I'm not sure why people leave me." Her voice teetered on the precipice of tears. "My birth mother even abandoned me."

Yes, she told him all she knew about her adoption, too.

York listened raptly. He said not a word. In the parking lot of Bed Bath & Beyond, Elizabeth watched streetlights blink on as she unburdened herself. When she was done, she nervously chewed on her lower lip. The silence was so complete she was convinced York had hung up long ago.

"Are you there?" she meekly asked into the void.

York then said two words that meant everything to her: "I'm here."

For the first time in a long time, Elizabeth saw a future without clouds.

"I live in a fifth-floor walk-up in Washington Heights," York said. "With two roommates. My view is my neighbor's brick wall. Living in a pool house would be a *luxury*."

"It's moldy," Elizabeth replied.

"A water bug crawled over my foot while I was brushing my teeth."

"I smell like a gas-station air freshener when I get home from work."

"I'm an intern in my professor's office. I smell like his B.O."

"I make minimum wage."

"My parents still give me an allowance."

"I buy clothes on eBay."

"Clothes are overrated."

Elizabeth giggled. "I'm Jewish, too. Though I haven't been officially, um, *inducted* yet."

"When you are, will you teach me the secret handshake?"

Together they released belly laughs of kinship. York said, "Rich girls are boring. They live like they're in a reality show."

"Unlike me who is just in *reality*?"

"Precisely. Genuine life is riveting."

He had a point. After all she'd recently learned about her birth family's history, Elizabeth couldn't wait to pull together the final pieces. To see the whole riveting picture.

"Did you honestly think I would dump you because you're not rich?"

Unable to stop smiling, she honestly answered, "No."

After hanging up, Elizabeth backed out of the parking space and drove to the exit. At Ventura Boulevard, she turned right and began her journey home. To the pool house. Green lights at every intersection.

## ⋯◦⟨ CHAPTER 48 ⟩◦⋯

NORTH BEVERLY PARK

*Present*

Valerie had the afternoon off. Elizabeth swapped hours with a coworker to end her shift at noon. She hurried home to the pool house and made two turkey breast sandwiches. She filled a thermos with iced tea.

"I'm taking you to lunch," she said when her mom came home.

"To what do I owe the honor?"

"To you."

Val beamed. She scampered into the back room and peeled off her uniform. "Dress or casual?" she called out.

"Shorts," Elizabeth said. "And flip-flops." Though fall was approaching, L.A. was stuck in its perpetual summer.

They drove to Balboa Park. On a patch of grass by the lake—away from the squawking geese—Elizabeth spread out two beach towels. She unpacked their lunch. As Val settled in next to her daughter, she asked, "Is this about the mysterious boy?"

Blushing, Elizabeth said, "So, you know."

"Of course I know. I'm your mother. I have eyes in the back of my head and ears in the front. I am a Picasso."

Elizabeth laughed. In spite of her guilt. She hadn't mentioned York because, how could she? How could she tell her mom how they met without confessing her many sins—swimming in the Adells' pool, sneaking down the hill, drinking alcohol? Instead, she'd said nothing. Even as her mom eyed her askance each time she slithered outside to make a private call.

"Here's the thing," Elizabeth began, taking a deep breath.

Out it all spilled. The truth. About George, anyway. The Duke of York. The rest was harder to say.

"He sounds nice, honey." Valerie took a bite of her sandwich. "Though I should ground you for drinking."

"I only had one. And it was pink. And I wasn't driving."

"You'd better not! No more sneaking into the pool either. You want us out on the streets?"

Elizabeth sighed. "It won't happen again."

"No. It won't."

They gazed out at the twinkling lake. A hidden gem in thirsty Van Nuys. Elizabeth's idyllic retreat. Her private club. Where she used to come with Shelby. Back when they were best friends.

"Too bad you two live so far apart," Valerie said. "When will you ever see him again?"

Elizabeth looked down at her long toes. So different from her mom's. "That's the other thing," she said, softly.

"Oh?"

"Well—" Surprising her, tears began to well.

Valerie set her sandwich aside and reached over to tuck her daughter's hair behind her ear. Elizabeth opened her mouth, then closed it again. What could she say? How could she admit her secret search? How could she confess how long she'd wondered about her birth mother, how often she'd tamped down her curiosity? For years, when she couldn't sleep and the murky light before dawn bathed her bedroom in shadows, questions rained upon her. Had her natural mother fallen overboard? Was she *pushed*? Had she flailed her arms and cried out for her baby?

*Elizabeth!*

Was her name—her original name—the last word on her birth mother's lips as she sank to the bottom of the sea? How could Elizabeth now hurt the mother who had actually *mothered* her?

"You've found out who your birth mother was," Valerie said, gently.

Elizabeth looked up, shocked. Valerie's eyes were damp, too.

"Is that it?" Val asked.

"Sort of."

She looked so vulnerable Elizabeth didn't have the nerve to say more.

"Tell me," Valerie said, almost in a whisper. Leaning across the beach towel, she wrapped her fingers around her daughter's palm. In the warmth of her mother's touch, Elizabeth felt her permission. From the crown of her dark, curly hair to the tips of her bony toes, a sense of peace floated over her. She opened her mouth and released the history as she knew it. The South Fork Fishing and Hunting Club. The flood. The aftermath.

"They still live in Johnstown, Pennsylvania," she said, spent.

"Who does?"

"My birth mother's family."

Valerie reeled back, as if blasted by a gust of wind. Her hands flew up to her chest. She pressed them against the cotton blend of her T-shirt. The one that read YES, I AM A SUPERMODEL.

"Have you contacted them?" she asked.

"Yes."

"Do they want to meet you?"

"Yes."

Valerie inhaled and blew it out. Twice. Her eyebrows knotted together, then they smoothed themselves out. In a what's-done-is-done sort of way, both hands slapped her knees.

"Okay, then. Let's get you a plane ticket."

# CHAPTER 49

SOUTHERN CALIFORNIA

*Present*

No one looks powerful in socks. That's what Elizabeth was thinking as she peeled down her jean jacket and kicked off her shoes at the heel. Standing spread-eagled in the giant X-ray machine, with both hands over her head, she understood the awkwardness of plane travel. Airports are a great equalizer. Even first-class passengers are treated like possible terrorists.

Not that she was flying first class. Elizabeth's cheap seat was at the back of the plane. In the middle of the middle section. By the time her group was called to board, first-class passengers were already sipping champagne.

With her carry-on backpack bobbling in front of her, Elizabeth shuffled to her seat. When she got there, she was surprised to see that her overhead bin was jammed full. Weren't they supposed to provide storage for one bag? Wasn't that included in the price? Not sure what to do, she stood in the aisle with cheeks blazing in embarrassment.

"Allow me." A man stood and took her backpack, stowing it over his seat next to the bathroom. Elizabeth was so grateful she didn't have the heart to tell him her book was still inside it.

"Thank you," she said instead. Then, somehow, she managed to climb over the other passengers in her row just as the flight attendant announced, "We're cleared for takeoff." Elizabeth plopped into her seat and buckled up. Even if she were dying to pee, no way would she have the guts to move now.

The plan was simple, though exhausting. With her mother's help, she hadn't needed to spend all of her laptop savings. Just *most*. Still, it was worth it. Elizabeth booked the cheapest flight to Pittsburgh. A redeye there and a redeye back to save the cost of a hotel. The train ride from Pittsburgh to Johnstown was an hour and a half long. There was one train into Johnstown in the morning, one train back to Pittsburgh in the evening.

Her visit would be a surgical strike. Meet her birth mother's family, take a tour of the town, have lunch, snap photos, get back on the train. No time to feel anything but tired.

In the plane, the lights blinked off and the engine revved up. Elizabeth's heart thumped. Trying not to let her head touch the white doily on the headrest—when was the last time they changed that?—she pressed her back into the seat and silently counted.

*Four, five, six.*

"Virgin?" The man seated next to her smoothed his tie.

She blushed. Was it that obvious?

"First time flying?" he asked, clarifying.

"Oh. Yeah."

He said, "Relax. It's safer than driving."

Elizabeth wanted to inform him that *thousands* of people died in car accidents every day, not to mention those that survived but were so maimed they wished they were dead, but she knew he was only being kind. So she smiled and nodded and swallowed her rising fear that she would miss the one and only daily train from Pittsburgh to Johnstown. If she missed the train, she'd have to spend the night in Pittsburgh and catch the train the following morning. Her plans—and her budget—would be blown to smithereens.

"When do they bring the peanuts?" Elizabeth asked instead, hearing her stomach rumble.

"Ha." He guffawed, thinking she'd made some kind of joke.

THE SUN WAS up by the time they touched down. Elizabeth had slept sporadically. The rumble of the engines soothed her into semiconsciousness. She even managed a brief nap during the early-morning layover at Chicago's O'Hare airport. Back in the air, as she was dreaming of floating on a raft in the ocean, the flight attendant woke her with the announcement that they were beginning their descent into Pittsburgh International Airport. Incredibly, they landed fifteen minutes early.

As soon as she was off the plane and in the airport, Elizabeth made a beeline for the bathroom. Her reflection in the mirror was a fright. How could *sitting* for hours make you look so racked? Her skin was both pale and blotchy. Her hair looked deranged. Mascara goo sat like an oil spill in the corners of both eyes. Why did people like traveling? So far, it had been embarrassing, frustrating, squished, starving, and mortifying. And she had only just arrived.

Splashing cool water on her face, Elizabeth ran a damp tissue beneath her lower lashes, brushed her hair, peed, washed her hands, applied lip gloss, popped a breath mint, and rejoined the flow of humanity.

"Elizabeth!"

She heard him before she saw him. His voice had the casual confidence she'd come to love. Dressed in Levi's, Converse sneakers, a heather-gray T-shirt beneath a charcoal pullover, with his dark curls spilling rakishly over his forehead, he somehow blended into the black-suited drivers who stood around him holding up signs with printed names on them. Elizabeth's heart tap-danced in her chest. He was every bit as delicious as she remembered.

"You're here," she said, shyly.

York took her backpack. When he grinned, she saw the three divots she had longed to see again: two dimples and a cleft. His teeth were white, but not blinding. His fingernails were the perfect shade of baby pink.

"I had a test today. I'd do anything to miss it."

"Ha ha."

As they walked outside to meet the shuttle that would take them to the Pittsburgh Amtrak station, York said, "Who doesn't love a good mystery?"

The warmth of his hand on her back melted the stress of her journey. It was morning. A new day. By nightfall, she would know all.

# ·❦[ CHAPTER 50 ]❦·

## THE ALLEGHENY MOUNTAINS

*Present*

Elizabeth tightened her grip on the backpack in her lap. Through the train window, she watched the branches flickering past. It had rained that morning. The green trees looked washed. High on the mountainsides she spotted flashes of fiery red and orange. The fall colors everyone talked about. *In a few weeks,* she thought, *the Alleghenies will be spectacular.*

"We're almost there," York said, beside her. "Two more stops."

*We.* Elizabeth liked that pronoun. When she first told York she was flying to the East Coast, he said, "Where do you want to meet?" She didn't stop smiling for a week. Now, awash in so many emotions, she was finding it hard to breathe. York was next to her, her birth family was ahead. *Was this really happening? Would she wake up on a moldy couch in a stuffy pool house?*

As if to mimic her agitation, the train's whistle blared. Her body felt the pull of the locomotive as they neared Horseshoe Curve.

"Whoo, whoo," York chirped, on the seat next to her.

Elizabeth reached up for the air control vent and turned the knob. A rush of mountain air cooled her face. She let her eyelids fall shut. For a wisp of time, she felt free.

York poked her arm. "The loop," he said. He'd read about the sharp U-turn curve, how tourists took the inclined plane at Kittanning Point up to the train tracks just to see the engineering feat. Elizabeth opened her eyes in time to see the front of the train circle all the way around the tip of Altoona's old reservoir. She felt the train car list as it curved in on itself. This high in the Alleghenies—swollen with forests of white pine and black cherry and foothills blanketed in yellow oxeye and lavender musk mallow—the view was calendar perfect. York clicked a photo with his iPhone. A deliciously woodsy aroma twirled around the floral scents that infused the air.

Elizabeth felt her panic easing. Fresh mountain air was a tonic.

FINDING HER GENETIC relatives had been surprisingly easy. Once Elizabeth had a last name and a city, her search went quickly. She found Haberlin descendants in Pittsburgh via a LinkedIn search.

"You're in luck," one Haberlin e-mailed her back. "My grandson did one of those Ancestry.com searches. He's the one you want to talk to."

He's the one she did talk to.

"Elizabeth Haberlin married Eugene Eggar in Johnstown,

Pennsylvania," he told her. "In 1891. They had a son, Silas, and a daughter, Victoria."

Wow. There it was. The woman in the photo came alive.

"Their descendants still live in Johnstown."

"No way," Elizabeth had said.

"Want an address?"

Just like that, Elizabeth Parker had the name and address of her birth mother's sister. Her *aunt,* Vida Eggar. Hiding it from Valerie, she wrote her biological aunt a letter. Vida e-mailed her back. On the subject line were three letters: "OMG."

"Can I call you?" Vida asked in the e-mail.

Elizabeth replied, "It's best if I call you."

Vida immediately sent her phone number. The next day, in the break room at Bed Bath & Beyond, away from the eyes and ears of her mom, Elizabeth sat alone in a chair by the lockers. With her heart ready to leap out of her chest, she made a call into her past.

"You sound just like her." Vida burst into tears the moment Elizabeth spoke. "I never stopped wondering what happened to you."

Upon hearing Vida's voice, Elizabeth's first impulse was to hang up. Her thumb flicked over to the red exit icon. *Who was this woman? What was she doing?* Guilt washed over her. Valerie didn't deserve this. After her mom's hellish year, she was going to dump this on her, too?

Still.

"You must have a million questions," Vida said.

She did. Of course she did. As any adoptee knew.

"I don't know how much you know," Vida said. "Do you know anything?"

"Not much. Well, a little, I guess. My mother, I mean, my *birth* mother, drowned, right?"

"Right." Vida sniffed.

"And my name was—is—Elizabeth. Maybe after Elizabeth Haberlin?"

"Wow. How did you find *that* out?"

"Long story."

Exhaling, Vida said, "There are a lot of long stories in our family." Then she asked, "Where do you live? Can we meet? Like, for lunch or something?"

"I live in California."

"California? Vera would have been horrified." She laughed. "She always wondered how people could live with so much sunlight."

At the mention of her birth mother's name, Elizabeth felt a surge of electricity shoot down her arms. "My mom's name was Vera?"

"Yes," Vida said, softly. "Vera Sinclair Eggar. An old family name."

# CHAPTER 51

*Photo Credit: R. A. Mauer*

JOHNSTOWN, PENNSYLVANIA

*Present*

From the moment Elizabeth Parker exited the train in Johnstown, Pennsylvania, she stepped back in time. The red-brick station was a striking homage to the past. Recently restored, the old building looked freshly scrubbed. In the original waiting room, the ceiling rose up like a cathedral—all light and celestial air. Dark wood pews sat in tidy rows on the shiny stone floor. A raised mural in the grand hallway depicted the city's history. The sweat of the workingman. The making of steel. And, yes, a massive tidal wave that washed it all away, only to be rebuilt, restored. Returned to work.

"My God." A woman about Valerie's age, with hair the color of burned walnuts and eyelashes as thick as paintbrushes, ran headlong up to Elizabeth's face. She bookended Elizabeth's cheeks in her hands.

"I cannot believe how much you look like her."

As she had over the phone, Vida burst into tears. She flung her arms around Elizabeth and said, "I'm your auntie. You don't have to tell me who you are. It's so obvious."

Tongue-tied, Elizabeth stood like a telephone pole and tried to smile naturally. York stepped forward with an extended hand. "I'm the boyfriend," he said, leaving her even more speechless.

In a flurry of sniffing and hugging, Vida sidestepped York's hand and threw her arms around him, too. Elizabeth snatched glances at Vida's face. While she resembled her more than Valerie did—same dark hair and eyes—Vida's cheeks were rounder, her nose was larger, her lips didn't peak up the way Elizabeth's did. Looking at Vida was nothing like looking in a mirror.

"Dad is at the house," she said, "but I thought you might like a little tour around town before lunch."

Without waiting for a response, Vida grabbed Elizabeth's backpack and chugged to the exit. At the door to the outside, she abruptly stopped and wheeled around to stare with wet eyes. "It's like my sister has come home."

Elizabeth summoned a smile even as dread settled in her stomach like a ball of pizza dough. Now that she was here, she wanted to be *anywhere* else. Her feet itched to turn around and run her body back to the platform. The train was already gone. Still, she could hide behind a pillar until the next train pulled in. It didn't matter where it was going, as long as it would take her out of here. Away from this soggy-eyed woman who wouldn't stop touching her. This person who was a total stranger and should act like it. York would understand their escape. It would be fun. They would have a wild adventure in the Allegheny Mountains.

In another wave of emotion, Elizabeth suddenly missed her mom. Her *real* mom. Valerie. The woman who was probably shedding tears of her own in the pool house. Like a lost child at the mall, Elizabeth felt panicked guilt. As if she'd been told to wait by the information booth—"Don't move!"—and had been lured away by the smell of popcorn. Now everything was unfamiliar. She might as well be on another planet.

How could she do this to the only mother she'd ever have?

Valerie was her mom. The *best* mom. She'd gone through hell to get her: years of trying to conceive, a loan for the failed IVF treatments, do-it-yourself fertility boosters she found online. No coffee, no alcohol, piles of edamame, spinach, bananas, yogurt, and wheat germ. She bought ground Peruvian maca root at a health food store and spooned it into smoothies. She checked the stickiness of her cervical mucus and meticulously tracked her basal body temperature.

"Can't we just *do it* for once?" Gil had asked.

Valerie checked her chart. "Tomorrow," she said. "Sperm can live inside me for three to five days. I won't shower."

Though she admitted it to no one, Valerie suspected that her husband's drinking was part (if not all) of the problem.

Adoption—at last—was Val and Gil's way to succeed amid all their failure. Still, it took years of effort to find a baby. But they persisted. When their daughter finally arrived, she was so perfect they both wept.

"Gil, look at these little feet. And her hands, like teeny tiny pillows."

Lee Parker was loved instantly and completely and felt it.

How could she now slap her mother in the face?

"Vida, I—"

"I know, I know," Vida said, pulling a wadded tissue from beneath her sleeve and wiping her nose. "You're starving. We'll take a *quick* drive around town so you can see where you came from."

Elizabeth's thought: *I'm from* California.

"I'd love a tour," York said. "This place is a trip."

Without a clue what else to do, Elizabeth followed them both to Vida's car and sat, shotgun, in the front seat.

JOHNSTOWN'S TOPOGRAPHY WAS striking. More than a valley, the town sat in a *pit*. It was impossible not to feel swallowed by the mountains. On all sides, the Alleghenies rose up like huge piles of broccoli. Orange, yellow, and red foliage was dotted throughout. Fall was on the verge.

As they crossed over the Conemaugh River—which now

flowed placidly west—Elizabeth glanced east. Where the wall of water had barreled down from the mountaintop on that horrible day in May. It was obvious that the mountain lake had once been practically overhead. As Elizabeth had read, the people of Johnstown once looked up to see sailboats criss-crossing the sky. *What curious geography,* she thought. *A lake in the heavens that caused such hell.*

"Down there is the old Cambria Iron building." Vida pointed through the windshield. "That Gothic steeple in the distance is the only downtown church to survive the big flood."

They drove along Walnut Street in the shade of mature elms. *Fourteen, fifteen, sixteen . . .* Elizabeth fell into the comfort of counting. Vida steered past the stately Flood Museum that was once the Cambria Free Library. Its goldenrod-brick building was built with funds donated by Pittsburgh's titan of steel, Andrew Carnegie—one of the few members of the South Fork Fishing and Hunting Club to attempt to make amends for the destruction his club had wrought. The museum's silhouette etched the sky with its pointy dormers and fluted chimneys.

Breathing with deliberate evenness, Elizabeth kept asking herself, *Am I really here? Was* Elizabeth Haberlin *really here? My birth mother, too? Is this really happening?*

" . . . an historic block," Vida continued. "The old post office is on that corner, City Hall is on that corner, an apartment building from the 1900s, one of our first theaters . . ."

Elizabeth listened through the loud pulsing in her ears.

Vida steered the car along Locust Street, past a perfectly square park with a starfish-shaped pathway in the grass. All points led to the round fountain with its gurgling water arching from—*one, two, three*—Elizabeth counted *four* open mouths of watchful marble lions.

"Our Central Park," Vida said with a sweep of her open palm. "Not quite New York City, but home."

At the mention of the word "home" Elizabeth winced slightly. Next to her in the front seat, Vida noticed.

"This must be overwhelming," she said.

From behind her, York rested one hand on Elizabeth's shoulder and squeezed. Elizabeth confessed, "It is a bit surreal."

Slowing, Vida said. "I have an idea. Can you handle a small detour?"

"Um—"

York asked, "Where to?"

"Someplace that will make it more real."

From the backseat, York said, "I'm in."

Despite her nerves, Elizabeth laughed. York was so easygoing, so sunny, so very like Valerie, what was he doing with a dark cloud like her? She shrugged. Then nodded. She was in, too. Of course she was. After coming this far, how could she not go all the way?

After circling the square park, Vida backtracked down Main Street to Market. Then she took a left. At Lincoln, she made a right. Elizabeth stared out the window and breathed. *In. Out. Repeat.* She had never seen such an old town. Sturdy square brick structures with arched windows, slate roofs, buttresses,

peaked dormers, rectangular columns. And she thought the
Beverly Hills Library—built in the 1960s—was old!

"What the . . . ?" At the end of Vine Street, York leaned
forward. Elizabeth tilted closer to the windshield. She, too, was
agog. Ahead was an extraordinary sight. She'd never seen anything like it. A long, thin strip of railroad track ran *vertically* up
the side of a steep mountain.

"That can't possibly be a train track," York said, astonished.

Vida grinned. "You'll see."

She steered her car straight to it. At a small kiosk at the base
of the mountain, Vida bought a ticket. Then she slowly drove
into the belly of a single railcar at the base of the mountain
and cut the engine. Other cars were parked inside the rail
carriage, too. With a small jolt, the railroad car began to rise.
*Straight up* the mountainside. Impossibly, they were all being
ferried up the hill. Seemingly floating upward in midair.

"Is this even possible?" York asked, grinning.

"It's called the Inclined Plane. Our version of an express elevator."

"Like the one at Kittanning Point near Horseshoe Curve?"

"Similar, but steeper. Wait till you see the view."

She was right. At the top of the mountain, Vida drove out
of the railcar and parked. They exited the car into a perfectly
warm day. Outside, Elizabeth felt the sun on her face and the
mountain breeze ripple through her loose hair.

"Check this out." Vida waved them over.

An observation deck jutted out from a ledge in the mountain.
At its railing, Elizabeth and York saw a truly stunning sight.

The whole of Johnstown stretched before them. They were so high up, the buildings looked like Monopoly pieces. "That's the library down there," Vida said. "The Flood Museum over there, *way* over there is the old iron works, and around that little bend . . . see it? There's the stone bridge."

"*The* stone bridge?" Elizabeth's jaw dropped.

"Yep."

York asked, "What about it?"

"If not for that old bridge," said Vida, "there would be no Elizabeth and no me. For us, that bridge connected two worlds." She paused to let the notion sink in. Then she added, "Speaking of which—" With a wave of her hand, she motioned for Elizabeth and York to get back in the car.

In silence, they snaked through fields of pink and white mountain laurel, past dirt paddocks and farmhouses. In the saffron sunlight, Elizabeth felt herself relax. Her outing began to feel more like a great field trip than a journey into her genetics. Vida, while still a stranger, was nice. Now that she'd stopped pawing her.

Onward they drove. Through shade tunnels of yellow birch dotted with the flickering green tails of the towhees. Dogs barked from front porches as they drove past. Neighbors acknowledged one another with nods. At the crest of a hill, Vida slowed and flipped on her turn signal again. The tires made a crunching sound as she veered off onto a patch of gravel and parked. Again, Elizabeth's jaw dropped. "Is that—?"

"Can you believe it's still standing?" Vida grinned.

"What is that?" asked York.

"The *clubhouse*," Elizabeth said in a near whisper. "Oh my God. I saw pictures of it online, but I didn't realize it was still here."

Opening the passenger door, Elizabeth stepped out of the car and into the past. Almost in a trance, she walked across the gravel parking lot to the side stairs. She stood where Elizabeth Haberlin had stood—at the foot of the clubhouse stairs, where debutantes chattered with one another, gazed out over their lake, waited for servants to bring tea cakes and lemonade. Where the moneyed once met for croquet and archery. Where Elizabeth's great-great-great-grandmother turned her back on her birthright.

"In a way," Vida said to Elizabeth, "you began right here. As did I."

The clubhouse—long abandoned—was now a sagging three-story structure of splintered wood. Locked to visitors, it was owned by the National Park Service. Elizabeth ventured up the front steps onto the weathered porch that ran the length of the building. She turned and stood at the railing as Elizabeth Haberlin had for so many summers, so many years ago. She looked at Lake Conemaugh. Only now, impossibly, the dry lakebed was filled with houses. A whole *neighborhood*. In the gently sloping valley that was once the bottom of a lake, there were backyards and tipped-over bikes and barbecue grills. Sidewalks and roads. The muck at the bottom of the lake was now patches of front and back lawns.

*Is this really happening? Am I really here?*

"The boardwalk was *here*." Vida pointed to a residential

street in front of the clubhouse. "Over there, the stables. Back there, the outhouse."

"And the dam?"

"Down that way. It's totally gone now. But Colonel Unger's old farmhouse is still on the north shore, so to speak. The Park Service bought it after he died."

"He *lived* there after the flood?"

"He did. He returned to South Fork and, for the rest of his life, he walked out of his house to see the gaping hole that was once his lake. I think he probably stayed here to pay penance for what he did, or what he allowed to happen."

York was bursting with questions, but he wisely remained mute. They had a long train ride back to Pittsburgh that night. Elizabeth would explain it all then.

"Want to see a cottage?" Vida asked.

Elizabeth's heart pinged. "The Haberlin cottage?"

"I *wish* we still had that house in our family. No, it was torn down years ago. As far as we know, after the flood, Elizabeth Haberlin never came up here again. Her family cut her off when she refused to return to Pittsburgh. And when she married Eugene, well—"

Nothing more needed to be said. Elizabeth Haberlin had done the unthinkable in those days: she chose love over money.

"Follow me," Vida said. Elizabeth and York followed.

As they walked along the narrow road that was once the boardwalk at the edge of Lake Conemaugh, Vida led Elizabeth and York on a journey into the late 1880s. "Elizabeth Haberlin was an amazing woman," she began. "When she married Eugene Eggar—a blacksmith from Johnstown—her parents disowned her. As did everyone in her social circle. I heard there was an attempt at reconciliation after their son was born."

"Did they?" Elizabeth asked.

"No. Her mother could never accept the new life she chose. Her brother visited once, years later. He became some Wall Street bigwig. Ever hear of the Haberlin Fund?"

Elizabeth and York both shook their heads no.

"Henry Haberlin made fortunes for all his friends before losing everyone's money in the stock-market crash of 1929."

"Ouch," said York.

"Yeah. Though it was hard at times, Elizabeth Haberlin had a happier life. Did you know she worked with Clara Barton?" Vida asked.

"Sort of. I knew they met here."

"Clara stayed in Johnstown for five months after the flood. She supervised the building of five Red Cross hotels. Elizabeth Haberlin helped her run them. She brought her piano down from the cottage and hosted elegant teas each afternoon. Clara—and Elizabeth—both believed in the healing power of civility. Wouldn't the world be a better place if we all thought that way today?"

"Tea instead of Kalashnikovs," said York.

With York a few steps ahead, they wound around the neighborhood that was filled with the chirping sounds of kids playing.

"Throw the ball! Catch it, catch it!"

*How many of those kids know they are playing at the bottom of a lake?*

Elizabeth wondered. *Do they pass by the clubhouse so frequently they don't even see it? Does anyone still care about what happened here?*

"There." Vida pointed up a small incline. "One of the remaining cottages."

York laughed. "That's a *cottage*?"

Resembling a turreted castle, the three-story maroon-brick house had a pointed roof, peaked dormers, and a wide slatted veranda that ran the length of its front façade.

*Always a porch,* Elizabeth thought. *Where her blood relatives sat and rocked and stared at the ripples in their private bass-stocked lake.*

"I think there are six cottages left from the original sixteen," Vida said. "Some of the flood's homeless survivors eventually made their way up to the abandoned cottages, but Eugene Eggar was a blacksmith at the steel mill. He would want to live in town. And, when his son grew up, he, too, worked at the mill. As did Eugene's grandson. They considered it the family business."

York was impressed. "Cambria Iron kept on kicking."

"Thank God for that mill. *Generations* have worked there. A few years after the flood, it became Cambria Steel, then Midvale Steel, then the biggie: Bethlehem Steel. Our mill helped build America. My dad—your granddad, Elizabeth—was a machinist there until the mill closed for good in the 1990s."

Elizabeth swallowed at the mention of a grandfather. How could a man she'd never met be her grandfather?

"Ready for lunch?" Vida asked. She reached up and ran her long fingers down the length of Elizabeth's wavy hair. They both knew what "lunch" meant: getting back in the car and driving down the mountain to the Johnstown, Pennsylvania, home where Vera Sinclair Eggar was born, grew up, lived, loved, and (maybe) conceived her.

Elizabeth Parker—daughter of Val and Gil, sister of Scott, niece of Vida—felt a surprising rush of calm.

"I'm ready."

Beneath the impossibly blue sky in the stunning Allegheny Mountains near the old South Fork Fishing and Hunting Club, she was—at last—prepared to hear the rest of her story.

# CHAPTER 52

JOHNSTOWN, PENNSYLVANIA

*Present*

The Eggar home was a brick box of a house compared to the spacious cottage up the mountain. As they pulled into the driveway in the seasoned residential neighborhood— alongside other compact homes with a similar look—Vida said, "Eugene Eggar built this house after the flood. Dad has rebuilt it over the years."

Once again, Elizabeth was stunned to see a structure from the nineteenth century still standing. And the same family living in it. In Southern California, so few people even had an old *face*. And if a building wasn't shiny and new, developers tore it down to make it so.

"Progress," they said. "Evolve or go extinct."

It was a comfort to see residents living *with* history. How narcissistic to believe that *now* was the only important moment.

Vida cut the engine and stepped out of the car. Elizabeth and York followed. A bursting apple tree grew in the center of the yard. The one-car garage—obviously an addition—was open and filled to capacity. A large workbench occupied the car space. Every imaginable tool was hung neatly on pegboards along all the walls. A lawn mower, circular saw, lathe, and air compressor were lined up on the cement floor like eager employees ready to go to work. A metal garbage can was filled with wood scraps. York gawked, openmouthed.

"There you are." A man in his seventies pushed open the front screen door with fingers bent by arthritis. His hair was fog gray and wispy; his eyes were two green grapes.

"Dad, meet Elizabeth and York."

"Elizabeth," he said, gruffly. "I see."

Vida climbed the front steps and held the door. As Elizabeth opened her mouth to greet the old man, Gene Eggar turned his back and walked into the house. Vida shot Elizabeth a commiserating look. York was undeterred.

"Nice to meet you, sir." He marched into the living room with an extended hand. Gene was already seated in his favorite chair. "Looks like you're handy with power tools."

Gene grunted and shook York's hand before flicking his wrist as if to invite them to sit anywhere. Elizabeth's heart pounded so loudly she was sure everyone could hear it. The tight room was crammed with mismatched furniture. A sagging brown plaid sofa, Shaker-style rocker, a frayed easy chair with a red velvet pillow on the seat. It smelled of lemon Pledge and stale cigars. Something garlicky? An old upright piano blocked a portion of the front window. Gene sat on a vinyl recliner and stared at his

Velcro-strapped shoes. Vida said, "Make yourselves comfortable. Apple cider? I made some this morning from our own
apples."

"Wow. Yes. Please." As before, Elizabeth had the strong
urge to flee. Real cider or not. How far was that train station?
Walkable? Runnable?

"Sit, sit," said Vida as she disappeared into the kitchen. "I
won't be but a minute."

They sat on the brown plaid couch. York leaned forward
with his elbows on his knees. Elizabeth set her backpack on
the floor at her feet. She breathed with deliberation. *In. Out.
Repeat.* Scanning the dingy room, she noticed a smattering of
framed family photos on the mantel over the fireplace, its brick
facing blackened by use. A surge of electricity shot down her
arms. Was her birth mother pictured there? Had she sat exactly where Elizabeth was sitting now?

"Original oak?" York bobbed his head toward the staircase
to the left of the front door.

"Throughout," Gene said.

"These old houses were sure built to last."

Gene grunted again. "I've fixed it up here and there. Though
I wouldn't call linoleum an improvement."

York chuckled. Elizabeth fiddled with the sharp spike of
a hangnail on her thumb. Glasses clattered in the kitchen.
Abruptly, Gene looked straight at Elizabeth and said, "Vida
tells me you live in that godforsaken state, California."

Elizabeth's cheeks reddened. "I do, for now. But I don't like
it very much. Too sunny."

"Your mother also disliked the sun."

At the mention of her birth mother, another current of electricity shot down Elizabeth's arms. Again she felt disloyal to Valerie—the only mother she'd ever known.

"You're the spitting image of her," Gene said, flatly. "But I guess Vida told you that." Twisting his neck toward the kitchen, he shouted, "Vida!"

"Coming."

York asked, "Have you lived here your whole life?"

"No reason to go anyplace else. Vida!"

His daughter scuttled in with four sweating glasses on a tray. "Here we are," she said, breathless.

"Let me help you with that." York stood and flew over to her. Elizabeth sat like a wart on a witch's nose. She felt paralyzed, unable to do more than furtively examine Gene Eggar's face for traces of herself. Had his genetic pool contributed her cheekbones, the slight ridge at the tip of her nose? Would her fingers look like knotted rope when she was old? Gene glanced at her with a downturned mouth.

"The chicken is almost done," Vida said, looking slightly sweaty. "A few more minutes in the oven."

Elizabeth nearly groaned out loud. She was roasting a *chicken*? It was so formal, so time-consuming. No way could they swallow a few bites and run. York set the cider tray down on the oak coffee table. Vida sat on the red velvet chair. Elizabeth tried to help in some way, but she didn't trust her hands to grip anything. They, too, felt numb. Her ears buzzed. She'd made a huge mistake. *What exactly had she hoped to find here?*

York took one sip of his apple cider and his eyes fluttered shut. "Now, *that's* what I'm talking about."

Overlaughing, Vida said, "Our apple tree is over a hundred years old."

"No need to waste money on dormant oil," Gene said. "You can make your own with canola and baking soda."

Without a clue what he was talking about, Elizabeth grinned idiotically. Gene grabbed a cider glass and took a large, loud swallow. Had elegant Elizabeth Haberlin married someone like *him*?

Setting his own glass back on the tray, York asked Gene, "Any chance I can get a tour of your workshop? I'm a bit of a carpenter. In my dreams, anyway."

When Gene Eggar pulled himself out of his chair and left the room, Elizabeth wanted to kiss York on the lips.

"Call us when lunch is ready," Gene said over his shoulder. With York on his heels, he made his way to the rear door without looking back at Elizabeth once.

"He hates me," Elizabeth said as soon as they were out of earshot. She sipped her cider and felt the cool, sweet liquid stream down her throat.

Vida stood and walked over to the fireplace. Picking up a framed photograph, she brought it to the couch where Elizabeth sat.

"He can't even see you. He only sees *her*."

There she was.

Elizabeth took the photo into her shaky grip. She looked down and couldn't believe her eyes. Wearing Capri jeans and a spaghetti-strap top, was a woman with her face and build. Tall, slim. The woman stood in front of a brick wall and stared at the lens as if she were looking straight through it. Her smile was faint, yet intense; her eyes and brows were as dark as coal. There were two peaks in her upper lip. Her jaw was a jutting right angle. An ebony mane tumbled messily down her back. A profound sadness emanated from those eyes. Elizabeth wondered, *Was I already growing inside of her?*

"Freaky, isn't it?" Vida said.

"She seems so, so—"

"Intense? Yeah, Vera felt everything deeply. Too deeply." Then she added, "That photo was probably taken in the morning. Vera never fully woke up before noon."

Elizabeth stared at the picture. At the woman she'd wondered about since she was old enough to wonder. There, in her hands, was a photograph of the person who created her, carried her inside for nearly a year, cradled her in arms—for a minute or two, at least. There, at last, was the mother who had first counted her long fingers and toes, examined every inch of her face in search of similarities. *My eyelashes. My nose.* Elizabeth breathed in the moment, eighteen years in the making. She waited for the magical connection to transport her into the picture, next to her birth mother. She braced herself for the jolt of cellular attachment.

Yet she felt something else entirely.

*Here is a relative who looks like me.*

A relative. Not a mother. Valerie Parker was her mother. The morning person with light eyes and blond hair and a disposition as sunny as Southern California.

Maybe DNA *wasn't* destiny after all.

Vida sat next to her on the couch. She leaned forward and pulled open a drawer in the coffee table. She retrieved an old photo album. It smelled like a vintage purse. It opened with a cracking sound. On the first page was a wedding photo. The bride wore a simple white gown with a gathered skirt that dusted the floor in a plain ruffle. Flowing down the back of her head was a long veil topped with wispy white flowers. She held a petite bouquet of asters. The black vest of her husband's suit was buttoned high. His stiff color was fastened with a white bow tie.

Elizabeth sucked in a breath. She pressed her palm against her chest. *Now* she felt a connection. There was the woman in the photo—the familiar face and body she'd seen in her adoption file. The blood relative who had started it all: Elizabeth Haberlin. Next to her new husband, Eugene.

"Eugene Eggar's entire family was killed in the flood," Vida said, softly. "His young sister, Elsie, his parents. They never even found his mother's body. Which wasn't that unusual. More than seven hundred and fifty people were so mutilated by the barbed wire and glass and *stuff* barreling down on them, they were never able to be identified. Lots of poor souls were buried so deeply in the mud no one ever got to them."

"You mean—?"

"Off Millcreek Road is the Johnstown cemetery. There's a Plot of the Unknown there. But no one knows who may still be beneath our feet."

Elizabeth's forehead creased in sadness. Vida pointed to other old snapshots. "That's their son, Silas. And their daughter, Victoria." She looked up. "You know we're Jewish, right?"

"Right." Elizabeth nodded. "Ashkenazi."

Vida's eyebrows peaked. "I'm impressed. You're Jewish, too?"

Elizabeth laughed. "I'm not very good at it yet."

"Me neither. A seder at Passover is about it."

*Ah yes,* Elizabeth thought. *The bitter herbs, ground-up fruit-and-nut paste, middle matzo.*

"I was named after Victoria Eggar, and your mother—"

"*Birth* mother."

"Yes. Sorry. Your birth mother was named after Vera Sinclair. You, of course, were named after *her*." She pointed to a photograph of Elizabeth Haberlin's back as she sat at a piano. Dressed in a dark color, her waist cinched, her spine upright, Elizabeth Haberlin rested both hands expertly on the keys. Her dark hair was wound neatly in a braided bun. On her wrist, a diamond bracelet sparkled in the light from the window beside her.

Elizabeth Parker knew *this* woman in the photo as clearly as she knew herself. The stillness of playing piano, the need for good posture, the ability to shut everything else out as you played. She fingered the vintage bracelet on her own wrist—the one she never took off. This woman in the photo was her. On the *inside*. The other woman, Vera—her birth mother—had similar features. But Elizabeth Haberlin—her namesake—had passed down her soul.

"Great-great-great," Elizabeth said, almost to herself.

"Isn't it?"

With a smile, Elizabeth explained, "I'd been wondering if Elizabeth Haberlin was my great-great-grandmother, or great-great-*great*."

"Oh." Vida laughed. "Yeah. Great-great-great. And she really was. Elizabeth Haberlin was extraordinary."

Finally, Elizabeth Parker found her peep.

From the kitchen, a timer went *ping*. Vida leaped up. "Lunch is calling." Elizabeth shut the photo album and rose to her feet, too. As she followed Vida out of the living room, she stopped by the window.

"This is it, isn't it?"

Vida turned around and nodded. "It's a bit clinky. No one has played it, or tuned it, in years."

"Mind if I try?"

"I'd love it." She grabbed a chair.

Elizabeth sat before the old upright piano and rested her fingers lightly on the yellowed ivory keys. She felt Elizabeth Haberlin's energy in her fingertips. With her back rigid and her neck elongated, she played Giovanni Marradi's "Just for You." Her favorite.

# CHAPTER 53

*Present*

The smell of roasted garlic and lemons saturated the Eggar kitchen. Elizabeth set the table while Vida stood before the open oven door to suck pan juices into a baster and squeeze them over the mound of crackling brown skin.

"You live here with your dad?" Elizabeth asked.

"For better and worse." Vida sighed. "I'm afraid there's no one else. I never married and I have no kids. Dad, well, he won't admit it, but he needs help. Without me, he would sit in that chair and starve. So, there you go. You do what you have to do. What about you? Brothers? Sisters?"

"One brother. Scott. He's twelve years older. A rebel. Right now he's living off the grid in Idaho. And my dad, well, let me just say that my mom is the only person who stuck around."

Looking slightly stung, Vida shut the oven door and hurried to the sink to rip lettuce for a salad. Just then, the screen door creaked open.

"Gotta oil that," Gene tossed over his shoulder as both men entered the kitchen. "Smells ready," he said to his daughter. To York he added, "Bathroom is second door on the right."

Without another word, the two men left to wash up. In a low voice, Elizabeth said, "He still hates me."

"He—" At the sink, Vida searched for the right words. In a whisper, she said, "Let's just say you're a *reminder*."

"Not a *happy* reminder of his daughter?"

Vida shook her head no. After glancing down the hall, she whispered, "Dad did exactly what Elizabeth Haberlin's family did. He disowned my sister. When she got pregnant, he kicked her out. When she needed him most, he turned his back on her. I was in college at the time, in Pittsburgh. I never should have left her alone."

"Alone?" Elizabeth asked. "What about my birth *dad*?"

Vida snorted. "That jerk took off the moment he found out about you. I don't even know his name. Vera told me they met at the Cambria County Fair. My sister, well, she didn't always make wise decisions."

Sporting a happy-go-lucky grin, York bounded into the kitchen and inhaled. "I have died and gone to heaven."

Elizabeth felt a wave of warmth for her newly declared boyfriend. Having him with her was the wisest decision she'd ever made. Never had she met anyone so comfortable in his own skin. That boy could be at home anywhere . . . except, perhaps, his own parents' home that was overstuffed with their expectations.

Incredibly—though it was only the *second* time they'd been together in the flesh—Elizabeth felt like she'd known York forever. The previous week, with Elizabeth on the West Coast and York on the East, they had pressed their FaceTime screens against their hearts to hear them beating in sync. How had she gotten so lucky?

Like a thundercloud, Gene blew into the kitchen and frowned. "Don't burn that bird," he said.

Too brightly, Vida chirped, "Okay, then. Elizabeth, will you please pour the dressing on the salad while I get the chicken out of the oven? And, Dad, will you do the honors?"

"I'll need to sharpen a knife."

"It's sharp enough, Dad. York, could you please bring our cider glasses in from the living room."

With a nod, York scampered off. Vida darted around the small kitchen like a chipmunk scurrying from nut to tree. She pulled the chicken out of the oven, forked it onto a cutting platter, grabbed tongs for the salad, handed them to Elizabeth. York returned carrying four glasses of cider in his two hands. "Don't worry," he said to Elizabeth's alarmed expression, "I know which glass belongs to which person."

Vida laughed. "Vera was a germophobe, too."

With a large knife in one hand and a big fork in the other, Gene looked momentarily confused. "Cut as many pieces as you can, Dad," Vida said. "Here, York, let me take those glasses. I'll pour fresh. Elizabeth, why don't you sit here. York, there."

Amid the scraping of chair legs across linoleum, they sat.

Vida set the salad bowl in the center of the table. She brought four new glasses from the cupboard and filled them with fresh cider from the fridge. In concentrated silence, Gene carved up the chicken. York gently squeezed Elizabeth's knee under the table. For a long minute, no one said a word. They scooped salad onto their plates and oohed and aahed over how good it all looked.

"Might as well tell her," Gene said, abruptly. "It's her past, too."

Elizabeth's breath stopped short. Her gaze shifted left, then right. From Gene to Vida. And back again. Gene set the carving utensils down and sat. With his own fork, he stabbed a piece of breast meat and set it on his plate. Then he reached for the salad bowl. Vida asked York, "Leg? Thigh?"

"I'm a thigh man," he said, his white teeth gleaming.

"Tell me what?" Elizabeth asked.

As Gene chewed with his head down, Vida looked exasperated. "Can we please just have a pleasant lunch?"

"No time like the present," Gene blurted with his mouth full.

York accepted the chicken thigh, then set about eating it earnestly. Elizabeth stared at Vida. "I'd like to know, really," she said. "Whatever it is."

With a loud sigh, Vida adjusted her silverware. She shot her dad a look. "Okay, then." She took a fortifying sip of cider. "What dad is talking about, well, my sister, your birth mother, she had, um, *issues*. She was depressed. She'd always been sort of *dark*. Even as a kid, she was permanently braced for disaster."

Elizabeth felt her cheeks flush.

"Medication helped," Vida went on. "But not enough. And after you were born, well, there was *postpartum* depression on top of everything el—"

"Oh." As if a ray of sunlight had just illuminated a cobwebby corner, Elizabeth suddenly saw clearly. "She drowned *herself,* didn't she?"

York's head shot up as Gene and Vida examined their plates.

"Yes," Vida said quietly.

Strangely, Elizabeth felt as though she'd known all along. "Where?"

"*Where?*"

"Where did it happen? Where did she do it?"

"Portland, Maine. I have no idea why she chose there."

Gene stabbed another piece of chicken.

"Somebody saw her climb onto a cliff with you," Vida said.

"I was *with* her?"

Vida nodded. "You were a baby, wrapped in a blanket. A witness saw the whole thing. He said he couldn't be sure, but it looked like she was about to jump. With you in her arms."

The only noise besides Elizabeth's involuntary gasp was the scraping of Gene's knife and fork on his plate. He never once looked up. York, too, chewed his chicken in silence.

"But she didn't do it, Elizabeth. I mean, obviously. She didn't jump with you. She set you down. She saved you."

Again, York reached his hand under the table to squeeze Elizabeth's knee. Almost in a whisper, Vida added, "Her body washed ashore about a mile away. But they quickly found you on top of that cliff, tucked into the hollow of a rock."

"A *lawyer* called me," Gene grumbled, now jabbing at his salad. "Damn lawyers."

Vida forced a smile. "She was thorough, my sister. She'd set things up."

"Didn't want me to have you," Gene said, coldly.

"She'd already signed adoption papers, hired a lawyer and everything. Explicit instructions were found in your blanket. A *closed* adoption. She didn't want you to know about her. She didn't want you to feel like you were genetically cursed."

Those two words hung in the air. *Genetically cursed.* Was she? Did the fact that she, too, was always braced for disaster mean that she was doomed to crumple under the weight of life?

"Vera insisted that her favorite photo was included in your adoption file. It was taken after the flood. Elizabeth Haberlin standing with Clara Barton."

"I saw that photo!"

"My sister loved that picture because it captured the resilience and determination of women. She wanted her daughter to take after Elizabeth Haberlin, not her. She wanted you to *survive* all the disasters that life will throw at you."

Elizabeth sat back in her chair. Her emotions were tangled into a hairball. Her birth mother had gotten what she wanted. Elizabeth *did* feel more connected to Elizabeth Haberlin than to her. Maybe she would emerge from her current crisis better than she was before. The idea of it cheered her. But, more than anything, she felt incredibly grateful. Her stormy birth mother had given her an amazing gift: Her sunny mom, Valerie.

"Did you make dessert?" Gene asked, done.

"Elizabeth hasn't even started her lunch, Dad."

"Oh." He sighed, gruffly.

Elizabeth smiled at her grandfather. Picking up her fork, she reached for the platter to stab a leg.

That was that. Now she knew.

For the remainder of their lunch, they chatted amiably about droughts and floods and ice storms and blistering sunlight that never let up.

## ···❧[ CHAPTER 54 ]❧···

JOHNSTOWN, PENNSYLVANIA

*Present*

One train in from Pittsburgh in the morning, one train out at dinnertime. After the chicken had been consumed down to its carcass, Elizabeth and York still had hours to kill. But they said their good-byes long before it was time to meet the six P.M. Pennsylvanian back to the city that sat proudly over the confluence of the Ohio, the Allegheny, and the Mononga-hela rivers. There was a lot to see in downtown Johnstown.

After lunch, Gene grunted farewell.

"Cordless drill is the only power tool a city dweller needs," he said to York. To Elizabeth, he said, "Now you know all that's worth knowing." Then he shuffled back to his chair.

Before they left the house, Vida took Elizabeth aside and said, "I have one more thing to show you." Scooping up her niece's hand, she quickly led her upstairs. In her bedroom, with its ornate ironwork bed frame and dark wood dresser, Vida opened a jewelry box and pulled out a roll of velvet. In the velvet's unfurling, a diamond bracelet was revealed. Its rose-cut diamonds sent flickers of light bouncing about the room.

"This initially belonged to Elizabeth Haberlin's grandmother. She took her own life, too."

"Wasn't Elizabeth Haberlin wearing this in the photo I just saw? The one at the piano?"

"Yes. She wore it everywhere. She never took it off," Vida said.

Elizabeth glanced down at her own wrist. Her own heirloom.

"This bracelet has been in our family for generations," Vida said. "Now I want you to have it. *Vera* would want you to have it."

Elizabeth took a step back, stunned. "It's beautiful, but I can't accept it. Thank you, but no."

"I don't have any heirs. I'm the last of our line. And it's too sentimental to sell."

"Sorry. I can't." Elizabeth made a motion for the door. Not wanting to hurt Vida's feelings, she didn't voice the thought in her head: *I have my own bracelet, from my own grandmother.*

Vida sighed. "I'll save it for you, then." She rewrapped the velvet. "One day you may have a daughter who wants a connection to your past."

Before Elizabeth left the room, Vida said, "One more minute." Then she walked over to a shelf by the window and pulled out a manila envelope. "Will you at least take this?"

"What is it?"

"Something to read on the train. An Eggar family tradition. We pass it on to our offspring. Meaning, it's now meant for you."

Elizabeth held the envelope, unsure what to say.

"No arguments. Put it away. Read it later," Vida said. "It's something to take with you . . . through life."

Elizabeth nodded. Vida hugged her niece hard and whispered, "Now that we've met, you're welcome to visit anytime. I'll always be here."

Surprising herself, Elizabeth threw her arms around Vida and hugged her—hard—right back.

As they descended the stairs to the front door, Elizabeth stopped and turned around. "Oh. I almost forgot," she said. "I have one more question. The breast cancer gene?"

Vida laughed. "That Ashkenazi thing? *Pfft.* You're probably fine. I've been tested, and I was negative. You can get tested, too, down the road. For now, forget about it. Relax and live your life."

Funny, that's exactly what she planned to do.

# ··◦]( CHAPTER 55 )[◦··

## THE ALLEGHENY MOUNTAINS

*Present*

B y the time they reached Horseshoe Curve around the old
Altoona reservoir, York was deeply asleep. The train shimmied side to side. Elizabeth listened to the sound of his breathing. It reminded her of the ocean. Ebbing and flowing. The
endless motion of life. The final sound her birth mother heard
before jumping.

Glad she'd come, Elizabeth was even happier to be going
home. She couldn't wait to open the pool-house door and wrap
her arms around her mom's shoulders, inhaling Valerie's apricot shampoo.

Quietly, she stood up and crawled around York to reach the
overhead rack where she'd stashed her backpack. With the sun

darkening to orange, she untied the top string and pulled the pack open. She reached in and retrieved the manila envelope Vida had given her. Then she shut her pack and carefully crept back to her seat by the window. In the fading light of the Allegheny foothills, she opened the envelope and pulled out a letter. An *old* letter—encased in a plastic page protector. Her heart lurched when she saw who wrote it: Elizabeth Haberlin, Johnstown, Pennsylvania, 1892. The heading read "Letter to my future child."

*Darling Son or Daughter,*

*You are almost born. Only two more months. At times, I am certain you are a boy for your strong kicking. Just as often, I am convinced that your father and I have created a feisty girl. Either way, we are both so very eager to meet you.*

*I am writing this letter in a moment of tranquility. The past years have been filled with many joys and sorrows. I have come to understand much about life from the depth of both emotions. I now know the heart's capacity to be filled as well as broken. I have seen propriety supplant love. I have also witnessed love triumph over all. One thing I know for certain is this: You will be born with the strength to survive whatever may come your way. You could not be our offspring otherwise.*

*In my imagination, I envision you with my dark hair and eyes. I fear you will inherit my stubbornness, too. And I pray you will grow up with your father's goodness and generosity of spirit. In all of the world, I could not have made a better match. God smiled upon me. Yet, of all the qualities your father and I might pass on to you, my dearest child, I hope you are blessed with one quality above all others: a mind that is yours alone.*

*Please remember this, dear one: Birth is not fate. You must create a destiny that is yours. Uniquely yours.*

*Many voices will seek to influence you in your long life. Sad experience has shown me that even family members can disappoint. And so, as I await your entrance into the world, I have but one request for you to hold dear. When those around you are shouting or commanding or cajoling, find a quiet corner away from all distraction. Still yourself long enough to hear one—and only one—voice. That is the voice inside you. The judgment of your heart. Forever follow your heart's direction and you shall never be led astray.*

*Yours Affectionately Forever,*
*Mother*

Leaning back against the soft cushion of the train seat, Elizabeth pressed the letter to her chest. Her heart beat into it. At that moment she knew one thing for sure: everything was going to be okay.

Suddenly an idea popped into her head. The topic for a new college essay. She would tell her story. Her *history*. She would pose the question she'd wondered for years: Is DNA your destiny? Now she knew the answer.

Beside her, York stirred. He yawned and stretched his arms

overhead. Elizabeth saw a flash of his tanned stomach, the ripple of muscle beneath his smooth skin. Seeing the letter, he sleepily asked, "Words of wisdom for you, Elizabeth?"

Looking into York's kind eyes, seeing his generous soul, she grinned. "Call me Lee. It's the name my mother gave me."

# ·◦❧ EPILOGUE ❧◦·

*On a train to Johnstown, Pennsylvania*
*Some years later . . .*

I was once a woman enamored with numbers. I don't know why. It has simply always been a part of me. Even as a child, I counted leaves fallen on my windowsill in the chilly breezes of fall, the number of steps from our parlor in Upper St. Clair to Father's medical office in an outbuilding on our property, the way certain birth dates added up to certain numbers, the manner in which a person's numerical age defined them or did not.

But after May 31, 1889—numbers I once would have added together to seek their deeper meaning—I ceased to care about sums and figures. Humanity is all that matters to me now. Human kindness. The simple understanding that we are not alone on this earth. Ours is a journey of a million hearts, beating as one. For it is *history*—not humanity—that remembers our horror in numbers:

**Ten:** Minutes it took for Lake Conemaugh and its gathered wreckage to destroy a town of thirty thousand.

**Three:** Days the fire burned uncontrollably at the stone bridge.

**Eighty:** Souls who perished while trapped, alive, in the fire and rubble at the bridge.

**Thirty:** Acres of the debris field at the stone bridge.

**Twenty million:** Tons of water in Lake Conemaugh that careened downhill to Johnstown.

**Forty:** Miles per hour the massive wave sped into town.

**Two thousand two hundred and nine:** Final tally of the dead.

**Ninety-nine:** Entire families killed by the flood and fire.

**Three hundred ninety six:** Children killed.

**Seven hundred and fifty:** Bodies too mutilated or burned to identify.

**Nineteen hundred and eleven:** Year the final body was found. *Twenty-two* years after the flood. Bodies were discovered as far away as Cincinnati—more than 350 miles away.

**Forty:** Additional deaths from the typhoid outbreak caused by unsanitary conditions following the flood.

**Zero:** Members of South Fork Fishing and Hunting Club who stepped forward to accept responsibility.

**Zero:** Owners or managers of the club ever held accountable for the negligence of the dam's repair and maintenance.

For me, I do not remember that awful day in statistics. In the misty gray light of that sunless day in May, on that fortress of a bridge, I witnessed sights so gruesome I cannot, to this day, speak of them without weeping. Nightmares are my constant companion. For years, I feared sleep. Yet I forced myself to relive—night after night—what we had wrought in the chilling vibrancy of my troubled mind. I would not—could not—turn away from it.

Yet, in the end, my biggest memory of May 31, 1889, is one of *birth,* not death. For on that day, in the aftermath of such careless disregard for human life, I, Elizabeth Haberlin, daughter of Dr. and Mrs. Stafford Haberlin, of the Haberlins of Upper St. Clair, Pennsylvania, was born anew. After I saw and heard and felt what occurred that day, how could I ever go back to being who I was?

I could not. I did not. And my soul is ever richer for it.

*The end.*

# ACKNOWLEDGMENTS

This novel could not have been written without the generosity and expertise of Richard Burkert, President of the Johnstown Area Heritage Association (JAHA). Enormous gratitude, Richard, for the incredible tour of your fascinating town. Many thanks, also, to Park Ranger Nathan Koozer for allowing me to walk in the footsteps of history inside the South Fork Fishing and Hunting Club clubhouse (wow!), to Ranger Doug Bosley at the Johnstown Flood National Memorial, Nikki Bosley and Caitlin Hucik at the Johnstown Flood Museum, Joe Koishal at the Heritage Discovery Center, and Kaytlin Sumner at JAHA, as well as Daniel Liedtke at the National Railroad Museum for their help securing the rights to the historical photographs. Thank you all for sharing your time and knowledge with this nosy writer.

In researching the modern-day parts of the book, my professional admiration goes out to author Elizabeth Brown Pryor for her meticulous biography, *Clara Barton: Professional Angel*. Thank you, as well, Andrew Vanderlinder of the American Red Cross. With your help, it was a joy discovering how amazing Clara Barton really was.

As every writer knows, from time to time we need a little change of scene to prime the creative pump. Mine was a week in Cape Cod at the beautiful Inn at the Oaks in Eastham, Massachusetts. Thanks to Lawrence Shapiro, for providing the perfect creative environment. Chapter 1 of *The Woman in the Photo* was written on an antique desk in front of the bay window in one of your lovely rooms.

As every *author* knows, it takes a team to transform an idea into a book. The words "thank you" don't come close to my appreciation for the care and stellar abilities of my agent, Laura Langlie, and editor, Carrie Feron. Without the two of you, I would still be fumbling my way through a story I couldn't quite figure out how to tell. Much gratitude, also, to Nicole Fischer for her cheerful finesse, and to everyone at William Morrow for making me *so* proud of my books.

Finally, to friends and family who expertly covered their confusion each time I said, "See, this lake was in the *sky*." And to the man of my dreams, Bob Hogan, who has never once said anything less than "Go for it." Endless love, my love, for taking the leap with me.

## About the author

## About the book

## Read on

Insights,
Interviews
& More . . .

# Meet Mary Hogan

Mark Bennington

MARY HOGAN is the bestselling author of *Two Sisters* (William Morrow), a novel inspired by her own sister, Diane Barbera Coté (1953–2010). Other novels include the Young Adult titles *The Serious Kiss*, *Perfect Girl*, and *Pretty Face* (HarperCollins), as well as a series of four teen books beginning with *Susanna Sees Stars* (Delacorte Press). Mary lives in New York City with her husband, actor Robert Hogan, and their dog (who has the soul of a cat), Lucy. Video proof of Lucy's cattiness can be seen on Mary's website: maryhogan.com.

# When a Story Calls

I'M NOT SURE WHY, but I felt *destined* to write this book. The seed was planted twenty-four years ago in an off-Broadway theater on the far west end of Forty-Second Street. My husband, actor Robert Hogan, was in a play there called *On the Bum, or the Next Train Through*. Written by Neal Bell, it also starred Cynthia Nixon and Campbell Scott. In one scene, two characters sit on a ledge high above the stage, supposedly on the edge of an empty man-made lake. Staring downward, they muse about the day in 1889 when that lake destroyed the entire town below it. Though I love a good disaster story, I was more intrigued by *geography*. I remember thinking, How could a lake be directly *overhead*? Doesn't a person look down at a lake from its shore, not up to a lake in the sky?

That scene, from that play, stuck with me. I was curious to know more about a lake in the clouds. So, I did what authors do: I went to the library. There, my mind was blown. Geography was the least of it. The real events of that tragic day in May 1889 were *epic*. It was a story of arrogance and indifference. The careless rich and the vulnerable working class. Billed by history as the Johnstown Flood, the destruction of humanity and property was really the result of a *tidal wave* more than a flood. The story of Johnstown, Pennsylvania, I felt in my bones, was one that needed to be told again. I had to write about it. Somehow. Someday. ▶

**When a Story Calls** *(continued)*

Fast-forward several years . . .

In Pittsburgh on a book tour for my first young adult novel, *The Serious Kiss*, I rented a car and drove into the Allegheny Mountains to finally see Johnstown for myself. It was an hour and a half away. I remember the drive vividly. Lush with black cherry, yellow birch, maple, spruce, and hemlock trees, the mountain highway is tucked into a valley that leads to a road that winds downward into a pit where two rivers meet: Johnstown. Mountains rise up on all sides. Instantly, I felt swallowed up.

Equally as memorable was the drive *up* the mountain road leading to the remains of the South Fork Fishing and Hunting Club—once the private summer retreat for Pittsburgh's elite. They were the owners of the man-made lake that was contained by the faulty dam that burst and set the tragic events in motion more than a hundred years ago. As I drove the path of the raging waters that caused such destruction and loss of life, I understood how easily the privileged class could ignore the threat their lake posed to the citizens in the valley below. They looked *up*, not down. Similar to the "one percent" today, they lived in a bubble. The very purpose of their summer getaway was carefree fun. They *hired* people to worry about such things as the failure of an earthen dam that would crumble and kill thousands.

Over the years, I would visit Johnstown three times. On each visit, I dove more deeply into its riveting history. Incredibly, the clubhouse that was once the center of activity in the South Fork Fishing and Hunting Club is still standing. As are a few cottages. The old stone bridge is still there, too! Though the lake is long gone, you can drive the pathway of its destruction. And Johnstown itself—rebuilt after the devastating flood—is a testament to the resilience of the working-class people who make America great.

In my research, I read many excellent books on the flood, including: David McCullough's *The Johnstown Flood*, Dr. Michael R. McGough's *The 1889 Flood in Johnstown, Pennsylvania* and *The Club and the 1889 Flood in Johnstown, Pennsylvania*, Richard A. Gregory's *The Bosses Club*, Curtis Miner's *Down at the Club: An Historical and Cultural Survey of Johnstown's Ethnic Clubs*, Les Standiford's *Meet You in Hell*, and Kathleen Cambor's wonderful novel, *In Sunlight, in a Beautiful Garden*. I also spent hours of discovery in Johnstown's amazing museums, and was given the tour of a lifetime by the president of the Johnstown Area Heritage Association, Richard Burkert.

Though my novel—including its main characters—is fiction, the actual flood and fire were so dramatic they required little embellishment on my part to bring that horrible day in May to life. There is written evidence that the club's president, Benjamin Ruff, was notified of Johnstown's serious concerns about the safety of the dam. Ruff famously ▶

replied, "You and your people are in no danger from our enterprise."

Still, the South Fork Fishing and Hunting Club was a private organization. While its membership roster is well known, including such luminaries as steel giants Andrew Carnegie and Henry Clay Frick, U.S. secretary of the Treasury Andrew Mellon, and U.S. senator and attorney general Philander Chase Knox, to my knowledge no record exists about who stayed at the clubhouse during which weeks, if ever. It is entirely possible that most members of the club never gave the dam—or the people of Johnstown—a second thought. It's hard to fault the general membership for the disaster. Their fees paid a caretaker to manage such things as maintenance and repair.

Ultimately, many small misjudgments—installing fish screens over the spillway, lowering the dam to widen the roadway, ignoring the engineer's report sent to the club's president by a representative from Johnstown—plus relentless rainfall led to the dam's catastrophic failure. I think of this often: how seemingly insignificant decisions can snowball into disaster. It is a cautionary tale for us all.

In this book, I have tried to be fair and accurate to both the privileged and working classes. As the character Vera Haberlin says, "A leopard that is born a leopard and raised a leopard will never be a house cat." If the story of Johnstown can teach us anything, my hope is that we *all* learn to be more mindful of the leopards and house cats that share the planet with us.

Finally, a word about fashion. I found myself dumbfounded by the endless nuances of fashion in the late 1800s. Countless hours of research were devoted to getting the outfits just right. Any blunders regarding corsets, bustles, hoop skirts, shirtwaists, sunbonnets, bowler hats, sack coats, and other frocks are sincerely regrettable. And any other historical missteps in this story are entirely my own. My intention was to honor the people who died on May 31, 1889, and to respect the current residents of Johnstown, Pennsylvania, who live each day with their town's extraordinary history. ∾

# Reading Group Guide

1. In what way, if any, do the events leading up to the Johnstown Flood resonate today?

2. One of the major themes of the book is the question "Is biology destiny?" Do you believe you are *born* to be the person you are meant to be? Or, can fate be shaped by human will?

3. If you were the product of a closed adoption (sealed records) would you try to identify your birth parents? If so, why?

4. Should the members of the South Fork Fishing and Hunting Club— essentially a timeshare—have been held legally accountable for the Johnstown disaster?

5. In 1889, a person's clothes instantly identified his or her class. Do you think it's the same today? Or are there other "class" identifiers that we use to judge people?

6. How many similarities between Elizabeth Haberlin and Lee Parker can you name?

7. Did Clara Barton become the historical figure she became because of her upbringing or *in spite* of it?

8. How did the confines of class affect the Haberlin family?

9. In a society where men held all the positions of power, in what ways did the *women* of this story make a difference?

# Have You Read?
## More from Mary Hogan

**TWO SISTERS**

One family, two sisters, a lifetime of secrets . . .

The third child in a family that wanted only two, Muriel Sullivant has always been an outsider. Short, dark-haired, and round, she worships her beautiful blond sister, Pia, and envies the close bond she shares with their mother, Lidia. Growing up in their shadow, Muriel believes that if she keeps all their secrets—and she knows plenty, outsiders always do—they will love her, too.

But that was a long time ago. Now an adult, Muriel has accepted the disappointments in her life. With her fourth-floor walk-up apartment and entry-level New York City job, she never will measure up to Pia and her wealthy husband, their daughter, and their suburban Connecticut dream home. Muriel would like nothing better than to avoid her judgmental family altogether. One thing she does quite well.

Until the day Pia shows up to visit and share devastating news that Muriel knows she cannot tell—a secret that will force her to come to terms with the past and help her see her life and her family in unexpected new ways.

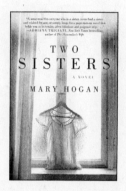